GRUESOME GROTESQ
VAMPIRES, WERE
OTHER BEAUTIFUL MONSTERS

Compiled and edited
by TREVOR KENNEDY

Published in 2017 by
PHANTASMAGORIA PUBLISHING

CAUTION:

CONTAINS ADULT CONTENT

COPYRIGHT INFORMATION

Dedicated to the memory of Michael Brennan.

Ten years gone, still missed and loved by many.

"Listen to them, the children of the night. What music they make!"

Bram Stoker, <u>Dracula</u>

CONTENTS

Editor's notes:

Many thanks to Jihane Mossalim for her wonderful cover artworks and Adrian Baldwin for his amazing cover design.

In the stories and poetry which follow, the authors' original spelling and intention have been retained, dependent upon their nationality (ie colour/ color etc).

FOREWORD

by John Gilbert

Nightmares Before Bedtime

We're in it for the werewolves, the vampires, the creatures that crawl half formed and gibbering from the ocean depths under a moon drained of colour. Yes, Horror fans have a penchant for the macabre, the bloody, the downright scary but, as an editor and author of more than thirty years standing, I would argue it is often acquaintance with reality that allows an author to expertly lead a reader into the Stygian depths of their own particular dark imaginings.

By rooting a tale in the familiar, the talented Horror writer can make their readers buy into one hundred waking nightmares before bedtime. Whether it's the chance meeting in a bar in Rachel Johnson's *The Slaughtering Seductress*, an academic newly installed in post at a university in *The Sign and The Sigil*, a sleeping house in *Death Pact* or what initially appears to be an idyllic holiday in Samantha Lee's *Hidden Depths*, many of the stories in this, the second in this series of Phantasmagorical anthologies, take reality and, like any good lycanthrope, transform it into something fantastical and monstrous.

Indeed, the werewolf and its cousin the vampire are both examples of the ordinary transformed, the mundane made supernatural. Less than two hundred years ago the wolf was a common enough critter in mainland Britain and America. Whereas now it is almost extinct in the UK and confined to the hinterlands of the US, in the past it was prolific and dangerous enough to be feared by the common populace. The legend of the werewolf grew out of a peasant need to cast blame for disasters. So, when cattle, sheep or even humans were savagely attacked by a wild creature the locals might blame and hunt down a human outsider for the crime.

These outsiders were ascribed supernatural powers through the principle of transference. Just as a witch might inherit their powers from the Devil and use transference - or sympathetic - magic to curse crops and livestock, so a vampire might or werewolf might be created through the bite of a similarly affected human. The fear of werewolves and other supernatural creatures led to the so-called Werewolf and Witch trials in Europe.

It may seem incredible that belief in such creatures continue to exist, though largely relegated to the pages of the horror story, even in this post enlightenment age. They have become during that time somewhat diluted and homogenised in classic supernatural tales with the beasts granted anti-superhero status in films, comics and novels. They are for the most part now somewhat of an entertainment, scary but containable within the imaginations of writers and even younger readers.

I would, however, suggest that there is a move afoot both in the UK and The States, to reset the horror story, take it back to its origins, sharpen the genre's intensity and ragged power to shock and scare.

The tales and poems within the second volume of this Phantasmagorical series of anthologies so ably collated by your host Trevor Kennedy, are cases in point. They are strong meat, packed with characters and images that will follow you off the page when you put the book down on your bedside table.

John Gilbert
Brighton, 2017.

INTRODUCTION

by Trevor Kennedy

It is a great honour, to not only be writing the introduction to this second volume in the Gruesome Grotesques series, but to also be helming such a high calibre compendium of weird fiction, from yet another sublime group of diverse and multi-talented creatives - a true and enriching team effort - from those beauteous covers, right through to the compelling verse and stories within.

Some of the old gang from the first collection are still thankfully with us, and the new additions to our ever-growing macabre world are some of the very best indeed - from right across the globe too - taking in the likes of South America, Canada, the USA, Australia, England and, of course, some quality homegrown talent here in Northern Ireland.

The first book sold reasonably well, all things considered, but more importantly, the critical feedback and praise received was powerfully positive and flattering, making all our collective toil and efforts very much worthwhile. After all, first and foremost, we are here to create entertaining and hopefully thought-inspiring literature of as high a quality as humanly possibly. Any other type of reward, be it financial or other, is a bonus, although also obviously a welcome one at that. But the art comes first and always must do. To get into this game for any other reason would be a sell-out and disservice to oneself.

If our Creator spares us, I plan on this to be a continuing anthology series, with around two editions released each year. The aim is for quality over quantity, as while it would be somewhat easy to repeatedly churn out the volumes, common sense tells us that the standard would obviously dip if the greatest care and attention was not given to not only the overall books in question, but to each individual piece that is published inside the pages. Each edition will have its own general theme and hopefully fresh take on the subject matter chosen. Some future overarching themes under consideration are the occult, science fiction and folklore, to name but a few. However, we shall make these sorts of decisions together as the team that we are.

The motif for this book - Vampires, Werewolves and other Beautiful Monsters - originates from my own personal love of these classic horror tropes. I have very fond memories of being a young boy and growing up watching old Hammer and Amicus films from the 1950s, 60s and 70s, with my horror-loving mother. A keen reader always, I also relished these types of tales in literature too. I have always found the creatures of the night in question so very fascinating, horrific and also rather tragic, especially the werewolf. For most of their time on Earth they are ordinary, decent, good people, but then, through no fault of their own, they change completely into rampaging monsters, taking with them the lives of many innocents. There is something so very heartbreaking (and painful!) about the metamorphosis David undergoes in *An American Werewolf in London*, and the one Jeff Goldblum's mad scientist experiences in David Cronenberg's superior remake of *The Fly*. Same rules apply for those quaint folk who become bitten and turn into vampires, although, in addition, I have always found the vampiric yarns of the drinking of blood and eternal life to be somewhat erotic and appealing.

As people, we all have our dark sides, so maybe these exaggerations of the nastier sides of fictional individuals have a fair amount of truth in them, and perhaps this is where the legends originated from in the first place.

Anyhow, I shall stop rattling on about my own reasons for compiling this superb collection and let the proof of the pudding be in the metaphorical eating of the poetry and stories ahead of you.

Bon appetit!

Trevor Kennedy
Belfast, 2017.

DARKNESS CALLS

by J.K. Wilde

Darkness unfolds its petals and I am alive
The cry of the night heralds through my mind
No longer do I sleep but am revived...

The thirst courses through my veins
Anger, hatred, deception; they are my friends
My self-torture leads only to pain...

If sin is whatever obscures the soul
Then I truly have sinned
For my soul is plagued by obscurity within the darkness...

Darkness swirls and bellows and I am aware
The pang of hunger slips deep within the pit of my core
Humanity has left my senses and all that I have is despair...

A tingle runs down my spine and my body trembles
Hunger, lust, greed; they consume my thoughts
Anguish riddles my existence...

Angst, oh angst...
Why is it you plague me tonight?

Silver beams dance wildly across tall blades
An owl cries out his sovereign desperation...

Why does he fear me and my presence?

Wolves howl and the pack convenes...

Commencement of the hunt rushes through their veins
Excitement, anticipation, hunger;
They are their allies...

Darkness blooms and I smell the fear
A rabbit cries and his death is felt
Warmth is a trickle that flows red down my chin...

Hands gnarled and grasping tightly
Eyes widening and then narrowing delightfully
Nostrils flare and I hear the growl...

A tremor, a shake...
Something chills me...

Adrenaline rushes and again I am alive
The wind whips through my clothes like I am standing still...

Darkness calls my name and I have answered
Hands now untwisted and trembling
Scarlet moisture tells the tale...

The bittersweet nectar trickles over my tongue
There is no retribution for what I have become...

INTO THE WOODS

by Ricky Mohl

Into the woods, so silent and still,
Lurks a presence, blood runs chill.
Down your spine, caress of finger,
Beware the whisper, it does linger.

A breeze kicks up, trees will shiver,
Branches dance, heart does quiver.
Through the dark, devoid of sound,
A forest of evil, a breeding ground.

Into the woods, so damp and alone,
No warmth found, cold to the bone.
So close behind, sounds echo near,
Panic looms large, insane with fear.

A breeze picks up, leaves will shake,
Blood runs cold, rapture does ache.
There is no running, no place to hide,
Here in the woods, all hope has died.

A MOTHER'S IGNORANCE

by Leanne Azzabi

Deep in the country,
Down an overgrown road,
Lay the remains of a castle,
Looking crumbled and old.

But down in the crypt,
Was a top secret lab,
War on their minds,
Trying to create something bad.

The best in the country,
Their secrecy sworn,
Thought they'd secured victory,
When the were-vamp was born.

They planned to groom and brainwash the creature,
Winning World War Three, that's were it would feature.
But they did not foresee, they just couldn't know,
How rapidly fast the were-vamp would grow.

Not only did the experiment blow back in their face,
They started the creation of a bloodthirsty race.
Control at the full moon, shape-shifting at bay,
Allowing more subtlety for luring it's prey.

To look on as human, it was beautiful perfection,
One could only describe as fatal attraction.
With the mix of genetics and correct DNA,
Allowing it to hunt in the broad light of day.

The killing spree began, blood, guts and gore,
That's putting it mildly, there was far worse and more.
Finally the solution and each one was dead,
Never killed women, but raped them instead.

But this was a secret no woman did tell,
As the government would put them through experimental hell.
Nine months later, some bore a child,
Who later in life would be crazy and wild.

Love part of their ignorance and maternal factors,
Unknowingly they created the new race of Lecters.

THE REASON

by Leanne Azzabi

I am the shadow,
From the side of your eye.
I am the voice,
When you hear the wind cry.

I am the goosebumps,
Raised on your arm.
I make you feel scared,
But I mean you no harm.

I am the dream,
That awakens you from sleep.
Strange noises at night,
That's while I creep.

When a dog starts to bark,
I am the reason.
I cross your mind,
When a room drops to freezing,

Deep down I am,
What you fear the most.
I am real,
I am a ghost.

MY VAMPYRE ANGEL

by Darren Webster

Her hair burnt red like a roasting campfire,
Leaned over me and said 'I am a Vampyre',
Her eyes were alive like the purest sapphire,
'You have been shot and will surely expire',
The pain was so bad, it felt like hellfire.
With her luscious bite I was 'saved' it did transpire,
But forever now a part of her Empire.

She was divine in crushed velvet all pure scarlet,
More like an angel than a vampy hot harlot,
She had saved me 'Yes', but at what cost?
I am her servant and She is my boss!

With bandages all neat and tied with a knot,
I lay there recovering on a gold silken cot,
I was so cold but the wound was hot,
Was I yet dead...or was I not?
But was safe in her castle, complete with a motte.

My 'life-giving' angel told me by the light of a lamp,
I was fully recovered, 'all fixed', but now a 'new vamp!'
But to bind it and bond us, there would be a pact,
A wild and abandoned 'all out' love making act.

Her body glowed amber, from the red of her hair,
Tied to the bed, I was prey in her lair,
She writhed as She rode me throughout the night,
Her breasts, her curves...what a gorgeous sight!
This was no 'act', for me it was love!
We fitted so perfect, just like a lamb glove.

I looked at her laying gently at rest,
I knew She was 'the one'...the very best,
I took photographic images with my mind's sight,
As we had to part ways before the sunlight.

My Vampyre, my Angel, my love.

THE WEREWOLVES AND HUNTERS

by Darren Webster

There they were in their glorious pack,
Set against a midnight sky so black.
They would sniff, hunt, prowl and attack,
The leader at the front, the young at the back.

Alerted to the sound of a twig and its crack,
The hunters came out of their woodland shack.
Prepared as they were with their guns and such tack,
But the werewolves were hungry and wanted a snack!

The shotguns set off with their great 'WHACK!',
Startled ducks flew up after the first 'quack!'.
The hunters would lose...in skills they did lack,
As the werewolves tore in – 'Fall back! Fall back!'.

Their guns never made it back to their rack,
Just body parts there where they'd got the sack.
And lately the erection of a memorial plaque,
To the failed werewolf hunters like Bill, Zac and Jack.

LOST FUTURES

by Jonathan Mooney

And there I saw it upon the horizon,
A deep darkness rising.
Swallowing all the lands before it,
Spreading fear and doubt and menace.
Turning brother against brother,
Setting sister against sister and sundering the heart of the
realm.
This great storm,
This evil,
This darkness flowing silken across the minds of men.

The horizon became black as ink,
Yet I could see it clearly.
The land fell under his sway,
Yet I could see it clearly.
The people tore themselves asunder,
Reaving hatreds deep and foreboding.
Changing faces,
Changing directions,
Changing cores,
Yet I knew them still.
He brought division where once a semblance of the future had
stood.

There came a man who spoke simply,
Who voiced craven thoughts that gave craven hearts sucker.
This man was unknowable,
Yet known for a fool,
He was a showman,
A conman,

A flim-flam artist of the highest merit,
And he gave the people exactly the mana they wanted.
But he was false,
As were the hearts he swayed, for his promises were false,
filled with lies and deceit and hate.
For it was in the hearts of the hidden craven that his doctrines
resided, cherished for its despair.

And I did despair,
For I had hoped.
I had believed.
I had found the truest of miracles came from the places deep
within others.
I saw the potentials of man and woman,
I saw a future.
Not of peace, but of harmony.
But a future of connection, understanding, challenge and
growth.
I saw man rise from his infancy and throw off the shackles of
ignorance.
And I saw this vision crumble to a forgotten glimmer.
I had hoped.
There came a darkness,
A menace to the souls of the pure.
A succour to those corrupt,
And a boon to those blind to honesty.

There came a darkness,
Insistent in its need to suppress opposition.
Desirous and covetous of all that shone,
For it could not shine.
It could not know honesty,
It could only devour.
And many stood before this darkness,
Not in unity of resistance,
But in supplication and a desire to be broken.
To be remade,
To be freed from the shackles of truth,
So they too could spread lies in the stead of facts,

So they could spew crazed shards of madness,
Thinking themselves righteous.

The world changed as darkness came,
And I knew not the direction for salvation.
I wept at the passing of the dream,
And mourned my lost futures.

SO THE STORY GOES

by Trevor Kennedy

The story, as it goes, concerns characters in a dream. Or should that be a dream within a dream? Regardless, the identity of the dreamer is unknown. The tale itself begins at Half Moon Bay, in the charming and picture-postcode seaside resort of Shannon in Northern Ireland. County Antrim, to be a little more precise. In addition, the events depicted in this anecdote are all completely true, partly true, or not true at all. It happened quite recently as well. So, let us waste no more time and engross and familiarise ourselves in the ripping yarn of Andy and Daphne's first and final date together.

Uncle Paulie's Ice-Cream Emporium, which was situated right on the seafront, could be best described as looking more like a 1950s American diner than an ice-cream shop, complete with retro jukebox playing contemporary pop songs. The attire of the staff also concurred with this era. However, this was just part of its charm. It was a well run and friendly place, popular with the local teenagers and somewhere for them to hang out that didn't involve underage drinking and/or recreational drug use, although the smell of weed could often be smelt from around the side of the business, and yes, this was also the same area where various grubby sexual encounters had occurred over the years too. The shop itself, which would have been the prefect spot to hold a jitterbug contest, by the way, served many confectionery treats of an ice-creamed nature, but the jewel in its crown was undoubtedly its succulent whipped ice-cream. I mean, regular ice-cream is good, but that of a whipped variety is the dog's bollocks. Not literally, of course. You just cannot beat a whipped ice-cream poke (as we call it here in Northern Ireland), with a flake and nuts on top, and Paulie's were arguably some of the best on the planet!

Paulie Esposito himself, who was naturally of Italian descent (his father heralded from the old country, settling in Shannon after meeting, falling in love and marrying a local girl in the 1940s), was a greasy, though amicable-in-nature, rotund man in his fifties, who had taken over the family business after his papa, named Haitham, had passed away of a heart attack in 1994. Paulie too married a local girl, named Alice. Remarkably, Paulie was not unlike that other Uncle Paulie in appearance, the one from the 1990 Martin Scorsese gangster film, *Goodfellas*, played with a classy and sinister grace by actor Paul Sorvino. Our Paulie, however, thankfully had no connections to the mafia or organised crime. Not that we know of, anyway.

On this particular night in question, as the story goes, twenty-one year old Andy was sitting in the pink-themed ice-cream palour waiting on his eighteen-year old date, Daphne, to arrive. She was ten minutes late and Andy was beginning to feel that he was being stood up...once again by a girl. Andy had often seen Daphne around the town and in the DVD rental shop where she worked at nights. She had always seemed a little strange to him, but there was something also very intriguing and mysterious about her too. Plus, she had the most amazing red curly locks and huge, deep green eyes that you could almost fall into, and a body to die for. Andy eventually got talking to her one night when he was returning *Batman vs Superman* to the shop, which was actually quite an enjoyable blockbuster, despite the critical panning it received when first released in cinemas. Lex Luthor, played by Jesse Eisenberg, was also a hoot in it. Anyway, they got chatting, tedious small talk really, with Andy quite enjoying Daphne's candor and directness. He soon had a 'fuck it' moment and asked her out for an ice-cream, despite already having a long-term girlfriend, whom he was somewhat getting bored of and now felt he needed a fresh 'challenge'. Daphne agreed to meet him on her night off, the Tuesday evening, which was Halloween night. Andy was delighted and even reckoned that his luck could be in on the night in question, if you catch my drift? He was certainly going to give it a try, as he reckoned the confidence with which she exuded, and the revealing outfits with which she wore, made her a probable goer.

Andy was about to give up the ghost and make tracks for home when Daphne arrived in a very relaxed and chilled out mood, apparently unconcerned at her poor punctuality. She didn't even apologise for being late. Andy let it go because his date was wearing a very revealing, and almost hypnotic, black top displaying quite a bit of her more-than-ample cleavage. This somewhat aroused and distracted Andy. The usual air kissing nonsense and social niceties were exchanged, before Andy went to the counter and ordered Daphne's choice of treats from Paulie's wife, Alice - a tub of mint choc chip and a can of Fanta lemon. Andy had a whipped ice-cream 99er and a Coke.

They soon got down to the serious business of idle chit-chat when Andy returned, putting their mobile phones away, whilst David Bowie's majestic apocalyptic classic, *Five Years*, crooned from the jukebox. The end of the world had never sounded so good! Andy was boring Daphne with talk about himself (he was a bit of a self-obsessed and egotistical bore, after all, but a generally decent spud, when all was said and done) and his work in Belfast as a semi-skilled factory operative in Collage Digital Colour, a printers. He was discussing the tedious details of his car journey to and from the factory, when Daphne decided enough was enough and cut in to begin a discussion about her own favourite topic - films. Specifically, horror films.

"So do you watch films much? I know you hire the odd DVD out at the store, but what would your favourites be then?" she began.

"Not big into movies, to be honest, love, but don't mind those superhero and *Fast and Furious* shows. I'm big into my cars, you see," retorted the disinterested and slick-haired

Andy.

"Cars don't impress me. Usually guys who are obsessed with their precious motors are just posers trying to make up for the fact that they have tiny dicks."

This both shocked and gobsmacked Andy.

Daphne continued, "Anyway, I'm not saying you're like that, but I prefer my guys to be a little more cultured, if you know what I mean? I do like my nights out to the theatre and am a big film buff too, but none of your all-action, big budget Hollywoodised shit either. I prefer the films of David Lynch, classic horrors like *The Exorcist* and *The Shining*, and some foreign films."

"Ugh! I hate movies with subtitles and black and white ones. Such pretentious nonsense, and too hard to follow as well. Never even heard of yer man, Martin Lynch," exclaimed the philistine that was Andy.

"David Lynch!"

"Whatever. I've no time at all for that sort of arty shite. I don't mind the odd vampire film though. Those *Twilight* films were pretty good."

"Are you for fucking real, mate? Those films are pure kak, and so are the books, and I've read them all, by the way. The acting is wooden, the plot is flimsy at best, and since when did vampires become sparkling, lovesick tweens anyway?"

"I liked them and the girl who starred in them, Kirsten or Bella or something, was pretty hot too."

"No way. Those films are truly awful and based on shite books too, just like that 50 Shades of whatever crap. And anyway, vampires should always be cold-blooded, evil, murdering bastard sons of monsters, not cute pin-ups that resemble David Beckham. It's ridiculous. We need to go back to how vampires were originally depicted in the early myths and legends, and the best vamp films were in the 1970s and 80s too, before Buffy, and to a lesser extent that *Interview With a Vampire* film in 1994, which made them all sexy, sympathetic and relatable. It actually makes me want to vomit. We need more Christopher Lees and less Robert Pattisons. Real vampires must be spinning in their undead graves at these great insults to their species! Is it any wonder they hate and have nothing but contempt for humans?!"

Daphne's ferocity and passion amused Andy greatly, and turned him on a bit too, as Batimora's *Tarzan Boy* emanated loudly from the jukebox speakers.

"You don't look or dress like a goth or emo girl, but I can see you are very enthusiastic about vampires. You do know there's no such thing as them though, right, haha? And don't even hit me with those silly blood drinking rumours about the murders last month on the edge of the woods. That was obviously the work of some escaped lunatic with a big knife or the like, hence the cutting up of the body parts."

"Then how do you explain the bite marks found on the victims' necks?"

"That was never proven and are just old wives' tales, for want of a better phrase. There's no such things as vampires, ghosts or goblins. That's a scientific fact, so it is. Anyway, what's your favourite vampire movie of all time then?"

"As I said, the older ones are by far the best, going back as far as Max Schreck as *Nosferatu* in 1922. Christopher Lee is also the quintessential Dracula to me, but Bram Stoker's original novel is the best of the lot, as most, if not all, book versions are. The stuff at the beginning, set in Castle Dracula, is some of the greatest gothic literature I have ever had the pleasure of reading. But, yea, I'm a big fan of 70s and 80s vampire and horror films. It was such a golden age for the genre. We had classic vamp flicks back then like *Texas Chainsaw Massacre* director Tobe Hooper's *Salem's Lot*, based on the book by Stephen King, *Near Dark* with Bill Paxton and Lance Henriksen, Romero's *Martin* and, of course, *The Lost Boys*, which perfectly balances the comedy and horror, just like *An American Werewolf in London* did a few years earlier. *Fright Night* was a joy to behold too. The recent remake was naturally a big pile of steaming dog turd, with David Tennant the only good thing about it, although I may be a little biased in that department. Out of the current batch of vampire films, most of them are pure shite, but the best one, and most realistic, would have to be the Scandinavian flick, *Let the Right One In*. Vampires have always been my favourite. Always."

"You know your stuff, love, I'll give you that, but to be honest, I've never even heard of most of those films."

"Why does that not surprise me?"

"I thought a girl like you would have been more into chick flicks and American high school comedies. Do you not like those?"

"To me, those sorts of films are complete and utter fucking donkeys' balls and an insult to one's intelligence! Does that answer your question?" before adding, "You think you're a real smooth ladies man, don't you, Andy?"

"Well, I can be a real beast in bed, you know?"

"Yea, well I'm not like other girls, so don't bother getting your hopes up, Mr Cool Dude. You hear me?"

They both laughed, making intimate eye contact and enjoying each other's company, despite their obvious differences. Daphne also chose to ignore Andy's irritating naming of her 'love'.

They chatted a while longer, mainly about where they liked to go for nights out and such, with the general agreed feeling that local club Xanadu was long past its best, but was still okay for a cheap night out. When a few kids dressed as a witch, Yoda from *Star Wars* and Spongebob Squarepants walked past the window, on their way to presumably go trick or treating, Daphne lamented how Halloween had become too commercialised due to the influence of American culture, and that it should return to its pagan and mystical roots. A good example of the rape and pillage of this ancient Celtic festival was, as she pointed out, the silly decorations ordaining the walls and window of Paulie's Ice-Cream Emporium. Daphne sighed. Andy didn't really know what she was talking about, but nodded his head in agreement anyway.

After a second helping of ice-cream-related snacks and soft drinks, Daphne told Andy it was time she was heading for home, as it was getting late and she had to be up early in the morning for an appointment. Andy offered to walk her home, with an ulterior, sex-related motive. Daphne agreed, although she did warn him that she lived alone on the outskirts of the town and it was quite a walk to her small flat, but they could take a shortcut through the woods beside the moors. Andy was more than happy to take whatever route Daphne pleased and the news of her having her own place made him even more eager, as he equated that this gave him even more of chance of getting the leg over, the horned-up young whipper-snapper that he was.

They walked hand-in-hand through the town, on what was an unusually mild and dry Halloween's evening, as dusk was beginning to settle in the cloudy sky above and more young 'uns passed by with their pumpkins in hand, whilst dressed up as skeletons and comic book heroes like Spider-man and Iron Man.

As they were passing Xanadu, they happened upon local character and joker, Michael Kane, who was his usual highly intoxicated and jovial self, his black curls stuck to his head by a drunken sweat. His eyes were as wild and crazed-looking as they always were. At this particular moment, he was being hassled by a couple of well-meaning male E-heads, obviously on their way to the Halloween rave at the club. They were telling him how much they loved him and that he was a great guy, shaking his hand firmly and hugging him intensely. Michael's response to their compliments was a simple hands thrust up into the air and shouting, "Ballix, lies, wankers!" before each party headed in their separate directions. Daphne and Andy chuckled at this amusing encounter, before moving on down the road, across the old moors, and towards the edge of the woods, chatting away happily about this and that. It was nice and felt good and right too.

"You know, these woods are pretty creepy, especially with it being almost dark. Please feel free to grab and cuddle me if you get too scared now," stated Andy jokingly.

"I'll keep that in mind, you big brave hero, you," responded Daphne sarcastically.

The moon was hanging in the sky, attempting to shine through the thick Halloween clouds and mist which had fallen suddenly, to light a way for the couple as they reached the middle of the woods, arm-in-arm. The place felt alive with damp nocturnal wildlife, while a sharp chill cut through the air. Daphne and Andy could now see their breath in front of them soon Andy slipped on a wet fallen tree trunk when they were clambering over it, resulting in him becoming even more damp and cold. He really wasn't an outdoorsy type at all. Daphne, however, was, and definitely much more adept to the woodland than her male counterpart.

As they approached and walked onto a more open greener area in the forest, Andy felt it was now the right time to make his move. He tugged Daphne's arm and pulled her around and towards himself, grabbing her by the waist tightly and squeezing his crotch area into her own, for added effect.

"Give 'us a lumber, love, wud ye?" he demanded in a totally unclassy manner, before leaning in to get his kiss, snog and hopefully a bit of a feel.

But he was left kissing the air when Daphne broke free from his horny clutch and fell to the ground, screaming and writhing in agony, grabbing her head and ears by her hands.

Andy was panicked and did not know how to react, so he simply stood back and watched, feeling and looking rather useless, as his date for the night began to contort and increase the volume of her now high-pitched screams.

"IT'S HAPPENING AGAIN! IT'S FUCKING HAPPENING AGAIN!" she yelped in apparent extreme pain.

What was to happen next sent Andy completely insane, the sanity switch in his mind simply flicked to 'off', as you would do with a light perhaps, his panic turning to sheer fear-induced terror.

Before Andy's very shocked eyes, Daphne's arms, hands and fingers extended, eventually becoming huge animal-like, razor-sharp claws. Her ears also elongated, became pointed and grew hairs alongside the other hairs which were sprouting up all over her greatly stretching and pulsating body. The clothes the teenage girl had worn on her date were soon ripping and falling off her now gigantic and masculine torso and onto the ground, including her sexy black top. The final part of her change happened when her mouth area swelled and grew, revealing huge pointed fangs in the place of her previously quite petite and very human teeth. As her eyes rolled back inside her now beastly head, she produced two new bright yellow ones. The creature formally known as Daphne then looked up at the full moon above her and howled the lycanthropic base wail of a creature of the night.

The last thing Andy would ever see in this world would be the eight-foot tall hulking monster hovering over him, before lopping off his head in one swift movement of its muscular right arm and claw, leaving his headless body to slump onto the ground motionless, aside from the large amounts of blood gushing from the part of his neck which remained.

The beast-creature that used to be an eighteen year old girl, pounced animalistically towards the human head it had just sliced off and grabbed it, holding it up to the moon like a trophy and howling repeatedly in a primal and terrifying screech.

That Halloween night, the creature claimed many more innocent lives throughout the idyllic-appearing small town of Shannon, in a massacre that saw the mutilation and devouring of their body parts and internal organs beyond recognition, leaving behind a trail of guts and destruction.

As is deep within the inherent nature of the werewolf, of course.

HUNGRY FACES

by John Gilbert

"Lisa?" Peter woke in chilled darkness with the echoes of her pleas still in his ears.

He ached, every muscle inflamed with the dull, sapping, throb of exhaustion. The raw rancid taste probed the back of his throat, combined with the coppery stink of oily sweat on his naked skin, threatened to make him vomit with every breath. He was weak, drained of life, and made no further attempts to explore the blackness beyond.

"Lisa," he croaked. The words broke in his throat as memories of her tumbled numbly back into his mind...

***

"Strange place for an exhibition," Peter said to the girl standing next to him.

They both pondered the monstrous canvas on the wall in front of them for a few moments more before the girl replied: "Art with a whiff of anaesthetic."

"Or at least antiseptic hand scrub," he laughed at what seemed to be her judgement not only on this painting - a male nude composed of thick slabs of dark toned oil paint - but also of the whole exhibition.

"What are you in for, then - if not this exhibition?"

He raised his thickly bandaged hand and attempted to

wiggle the pain stiffened fingers. "A&E. I saw the poster in the lobby and thought I'd take a quick look."

"A waste of time?"

"No," he looked across at her and smiled again. "Not a total waste. I draw and paint occasionally. Wouldn't call myself a serious artist but I like to look, convince myself I could do better. So what are you in for?"

She glanced back at the canvas. "I am an artist."

"Shit," he sighed, casting his eyes down to the floor. "I'm sorry if - "

"Don't be. I'm well aware of my meagre talents."

"Not so meager," he assured her. "I know very little about art, no opinion worth considering, and you're featured in a real live exhibition -"

"In a hospital," she reminded him.

They both laughed.

He leaned forward to study the bottom right of the canvas.

"What are you looking for," she asked, following his eye line.

"A name?" he said, straightening up.

"Lisa" she replied, holding out her hand.

When he didn't take it, she remembered the bandage. It was her turn to apologise and his to wave it aside. "Have you called a taxi home yet?"

He shook his head.

"Live far?" she asked.

Peter shook his head. "Cleve Park."

"Well, if you're interested, let me show you around the rest of the paintings and then I can drive you home."

He was interested, but in the next half hour paid more attention to her than the exhibits.

Lisa's slender oval face was crowned with short spiky white blond hair: She wore a blue leather jacket and tight black jeans that might have looked scruffy and uncaring on any other woman but on her seemed the height of carefully chosen tailoring.

She was what his father would have called petite; a girl on initial impressions but, the more subtle glances he took into her face, the more he realised that she was well into her mid-twenties, with a mind well into its mid fifties. But beautiful, yes beautiful. The sort of mellow beauty you could appreciate the more time you spent in its company.

When they arrived at the heart of the exhibition, he paused in front of a small unframed canvas, a view of the Scottish highlands painted in deep rusty browns and olive greens.

"Of particular interest?" she asked.

He nodded. "I think I've been there - or somewhere very like it."

"You're in to open spaces."

"Some," he mused. "Who's the painter?"

"Mr. Fellows," she replied, "He's a consultant at this hospital. Likes to explore out of the way places. He also runs the weekly art class I attend. Perhaps you've found a soul mate?"

His gaze lingered on the painting – on the ragged curves of the hills, the dark blue and white whirls that marked patches of water, rather than the artist's technique. It was a place he was sure he could never have been and of which he could certainly not recall the name. Maybe it was simply the memory of a dream, a location on TV or a picture captured from a roadside hording. Yet it felt more personal. A memory? He was not sure why he was drawn to the painting. It un-eased him and yet the place drew him in with its sense of quiet.

"A kindred spirit? Maybe. Maybe not." He gestured at the picture, "I might be interested in buying it. How much do you reckon he'd take for it?"

"Don't know, but I can ask - if you really are interested in it."

"Oh I am," he replied a little too quickly while at the same time wondering if he would ever be brave enough to ask her out.

He need not have worried; the opportunity came all too quickly. He had written his phone number on the back of her hand as they sat in her car outside the entrance to his block of flats.

She called that evening. "Martin's willing to sell the landscape. He suggested you meet at the art class on Friday."

"What?" he asked. "Why there?" He had, after all, thought of suggesting she act as go between, going out for a drink or dinner at which time he could hand her the money. That was after all his greater purpose. He was not so much interested in the painting as in her.

There was a pause on the phone line before she confessed: "I told him that you draw and paint. He was interested in seeing your work. I thought if you brought - "

"But you haven't even seen them. They could be rubbish."

"He's a better judge than I." Another pause. "Perhaps we could go out for a drink or a pizza afterwards."

A ray of hope. "He's not likely to rip them apart is he?"

"Of course not," she replied. "Have faith in yourself Peter. I do. Now are you coming or not? I can pick you up tomorrow evening around seven?"

***

The Friday night art group took place in a purpose built craft's room at St. Paulinus School, a space shared during the day by budding painters and sculptors where the smell of wet clay and turpentine mixed and lingered in the air like the sweat of dedication and endeavour.

When Peter and Lisa arrived the room was already full with the expectant, hushed voices of people setting canvas or sketch pads to easels. It was, as Lisa had promised, a mixed bunch. Some were still in their teens, perhaps students at the school who just could not get enough during the day. Others still wore suits - with shirts open-necked, sans ties - no doubt hot from work, while others were well into their sixties, making the most of their retirement. Nearly all paused to acknowledge Lisa as she entered and, no doubt, wonder at the young newcomer trailing behind her.

She pointed him to a chair and easel near the front of the class and took up position at the work station beside him. He had just enough time to deposit the small packet drawings he had brought along before a hush descended on the room and a tall man in jeans and an olive green roll neck sweater took his place at the front of the class.

Apart from the height that was reflected in every limb of his body, Christopher Fellows was unlike any surgical consultant Peter had ever seen or imagined, barring one aspect - the intensity with which the members of the art group followed his every move.

At another time Peter might have found this unsettling. But now he noticed the gentle, intelligent, blue eyes that reflected back all that rapt attention and the smile that continued to widen as he sat informally on the front of his desk in front of the group.

Fellows clasped his hands in his lap: "Welcome everyone, whether you are regular or a newcomer - " he smiled at Lisa and nodded at Peter. "As usual there are no hard and fast rules here, and most of you will have met our model for tonight, Abi Turner."

There was movement at the back of the room and Peter turned to see the subject of Fellows' welcoming hand gesture. A young woman of no more than twenty-three walked between them towards Fellows. She had long hair, so black that it seemed to eat the harsh artificial light in the room, and wore a cream robe that perfectly matched the soft textures of her face and bare arms.

Peter felt uncomfortable, not at her impending nakedness but rather with a rising doubt that he could capture her image in a crude pencil illustration.

He had no time for further worry as Fellows gently grasped her silk clad shoulder with his long fingers just long enough for Peter to wonder whether they were lovers. But, it appeared that the gesture was simply a signal for her to disrobe.

He had to admit, Abi had the perfect form, from the shallow curve of her breasts down to the carefully clipped wiry black hair between her thighs.

His cheeks swelled with heat but, he guessed, no one in this room would be singling out his reactions as she walked to a green chaise lounge to the left of Fellows' desk and stretched out across its length clasping her hand behind her head to best display her tits.

Peter let out a subtle breath with the rest of the room. The atmosphere had changed. While everyone had been momentarily distracted by Abi's appearance, the focus was now on the creative work ahead. Without any further words from Fellows, people began to pick up pencils and brushes. Peter did the same, not looking sideways at Lisa or glancing at the others around the room until Fellows voice woke him from the movement of pencil mark across paper. "Very good."

He drew his head back to survey his own work on the paper. Had he really drawn the svelte female figure of light and shade that gazed back at him from the paper? There was an intensity of shade and detail that he had never achieved before. Perhaps it was the emotional expectation of the group or, more probably, the desire to avoid public humiliation. Whatever the impetus, Fellows seemed genuinely pleased with the results.

Bending close to Peter's ear he spoke in a hush: "I understand from Lisa that we share an interest in wild landscapes. If you have any examples in that pile of work you brought with you perhaps you could share over a drink later?"

Peter nodded.

"In the meantime, perhaps you could go further with this new piece."

"Go further?"

"You've done well in capturing her image; now give her something to do. Give her some background, some action to perform. Bring the painting to life". He noticed Peter's frown. "Close your eyes and draw the first thing that comes into your mind," he paused to look down at the drawing before starting towards the next easel with one final suggestion. "Don't be afraid to change her pose in the picture. The lady up there, beautiful as she is, is only a model, waiting for you to clothe her with action, make her come alive."

Clothe her with action? Peter shook his head at Lisa as Fellows moved away and whispered: "What the fuck does that mean?"

Lisa leaned towards him. "He knows what he's talking about. Close your eyes; imagine her in a scene. Draw the first thing that comes into your mind".

"What if the first thing I think about is something that doesn't fit?" he laughed, "Like a kitchen or a supermarket."

"It will be suitable," she assured him.

He shrugged, closed his eyes and tried to turn off the noises around him. At first, all he could see was the light behind his eyelids but, as he lost a sense of the classroom around him, that light grew darker and a familiar picture rose unbidden from his mind. Copper brown and olive green, dark and old. Grey cloud boiled above the black panoramic curve of the horizon. He was a part of this picture, running close to the stubby grass and sticky mud, hot and heavy with breath...

Dizzy at landscape's power, he forced open his eyes and began to draw, hardly able to look down at the hurried invasion of black pencil trip across silk paper.

At last, he finished and looked across at Lisa with a smile only to find that she was already at his shoulder. Somehow disturbed at the sudden, frenetic pace of this work, she had already dropped her own work in favour of his. And what he saw in her face was not the return of his smile but a look of concentrated fascination. "Jesus," she whispered, "That's quite something."

Only then did he look down at the sketch pad and become conscious of what he had drawn. The landscape was a familiar one but the jagged execution of the pencil strokes made it wilder than had the smooth rich oils in Fellows' painting. Yet it was not the landscape but the female figure it contained that had caused Lisa's sharp exclamation.

Peter could not say for sure that it was the woman still posed on the chaise lounge at the front of the class, for he had redrawn her. The features and proportions of the life model were the same or would have been if they had not been cruelly distorted by the violence visited upon her.

She lay naked on the highland scrub, her face opened to the bone, breasts cleaved, arms and legs broken and rearranged at lunatic angles.

Fortunately, no one else had been roused by Lisa's sudden interest in his work, but Fellows had started to walk back in his direction and he was clear on one thing, he did not want this teacher to share this student's work.

He flipped the page over and had begun to build up the stiffly posed form of the model again as Fellows stepped up behind him. "Inspiration must have deserted me this evening," he said by way of hurried explanation.

"So it would seem," Fellows nodded. "But I'd still like to see the past work that Lisa said you brought along this evening".

***

"Do you still want to buy my landscape?" Fellows asked as he paged through the sample sketches that Peter had handed him.

"That depends on whether you're willing to part with it," Peter replied. To be honest, he had forgotten that night's original purpose and now he was not sure whether he wanted a reminder of his class work hanging in his flat.

If it had not been for the thought of later sharing some time with Lisa - and alone - he might have feigned an excuse to cut the night short.

"Lisa told you I was," his dark eyes narrowed, "But - you don't sound as enthusiastic as she described. Has meeting the man who painted it put you off?"

"Not at all," Peter protested.

"Then maybe it has something to do with your own work? What you were drawing this evening?" A subtle smile flickered on Fellows' face. "Perhaps what you discarded during the group earlier on."

"It wasn't worth considering," Peter insisted.

"I'm sure Van Gough and Rembrandt said that sometime in their lives. But, honestly, it's very often our initial attempts; those things we are driven to throw away that often turn out to have the most value."

"And what if they just turn out to be rubbish? Surely the artist is the one to choose what is to be discarded and what is to survive."

Fellows smiled. "Or maybe it's the art that is the final arbiter, and artists should just follow their hunger to create."

"You make it sound as if the art is alive, that is chooses to come into being, chooses to survive."

"M'be," Fellows replied, "And perhaps that is just what terrifies you, the hunger to survive."

"Hunger?"

"Yes, all artists are hungry Peter. Hungry to achieve, to be creative, to be known, to be acknowledged for what they create - or maybe what creates them. I told you to rely on initial impressions. Is it the thought of letting go that scares you? You will have to do it sometime; you'll have no choice - if you want to survive." Fellows held out his hand. "Can I see it?"

Peter was going to insist he had torn it up and left it behind in a bin at the school, but the look in Fellows' eyes showed he knew otherwise. He reached to the very bottom of his leather bag and drew out the crumpled sketch.

In the few seconds it took to hand the drawing over, Peter imagined all the ways in which Fellows could respond. Shock at the brutality on the page. Derision over the crudity of technique. Anger that he had been inspired by Fellows' own darkly rugged highland scene and introduced such violent chaos into it.

Fellows studied the picture for a full two minutes, smoothing out the creases, straightening the edges, running his fingers above the pencil lines.

"Finally he spoke: "It is beautiful. How much do you want for it?"

***

"I couldn't seriously sell it to him," said Peter on the way back to Lisa's dark blue Volvo.

"Why not?" she asked.

"It was all torn up. Not even worth the paper it was drawn on."

"Don't -" she stared at him over the roof the car. "Don't say that. It's obviously worth something to you."

He laughed and pulled on the handle of the front passenger door but found it still locked. "Okay, how do you work that out?"

"Because you drew it in the first place."

"And then I screwed it up -"

"No, you tried to hide it. There's a difference."

"I was going to put it in the nearest bin."

"So you tell yourself."

"And you know better than me?" He pulled at the locked handle repeatedly and glared across the roof at her.

Lisa sighed. "Maybe not," she offered meekly, before slipping behind the steering wheel and pulling her door shut.

They shared the journey towards his flat in almost silence, Peter looking out of his window at the near deserted dark streets until he said: "You know him. I was just wondering, why he would want a sketch drawn by an obvious amateur?"

"He collects potential, enjoys raw talent."

"He wants me to join the group - as a regular?"

"Maybe."

"So he can develop me?"

She shook her head. "He believes in the total freedom of the artist to develop in the way that they need."

"And what about you?" Peter asked.

She frowned. "What do you mean?"

"How did you meet?"

"Christopher? At the hospital. He was getting the group

together about two years ago, advertised on the reception notice board. I went along to the first meeting and got roped in, as you do at the start of these things."

"And what drew you in? The art or the man?"

"You want honesty?" she laughed, and then grew more serious. "Honestly, the man. He is -"

"A Svengali?"

"Captivating," she applied the brakes hard as the traffic lights turned red.

A wave of dizziness surprised Peter as he settled back into the passenger seat. It followed by a hard bitter ball of nausea rolling up his throat. He choked the nausea back but the dizziness rose in his brain, blurring vision and thought.

"Are you okay?" Lisa asked.

"Uh-huh," Peter assured her, but felt as if he was drowning and wondered if he would be able to leave her at the end of the journey without messing up her carpets.

He tried to relax. "You were saying?"

"About what?"

He tried to remember. "Captivating."

She threw him a puzzled look, "Christopher?"

"You said he was captivating."

"He is. He can take such an interest in you without all the usual baggage that goes with it."

"Baggage?"

"What you really want to know is if he's seduced me."

"No-no. It wasn't that -" and with his protestations came a fresh wave of nausea.

He rested his cheek against the cool window, watching the night of amber flares drift in and out of spiralling, shrinking consciousness until his eyelids shut and, next to him, he thought he heard Lisa whisper, "Sorry"...

***

Ripples of mottled light race amongst gorse, heather and bulbous outcrops of moss stained rock. A grey sky tilts towards him as he raises his head, weary of his own ragged breath.

His sore belly brushes the spiky undergrowth, his legs pound at the hard ground beneath them. Despite the tiredness of the almost finished night, he is still light, fleet footed and as relentless as his pursuers. In another life, another form, he would know who they are: friends, neighbours, colleagues. But now all he knows is their lust, their hunger for revenge.

He is not ready for atonement. His only thoughts, as insistent as his pounding legs and heart - before him freedom, behind him, captivity or, more certainly, death.

The Outcrop is up ahead: a chance to climb, to turn, leap, gouge and tear at his pursuers, to purge them of life or, as was his curse, of their humanity.

Cunning, spiced with cruelty makes manoeuvring easy on the hard, rising, rock. Claws skitter to a halt as he turns to peer through the darkness down from the sharp overhang.

The still, thick, air is polluted with the clatter of horse hooves. Two, three, four? He could not guess at the number of riders, but his muscle-packed joints were more than a match for any horse or rider.

He leaps and is engulfed in an eruption of blood soaked flesh and splintering bone.

***

Peter woke in darkness, the copper tang of blood in his dry mouth. It took him several panicked moments to realise it was his own. It took longer to realise that the oily stink of sweat came from his nakedness.

Pain flared in his arm as he reached out into the solid darkness for even the bandage that had cocooned and protected it was gone and the stitches gripped at the long, ragged, wound like steel wire. He winced but continued to reach out, splaying his aching fingers against the cold concrete floor.

The unnerving euphoria of the dream - could he really call it a nightmare - had already melted into the swelling darkness of his mind as he recalled what had gone before. The thick throb of the engine, the vibration of wheels on tarmac, the jolt at the traffic lights. The swell of vomit in his throat. The dizzy heat. And her voice.

Lisa.

Had she - ?

A patch of white light widened on the floor as a panel above his head slid open. He glanced up just long enough to note heavy metal bars before screwing his eyes shut against the screaming white light.

A breath-length pause. Movement. Shadow against light.

Peter lowered his hand from his face, turned his eyes upward towards the bars and tried to focus beyond them. The sharp light parted and formed two indistinct silhouettes that solidified into two shadowy faces - faces that he recognised.

"Fellows?" The name came as an ugly croak from his parched throat.

His question was answered by a voice just as familiar, though not one directed at him. "He's fine," Lisa sounded relieved, though, given the circumstances, he doubted it was purely out of concern for his well being.

"Well, I can't see the point of his being conscious yet." Fellows replied.

"We have no idea of the effects of the drugs in his system - even in the short term. You do want him alert and active later."

"Of course," said Fellows. "The livelier the better."

Peter tried to force focus into his eyes, but the figures beyond the bars of this cage still shimmered in the piercing cold white light.

"Lisa, please." It was little more than a whisper from the prisoner, but Fellows response showed that he had heard.

"Put him back to sleep," his voice was cold and stung as much as the dart of pain that pierced the skin of Peter's naked shoulder. He opened his mouth to cry out but was unconscious before the sound could project beyond a rough grunt at the back of his throat.

***

The wound is the centre of his world, a dull throb that becomes a heartbeat before which reality dances with dream.

He is no longer chained by soporific drugs, free to stretch his aching limbs, but only as far as the confines of the cage that is now flooded with light on all sides. There is enough room to pace, still naked, several feet on all fours, like a lion or bear in a zoo or circus enclosure. He can make no more sense of this than he can the strange world beyond the bars. A cavernous, low ceiling room, illuminated by a combination of spots and up-lighters.

A bubble of noise to his left, though he can no more see the people hidden as they were in shadow, as much he can distinguish the nature of their hushed conversations.

Is that awe in their voices? If so, at what? Perhaps the figure who stepped into his field of vision and now stooped towards the bars to speak to him.

"You must be terribly confused by now," Fellows offered him a mock pout of consolation and nodded down at the throbbing wound in his shoulder. "Not had much luck since your accident. Can you still not remember how it happened?"

Peter lashed at the bars but Fellows did not even flinch. Instead, he leaned closer, consolation replaced by a provocative smile. "Perhaps it's best not to remember the attack, all that fear and pain."

A vision of a dark street soaked in the thin glare of sodium lamps. Running, panic - he could not remember the cause. And then a blow from behind, the breath beaten from him, the agony slicing up his arm followed by a hot gush of blood that swallowed his consciousness.

Fellows nodded as if he could follow every thought. "Best not to dwell on it. But I would like you to at least understand what happens now. It won't do you much good as far as your freedom is concerned but I would like you to understand the motivation, that all this is more than kidnap and torture."

Peter glared up at Fellows from the discomfort of the concrete floor, his fingers still tightly wrapped around the bars of the cage. But he refused the urge to make another push for escape that he knew would be futile.

"Those bars were built to hold something far more powerful than your feeble human strength," Fellows again appeared to read his mind. "A transformation my select group of friends gathered here are keen to see - hungry to portray."

This time Fellows did step back to allow him sight of the room beyond. Peter's eyes had now become so accustomed to the light and shadow that he could easily make out the small group of people, conversing, nervously it seemed, drinks in hand and before them an array of easels.

"Transformation?" Peter croaked. He reached up with his right hand and played his sweat slick fingers against the ragged landscape of the tear in his arm. The wound now seemed to pulse, keeping pace with the dull irregular beat in his brain.

His fingertips began to throb, nails lengthening, narrowing, while the knots in each joint grew thick and red as if burdened with arthritis. But, rather than weakness, his fingers were flooded with power, a power that bit deep into the thick bars of the cage, yet not enough to break them.

"Transformation," Fellows repeated. "The first time I encountered it I was surprised the human frame could take it. Now I understand it's a matter of survival. And that is what my friends here have paid so much to witness and record. Savagery for art's sake. The beast in repose".

Peter screamed as the tendons in his legs and arms constricted. He released the bars and collapsed backwards in convulsions that at first seemed to be shaking his body apart. No, he was changing; feet and fingers elongating, legs and arms thickening, the taut muscle of stomach becoming a ribbed underbelly that sweated and throbbed beneath a dark pelt.

He raised his head, sucking air through flattened nostrils into lungs that had filled his chest cavity, releasing it up into his throat where a simmering growl became a howl.

***

Peter woke again to the rattling of the cage bars, a rise in the light levels and a soft voice before him.

Lisa.

He scuttled back again with a whimper, raised his fingers to blot out the light and realised that he was himself again.

"I'm not going to hurt you, or could hurt you". She hushed and soothed at his nerves.

But he could not forget her betrayal. "You already have," he replied with a growl that was all too pathetically human. What had happened? From the moment he had passed out in the car, through the violent pain of transformation to here, now. A dream, a vision made wild by the drink he had consumed at the pub. Perhaps drugged by Fellows, but for what reason?

"It wasn't – isn't - a dream," she said. He must have spoken aloud – unless she could also read his thoughts.

A bitter, surgical smile cut into his face. "Why would you want me to believe that I'm – what? – a werewolf?"

"Belief has nothing to do with it," she replied in a hurried whisper. "It's what Christopher wants, has always wanted. To capture something unique."

"The beast".

"I saw it: saw you. So did the others..."

"Others?"

She looked behind her, as if she had heard a noise that she

wasn't expecting. "The others who came here to paint you, your transformation."

"To paint me?" he asked. "A portrait."

"Not of you, of what you've become after the attack." When she looked back at him her eyes were filled with fear. "I have to get you out of here. We have to move."

"What? Before he wheels in another group –"

"There won't be any other group. They were the richest, the most powerful, but I don't think the money was that important to Christopher. I didn't - didn't understand," Lisa worked hurriedly on a lock that was out of sight below the cage. She whimpered and hit the bar with the thick key in her right hand. "Damn." She looked him closely in the eyes. "He's going to kill you."

"Kill -"

There was the sound he had heard before, a silence bullet or the phut of a pellet being released from an air gun.

Lisa looked at him with a mixture of pain and terror that slowly drained away into unconsciousness as she slumped before him. Behind her stood Christopher Fellows, the snub nosed pellet gun extended towards the cage, the nozzle moving from the figure prone on the floor to the one, naked and tattered lying at the back of the cage.

"Don't worry, she won't be out for long," Fellows assured him. "Do the dreams make sense yet?"

Peter frowned and, for all the fear focused on the gun before him, shuffled closer to the bars.

"Dreams of racing through open spaces, being pursued, becoming the pursuer: the hunt, the kill." Fellow's voice

56

became almost sibilant and with every word stepped towards the cage and Lisa's slumbering body. "My dreams, shared with you."

"Shared?" His eyes widened as he understood and finally accepted the truth. "You - it was you who attacked me and made me into this –"

"Yes – this," Fellows gestured at himself, "But don't for one minute believe I attacked you out of some uncontrollable bestial lust. True, one eventually finds some solace in rending human flesh, but I'm hundreds of years old; I can transform at will, though am still also affected by the cycles of the Moon. I can subdue my nature for a while but eventually it will out. At such an age the hunt, the kill, soon become secondary pastimes."

"So why?" Peter asked, hoarsely. "Why attack me? And why not kill me?"

"Eventually even the beast tries to evolve, to make an effort to study its nature perhaps to subdue and overcome it completely. During the past decades I have 'turned' others – men, women and even children - in order to study them, measure, probe and dissect the beast when it appears. But – well, what would you do if all you found was that there was no possibility of salvation?"

Silence between captor and captive until, at last, Peter pleaded one more time: "Why?"

Fellows gestured at the easels, paints and cameras beyond the cage. "Those who sat there and witnessed your first transformation tonight, who quickly set to capturing those images on canvas and film – they are all able to do so because they are rich and powerful. I offered them a unique experience that they did not quite believe would happen until they were here and witnessed it. But my aim isn't to make money from them. No, the nature of the beast soon strips all that money and power away as baser instincts come into play. My aim? To watch and study them as in the coming years they lose everything they have to the nature of the beast. Tonight I will turn them as I turned you then watch as they face their first transformation, unable to touch me or report me for fear of what the wider world would do to them."

"Revenge?"

"Nothing so simple. Call it a need to know that there are others in the world like me and, despite all their power and position, that they, like me, are unable to change the nature of the beast, what it makes them do."

He drew closer still to Peter and looked down at Lisa's still, silent, form. "A pity. She had it wrong. I don't want to kill you...brother."

***

"Lisa?" Peter woke in chilled darkness with the echoes of her pleas still in his ears.

He ached, every muscle inflamed with the dull, sapping, throb of exhaustion.

A raw rancid taste probed the back of his throat, combined with the coppery stink of oily sweat on his naked skin threatened to make him vomit with every breath.

He was weak, drained of life, and made no further attempts to explore the blackness beyond for he knew what it held.

"Lisa," he croaked. The words broke in his throat as memories of her tumbled numbly back into his mind...

HIDDEN DEPTHS

by Samantha Lee

Daisy looked up from her book and there he was, powering across the bay like an Olympic athlete. He had the elegant, fluid rhythm of all good swimmers, his strong arms slicing through the flung spray like a knife cuts through butter. At the farthermost end of the beach, where the shingle rose sharply to a granite headland, he turned in a smooth arc and began to breast stroke lazily back.

It was a glorious west of Ireland day, the sort about which poems are written. No cloud troubled the hyacinth curtain of sky which dropped, satin smooth, into an almost amethyst sea. A nectarine sun hung, hot and sultry, over the isolated crescent of white sand.

Daisy shifted onto her elbow, shading her eyes from the noonday glare the better to observe the swimming youth. She felt a trickle of interest in the damp nest of her pubic hair. She'd been feeling randy all morning. Must be the heat. Anyway things were looking up. She hadn't been remotely interested in anyone since Sean had dumped her unceremoniously and gone back to his pregnant wife six months ago. But this gorgeous creature could certainly tickle her taste buds. He was very young of course. Too young for her. Not exactly jail bait but as near as made no matter. Seventeen at most and her all of twenty eight. Old enough to know better.

The discrete object of desire came to a halt opposite her and began to tread water. Noticing her for the first time, he raised one brown hand in greeting, sweeping the other through hair that cascaded like sea-wrack from his neat round head. It was a fine, dark bronze with a tinge of green and it hung across his muscular shoulders in a silky waterfall.

Very unusual for this neck of the woods where the short back and sides was still in vogue and most of the men were dark and dour. He reminded her of a painting by Dante Gabriel Rossetti. Something called 'The spirit of the sea' perhaps? Of course Mrs O'Rourke wouldn't approve at all. Baby snatching, she'd call it. Still...Mrs O'Rourke wasn't here...and anyway, it was none of Mrs O'Rourke's business.

Daisy grinned and waved back.

"Are you coming in?" The boy's voice was soft and warm as the May wind. It carried across the still surface of the water and wrapped itself around her loins like spiced wine.

Daisy was a city chick, born and bred. She could programme a computer, drive anything on wheels and boogie til the cows came home, but water was not her medium.

"Can't swim," she called, embarrassed at such a confession, but the boy just laughed.

"You can paddle, surely?" he said. "Come on. I'll give you a free lesson."

"Daisy cursed her luck. Three weeks she'd been here in this enchanted place and tomorrow she had to go home. Back to the rat-race, the rush-hour, the burn-out that had sent her, after the abortive affair with her bastard boss, on retreat to this remote backwater. The split with Sean had hit her like a ton of bricks. The intensity of her feelings had taken her by surprise and left her fit for nothing. She couldn't stop crying. A complete break, the Psychiatrist had said, or she'd be for the funny farm. Three weeks. And on her last day, she meets this Adonis lookalike.

Wondering whether he was a visitor or a native, attached or

available, she stood up and brushed the sand from legs tanned by twenty one days of incredible weather. Her long blonde hair shimmered in the heat haze like spun gold. She was looking good. And she knew it.

Just as well he hadn't materialised before, she thought. If he'd seen her when she arrived, thin as a rake, white as a ghost, he'd have run a mile instead of inviting her in to play. Three weeks of Mrs O'Rourke's mothering and the peace of the deserted beach had turned her into something more like a human being. Mrs O'Rourke with her enormous meals and her tales of the Enchanted Isles out at the edge of the horizon. Of seals who shed their skin at night. Of hobgoblins who stole children out of their cots, leaving one of their own changlings in return. And of the Finn Folk who, if they hadn't captured a human heart before they came of age, were doomed to become old and raddled and monstrously ugly. All nonsense of course but very seductive on a moon misty night sitting in a rocking chair on the deck of an isolated house with the seals serenading you out in the bay. An old echoing house that had neither TV, nor wifi signal, nor land-line nor any other form of communication with the outside world. She'd only found it because she'd taken a wrong turn in the road.

The boy beckoned her into the sea once more and she padded down the sand and waded into the shallows up to her knees, then stopped. Despite the heat of the early afternoon, the water was freezing.

"Come on," he coaxed. "You won't melt. I'd come out and get you but I'm not wearing any trunks."

The thought shocked her nipples into prominence. They stood up against the thin fabric of her bikini like organ stops. She felt his sly look and crossed her arms over her breasts to conceal her obvious interest. He grinned, putting his hands over his eyes and peeping through the fingers like a naughty schoolboy. A hiccup of laughter propelled her a few more feet before she stopped once more, drawing in a deep breath as the water lapped at her thighs.

Young Adonis held out encouraging arms.

"Nearly there," he said...and he smiled...a hint of pink tongue behind strong white teeth. Close to he had the face of an angel carved in amber. A profile fit to decorate the prow of a ship or capture a lonely woman's soul.

Daisy's pathological fear of drowning (triggered by a sadistic brother who used to hold her head under water in the bath), evaporated. As if by magic she found herself suddenly beside him, breast deep in the violet sea. She glanced down to see if he really was naked but her hair fell over her eyes as he leant forward, circling his arms round her to unhook her bikini bra. Holding her in thrall with his sea green eyes, he slowly dropped the sliver of scarlet lycra into the water. Shocked in spite of herself, Daisy stepped back apace, the movement agitating the sea bed, churning up sand and silt, obscuring her view.

Titillated though she was, she still hated not being able to see her legs. If she couldn't see *them,* she couldn't see other things that might be lurking down there. Sea-slugs and jelly fish and such. Hadn't Mrs O'Rourke said that they'd even had a basking shark one summer? She shuddered, the panic plain on her face.

"Don't worry," he said, taking her hands. "You're with me now. Trust me. I won't let you go. Turn round and lie back, why don't you? I'll hold your head. All you need to do is kick your feet and you'll be swimming. It's as easy as shooting fish in a barrel."

Somewhere in the back of her brain, where civilisation lurked, Daisy felt she should protest. Instead, led by the most primitive instinct of all, she did as she was bid, sinking gingerly into the swell. He cupped one hand under her neck, sliding the other down the soft skin of her belly. His fingers moved into the top of her pants massaging the flesh in circular strokes. She felt the sticky surge of warm liquid trickle from between her legs, knowing she should stop him but wanting him to go on. Thoroughly aroused now, she reached back, hoping to touch the erection that she knew must be there.

"Daisy!" Mrs O'Rourke's voice, urgent, shrill, bounced across the water like a skimming stone, coming to her from another time, another place.

A pang of guilt shot through her. What was she doing? What was she thinking? Cavorting around half naked with a man she didn't know from a hole in the ground. She shook herself free and sank under the swell, inhaling as she went. A sudden rush of water surged up her nose and into her mouth. As the sea closed over her head, she opened her eyes in panic, catching a fleeting glimpse of a flash of silver close to the ocean floor. Terror shot her to the surface again gasping for air.

"There's something underneath us," she spluttered, memories of 'Jaws' hot in her head. Just when you thought it was safe to come back in the water. "Something big. A shark."

The young man received this information calmly, taking her face between his hands, his lips curling in a slightly sinister smile. "Relax," he said. "I've got your back."

In his eyes, limpet clear as rock pools, she saw the reflection, not of herself but of cool green caverns where seals sang and nobody owned a mobile phone. Then he pulled her gently beneath the waves.

And Daisy realised that she wouldn't be going back to the city after all. No more rat-race. No more struggle. No more faithless paramours. No more regret.

In the tranquil underwater world the bronzed body had taken on a luminous sheen. At least down to the navel. Below his groin the sleek fishtail tapered in translucent splendour down to the undulating, feather-like fin.

He reached forward to stroke her with a web-fingered caress and she was conscious of a sudden, sharp tearing in her breast not far removed from the sensation she had felt when Sean announced that their affair was dead in the water. Her silent scream rose in a rainbow of bubbles, drifting like soapsuds to the dappled surface. Just before the swirl of blood obscured him from view she saw him hold her heart, her all too human heart, in scaly triumph above his ugly, fish eyed head.

And Mrs O'Rourke, who had seen it all before, stood on the sand-dunes as the scarlet stain slowly spread outwards and sadly shook her head.

"Don't say I didn't warn you," she said to nobody in particular.

Then she went inside to get rid of the suitcase.

MANIPULATION AT MIDNIGHT

by Allison Weir

The world can be a beautiful place. I sit there watching it go by and come back to life again most days. At the same time, this cosmos co-exists in a very ugly manner.

I mean the world itself isn't ugly, no. God no. Far from it in fact. I am referring to the sick species with which it is unfortunately lumbered. The same said species that somehow remain el-bent on fucking it up and sometimes without even realising it.

The globe in which we live is immaculate. Into the one hundred billion (or whatever) days of its existence and it's still flourishing. Lush beyond belief. And not one hidden wrinkle. Shame I never get to see a single strip of it, least not fully by daylight.

It's just me and my sibling Celia left in our family. She has my back and I have hers and I've been in this condition for about thirty-five years now. I managed to turn her despite my reservations about effacing her from the living. I could not bear the thought of out-living my lil' sis.

Forgive me. Just spotted a bunny and I am absolutely starving!

I haven't been to many funerals in my lifetime. I'd like to keep it that way too. Man oh man they're depressing. When I am ready to leave this world, I want people to get a band playing, defy the drab dress code with purples, reds and yellows and just be their God damned happy selves.

This is the second funeral in the space of four months and I am still in mourning from the first. My beloved Lacey. Cruelly snatched from this world by the 'c' word. And I am not being blasphemous.

Her last few months were excruciating. Both for me and for her, in her state of pain. We tried many options, pursued all avenues for some miracle cure, alas we live in an age where one has yet to be discovered.

There are some days where I just break down and cry. I literally let it all out. I get naked and curl up in bed, imagining her lying next to me in her nakedness too. I have phoned in sick because I cannot even leave the house at times. I am constantly shrouded in pain when I see her petite ivory face literally everywhere.

My best friend Mitch has been a godsend in getting me through life since her passing. I cannot pinpoint exactly what he does to release me from my set ways of being cocooned in a blue funk of misery but he does it. And wonderfully so.

Unfortunately he is not here today to support me but I know a few in attendance so I will mingle with them.

It is St Gertrude's where they're burying my neighbour Maggie I believe. A place I have been to only once before.

Anyway, my name's Vernon. Just to let you know, I am not quite all there at the moment. Mentally and physically. But I am coping slightly better day in day out.

I love life and I don't want to be taken away from it just yet. Rather than me join Lacey in her restful state up in those utopian clouds, I would prefer her being back on dump shit earth, hating every second of her job and family. Now that sounds quite selfish, however she loved the nuts off me, of that I'm sure.

Bloody hymns. Great. My deep voice is way too hoarse to participate in the collective karaoke of melancholia. It would just sound ridiculously undulating so I keep on with my miming act.

Three hours later and I am as good as anyone's. Geez I don't know what stuff they're pulling at the bar but it's at least 10% per pint! Biggles Nest you call it. But I won't be going overboard today as I've got to start work at the crack of dawn.

"Vernon. You're ridiculously late. Wake up!"

I somehow stir at the bastard demands and urgency in the voice of my old school mate, Sam Jones. Why oh why have I wound up at his place?

Slowly but surely I nod in agreement and gesture for him to leave me be whilst I lean over to the window and light my first fag of the day.

Sam Jones is a mortician. Eurgh, right? Some poor arsehole has to do it I suppose. Within his job, he's rather apathetic.

Just going to that funeral made me want to heave. Well the drink probably had an effect on me there too but there's absolutely no way I could do what Sam does – embalming corpses and re-dressing them and all that? Grotesque!

"I'll get you egg and toast." Sam hastily cut into my thoughts as he tended to.

Within a minute, I am in the power shower. I dare not let my mind take heed of the loneliness as nothing otherwise occupies this makeshift vast void. The shower gel is good stuff. I imagine being under a bubbling waterfall in a faraway place, the spiced oranges manipulating the fish who bounce up and down in the cascading lagoons below. Or being on a desert island with everything I could want in life – the balmy water sluices over my rubbery skin at the shore back and forth, again and again.

Within ten minutes, Sam is true to his word, as the soldiers are ready to be dipped and swiftly consumed.

"Here mate, give this a whirl."

Another role play game for which I have no genuine interest. Trying to concentrate on anything at the moment would be a benediction.

"Don't write it off," he shoots back. He is hasty to hand me a plain looking DVD entitled 'Necro Nemesis,' and he just as quickly watches my reaction. "Guy in work lent me that.''

Pure filth. Even I can't help but chortle at the very basic blurb.

"Funny shit!" I exclaim between mouthfuls of runny yolk. "You expect me to get a thrill out of this?"

This of course had Sam in stitches and he would not reveal another thing other than, "Watch it!" which is what I did...

Nobody comes to St Gertrude's these days really. Whether it is because I am here that they are deterred or that they actually come and go in order to grieve with me being unawares, I couldn't be too sure.

"Delores!"

It can only be Celia – yes, my justifications are accurate as she swoops into view having been astray for a while.

I move over to her spiritedly. "Destroying angel, how are you?"

"Blissful," comes the answer. She quickly pelts a sparrow to the ground with her stone throwing catapult and more slowly, takes the time to yank its head off to ensure she misses no juicy goodness.

I always check the coast is clear. God forbid if some human stumbled upon us at a moment's notice... I would have no choice but to destroy him or her.

Celia on the other hand is a very different story. She has no human barbarity in her wax-like skin. She flies on the care-free side whereas I... I am much more prudent.

"It completely slipped my mind, sis," she started cheekily, "but there was a stranger sighted at East Chapel at approximately 1 o'clock this morning."

Oh frig. The words she delivered were completely superfluous. As superfluous as the stranger with whom I shall contend if a return visit to our strip is on the cards for that unfortunate human.

Over the years, we've had a minority of visitors to St Gertrude's. Naturally they have every right to pay their respects to bony dead relatives but others come here to merely abuse this place of rest. I like to remove these degenerates. That is my job – to more or less punish the living and help the dead. I guess I am in the middle somewhere on that one.

"What did he look like?" I assume this person's male because females other than ourselves would not be caught alone in this graveyard! "And how did I not see him?"

Celia was quiet upon my questioning and she flew to a high branch to shield her delicate thoughts. I have her down to a tee. She's taken a shine to this fellow!

"Good looker was he?" My grin spread as far past my fangs as you could imagine.

"I wouldn't know," she lied, the dimples forming even deeper crevices in the creases of her cheeks. "I didn't see his face too much. Just his arse and back mostly."

Cripes, my sister certainly has a way with guys. I pause

and await a further explanation although I may not be getting one.

"Look I was on echo-location at the time," she began in a huffy tone. "It looked ever so like Annabelle Finchley's grave but I couldn't be too sure..."

Right, that did it for me. That was all I needed to dart over to the East side to check out 'said' grave.

Annabelle Finchley. Died 13th February 2017. The monument above her grave has been removed within the last twelve hours due to the stone texture that I can see and possibly from the outset, the body exhumed from the shallow coffin. I mean, my methods are superior I have to say. As I dig with my rat like arms to get to the soil beneath using my dad's old sickle, I further notice that the clay has been disturbed.

I am almost unsettled as I use my bare fingernails to prise off the lid of the coffin, hands of which now resemble those of a spindly old witch's. Brittle and skeletal.

Annabelle is lying in wait. Like a dumb damsel in distress. The first thing I notice about her appearance is the out of place hair and most importantly, the positioning of her putrefied body. I mean, my sense of smell is off these days but even I can sense that this is too festered and horrific for a corpse so young. I do not wish to tamper with her smart sassy outfit but if what Celia said was true, then I fear the worse.

For a laugh, Sam has dared me to go out to the graveyard and perform one of those amorous acts on a random corpse. I'm guessing he has been duped into this through work and though sick, I can see the addiction to this fetish after watching that mad movie.

Tonight I am out with Mitch for a few pints. This is all I can do at the moment (in terms of socialising) — go out drinking. I really am unable to focus on a voluntary sober conversation. Poor Mitch. He has his own life and shouldn't have to babysit me.

"And what's the bizz with you?" he demands in his harsh talking style. I realise he's trying to 'normalise' things...

"Yeah," I start, an extremely weak smile in my even weaker attempt to feign a good week's work, rest and play. "Going okay this end."

Geez, who am I kidding? I mean, it's okay to be shit scared and vulnerable and down, Vernon. It is still too soon and people grieve for months on end. Don't they?

"...Beverley's prone to doing that as you know, the daft bird. And then little Janey took matters into her own hands by spraying everyone with water! What a rascal, eh? Ha ha!" He looked at me for a response, except he wasn't getting one. I had no idea what he was saying.

Angrily, I leapt out of my seat and rushed to the entrance, completely unaware of what I was actually doing. Supposedly fresh air would help. Nah. Bollocks it would. I didn't even want a fag!

"Are you okay mister?" A small figure down below tugged at my jeans, near enough on top of my gnads. "You look sad."

"KATIE!" snapped a voice at once, horrified to see the entire scene play out. A woman emerged from the shadows and sighed instantly. "Sorry pet. She does that to random strangers!"

Which one? Tugging at stranger's balls or going up to console them?

I force a smile and move on to the patio. Mitch must wonder what the fuck is going on with me. I ask myself the same question repeatedly. Then I see her.

Lacey.

If one were to describe her in food form, she would definitely be the deluxe edition of a white chocolate ice-cream with cookie sprinkles, mini marshmallows, chocolate sauce and a smattering of frozen strawberry pieces thrown in for good measure. She matches up to my idea of food heaven as she delicately glides across the car park, her wild dress flowing about, accentuating her curves of loveliness.

And then, she disappears. Mitch is at the door and observing my every move.

"Come on hotshot," he grins, steering me back towards the bar. "What you need is another set of liquor. Yes you do!"

And that's precisely what he delivers in the next three rounds. There's an ongoing but steady supply of bar juices that are just waiting to be discovered. I suppose a few won't hurt – but a lot can kill you.

Whilst the evening flies in, I think about going to bed. I am genuinely tired, depressed and the drink is a strong contributing factor to all the mayhem.

"So... Vernie Vern. Let's head on to The Wickerman. Lock in!!!"

Mitch often shouts when he's on the way to 'tanked up' land. He's a big fellow.

"Mate, I am going to make a move," I start with a raised voice. "It's been a long old day..."

Immediately he grins and shoves me back down in my seat. Soon after, he's up to the bar to get another jager-bomb.

"Mate, seriously," I begin once again. "I can't drink anymore. Not right now anyway."

Ah what's the use? He is well gone and not even listening to me. So I just stagger to my coat and make my way out of the crooked door in a rather hastily fashion.

Within a minute, Mitch is hot on my heels and chasing me down the street, laughing uncontrollably.

"The night is young!" he barks in excitement, now

picking me up as if I were his little daughter. "We still have much to complete in our Ver-Mitch rostra of shenanigans!"

"Ack, Mitch!" I slur and protest my words simultaneously, watching the upside-down car headlights and street lamps go by as he jogs me down the lane over his shoulder. I have no idea why we're going this way.

The night has become eerily cool. The previous street lamps are now faint as we enter this bone-chilling mist that envelopes the pair of us into its midst.

I barge my way out of Mitch's grip and make for the nearest drain. Yep, it's barf time!

By the time Mitch has turned around and noticed, I am wiping the sickly vomit away from my chops. Ah, what I'd do for a glass of water right now.

Suddenly I hear a sharp rustling sound beyond the wall which initially startles me. Yes, St Gertrude's... I've grown numb to that place for a plethora of reasons.

However Mitch bounces on ahead and leaves me to follow in his Neil Armstrong footsteps. He just keeps plodding on through the chapel area. Until he stops. And there is a jolly good reason for him stopping.

"Holy shit!" he breathes, gesturing ahead for me to check out his findings.

Lo and behold, and before my very eyes, is a sight definitely NOT for sore eyes.

Sam Jones! The Sam Jones I remember from school. He is zombie fucking.

A zombie, lying on the ground and writhing round. No way. I mean, am I imagining this in my drunken stupor? And then to re-confirm my suspicions, Mitch does what I don't have to and speaks:

"Jesus Christ! That guy is bonking a dead chick... Get out of here! Urgh! That is sick, man..."

I stand their helplessly watching a friend taking part in rigor-coitus!

"Sam?!"

Sam's attention is soon drawn towards me and he cannot do a thing other than gawp at me and realise I am not just any stranger. I am Vernon Stokes.

This sickening shit is happening. I sit and patiently watch the culprit with the pathetic Annabelle and then, his mate turns up for a piece of the action. These humans disgust me. I cannot believe I used to belong to their kind.

Before I know it, this Sam is moving towards his friend as I listen in to their exchange of words.

Oh, his friend is very sweet looking I must say and no, it appears this hunk of flesh is not favouring the dead tonight. Focus Delores, focus! He is cute but he is also a ghastly, foaming human.

"Celia!" I silently squeal to my sister who is a few hundred metres away. "Get ready to put that body back if these guys run away. I'll deal with this myself."

Focussing on the task in hand it appears that there is a commotion below. Sam is now being confronted by this 'stranger' and there's some altercation.

"Vernon, why the frig are you spying on me?" Sam demands. It appears he has no fear of being caught illegally cavorting with the dead... "This is my watch! She's my lover."

Ah, the cute guy is Vernon then? Interesting! It must be at least a minute before stranger number two responds although he does look worse for wear.

"It better not be my Lacey down there, Sam!" Vernon

growls, resisting the struggles of a third man. I don't know his name but he's one big brute!

"You don't understand, Vernon!" Sam cries out, waiting for Vernon to be led away. "You've had too much liquor son. Go home!"

Vernon still appears to be fighting against this third man although he is no match for him and in the end they hastily depart, as does Sam who is yelling some strange sounds. Thankfully he moves in the opposite direction and the entire mad crowd leave me and Celia in peace. Weird night. I will be monitoring this place 24/7 from now on, and mark my words, should there be a lucky third occasion, me and my wonder serum shall intervene.

"Did what I think happen last night, actually happen?"

I ask myself the same question aloud at least three times and then decide it had to have been the case. Mitch was even more pissed than me but he is in denial and assumes we hallucinated the entire corpse ritual. Unlikely!

I cannot stop thinking about the dead body Sam had exhumed. My friend Sam from school who has seemed so normal all this time. I know I didn't get a good look at the body but Jesus Christ... Was it someone he even knew? Or just a random deceased girl he decided to bonk?

Infected thoughts are pulsating through my mixed up mind. Someone he knew? Well he knew my Lacey fairly well... Oh fuck! I cannot be sure that it wasn't her. I cannot picture where exactly we were in the graveyard when Mitch and I staggered across Sam's depraved love act.

My mind has gone blank. The only way I'll ever know is if I go back to St Gertrude's myself.

Tap. Tap.

I look up, half expecting someone to be at the bedroom door – but who would it be? I live alone, regrettably...

Tap. Tap. Tap.

Okay, this is like morse code being signalled and I've now worked out where it's coming from. The window.

It could be a tree branch starting up its antagonising dance as the wind makes it swish and sway. Although when I open the window, there's not a thing against it. Very peculiar...

Looking ahead to tonight's jaunt I re-assure my paranoid self that nothing dodgy happened to my beloved. I am almost ready to head out – as soon as I re-watch 'Necro Nemesis' and get into the mind of that sick fuck.

Ah, Celia is a good girl. Nobody could assume a soul had trodden the personal ground of Annabelle Finchley. This is her patch and it shall be respected.

No more antics from any of these wanton types this evening. I have been contemplating a trap that my sister and I worked on many years ago when our herd were threatened in the region. Tonight its virginity shall be lost.

The time is nearing half past midnight and I am ever so slightly regretting this. I have told nobody of my intentions and neither have I seen nor heard a peep from Sam or any other random visitors.

Lacey Chambers was my fiancée. We found each other in the summer of 2010 and were supposed to get married next month. It didn't matter if we rollicked around in wealth and champagne when health was more important. Being married wouldn't have saved Lacey, not at this stage...

Quietly I begin digging away at her grave and soon

make my way through the moist yet satisfying earth of decay. I have to be sure she remains untouched.

I am almost a stone's throw away from being re-united with my dearly loved when I hear a faint rustling sound, almost like a scratching of some kind.

It's all muffled and hidden away. Literally it is coming just two graves away from Lacey's...

Oh God, is someone stuck below the ground?

No way... On second thoughts, it's probably kids on their phones mucking around.

So I go back to digging and ignore it however this time, the sounds become more ferocious and there is a hollow thumping. A repetitive strike which seems to get ever so slightly louder each time.

"Hello?" I shout.

Immediately the thumping stops for a minute or two and there's a buzzing sort of sound. Ack Jesus, a trapped animal for sure!

That's it. I'm pretty curious now. Before I can dig at this neighbouring grave, I feel something land on my cheek. Like a large mosquito with piercing fangs.

"Ouch!" I actually yell out which causes the noise to cut out entirely. I throw the thing to the ground and feel ever so slightly woozy however I am now digging at this mystery grave until I have unearthed the truth.

And the truth is... There's a body quivering before my blurry eyes. Dear God rigor-mortis is happening. Shit no – it's not!

The corpse's steely blue eyes snap open and within a second, the mouth is widened to reveal a plethora of yellowed sharp teeth and a hissing sound that comes from beyond. What the fuck...

Before I can defend myself from this now arising skeletal zombie, I feel my knees buckle from beneath. And then with no ounce of energy, I crumple to the ground like an exhausted leaf.

"Vernon. Vernon... Is that you, Vernon?"

I can feel a strange sensation across my face, perhaps the splashes of water but my body feels even stranger. My bloodstream is incredibly heavy, almost like it has been replaced with lead. In fact, on attempting to move, my whole body is feeling that way. Heavy.

"Vernon?"

I hear my name for the umpteenth time but wherever it's coming from, I haven't figured it out. Until I attempt to zone in on what I believe to be a familiar shape. Hell no... It cannot be.

"Lacey?!"

"Vernon," she replies, moving closer for me to blur her into focus. "It's your Lacey, back the way you remember her..."

"Her?" I started dazed. "But she's dead..." I'm mildly freaked out now.

Yes," Lacey went on. "And you can join me now. All it takes is one juicy kiss."

By the time I put two and two together, I'm engaging in this snog with my beloved Lacey. Except it doesn't feel right. Not her warmth, nor her smell. Nada. I am not getting the same vibes I once did. What has happened to my little cherry pie?

My brain is only just registering as my tongue becomes wrongly entwined with something else. My eyes gaze into those of a bloodshot content and I instantly back away to find it is not Lacey I have made human contact with. But a malignant spirit. No, worse than that. A rabid monster. A perilous vampire. And she's going right for the jugular.

"NOOOOOO!" I scream, holding my arms up to protect myself.

I look round and she's simply staring back at me. She no longer even resembles the blond of Lacey but a dark haired grey skinned bony woman.

"No what, cutie pie?" Her blood red lips reveal this cheeky grin that further reveals a profusion of pointed teeth. She appears confused by my reactions.

"You aren't going to devour me then?" I lower my arms and upon asking this, feel like the wimpy scrawny kid who fears the school bully's wrath. "You went for my neck!"

The vampire woman threw her head back and laughed in the most petrifying manner. Whilst this was happening, another vampire slid into view and stood there grinning at (possibly her friend's?) reactions.

"Nuh-no. Delores was merely sniffing your aftershave scent, guy," the latest visitor revealed saucily and with a slight snicker too. "She has had her eye on you a bit recently!"

"Celia!" Delores exclaimed aghast. She looked back at me and delivered this weirdly sexy smile. "My little sister, haha. She lies not on this one."

My head is spinning and the dials on my watch are making no sense at all. I'm guessing it could be 2.30? I feel drugged up to the hilt, it's strangely warming up in this eerie graveyard and I am insanely tolerating the presence of two temptress vampires who may still eat me.

"Look, I was here to check that that son of a bitch 'mate' of mine had not touched the corpse of my fiancée," I started confidently, backing away from the moonlight slightly. It's blinding tonight! "That's all I came here to do. I am sorry to have disturbed you ladies." As I turn to walk away, I feel a change in my hands. Not just in temperature but in appearance. They're more pointed. As are my feet which are struggling to stay in my shoes! What the hell is happening to me?

My lower cheeks expand slightly and as I go to feel them, I fear the worst. Protruding fangs! Two sets of them!

Celia and Delores walk towards me and continue to watch my freaking-out behaviour. All it takes is Celia to feel about her person and hold up a tiny ancient mirror to my face.

"Welcome to St Gertrude's."

DEATH PACT

by Soraya Abuchaim

The night was cold without stars. The lightnings that cut through the dark sky were the harbinger of a storm. The house where Deborah lived was silent; on the outside, not even the insects seemed interested in manifesting themselves.

In the huge living room, the old-fashioned wall clock hit vibrant twelve ticks, while Deborah slept a dreamless, heavy sleep.

In the middle of the pitch black room, a translucent, female shade sneaked silently into the new resident's bedroom. The female shade stopped beside the bed and watched Deborah lying placidly, her chest rising and falling through her heavy breathing. She gave a diabolical grin when, without blinking, she threw herself at the lean figure that was snoring on the antique canopy bed.

***

Deborah opened her eyes suddenly, pulling up her body and sitting on the bed, still tangled in the linen sheets. She felt a powerful force taking care of her, as well as an excitement that made her groin tingle. Carefully she got up and walked to the dressing table at the far end of the room. A light curtain swung through the half-open window. It was late dawn.

She sat on the bench and looked at the reflection illuminated only by the dim light that came through the window. She didn't recognize that woman in front of her: black hair, very different from her blond curls; a scarlet and fleshy mouth, full breasts, outlined and tempting under the white silk nightgown. Deborah touched her hair; it was soft, it seemed made of some material she did not recognize. The woman's eyes in the mirror were violet, and although the room was dark, the image became fully visible, as if emanating its own light.

She did not panic; she felt herself well and young, showing none of the wrinkles of her forty-five years of age. That beautiful woman in the mirror couldn't be more than two decades of life.

When lightning cut through the sky and heavy raindrops drummed on the roof, she murmured mechanically, as if she could not contain the words that came out of her soft lips: "It's time."

Deborah did not know what was going on, nor who was guiding her when, in the midst of the storm, she left the house, her nightgown becoming glued and transparent, showing all the curves of her newly discovered young body.

She walked directly to the small town tavern; her hair dripped water, but she did not feel cold. On the contrary: the tingling sensation in her groin continued, releasing excitement shocks and burning her body.

The tavern was empty, except for three or four drunks who were waiting for the rain to pass. She went silently, no one seemed to notice her.

Deborah looked at her victim: a tall, muscular black man, bald, but with a thick beard. She walked to the table, insinuating her wet breasts on his face and putting her violet gaze over his eyes; without saying a word, she pulled him by the hand, and he dutifully escorted Deborah back to her house, having as company the rain and some audible thunders.

She was safe. She pulled the man into the house and closed the heavy door behind her.

The sun broke into the room where Deborah snored. There was no cloud in the sky; it did not even seem that there was a storm the night before. She stretched languidly, sitting up and rubbing her eyes. There was in her brain the remnant of a strange dream where she killed a man. As she remembered, she felt a shiver run through her body, but she pushed the thought away and stood up, taking care of her daily activities. When, however, she looked at herself in the mirror, it seemed that some of her wrinkles had disappeared. Restful sleep, she thought.

***

Deborah followed the day as usual, working on her paintings in the room she'd turned into a studio. She was enjoying the life greatly in the quiet town, the property where she had come to live had been inherited from an unknown uncle, its location in the countryside of São Paulo, about three hundred kilometres from the capital. As a visual artist, the inheritance was the solution to the rent problem that was destroying her in the capital. She paid huge sums for housing in a stinking alley, with no prospect of better living, earning scarce change in return for her hard-fought art.

After lunch, she got into her second-hand car and drove on the dirt road leading downtown, which was not far. She needed some things to fill up the fridge.

Deborah parked the car on the curb in front of the city's only emporium; the place was crowded, it looked like there was going to be an apocalypse and people needed to stock up on food to survive. In the narrow and dimly lit aisles, she managed to fill her basket with the basics and, without patience, went to the checkout line.

There, she listened to the conversations around her. She found, indifferently, that one of the women, who was waiting to pay for groceries, husbands did not come home the night before, and she was annoyed that he was always making sudden disappearances. The woman was very beautiful, her skin was olive-toned, and her eyes were very black, but she seemed wrathful, talking to a friend in a high tone:

"Wait until he arrives home with that remorseful puppy face. I'm going to put him out!"

Her friend laughed, Deborah shrugged and paid for her purchase.

She spent the afternoon painting, her new painting was brightly colored, especially red, and she admired each new touch of the brush, still having no idea what shape it would take. She felt transported into that painting, she had never brushed with such will.

When night fell, and the temperature dropped, Deborah was exhausted. She prepared something quick to eat and decided that tonight, she would read a book in the library.

The house was silent, though it creaked constantly in several places. It must be at least five decades old, and the former owner, an uncle she had never met, left it furnished. Deborah still had neither the time nor the willingness to explore it in full.

She entered the dusty library making a mental note for a cleanup the next day. She felt an itchy nose and sneezed, but she could not help but admire the huge collection of books. An intellectual, she thought.

Walking slowly, like an appraiser of rare works, she stared at the spines on the shelf, when something caught her attention: a thick bulk, a leather cover, a golden thread hanging down from the middle of its pages. It looked like a different leather, and she thought, for a brief moment, that it might be human skin. She had heard that it was a practice known in the 1800s.

She shook her head away from the thought and took the book, as it had greatly entranced her.

She started to leaf through the pages and realized that it was a diary, written in a far-fetched letter, probably with a fountain pen.

On the back cover, a name written in blood-red: Laila. That was all.

Deborah felt excited. Who could that woman be? What secrets had she kept in such an elegant diary?

Sitting in the dusty armchair, she began to read, and did not notice when the night advanced.

***

"September 1891,

I don't know how long I've been locked down here. The days must have turned into weeks and I have lost track of time. I feel weak and outraged to learn that he wasn't there for me when I needed him most. I know I'm nearing the end of my life. What irony. I do not feel like I have sorceress's powers, just as I was accused of being one, I just perceive my body withering away and I am able to fight against it. He says he wants to keep me from the people's hatred in this town, that it's better than being locked up here than burned at a bonfire. I hate him with all my strength, because this is not to preserve me, it's to kill me slowly. I hardly eat, I do my physiological needs into a filthy hole, I feel worms eating me. The water in the bathtub is cold and dirty, I do not know if I will ever be able to take a bath or if I will keep exhaling this horrible smell that causes disgust even in myself.

I hate him and the men he calls fellows. I'm here rotting because of them. Witchcraft! How could they call me a witch when all I did was to help this pathetic town? Didn't I heal the wounded? And all I got in return was to be locked up in this hidden basement where they will never find me. And only he knows where I am, without anything to help me.

But I'll do one last spell, if that's what he thinks I'm capable of. This book will stay on his bookshelf, for anyone who reads it, to know the truth about Laila Borges and her terrifying end."

Deborah closed her eyes as she read the last sentence. The writings ended there. The diary was filled with pain, frustrations, and the fear of a woman judged as a witch, a sorceress, only because the knowledge she carried with her which was beyond what the human being presumed to know.

She became sad about her situation, and curious to know how the diary had ended up on the shelf. Judging by its condition, it had not left there in the years after Laila's death.

Deborah felt drowsy, despite the surprise of reading the shocking narrative. She had so many questions to ask, so many things she wanted to know, but for now, she'd just get some sleep. The next day she would try to find out who were these men who caused so much harm to Laila.

Deborah crashed as soon as she laid her head on the pillow. There would be no dreams at the crack of dawn, but she had now entered a story where there could be no turning back.

The following day, it was cloudy and rainy, and Deborah woke up with a strange feeling. The house looked heavy, but not in a bad way. It was as if she was no longer alone, as if there were people there, in routine movements.

She wanted to get into Laila's life further, but she felt a crazy desire to finish the painting she started also. She walked into the studio, put on her dirty apron of multiple colors of paint, and took the brush.

On the portable radio, she put on some melodious rock music, as she was tired of the silence of the house that had been chasing her since she arrived there two weeks ago. She began singing and painting madly, using the paints on the canvas as a lover would use a beloved woman's body. She felt excited, it looked like she was going out of herself, moving to another dimension, her hands frantic, her body shivering, the canvas gaining color.

When it was over, she was tired, as if she'd been through a one-night stand. She came around to herself, the radio still playing the heavy and soft melody at the same time. When she looked at the picture, Deborah was startled: unlike anything she had ever painted, there was a picture of human sacrifice, neatly drawn, pieces of bodies and blood scattered beneath a chunk of human body hanging from a rope.

She started to cry, the radio turned off suddenly, the lights went out and she found herself there, desolate and lonely. The air was still, but Deborah felt a wind kiss her face, and slowly, she was calming down. That was the most macabre and most wonderful painting she had ever painted. If she could sell it, she would make a fortune, something told her.

The lights went on again, and Deborah noticed that the night had fallen completely. She could not sense the passage of time in this house, she thought.

She felt her muscles aching, as if she had run a marathon. She took a hot shower and went to bed.

The shade visited her again that night, and Deborah became the seductive woman who decimated the fool who dared to fall for her charm.

She did not even go near the bookshelf in her wanderings through the library in search of more of Laila's writings. The only thing she found related to the witch was a portrait beautifully painted by an artist, that carried her name behind.

Laila was beautiful, any man would fall in love with her without any spell.

After a couple of nights, dreaming of sex, mysteriously dyed of blood-red, Deborah woke up with a loud noise coming from downstairs right at dawn when the sun was trying to make space in the sky. She jumped up, her heart racing. What was happening? Fearful but curious, she wrapped the robe around her waist and tied it, hugging her own body. She could not quite make out where the noise came from, but as soon as she went down the stairs, she noticed what had happened through the wide office door: one of the shelves had collapsed, knocking down books all over the place. Deborah approached and did not need much to realize what had happened. There was a multitude of termites eroding the exposed, brittle wood. *How could I not have noticed these insects before?* she thought incredulously.

Deborah stared in disgust at the little critters and their repulsive form. Obviously, something would have to be done, she would have to call a specialist to fix it. Just thinking that a stranger would enter her habitat, she tensed, but there was no other choice.

She left the room hoping the termites would not dominate the whole house until she got help. She looked for a phone book, but found none. Then she went to town after having a cup of coffee and taking in the sun, now fully awake, through the kitchen window.

Where would be the best place to find the fumigation professionals? She returned to the emporium again, and it did not take long to find the man who does the dirty work of home debugging. To respond her demand quickly, he charged her a small fortune that she did not have, but Deborah did not want to sleep knowing that she would be veiled by tiny, filthy, silent creatures that corroded everything without nobody's noticing. The man could come to her house in an hour. She waited anxiously.

When she returned, Deborah did not feel like painting. She went to the studio to look at her latest work, however, hoping the inspiration would reach her.

The paintings were all hung on the walls. She did not notice how fast she had produced them (a personal record) and how they, side by side, formed almost a bloody story. Since when had she become interested in massacres? Blood was the element that prevailed in the paintings. One complemented the other in scenes of human offerings and brutal murders. They were beautiful, and Deborah did not doubt their great value.

She was awoken from her reverie by the old-fashioned bell she had never heard. The insect exterminator has arrived. Thank God!

***

Deborah offered coffee to the man, who declined rudely. She heard him curse and complain about the condition of the furniture there. Idiot, she thought bitterly. He'd been mumbling since he started work, probably thinking he should have charged more for the effort. He was carrying a cylinder from wherein toxic fumes came out. He turned on the hose that splattered the fumes throughout the room, making a fussing noise. When he bent down to reach the lowest places, Deborah could see part of his huge butt coming out his shabby jeans. It was the vision of hell.

She was still standing at the office door, even with the bothersome smell of smoke, holding the empty coffee cup. She was so lost in random thoughts that she was startled when the fat guy said:

"Madam, I'll have to pull down the shelves. The situation is ugly. I think the lady better get out of there."

She nodded, leaving. She would try to paint something

instead.

Forty minutes had passed when, in the middle of her new painting, when Deborah heard a terrified scream coming from the office. In fact, it could only have come from there, because the man was working in that room, but she found his voice too muffled.

Afraid of what might have happened, she ran off, without even taking off her apron, and in the doorway of the room she stopped astonished. The man, pale as a ghost, with sweaty, sticky skin stared at her angrily, standing in front of a small narrow door that Deborah had never seen before. He brought his hand to his heart, as if he were about to suffer a heart attack (which could well have happened, since it was clear that this man was a lover of bacon and suchlike).

When she approached to see where the door went to and why the man had shouted, he screamed, pointing his fat little finger in her direction:

"Don't come near me, you're crazy! I'm calling the cops!"

Deborah did not understand anything. Leaving his threat aside, she said, arrogantly:

"Look, I have no idea what you're talking about!"

"You lying cow! This basement is a freak show."

He shook himself theatrically as if to show how shocked he was.

Deborah still did not understand, and at that moment, she had no idea what there was behind that door. But she would find out.

"Look, sir" - she said through her teeth, controlling the desire to wrench that half smile from the man's face - "I recently inherited this house, and didn't even know of the existence of this basement. Or how about you tell me what it is..."

"Or what?" - he interrupted her. "Are you going to kill me!? Killer! I knew it was a bad idea to accept this job. Do you know what they say about you? That you are weird. To be polite. No one knows how much! My God!"

He put his hand between his hair, pulling the strands so that his forehead became distorted. Deborah was shocked, less with the discovery of the basement than with the villainous language of the residents, they should have plenty of time to speak ill of others.

She felt angry. Without blinking, she moved towards the door, making the man leap to the side, and came in, holding her breath as she looked at what was at the bottom of the stairs, the man right behind her, as if to check her reaction.

The basement was practically a human butcher's shop. There were pieces of human bodies and dry blood everywhere. Flies and worms were feasting on the poor dead. A dirty, peeled bathtub was filled with blood, which lazily flowed into a puddle on the floor. The putrid odor was unbearable, and Deborah held her cry, but she could not prevent the vomit from being expelled with violence on the floor, making her dizzy.

The man, just behind, moved forward on Deborah, screaming: "Murderous bitch!"

As he went to attack her, something made him freeze, in a funny position, as if he had suddenly turned to stone.

Deborah could not remember whether she cried or ran. What happened there? Despite the dry blood, they did not look like ancient deaths, the bodies were just beginning to rot. And why was the man frozen like magic? Was she dreaming about all that?

She remembered Laila, the witch who had been locked away. It was there! The cot, the bathtub, the table...she was in the place where Laila had died!

As soon as Laila's image, as she had seen it in the picture, showed up in her mind, a spectrum of the woman materialized in front of her eyes, making the whole scene seem even more bizarre.

"Hello, Deborah."

The woman's voice was as sweet as a melody, one that pulls tears from the listener with no reason.

"What is going on here?" - Deborah shivered, her voice faltering. It sounded like a fantastic teenage dream.

Laila - the witch - faced her with violet and sparkling eyes. Within seconds, the memory of the bloody nights came to Deborah's mind in sharp flashes, and she remembered everything she had done with those hands that reproduced blood on the canvases painted in her studio. She had become Laila - the hair, the eyes, the seduction pouring through every pore of her body - her attracting of men, the nights of sex, and then the killing, the bloodbath.

A particular scene began to be projected in her mind and she could do nothing to stop seeing clearly what she had done:

She was wet, she arrived at the house on a stormy night with a company of a handsome black man. Deborah gave him a kiss on the lips, feeling the taste of beer that he exhaled; he had been in the tavern, she had seduced him. He remained oblivious to anything but her mesmerizing glance and Deborah, taking advantage of the situation, led him up the stairs to the room where she used to sleep peacefully.

She pushed the stranger into the bed and rode him savagely until he exploded with horn. The man was surrendered to his mysterious self, his hands trailing the curvy body with obvious lust, while his penis thrust her increasingly harder until she reached the climax.

When it was over, Deborah stepped off him wearing her torn-off nightgown, and, once again, she stared at him with flashing violet eyes. He was under her domain.

She walked the hall of the big house and down the stairs, the man following her like a puppy. She passed through the living room and into the office, a place full of shelves packed with books. There, where she rarely came in during the day, was a small door behind one of the shelves, which she opened effortlessly, because it was scenic, though it looked very real.

She entered through the unlocked door and went down the stairs into a huge basement, the same one were she was now and that it was all so strange to her. That place was not even in the original layout plan of the house when she inherited it, she remembered. However, on that first night, she showed familiarity with the place. There was a cot and, dangerously near, a smelly hole on the floor. In the other corner, there was a large table with dirty personal objects, and beside it, there was an old bathtub made of cast iron and painted white, already showing signs of peeling. At the other end of the room, there was an old round table with three chairs all around; there were some steel forged knives and a saw. Deborah seemed to know exactly where everything was.

Without a word, she gently pushed the huge man by his chest until he fell into the bathtub and, in a clear movement, she picked up the knife and moved in on him, who made no sign of protest. She whacked him on the jugular, the blood squirting with strength into the bathtub, dripping viscous by the light, dirty metal.

The man gradually withered away; inexplicably all of his

blood flowed out of the open wound, filling the bathtub with shiny, viscous, ruby-red liquid. Deborah undressed, her skin bristling, her black hair covering her breasts in a cascade with violet reflections that had the tone of her eyes. On the opposite side of the man, she lay in the bathtub with sensual movements, letting the blood cover her body and face, feeling waves of pleasure run through her skin.

Deborah shook her head, returning to reality, her eyes shedding thick tears, while the man remained paralyzed, and Laila just waited, graceful, for her to recover from the effect of the memories that had been projected on her mind. When the profusion of weeping ceased, Laila said:

"My beloved, we have merged into one since I saw you walking in this house for the first time. You served my purposes, but this man can give everything away. It was a dangerous move."

Deborah did not know how to react. That woman had made her, in a way she would never understand, commit barbaric crimes, dirty her hands with blood, and still blamed her for the discovery. It was nonsense!

Laila seemed to read her thoughts, which did not surprise the painter:

"It's no use to victimize yourself. You needed me as I needed you. Do you have any idea how much your paintings are worth today?"

"N-no..."- but she imagined.

"A lot, my dear. Try to sell them and you'll be rich."

Deborah kept her eyes wide open, she could not believe what she was listening to. Laila continued:

"And there's more: I can give you back your youth."

It was like a shot of mercy: Laila picked up on a critical point of Deborah's psychological side, the fact that she hated getting older, watching life go by, wrinkles showing up and still alone, without money, pathetic.

She had already gotten her hands dirty, and the witch's offer was too tempting. On the other hand, would she be willing to sell her soul to the devil?

Her thoughts were abounding, her heart was racing, and she noticed that the living statue of the man was gradually moving again.

Laila spoke with the tranquility of one who knows on what ground she is stepping on:

"It's your call. Wealth and youth, in exchange to continue helping me in my revenge or return to your deplorable life. You will need to choose... now!"

Laila disappeared and the man moved again. Deborah had milliseconds to think, and without concatenating the ideas right, she moved on him, taking him by surprise and knocking him down with a thud on top of one of the bloody bodies of the basement.

The man shouted. Deborah groped on the table, turning around without taking her eyes off him and reaching one of the weapons. With the weight of the cylinder on his back, he could not get up, shaking his legs in a comic manner. Deborah moved on him and struck him on the chest again and again, his face sprinkled with blood, until he stopped moving. The ruby-red liquid flowed to the floor and the man softened. It was done. Deborah had made her decision.

***

The painter from the interior of São Paulo gained national fame with her works. She was known for the precise and realistic strokes in the painting of death.

Laila still took revenge on men, but with diminishing periods. The bodies were buried in a huge open ditch in the basement. One could not live with rotting corpses and exhaling fetid odors.

Deborah felt young, beautiful. She looked at herself in the mirror and saw her skin increasingly smoother, her hair shiny, her eyes vivid.

In the town, everyone talked about the mysterious neighbor. However, the fame of stranger could never have been perpetuated due only to the morbid subject of her paintings.

What most intrigued the locals was, in fact, the way time seemed to pass differently for her.

THE NOISE COMING FROM THE MACHINE ROOM

by Vitor Abdala

The persistent ringing of the intercom woke Ariovaldo up. As the manager of that building, he was accustomed to the fact that other residents woke him up in the middle of night. There was always some problem to be solved. Whether it was a sewage leak or the puritan spinster annoyed with the smell of marijuana that came from the neighboring apartment.

He asked himself if there would be time for a piss before he answered the intercom call. He decided not to pee. He had to interrupt that irritating ringing. After that, he would empty his bladder.

"Hello!"

Nobody answered. He just heard crackling sounds coming from the other end of the line.

"Hello!" Ariovaldo tried again, before he angrily hung up the intercom, as he noticed that only the crackle responded.

With a dry feeling in his mouth, he went to the fridge and got a bottle of water. Sleepy as he was, he tried to put some water in his glass, but half of it spilled out when the intercom rang sharply by his side.

"Son of a bitch!" he roared, before he answered the intercom and said *hello*.

This time, a feeble voice on the other end of the line greeted him. Ariovaldo made some effort to hear it.

"Mister manager," it was Miss Isaura, an elderly ninety-year-old woman that had the bothersome habit of addressing Ariovaldo this way, "there's a strange noise coming from upstairs."

She lived alone in an apartment located on the tenth floor, the highest floor of that building. Her home had two bedrooms, but she insisted on sleeping in the maid's room. A room that was located near the elevator and therefore was the noisiest place in the apartment.

"Good evening, Miss Isaura. Are you referring to the noise coming from the elevator machine room?"

"Yes, my darling. That sound's driving me crazy."

"Miss Isaura, the elevator machine room makes noises every time the lift goes up and down."

Ariovaldo almost added: *instead of sleeping in the maid's room, why don't you throw away all those useless old things that clog your two bedrooms and sleep in one of them, like a normal person?*

"You don't understand, mister manager. I'm not referring to the elevator's engine noise. I'm used to that sound. It even helps me to sleep, when I'm insomniac. I imagine whoever is arriving or leaving home, every time the elevator moves. It pleases me, you know? I'm talking about the other noise."

Ariovaldo impatiently rubbed his face. All he wanted was to take a leak and go back to sleep. Although he was a retiree, he enjoyed to wake up early and to go for a walk nearby. His cardiologist had suggested he engaged in physical exercises, after he had been hospitalized because of a preinfarction.

"What other noise?" he asked, regretting immediately after

doing so. It would allow the old woman to keep complaining.

"It's a noise that's driving me crazy..."

You've already said that, Ariovaldo thought, almost running out of patience.

"It's probably the elevator engine. It really makes a deafening noise."

"The elevator engine doesn't crawl on the ground, mister manager. It doesn't pant either."

Ariovaldo felt goosebumps on his neck and he almost peed on his pants. For a moment, he heard only the crackles coming out of the intercom.

"I beg your pardon. I don't get it, Miss Isaura."

"There's something upstairs, my darling. That thing has been creeping and breathing, breathing heavily. I can't sleep."

Ariovaldo knew she could hear the sounds made by the elevator's traction mechanism. It was an old engine and it creaked a lot while it pulled the lift. And part of the machine room was located exactly above Miss Isaura's maid's room, even though the engine itself was located above the elevator.

But he didn't think that the old woman was hearing anything crawling or breathing in the machine room, even if there was really something doing that upstairs.

Then he listened to the request he didn't want to hear.

"Mister, would you mind to take a look upstairs, to see what's going on?" asked the old lady. "It's really disturbing me."

As there was no doorman in the building after 10:00 pm, the

manager had to solve every problem after that time.

He couldn't believe it. He should have pissed before he'd answered the damn intercom. He needed to think fast in order to get rid of the old lady. There was no way he would go up to the machine room at that time, to check upon some noises that a crazy old woman had supposedly heard.

"Ok, I'll take a look," Ariovaldo lied, hanging up the intercom afterwards.

Going to the bathroom and taking a leak were the first things Ariovaldo did after ending the call. He was relieved after emptying his bladder, but, at the same time, he regretted for having lost his sleep.

It wasn't midnight yet and he was already sleepless. He made some coffee and turned on the TV. He watched a strange movie and, then, half an hour later, the intercom rang again.

"Oh, lord, give me patience," he grumbled as he stood up to answer the intercom.

The old woman didn't sleep and decided to turn his night into hell.

"Hello!"

"Darling, did you really check up on the machine room?"

"Yes, madam. I could find nothing there. It's probably the elevator's machine disrepair. I'll call the repair company tomorrow."

"Mister manager, I'm ninety years old. I know when someone's lying to me." Ariovaldo didn't expect that sort of reaction from Miss Isaura. "The noise got worse. Besides the creeping and panting, *whatever is upstairs* has decided to dig."

"Dig?!" he asked in surprise.

"Yes. It looks like it wants to excavate the floor and come out here, in my apartment."

"Miss Isaura, why would anybody dig a hole in a concrete slab to get into your home? Wouldn't it be easier if this person rang the doorbell?" the manager asked, running out of patience.

"Don't get funny with me, mister manager," Miss Isaura said reprehensively.

Ariovaldo had regretted starting a quarrel with the old lady, but he knew she wouldn't give up until he complied with her request.

"Alright, Miss Isaura. I'm going up right now. And I'll call you from upstairs to tell you I found nothing besides cables and engines."

"I'd appreciate that, mister manager."

Ariovaldo hung up the intercom, put on a shirt, got his cell phone and took the elevator to go up seven floors. After he reached the tenth floor, he climbed the stairs to get to the machine room.

There was no light in the last flight of stairs or in the area outside the machine room. So he had to grope for the walls. In the last step, he stumbled, but kept his balance and didn't fall on his face.

"Fuck! Why haven't I placed a light bulb here?" the manager complained.

Although there was a *authorized personnel only* sign, the machine room door was never locked. Closed, but not locked. He stood in front of the door for a while, until he gathered his courage to open it.

Ariovaldo was a fainthearted man. He was afraid of almost everything: animals, criminals, ghosts. And what if Miss Isaura was right? What if there was really something creeping and panting inside?

He imagined a horrible creature, with huge claws, digging at the concrete floor in the machine room, trying to make a hole and get into the old woman's apartment.

Twice, he thought of running downstairs before he opened the door. But he took a deep breath and decided, once and for all, to get into that place, into that room where something had supposedly been creeping and disturbing Miss Isaura's sleep.

Ariovaldo slowly pushed the door. The harsh squeaking sound of the door hinges made him even more scared. However, there wasn't any sound besides the hinges. The place was silent. His hand groped for the walls, trying to find the switch, for a moment that seemed too long for his inventive and frightened brain.

The situation got even scarier when his finger pressed the switch and the lights didn't turn on.

"Son of a bitch!"

Although he had already peed before he left his apartment, the manager felt that his bladder was ready to explode again. He regretted coming to that place late at night. He also regretted forgetting his flashlight.

He took his cell phone out of his pocket and pushed a button that lit up its screen. The light wasn't enough to illuminate the whole room, but that was all he had for the moment.

Ariovaldo pointed his lighted cell phone screen toward the floor and started to walk, leaning against the wall.

After seven steps, the elevator was set in motion and the engine made a deafening sound. The manager got startled and put his hand to his heart. Gasping after the fright that almost killed him, he bowed in order to catch his breath.

Ariovaldo got a bit worried after the fright. The first time he had a preinfarction, he had survived thanks to the help of the doorman, who talked to him during the time he felt the chest pain. He was afraid he wouldn't make it if his heart played a trick on him again.

His mobile light switched off and he had a hard time turning it on again. The sound of the engine stopped, but Ariovaldo got ready for the noise that would come next. After all, somebody would go into the elevator, would press a button and, soon, the lift would be moving again.

The manager stood leaning against the wall, waiting for the sound that would come. One minute went by. Then, two minutes. But the elevator didn't move again. During this time, he had to light up his mobile that switched off every thirty seconds. *Somebody probably took the elevator on the tenth floor and went down to his destination, on the ground floor, therefore it won't move again*, he thought.

His heartbeat slowed down and he was able to straighten up his body. Then he started to examine the room with the help of his mobile's dim light. He directed the mobile light to his right, to the empty corners of the machine room.

He didn't find anything on that side and prepared to point the illuminated screen to the elevator engine, but before he could get there, the light switched off again.

Ariovaldo unsuccessfully pushed the mobile button several times. While he fought against technology, he heard a noise that was like a grunt coming from behind the machinery. The manager looked in the direction with his eyes still trying to get used to the darkness.

He couldn't see much, just the silhouettes of the engines and the components of the traction cables. However, another grunt came from behind the machinery.

The manager, who was more concerned with suffering another heart attack than with looking for an imaginary creeping creature, got frightened again. Frightened to death.

He heard the grunt one more time. His finger desperately pressed the button in order to light up his mobile screen. He felt his heart beat dangerously faster with the adrenaline rush.

Please, calm yourself down, calm yourself down. Nobody will save you here, upstairs, Ariovaldo thought.

At the moment he finally managed to light up his mobile screen, his hand was pointed to the machinery and he could see a shadow rapidly moving away from the light.

"What the fuck?" Ariovaldo screamed.

Whatever was behind the machinery went back to the darkness and let out another grunt, this time a stronger and more menacing grunt.

Ariovaldo, still trying to keep calm, attempted to follow the shadow with his mobile, but had no success. The mobile light switched off again. And again his finger tried to quickly switch it on. Another grunt made Ariovaldo feel a strong chest pain and he dropped his unlit phone on the floor.

Although it was dark, he noticed that something came from the shadows and moved in his direction, at the same time he searched for his mobile on the floor. And it grunted.

The pain in his chest got stronger, as he tried to move away from that thing that his eyes strove to see in the darkness. Ariovaldo lay weakly on the floor and started to crawl to the empty corner of the machine room, panting.

The creature in the machine room was coming close to him. He could fell it was right behind him.

Ariovaldo kept crawling, grasping for air, striving to remain conscious and fighting for his heart to keep beating. He broke out in a cold sweat, as he heard the grunt drawing near.

Unable to scream, Ariovaldo felt something grabbing his ankle, something that prevented him from moving. Ariovaldo desperately dug his nails onto the floor and tried to pull his body with them.

But he was unable to move. His fingernails kept rubbing the floor, but he didn't move. In desperation, the manager started to scratch the concrete floor. It was like he was trying to dig in order to get to the lower floor. He was aware that he wouldn't be able to dig that concrete slab, but it was an unconscious and instinctive attempt.

At the same time he used his final strength to scratch the floor with this nails, the pain in his chest got unbearable. Then his eyesight became cloudy and, seconds later, he was unconscious.

This time there was no one to save him and take him to the hospital. Ariovaldo died in the machine room.

Simultaneously, down the stairs, Miss Isaura noticed that the strange noises coming from the machine room had suddenly ceased. Before she could finally sleep, the elderly woman spoke in a low voice, in the dark maid's room:

"Thanks, mister manager."

THE SLAUGHTERING SEDUCTRESS

by Rachel Johnston

I met him in a bar. It was crowded and the atmosphere was electric. We danced the night away, he laughed at my corny jokes, the attraction was mutual. The fool looked into my eyes and told me I was beautiful (the eyes are the window to the soul, you see). He said - and how gravely mistaken he was - 'Why don't we go back to yours for a coffee?' I agreed. He grinned and I could tell he was excited and more than willing.

We arrived at my flat. I gave him a glass of my favourite wine and we chatted long into the night. Lots of foreplay on my sofa soon after - kissing, fondling, playing, you know the drill. I led him breezily into my bedroom. It wasn't long until we were stripping each other naked. I kissed him longingly all over, starting with his feet and slowly - very slowly - working my way up to his red lips. We kissed intensely and passionately. He stroked my naked body, becoming more and more aroused. I climbed on top of him and we made love with a wild abandonment and base lust.

It was around this time that I grabbed his neck. He urged me to squeeze harder on it. I obeyed his wishes, of course. Little did he realise the error of his folly and the profound regret which would soon ensue him. But by then it would be too late for this pathetic little mortal soul. I lay my bare naked body flat on top of him and stroked his neck gently and slowly, making love to him all the time.

I waited until he was at the point of climax before the real me - the pure me, the demon which lies beneath with baited breath - emerged once again for the consideration and debasing of my next victim. I was thirsty, thirsty for blood. I opened my mouth and sank my fangs into his jugular. The feeling of the warmth of his blood pouring into my mouth and running all over my bare torso caused me to climax in the intensity of an extreme orgasm, the likes of which I had not had in quite some time. I had claimed my next victim. I was drinking his blood like someone desperate for water in the desert. I looked up and smiled. I was hungry now, so it was time to feed.

Taking my sharpest knife from the kitchen drawer, I began the operation of tenderly slicing and dicing up his flesh, cutting him into little pieces. I wanted to taste him. I took the pieces of bloodied flesh to the frying pan on the cooker, which was hot and ready for my evening supper. I threw these varying chunks of sinew into the burning hot pan and waited, as I had done so many times before. Were you aware that human flesh when cooked turns white like chicken? Every day's a school day, eh? When my meal was finally ready I put it onto a plate and drizzled it with some of his warm blood which remained. I devoured with relish. Orgasmic ecstasy once more!

But still, my appetite is always insatiable. Who will my next victim be?

It could be you.

SHADOW WOLF

by Raven Dane

A shadow that needed no light to exist, seeped from the ground, weak and nebulous as morning mist. The depths of the earth teemed with microscopic life and this had given it the strength to rise after countless centuries. As it crossed open ground, a colony of ants turned against each other in murderous fury. The shadow strengthened.

After passing through a forest, leaving wildlife carnage in its blood-stained wake, it was now strong enough to tackle more complex prey. In a car park beside the woodland, it found two humans in the throes of lust in a steamed up car, oblivious to anything beyond their urgent needs. The shadow passed over the car. To unheard screams, the woman turned savage, bit down hard on the man, severing his erection. Drenched with his own gushing blood, insane with pain and fury, the man groped for a weapon, plunged a blunt screwdriver into her neck. Yet more blood mixed with the steam and ran down the car's windows in wide scarlet ribbons.

Stronger, bigger the shadow moved on to more quarry ....

What was wrong with his home town? After Colorado, he expected it to look small, cramped and overcrowded but this was still a good place, a town to put down roots and raise a family. So why did it now give him the creeps, make him shudder for no obvious reason? Jet lag? Rob Helson pushed aside his unsettling observation and paused outside the boozer, here for the first time in four years and nothing had changed. The same stench of stale piss and spilt beer, dusted with cigarette ash and butts from the pariahs banished to the pavement outside. He smiled to himself for feeling a little nervous about the reunion with his childhood friends waiting inside for him.

Not that they would seem strangers after a long absence, Facebook and Skype took care of that. They had miraculously managed to grow older together, the old bonds stayed linked by the cyberverse, Helson only hesitated because he did not want any fuss, nothing beyond a manly handshake and everything back to how it used to be before he went to the States to pursue his high flying academic career. All he wanted was a relaxed gathering of good mates, equals in every way, some sort of normality to chase away the disturbing dark shadows invading his soul since his arrival back in Weltham.

He strolled in to find them at their favourite table furthest away from the toilets and closest to the bar. Mr Sensible Jenks, Baxie the perma-stoned aging hippy, Dan the Man and Mike. The guys who'd shared their first cigarette behind the clichéd school bike shed, who'd passed the first crudely rolled spliff at impromptu overnight camps in Lockley Wood. Who'd all cram into Baxie's battered estate car, the brown and rust coloured one with the trailing exhaust held up by wire to go clubbing in High Wycombe.

He sat down, with a nod of thanks as the first of many pints of Green King was pushed his way. Sunk in one as ritual bravado to boyish cheers from the men they'd become together. Overcome by a nostalgic surge of affection, Helson watched them over the rim of the next pint.   He was closest to Mike who had come out two years ago first to the group, then to his parents and family before finally announcing it to a mainly unsurprised world. Mike was slight of build, quick of temper and the best man to have at your side in a fight caused by...

'Oh look, The Brainiac has returned. '

Nigel. Or as Helson called him 'That Bloody Nigel.' No one

would own up to Nigel, he did not belong to the original group of friends, somehow over the years he had insinuated his way into their laid back company and never left. Already the sensation of fingernails scrapping along a blackboard invaded Helson's relaxed mood, the man's sneering tone and superior manner setting his teeth on edge.

'That is Professor Brainiac to you, Eelman.'

Helson felt petty minded but couldn't help enjoying the narrowing of the man's pale eyes, the slight tightening of the mocking, thin smile at the mention of their old, hated nickname for him. Helson did not want to ruin the reunion with spite but was satisfied by the shared amused glance of secret agreement between the others. Dan fetched in another round and the gathering settled to their time old relaxed mixture of banter and catching up with recent news including the unsettling, gruesome deaths of a courting couple outside town the night before.

The noisy pub fell silent as new arrivals strode in, picking up the volume once they had found a table and settled down. Nothing threatening about them, another group of Weltham locals, just friends not out for any trouble. Helson's mood sank as Nigel owned up to knowing the newcomers. Of course he did, Nigel knew everyone and everything. The font of all knowledge and all of it bollocks.

'See those lads over there,' he announced, in a voice too loud for anyone's comfort, 'they are all LARP nutters. Dress up as bloody elves and orcs, run around wet woodlands all weekend with bows and arrows.'

'Nothing wrong with that, Nige,' sighed Baxie, 'actually looks great fun. I'd have a go if I had the dosh.'

Nigel laughed at the prospect, 'I can just see you dressed as some stoned druid or wizard.'

Baxie nodded agreement with a wide grin, hoping the men in the corner did not think they were laughing at them. Nigel's runaway mouth and obsessive bragging had led in the past to fights. Not that he was ever there to see the results of his winding up, he was so slippery and quick to escape, hence the nickname, Eelman.

'That big blond lump is completely barking,' Nigel continued, prompting the others to hastily drink up their pints, time to leave the pub, 'thinks he's a real fucking Viking. Worships bloody Thor and Odin, says he can speaks old Norse, crazy.'

While the others squirmed in embarrassment, Nigel turned in his chair, 'Oi, Big Eric,' he bellowed to the newcomers, 'where's your helmet with them big pointy horns?'

As one, the friends stood up, smiled apologetically to the LARPers, definitely time to leave. Eric, the big man's demeanour caught Helson's attention, visibly shaken up, nervous and nursing a crudely bandaged wound to his arm, seeping fresh blood. A man in no mood to even notice some passing idiot's mockery.

Normally the young women and their boyfriends all went out together, including meeting up at live action role play weekends or Sci-Fi conventions, activities they all enjoyed equally. But with all their menfolk out on a pub crawl, their girlfriends were determined to have a wild night out of their own. Not a hen night complete with tacky haloes and glittery fairy wands but a proper evening out on the lash, carefree and silly with the whole long Bank Holiday weekend to recover from the deliberate excesses. Avoiding the pubs where their other halves planned to visit, the young women had taken a taxi to a large Chinese restaurant on the edge of town that also held a disco on Friday nights. A safe place to let their hair down and have fun.

Unsatisfied by the continued weakness, the shadow became insatiable for mayhem and madness, the spilling of blood it needed to return to living form. Unable ...yet... to kill for itself, it used powers inherited from Loki, its deity father to influence and corrupt minds to commit acts of horrific violence. The inner savage locked within every human being was the key to the shadow's survival and victory over its treacherous enemies, those bastards dwelling in smug celebration in the unearthly dimension known as Asgard. Nothing would taste sweeter than their total defeat, rent apart by his regenerating fangs.

'Something heavy going down,' Mike muttered as he applied the brakes to his black Audi sports car. Ahead of them was a blaze of flashing emergency lights, police and ambulances, a wide area of road and pavement outside Tangs taped off with the familiar blue and white strips that warned of a serious incident.

Helson shuddered without knowing why, as he had earlier at mention of the courting couple deaths. Weltham was a quiet town, crime meant the occasional burglary, boy racer speeding and late night, drink-fuelled petty vandalism. But emergency barriers around an expensive Chinese restaurant? As Mike paused waiting for the cars ahead to ease past the scene, a rivulet of dark liquid flowed from the restaurant car park and into the road close to the Audi. In the flare of a policeman's torch, the liquid glowed bright red...fresh blood?

Finally able to move away, a tall figure caught Helson's attention, standing among the gawping sightseers behind the tapes was the one Nigel called Big Eric. Horror-struck and white-faced, the man was howling with grief. A primal, heart-rending sound that sent shudders through both men. Two bloody incidents in as many days, what the hell was going on?

'There's nothing we can do,' Mike sighed, 'best thing to do is go home. No doubt this will be all over the news by morning.'

Helson's decision to come home from the States on a short

visit now felt tarnished, nothing bad was supposed to happen in this sleepy, old market town in Bucks. Waking the next morning to the aroma of a welcome mug of fresh coffee, Helson thanked his host, Mike and joined him on the living room sofa. The TV was on, and a news flash brought familiar local sights to jolt both men to shocked awareness. Tang's Chinese restaurant had been the scene of a horrific massacre. A group of young women attending the after hours disco had raided the kitchens for knives and meat cleavers to set about attacking each other with crazed brutality.

Their insanity was contagious as staff and clients turned on each other using whatever they could to attack and kill. Out of fifty people, only ten survived, three in intensive care, none able to recall anything of the night's madness fuelled terror. The police spokesman asked for calm, refusing to be drawn into conjecture on the possible cause of the murderous lunacy or any connection with the courting couple's gruesome deaths the night before. Helson shuddered as a premonition cast a further dark shadow over his soul.

'Now the media circus will take over,' muttered Mike, 'plus coach loads of bloody ghoul sightseers with cameras. You've picked a bad time for a reunion, Hellboy.'

He put down his coffee and stared directly into Helson's eyes, 'Or maybe a good time. Are you still going... you know... to that other place?'

Tactfully put as ever, Mike was the only one he had ever confided in over his bizarre visions, vivid and real as if he actually dwelt in another dimension, a place of deep, old earth magic, human heroes and powerful but contrary gods. Dreams that always seemed more tangible than everyday life. Helson's past nightmares remained hidden, firmly locked in a strongbox in his mind. The basic facts of his life, orphaned as a baby, raised in several foster homes and now a renowned and respected Professor of Norse History in Colorado, all this normality seemed unreal as if he was living someone else's life, inhabiting a shell of a body that did not belong to him.

'I've done all I can to shut all that crazy crap down, to turn my back on it,' Helson confided, relieved when his host switched off the television. 'Guess I was not good enough, I've been plagued by a sense of great wrongness since I got back to town. A darkness over the town, something very bad that may be connected to me.'

Mike's silence and look of incredulity was to be expected and Helson was relieved when the first of the their phones began to ring as the others learned the news. The friends agreed to meet over coffee in town. 'I am not surprised,' said Mike, grabbing his coat and car keys, 'must be some old instinct at work bringing us together. All those people killed or hurt at Tangs? This is still a tight-knit community, there will be people we know among them.'

'I hope bloody Nigel won't turn up,' Helson added, his mood sombre, 'if he starts making crass remarks, I swear I'll deck him.

'No you won't,' Mike kept walking out of the house without looking back, 'because I'll have already done it.'

As they entered the outskirts of town, Helson had never seen Weltham like this. The rain-lashed streets seemed drained of colour, of life, with far fewer people out and about, even for a wet Saturday morning. Both men knew why, like the residents of the town, they too were frightened. Mike parked and they met up with the others at Gio's coffee house. Jenks was there with his wife Penny. Baxie already stoned and Dan with his latest girlfriend, Angel. The women looked up, gave brief, tight smiles when introduced to their partners' old friend from America. Penny's face was washed clean of makeup, eyes red–rimmed from crying. Unlike the streets, the coffee house was packed but mainly with strangers, press and TV crews getting out of the chilling, hard driving rain. Many had been up all night outside Tangs.

'I hope the bastards will leave us alone now,' Dan glowered around him, 'I've had words. When we arrived they pounced on us looking for some local reaction. Well bugger them. Penny has lost her best friend from school last night.'

'Baxie's aunt was one of the victims too,' added Jenks, shaking his head in disbelief, 'they haven't officially given out a list of casualties, but word gets about.'

'Hope you are not planning to get away, Professor Brainiac. '

Helson's fingers curled into tight fists as Nigel sauntered in, nodding and grinning to the press, 'this town will be closed down tighter than a duck's arse any minute. Men in hazchem suits, quarantine, secret autopsies...'

'Just for once, shut your big mouth, Eelman,' growled Mike, putting a protective arm around Baxie's shoulders. Nigel's mood darkened but the stern faces of the others for once reined in his mocking banter. He pulled up a chair and joined their table but no one went to buy him a coffee.

'I meant it, lads,' he continued, as always ignoring the women, 'something like this has to be some contagion or biological weapon. Why else would make sweet little old grannies batter each other's brains out with wooden chairs at a church union meeting?'

One glance at the others and he gave a smug grin, 'you lot haven't heard, have you? It has happened again...this morning over at St Edward's.' The shocked silence gave him his answer. 'I walked past the latest incident as it was happening, heard the screams,' Nigel continued, 'saw something strange too. Bloody great grey shadow...huge. Up on the church roof like some sort of crouching animal but see through like a ghost.'

This statement would have once triggered guffaws from the others, Nigel's outrageous exaggerations and wild stories were the stuff of legend among the group. This time the men were silent, uneasy, reality upturned and therefore anything was believable. Helson shuddered, deep dark memories, if that is what they truly were, stirred within his soul, threatening to erupt to the surface after years of suppression,

'This animal, Nigel,' his voice barely above a hoarse whisper, 'could you tell what sort of creature it was?'

Shocked to be believed for once, Nigel nodded, 'Yeah, Prof. I reckon it looked like a bloody great bastard of a wolf.'

Without waiting for a reaction, Nigel stood up and addressed the huddled press nursing their latest fix of much needed caffeine, 'What are you lot hanging around here for? Been another massacre while you've been sipping your mochachinos. Better head off for St Edward's before your editors find out.'

For once, the friends were grateful for Nigel's runaway mouth as the coffee house cleared of all but even more distressed locals. Many abandoning their fare and hurrying home, calling up loved ones on their mobile phones.

'That's better,' he smirked, 'now we can talk properly. Work out what really is going on....over to you, first, Professor.'

Helson had more than enough, stood up abruptly to leave, what did Nigel think they were, the bloody Scooby Gang? Decent ordinary people becoming violent mass murderers? Ghostly monstrous wolves? What could they do against that? He stood up, 'Sorry, I need some air'.

'I didn't take you for a ghoul, Brainiac....off to see some battered granny bodies?'

Striding out of Gio's, he didn't look back, knowing Mike would probably have the creep pinned up against the nearest wall by now, the women urging him on. Hopefully Eelman was getting an overdue lesson in decent behaviour. Outside, the street was deserted, Helson could hear the wail of many emergency sirens, not all heading towards the church. What the hell was going on? With a waft of perfume preceding her, Angel ran out, eyes wide with confusion and fear. 'They are closing all the schools, I've got to collect my little brother.'

'Do you want me to help?' Helson offered.

'No worries, Dan is coming with me, he's just paying for our coffee. Thanks though.'

Angel looked so young in the harsh light of the grey morning, vulnerable and frightened. She put her hand briefly on Helson's arm, 'Bet you wished you'd never come home, this is so unreal, insane.'

He watched as the couple scurried away to Dan's car, the traffic was heavier now, reckless and fast as parents raced to pick up their children from their schools. Had something happened at one of them? Helson was a spiritual man but not religious, at least he thought he was. He found himself praying to anything that would listen that the town's children would be spared. All this chaos and bloodshed in less than twenty-four hours, what the hell was happening?

So close now, the shadow form had gained more solidity and revelled in new sensations, feelings it had been denied for millennia. It was dense enough to feel the wet caress of the teeming rain running icy fingers through its growing pelt of grey fur. It could not taste or smell yet so had to forgo the pleasure of rending flesh and bone with its long, curving fangs but it would not be much longer. It insinuated still smoke like in movement past a school playground. How sweet that young flesh would taste! This would be its first great feast of celebration...a heinous crime that would alert the fools in Asgard. This time they could not use their only weapon against him, deception. This time the Great Wolf would prevail and win.

Helson's walk through the town had no direction, no purpose but awareness of the oppressive atmosphere of latent violence hung in the air, tangible and growing in strength. Nigel's comment about contagion did not seem so risible now. Had some deranged bastards with a grudge released something deadly into the peaceful air above Weltham? This was a crazy, angry world now, anything was possible. More screaming sirens rent the morning air, two police helicopters hovered like metal dragonflies above the town.

Now Helson felt truly frightened as the notion of a terrorist strike strengthened. He could be infected, they all could. He hesitated, perhaps being alone was the only sane option, this gas or toxin could make him turn against his friends, kill them in the same mad rage as the clients at Tangs or the gentle, elderly women of the Church Union...no one would be immune.

An authoritative voice boomed from a helicopter, ordering everyone to return to their homes, lock the doors and remain inside, commanding that there must be no gatherings or meetings for their own safety. Only Helson did not have a home and he did not want to be a danger to Mike...or Mike to him. He decided to keep away from all people, wait out whatever this was beyond town. The rain refused to relent but Helson would rather be cold and wet than slash open a friend's throat with a blunt cake knife. The police order had worked well, the town's folk were frightened, eager for guidance, for rescue. Helson did not see another soul as he headed for the park on Weltham's outskirts which lead to open countryside.

There was just the ring road around the town to cross to get into the park but this main artery was still, an untidy blockade of abandoned cars and lorries. Built in the centre of a deep valley, with few roads leading out, the town was easy to cut off, isolate, what was part of its charm was now a trap. With the police no doubt concentrating on sealing off Weltham and its inhabitants, Helson was not challenged as he ran through the park, careful not to trip over the overturned scooters and tricycles abandoned when mothers fled home with their toddlers

At the crest of the hill, Helson paused for breath, turned back to look down on Weltham, by now eerily silent and still beyond the now constant sirens and loud, insistent drone of the helicopters. The oppressive miasma had not faded, spreading to the park and Helson's old unwanted instinct kicked in as he realised this homicidal insanity was something supernatural in origin, not a terrorist attack.

Up here, above the town, he was not alone. Others had the same idea, escaping whatever was swiftly killing their town. A sodden group of people, suspicious and frightened moved away from him, heading towards one of the few other routes out of Weltham. Helson relaxed as they left, it seems only he wanted to head into the deeper countryside. The sky was a low canopy of pewter clouds, slow moving and laden with more rain but Helson made out a darker shadow travelling against the wind direction. A contradiction in nature itself. Impossible. Its movement was not cloud-like either, a sinuous, stalking manner like some vast prowling animal.

He watched, transfixed as the shape seemed to gain in size and solidity, swooping down to the High Street , becoming a huge wolf loping down the centre of the road, yellow eyes lit by an inner demonic fire, eyes that blazed with intelligence and malevolence. It opened its jaws in a lupine grin, exposing long yellow fangs dripping with glowing saliva mixed with human blood and torn flesh. Shaking from the impossibility of the monstrous entity, Helson whimpered with relief as it headed away from Gio's and his friends. He felt a complete shit leaving them in town while he headed for the hills but was this creature responsible for corrupting people, turning them on each other? In which case he was a potential danger to the other lads...and anyone else in his path.

Stumbling, sobbing, someone approached, Helson turned to see the dishevelled form of Big Eric, the Viking heading towards him. His eyes were blurred with tears but Helson sensed no fury, no crazed anger in the man, nothing that screamed infection and so stood his ground.

'My fault, all my fault....I did this...killed my Anna...so many others...all my bloody fault.'

The man fell heavily to his knees, began to bang his head against the ground, sobs turning to hysteria. Helson dropped down beside him, struggling to find a way to comfort him and eager to make sense of Eric's words. Was this grief-driven madness? Or a clue to the nightmare consuming the town, anything was possible, Helson had decided when a fever-fuelled nightmare became stark reality. Without daring to take his gaze away from the monster still prowling through the town centre, Helson put a comforting hand on the distraught man's shoulders. He looked up at Helson, eyes red and puffy with weeping. 'I did it...brought this horrible thing into our world.'

Big Eric ripped off a silver medallion from around his neck and threw it onto the grass. 'I have always been fascinated by the tales of Fenrir, I thought the Great Wolf was badly treated by the Gods...I became obsessed with him, read all I could. Learnt all I could.'

Interrupted by gun fire and screams from the town, both men paused, ready to run from their lives should the monster head towards the park. They were horrified to witness bloody carnage... a group of armed police had confronted the beast only to turn their weapons on each other. Weltham's High Street ran with freshly spilt blood mixing with the rainwater to pool in crimson lakes.

'Shit, shit,' Eric wailed. 'What the fuck have I done....'

Helson reached down and picked up the medallion, held it in his right hand and was overcome by a sense of ownership, a feeling deep into the very core of his being that it belonged to him. The old dreams came back, more vivid than ever before. He questioned Eric about the object, whether it gave him dreams too but the man still sobbing shook his head.

'No, nothing. I sold my soul to buy the accursed thing, that was all the old man in a weird antique shop wanted. Said I was the first person in fifty years to recognise the sigil designs, those of Loki, Fenrir and his mother Angrboða, the giantess. He said I could raise Fenrir's ghost to be my servant if I shed my own blood beneath a yew tree.'

He got to his feet with some difficulty and pointed to a distant tree close enough to the two to be lit by orange sodium lamps.

'So I put the amulet on the ground and cut my arm, let it bleed all over the surface, wished with all my heart that the Great Wolf would return to do my bidding. It was a lie. There was just some grey smoke that oozed from the ground, nothing more. I walked away, thinking I had failed...now this...'

Eric became hysterical, overburdened with his sense of guilt. Helson's attention was too focused on the town to be of any comfort to the distraught young man. The increasingly solid shape of the wolf had finished with the police defenders of the town and had turned back towards the centre, towards his friends. Helson held on tight to the amulet, pulses of energy radiated from the metal and engulfed his body, his mind. His past life became a disjointed dream, the once certain memories distorted, fading and replaced by older, deeper and infinitely stranger ones. He was still Helson but someone much more than a young academic, someone far less vulnerable, less human.

He ran back towards the besieged town, fuelled with a curious sense of ancient destiny, that this was meant to be. The exertion fogged his mind and clogged up his lungs in pain but still he drove on, running to head off Fenrir. His arrival at Gio's was not a moment too soon, with the monstrous beast blocking Weltham's far exit, the coffee shop had become a refuge for the many caught out of doors and far from home. Dan had returned without his girlfriend but the others were there, none too pleased to see him.

'We thought you were safe,' Baxie slurred, clearly hitting his secret stash hard to blur the awful reality of this blood-stained scenario.

'Or made crazy then devoured by whatever is out there,' sneered Nigel, more out of habit, his hands were shaking, his usually pale face now a chalk-like mask.

'I know what it is,' Helson announced, as he struggled to catch his breath, 'and I think I may be able to stop it.'

He ignored the derisive slow handclapping, not even bothering to look up to know who it was coming from. Helson was no hero but the medallion had spoken to him, made it his and he was all humanity had against a creature even the Norse gods could not truly conquer. With no strong drink on hand to bolster his failing nerves, Helson stumbled back out onto the street. Already he could feel the hot breath of the wolf blast down the body-strewn street, its heavy, prowling footfall betraying its now totally corporeal presence. Helson's legs weakened at the size of the thing, as tall now as the tops of the town's old buildings, eyes huge, hypnotic with ancient cunning and relentless ferocity.

Helson knew he could die from this encounter but it would be a quick death, instantly crushed by the beast's dripping fangs. Much preferable to losing his mind and killing people he loved in a possessed frenzy. He stood his ground and as he held up the amulet, it began to glow with a cool silver light. Knowledge flooded through him, all the bonds of hidden secrets broke away and disappeared. Empowered, Helson announced to his monstrous foe in the old Viking language that he was born of Fenrir's sister, Hel and he commanded Fenrir by the power of the amulet. One forged for the Great

Wolf's father, the god Loki.

Fenrir's howl shattered windows, caused the earth beneath the town to tremble and heave. Helson fell to his knees from the shuddering but stood up immediately and repeated his challenge. It halted in front of him, allowing the full force of its physical and eternal power to wash over the impudent primate possessed by some suicidal impulse and death wish. What it found instead made Fenrir shudder, whimper like a wolf cub and back away.

This creature does have power over me! This cannot be. But it bears the command of my father, is of my lineage and therefore cannot be disobeyed. I have a choice, to become new born again, live and grow in the service of this creature, to bide my time before I can break free and steal the amulet for myself. I have eternity. Or allow myself to die now, dissipate to true nothingness, be a fading memory to Man with no hope of return or a place in Valhalla.

Helson moved away from Weltham briskly not wanting anyone to quiz him over what happened, especially his old friends whom he must abandon forever. Questions would be asked over what happened to Nigel. But for a pact with the Norse Old Ones this solemn must be sealed in blood. Nigel's loss was an unfortunate necessity, a sacrifice to save many lives. There would be police road blocks everywhere but with his new strength and agility, he could travel easily across the surrounding fields, not stop until he was far from the scenes of tragedy and what would be endless speculation. Let them find some prosaic explanation, a mind-warping gas or mysterious ailment. No evidence of the reality would remain. It was over now.

For the first time in his life he was content. Helson's destiny had been revealed, the dreams and memories of his old life as Rob might never return. It did not bother him now. Only the future as Helson mattered. Inside his coat, something warm wriggled and whimpered. A tiny wolf cub with soft grey fur and amber eyes bright with the innocence of the very young. Fenrir was reborn and was his.

THE MASSACRE OF THE LAST OF THE LITTLE ATLANTEANS

by Richard Barr

There were only two weeks left to the Christmas holidays, and the class was restless and noisy. Mr Stephenson, our History master, watched on wearily, his eyes raised ceiling-ward.

After letting out a long, wheezy sigh, he lifted his voice over the din.

"Class...class...quiet down there, now! Questions on the Little Atlanteans will be on next term's paper, and it is mandatory you pass it. And if you do not, you will be sitting back here in my class next Christmas, repeating the year!"

We all quietened at once and Mr Stephenson began.

"The Little Atlanteans, or LAs as they are commonly known, are a race of time travellers, come forward millions of years from the past. From the legendary undersea kingdom they came as refugees, escaping the terrible cataclysm that befell their gentle and fascinating people.

"Approximately ten million of them came through the spiral vortex seen over the skies of Norway on the 9th December 2009, fifteen years ago. They appeared before the people of Earth two days later, their leader Barnyubus taking the podium in the White House Rose Garden. From behind a specially built lens that rendered him enormous, this...diminutive man, standing merely six inches tall approximately, introduced himself and his people to Earth's inhabitants through an impassioned speech, beseeching that we modern day humans receive this diaspora with love and compassion.

"For the first few years we took to them with a great deal of affection, and not a little confusion at how our ancestors, emerged from the mists of time and before known history, could be so small. They appeared on popular American and European talk shows and many people the world over copied their quirky retro-futuristic sartorial style. People lapped up the fascinating trivia about them too, such as the fact their diet consisted of only raisins. We started to eat raisins at a far greater rate then, hoping we would somehow adopt the charm and intelligence of the LAs by doing so."

Stephenson paused here, looked pensively to the floor, then continued.

"But then stories began to circulate about the LAs dirty habits and greedy nature. The gutter press here in Britain ran scare stories about the danger they posed to domestic animals, and how world stocks of raisins had greatly dwindled since their arrival.

"It wasn't too long before groups hostile to the LAs sprung up. Yobbos in Tokyo and London began by destroying the reinforced perspex tunnels that were to be found running all through these big, populous cities; in the ensuing six months this practice would spread worldwide. The LAs, dependent on these tunnels to commute safely around civic amenities and shops without being trodden upon, had to up roots and re-establish their communities in rural areas. However, what they thought were quiet, pastoral idylls granted even less sanctuary than the cities did...

"*The Great Little Atlantean Holocaust* had its roots in Ireland. There, on the 15th of January 2019, groups of farmers released their hunting dogs into a sprawling LA community which lay right on the border of Cork and Kerry. That night the dogs ripped apart thousands of the LAs cute little duplex houses, leaving hundreds dead. Around the world this practice of releasing vicious animals into LA communities took hold, and by 2020 six million of them had been exterminated. A full scale genocide had unfolded. At last count scientists estimate there are only a few dozen of them left."

The bell then went and we all launched back into our talking and howling. Behind me some of the boys with more fascistic tendencies began to shout slurs about the LAs.

"Kill the vermin! Down with the LAs!" snot-nosed Kilroy bellowed.

"A pestilence upon them!" Posho Porter shouted as a rejoinder.

Stephenson tried to pick out the culprits among us, but gave up as we all bottlenecked between the wide oak door frame in our rush to exit the classroom. I, uncharacteristically, straggled behind, not wanting to get into the centre of the mêlée. Worry space was needed, for I had weighing on my mind the terrible suspicion that the last of these Little Atlanteans had taken up residence in my home, Stein Manor.

Grandmamma was the first to notice them. Sometime around the start of December she reported to Papa and I that she'd witnessed three of them carrying raisins into a little hole in the skirting board in the kitchen. Papa told her she was doting, while I came to much the same conclusion, noting as well that Grandmamma had a reputation her whole life for telling fibs.

However it wasn't too long before Mamma started getting in on the act as well, swearing she watched three of them (again!) abseiling down the leg of the dining room table, backpacks replete with raisins.

"One of them," she exclaimed, "with a thimbleful of our good brandy slung over his back!"

So with Mamma (so logical and honest) seeing them as well, I was more inclined to believe that maybe the LAs really were here. Knowing of their reputation for disease and greed I immediately began to make provisions for capturing one of the little shits. When Mamma and Grandmamma cottoned on to what I was doing they encouraged me in my endeavour, with Grandmamma prowling the mansion for hours on end, a butterfly net in hand and Mamma putting down raisins in the middle of big patches of superglue. Then, on the day before Christmas Eve, Grandmamma caught one of the blighters in her net.

"He was distracted, teasing Bonbon (the cat). This allowed me the opportunity to sneak up on him unawares and catch him!" Grandmamma boasted, breathlessly.

The creature was a callow youth of about sixteen. He wriggled violently in the firm grip of Grandmamma's bony old mitt. Mamma glanced about the living room, looking for something to put him in, finding at last an old hamster cage behind the TV.

Once in the cage we all scrutinised the LA carefully, and Mamma lifted my little brother Myles up to the table so he could get a look, too.

"Lil Atlan! Lil Atlan!" he squealed.

Alerted by the commotion, Papa appeared in the doorway. I turned to address him.

"How do you imagine we should dismember the Little Atlantean, Papa?" I quipped.

Without saying a word he strode vigorously across the room and struck me hard.

"Why, Papa...?" I whimpered.

"I have something to tell you all family. Let us convene in the dining room."

What Papa had to say made Mamma throw her hands in the air and exclaim, "But they're vermin! They'll kill us all with their diseases!"

"And they're greedy, covetous little pigs," said Grandmamma, feigning a swoon. "Why, I think they've been pinching my diamonds!"

"Nonsense!" said Papa, rankled by his wife and mother's ignorance.

Papa's admission was that this last three years he had been head of a secret movement, dedicated to giving aid and sanctuary to the last of the LAs. This surprised us, not least because Papa made his name as a bio warfare scientist and had no time for radical nonsense.

"In major cities all around the world members of this movement have left communiqués in and around storm drains, as it is thought the tiny people have fled to the sewers to avoid extermination. These communiqués informed them of the addresses of the places they could find protection and safety. And it just so happened that the last of these fascinating Little Atlanteans have emerged here, in our great city. Come family, let me introduce you..."

With this startling revelation Papa turned to the wall and, using a cacophonous mishmash of clucks, woos and hisses, began to speak in the native tongue of the LAs. Around three dozen of them emerged, some from the mouse hole in the corner of the room, while others from behind false fronts in the skirting boards.

Papa lifted them all onto the table. He released our captive from his cage and proceeded to introduce each by name. They were three families, the Prindinshires, the Binnowbrains and

137

finally the Zindleducks, to which the overall leader of the LAs, Barnyubus, belonged.

Papa took a magnifying glass from the inside pocket of his jacket then and put it in front of Barnyubus's face. At his tiny feet he placed a little tiepin mic, which he'd somehow wirelessly connected to the HI-FI speakers. For the rest of the evening Barnyubus regaled us with tales of Atlantis, and had us in hysterics with his unique Little Atlantian wit. The party lasted right into Christmas Eve morning.

Later that afternoon, Mamma swaddled Myles and myself up in our winter jerkins and sent us out with the LAs to play in snow. Much fun was had frolicking. By early evening little Myles was so exhausted Mamma carried him up to bed before supper.

After watching *It's a Wonderful Life* with Grandmamma I too retired to sleep well; a peace of mind granted me in my casting off of my prejudices and accepting the LAs for who they were.

Christmas Day arrived before I knew it and I jumped from bed like a whippet, giddily anticipating what Santa had left for me under the tree. Myles' bed was already empty, and I presumed the cheeky little imp had risen even earlier to open his presents. The scene that met me in the living room, however, told a different story. For there, under the tree, lay my pudgy little Myles, his chubby cheeks covered in raisin juice.

Papa, Mamma and Grandmamma entered then. Papa, on seeing this, scooped Myles up in his arms and shook him.

"What have you done, you silly little boy?!" he shouted.

"Leave him be," said Mamma. "He must've been hungry having been put to bed without supper last night."

The LAs appeared from out of their mouse hole in the corner. On seeing Myles they all groaned and wailed as one, so that even at our human height we could hear them. Papa implored them to calm down, but they dismissed him.

"...we will get you more raisins. There will be more raisins here!" he enticed.

Barnyubus picked up the tiepin mic and spoke.

"There are no more raisins in the house, and I've just come from our larder where I discovered that your child has eaten all the ones we'd stored," he admonished. "And, also, you will not be able to go out and purchase any as all your outlets are closed on Christmas Day! However, and contrary to your earthling misunderstandings, raisins are not our sole source of sustenance, despite the fact they are by far our favourite and will always be consumed by my people where they are available. We will eat other things when we need to, but rest assured we will eat without pleasure, through gritted teeth. And don't think of offering us any of your own food, we do not want it. But we will eat, and our bellies will be full on this your Christmas Day, and let me leave you with this: you will regret the insult you have shown myself and my people this morning." He tossed the mic at Papa's feet, and with that he led his people back in through the mouse hole and behind the wall, their heads bowed.

Papa ruined the rest of the day pacing round the house fretting over the offence we'd shown the LAs. After Christmas Dinner, he sent Myles and I to bed without any pudding. It was us, Myles especially, that he blamed for emptying the LAs larder, but he got it into his head that I'd been involved as well. Even Mamma was unsympathetic.

Upstairs in bed, I watched Myles roll back and forth on his little rocking horse Santa had brought him. The motion of him going, to and fro and to and fro as like a mesmerist's pocket watch, quickly lulled me into a dreamless sleep.

On awakening I was taken aback, and not a little miffed, to hear the clickity-clack of that blasted horse still going. I presumed that the noise of it had woken me, but then, on noticing the bright, fresh daylight pouring through the window, I turned to chastise bold Myles, thinking he'd stayed up the entire night on his new toy, imagining himself riding on some endless prairie.

However - and to my mortal horror - the image that met me was not my beloved brother, but rather his skeleton, his cherubic little face now just a grinning skull, not a pick of meat left on his short, white bones, which were instead covered in little teeth marks.

"Papa! Mamma! Grandmamma!" I squealed.

At once they all appeared in my bedroom. Mamma howled on seeing what was left of Myles, and Grandmamma started to beat Papa round the head and shoulders, screaming, "You stupid pig! Look what you've done, letting those little devils in this house!"

At Mamma's insistence Papa vacated our home and ran straight to his fellows in the LA liberation movement. She was never to grant him admission ever again to Stein Manor.

I spent the next week prostrate with grief, crying nightly. Then, in the week following, I set my heart on implementing a raw and raging revenge!

First I assembled some of Papa's pump and gas-compound equipment that he used in his capacity as a bio warfare scientist. Once concocted, I pumped a non-lethal irritant in behind the walls, where the little bastards lived, flushing them out, coughing and vomiting. Making sure they'd all emerged, I dropped the hamster cage down upon them all, imprisoning every last one of them.

My cruel vengeance could begin.

I started by separating all the men from the women, then all the women from the children. I herded them hither and thither using newly extinguished hot match heads. Once the men and women were separated in two cages I brought out the children, corralled at the bottom of Papa's large chemical beaker. Packed in above them was a thick, dense ceiling of hay, which I doused in lighter fluid. Then, before the adult LAs very eyes, I struck a match and dropped it in there.

When I returned some time later all that was left at the bottom of the jar was the scorched and tangled hay intermingled with the viscera of the LA children. The LA women cried and the men spat at me. But it was the women I dealt with next.

Taking an eyedropper filled with my own semen I inserted the nib into their private parts and squirted it up in there as they squirmed and pleaded. For the next two months I fed and watered them as my seed grew and flourished inside their bodies.

When the time arrived that I knew their small size could no longer house my human proportioned offspring, I brought them out in front of their Papas, husbands, brothers and lovers who bore witness as their translucent bellies popped, sending grotesque and underdeveloped foetuses spilling out. In a final insult I let the cats in the room, who fed eagerly and without hesitation upon the corpses.

At last it was the men's turn to face unimaginable and multifarious tortures and deaths.

To begin with I taped eight of them to the radiator in our grand front hall and turned the central heating up to its highest setting. Mamma and Grandmamma joined me as we watched them slowly, agonisingly die.

Six of them were buried up to their necks in the cats' litter tray. In two days they had either died of noxious poisoning from their faeces or been eaten alive by them.

Barnyubus's three sons I dropped into the toilet then shat and urinated upon them. When I was done I carried Barnyubus into the bathroom so he could watch me pore some of Papa's sulphuric acid in on top of them.

The last nine of them, not including Barnyubus, had hot matchsticks shoved up their bottoms and driven slowly through their bodies, right up into their skulls.

Barnyubus watched this indignity also. Then it was just him left.

Using lollipop sticks and sticky tape I constructed a little makeshift cross. I held him down upon it and drove thumbtacks through his hands and a third one through both his feet.

I placed the crucified Barnyubus outside our estate to serve as a warning to any other LAs who may have still been out there and come wandering by. Over a course of days he was slowly picked apart by ravens and the cats, and by week's end all that was left of him was a tiny six inch skeleton.

The other LAs I buried at the bottom of the garden, with Myles' little milk teeth serving as their headstones.

It was all I had to remind me of the heinous deed they'd done in eating him and my brutal and terrible vengeance in response to it.

PEEPING TOM

by Carl Redding

Mid fifties male looking at a half dressed girl through a window. Does that make me a Peeping Tom? I guess some people might think so, but on a cold December night, well, sometimes you can't help but look when it is the only thing worth seeing. Unfortunately, some things, once seen, cannot be unseen...

Bill and I had been in the pub, and when we left, we walked unsteadily across the car park and crossed the road. Bill wanted some beers and snacks to consume while we watched the DVD's he'd bought. Bargain basement horror films. So he'd called into the corner shop. Bill never rushed his shopping. I didn't like the shop much, it smelled of old newspapers and stale pet food, so I waited outside. An evening finished off with cheap horror movies and carry outs was a regular thing for Bill and I. The Christmas decorations and twinkling lights of the shop window display didn't hold my attention for long. I turned around. Opposite this side of the corner shop, across the road, was an abandoned estate agent's office. Above it were two windows, probably a flat. I vaguely knew the good looking young guy who lived there. I saw him sometimes at the pub, usually with his mates. I think he was Spanish. I think his name was Angelo. He worked at a nearby chip shop. I knew it must be Monday because Angelo was at home. The chip shop was closed on Mondays. This Monday Angelo wasn't alone. On this side, the flat had two windows. The left one, which I assumed was a bedroom, never had the curtains open. The right one, which I thought might be a kitchen, never had the curtains shut, and the light was always on. I'd noted this on many a wait while Bill shopped.

I could see Angelo was in the kitchen because I recognised his black curly hair. The rest of him was obscured by another figure. A female with her back to the window, pale blonde straight hair just a little longer than shoulder length. I could see her down to her waist. She only seemed to be wearing a bra. When she moved slightly, I could see more of Angelo. He didn't seem to be wearing much either. It is considered rude to look, to spy on people, especially people getting amorous. I should have looked away. I should, perhaps, have gone into the horrible corner shop and tried to hurry Bill along. What I shouldn't have done was to stand and stare at the impromptu live show. Maybe if I was sober I would have had better manners, but it had been a long time, and the people involved looked attractive, and this night I was weak willed.

The pair of them clinched together, her arms clasped behind his neck, his hands dropping below the level of the window to, presumably, grasp her bottom. As they kissed passionately, they moved around, still next to the window, so now I could see them in profile. She on the left, he on the right. From where I was standing, they both looked to be fine specimens in the prime of life. Angelo's hands raised, and she leant backwards to allow him access to her bra covered boobs. As he fondled her, they broke their kiss. It was at that moment, when Angelo was distracted, that she turned her head and looked directly at me. It wasn't as though I was hidden, I was standing out on the pavement silhouetted in front of the corner shop's gaudily lit window. Her movement was so quick I didn't even have time to avert my eyes. I was caught. Her face was beautiful. Her lips slightly parted, perhaps she was groaning in pleasure, but it was her palest of pale blue eyes that fully occupied my attention. As she met my gaze, I felt my heart bump. Not in pleasure, but in fear. It was the sort of bump a mouse might feel when confronted with a snake. Whatever language the girl's voice and body were communicating to Angelo, her eyes were telling a completely different story to me.

The look was cold and hard, and certainly held a threat of

danger. And hunger. There was definitely a look of hunger. I should have looked away. I wanted to look away. But those eyes transfixed me. Paralysed me. I couldn't have looked away at that moment to save my life. I fully expected her to scream or something. I expected that an irate Angelo might remonstrate with me. I felt like a dirty old man spying on the pleasures of young flesh. But that isn't what happened. Even now, I can hardly believe what she did.

Slowly and deliberately, she winked at me. Then she was facing her lover again, but from then on, I got the impression that she was putting on a show, not just for Angelo's benefit, but for mine also. Now she was pressing kisses along his jaw line, then down his neck to his chest, then down and further down, until just the top of her bobbing head was visible above the window ledge. Angelo's eyes were tightly closed, presumably concentrating on averting over excitement. Now she was working her way back up his torso, bra removed and a breast sometimes visible. Their bodies parted slightly, and she dropped a hand below window level, fumbling to make an adjustment between them, then her hands were back behind his neck, and gently they started grinding and gyrating their lower bodies. Her hands slowly dropped down his back until they were below his waist, pulling him to her, controlling his movements. His hands were on her shoulders, steadying himself.

This phase of their lovemaking didn't last more than a few moments before Angelo tilted his head back, obviously close to the end of his self control. In this position, her chest was perfectly visible in profile, and even though I was some distance away, I could see something odd about her breast. It looked swollen and red, engorged maybe. Then it looked as though something powerful and muscular actually slithered under the skin. I gasped involuntarily. I was aware that there was some kind of connection between her breast and Angelo's torso. Something that looked not unlike a bunch of red earth worms, or maybe tentacles, had emanated from around her nipple, and were rapidly spreading over Angelo's body. He must have felt it at the same time, his eyes opened and he glanced down between them, his expression no longer pleasure, but pure horror. Something in that breast pulsed.

The pulse travelled along the tentacles and into Angelo. He shuddered, whether in the anticipated ultimate ecstasy, or terrible agony, I couldn't say. I don't know if he pumped anything into her, but I got the distinct impression that she pumped something into him. His face went slack, his head fell backwards, and his eyes rolled up to show the whites. He looked as though his trembling body would have fallen, but the tentacles held him fast. Again she flashed me a direct glance.

This time there was something more in that cold hard stare. Maybe a look of amusement, and maybe a hint of triumph. Slowly she and Angelo dropped towards the floor, below the level of the window. Then there was nothing more to see.

I didn't watch the horror films with Bill. Couldn't face it. I never told anyone what I saw, or think I saw, after all, who wants to admit to being a Peeping Tom? It isn't as though I haven't been punished for seeing what I should never have seen. The nightmares have seen to that. I haven't seen Angelo since that night. His friends still come to the pub, but he is never with them. There is a job vacancy advertised in the chip shop window.

In the flat above the disused estate agent's office, opposite the corner shop, one set of curtains remains closed, the other set are open, but now the light is never on.

THE SIGN AND THE SIGIL

by Paul Green

My name is Arthur Montague. I am - or was - an academic, specialising in Renaissance esoterica, whose happiest hours as a student were spent in the reassuring presence of antiquarian books, whether on the shelves of my study or in the stacks of the Bodliean Library. Now, suspended from my post in the so-called Humanities department at this provincial university, I still try to find consolation in my fine editions of Cornelius Agrippa's *De Occulta Philosophia Libri* or G.S.R. Mead's *Thrice Greatest Hermes* while I wait for the authorities to decide my fate.

Given my age, I expect they will find some formula of redundancy or early retirement to discretely remove my embarrassing presence from the payroll. I have been asked if I want a union official to support me at next week's hearing, but I have declined, as the outcome is almost certainly predetermined - and perhaps irrelevant now. Instead, I find it imperative to write this account of my traumatic experience, if only to understand how and why it has befallen me - and others.

When I was appointed three years ago to teach basic courses in the history of philosophy, by then reduced to an insignificant enclave in the vast expanding empire of cultural and media studies, I was informed that it was essential for a lecturer to develop a 'presence', that students would regard me as a non-entity for failing to leave my cyber-footprint, that only regular interfacing in the digital world would validate my post-modernity. The electronic entanglements of email, the Internet and the babel of social networking had little appeal for me. But I was eventually forced to adopt these modes of communication by the pressure of my peers and the policies of the institution. In my very first appraisal Victoria Bormann, our ambitious head of department, reminded me that 'in today's skills-based environment, the customer expects an inter-active learning experience designed for the twenty-first century.' How bitterly ironic that my attempts to engage with the contemporary world have dragged me into a vortex of ancient forces.

Of course, I did my best to create a digital persona in the university. I responded punctually to management emails demanding ever-increasing amounts of assessment data to quantify my performance and set my teaching outcomes. I posted updates on Facebook about papers I'd published on Renaissance Neo-Platonism, which never gained the accolade of a single 'like' from either colleagues or students. I even created a web page on the university intranet, displaying my lecture notes, reading lists, assignments and seminar topics. I liked its stark monochrome simplicity and austere font, but it was rarely visited.

However my troubles really began at the start of the last academic year, when Ms Victoria Bormann summoned me to her office and informed me that my option modules on 'Philosophy from Heraclitus to Derrida' would not be running.

'Enrolment's almost nil this semester,' she announced cheerfully, totally empowered in her crisp trouser suit and her role as course leader for Multi-Media Cultural Studies. 'And frankly I'm not surprised, Arthur. Word gets out. You're really letting down the brand.' She produced a sheaf of student evaluations. 'Your lecture room style, all solemn as if you were high priest of culture. No Power Point or YouTube. Your endless digressions on Kabbalism, your enthusiasm for that horrible sexist Nazi Nietzsche. Nothing to prepare them for the real world. Our seats have got to fit their little bums, you know...'

I refrained from correcting her ill-informed slander of a great thinker, as the void of a zero-hour contract opened in front of me. I was also oddly transfixed by the pallor of her skin, the ripeness of her lips and the way she toyed with her long blonde hair as she fixed me with her over-bright blue-eyed stare, even though this performance was usually targeted at her younger male colleagues, not a greybeard in a faded corduroy jacket.

'Stop looking gob-smacked, Arthur. We have a solution. You can support the Multi-Media Studies programme with some background stuff. Marx, the Frankfurt School, you know, critical theory, semiotics and all that.' I may have vaguely protested that students couldn't understand the epistemological errors of Marx without tackling Hegel or the concept of idealism, and she probably said that I was simply being 'academic'. But one thing rankled above all, her parting shot:

'That boring web page of yours, Arthur. Anyone would think you were a dead white male. All text. No visuals, no iconography, no exciting links or inter-activity for the students. You've got to sex it up a bit. Your signage doesn't signify anything much right now...'

That evening as I sat in front of a blank screen in my dusty apartment, the numbing shock I'd experienced at Victoria Bormann's invalidation of my entire career was slowly transformed to a burning current of fury. How could this corporate harpy dismiss centuries of philosophical debate and speculation, how dare she demote me to serfdom, to peddle the half-truths and pious platitudes of critical theory? Clearly she expected higher education to be delivered as a kind of music video or a series of tweets.

Nevertheless, resignation was not an option. My pension was still several years away, so I had to sublimate my anger and keep my job. My immediate targets were to refresh my knowledge of critical theory and semiotics, and to re-design my course web pages, incorporating more imagery. There had to be a copyright-free picture of Marx or Louis Althusser that I could bodge in, and perhaps I could even create a simple diagram of Saussure's model of signification, depicting the signifier and its relation to what was signified.

Semiotics had always seemed to me to be the least unattractive element of the Cultural Studies programme, so I felt I might as well begin my lecture preparation by re-reading Roland Barthes' Elements of Semiology, a battered paperback I had not touched for decades. As I opened it, I recognised the neat italic signature on the title page 'Charlotte Cockburn' and felt a sudden resurgence of youthful angst, recalling the way she'd flounced out of my room at Oxford all those years ago, having hurled the book at my head in the course of terminating our semi-Platonic relationship. I had to read on quickly.

The key aspect of semiotic theory, I swiftly recalled, was that the signifier was an arbitrary symbol. The linguistic sign systems C-A-T or K-A-T-Z-E-N only referenced the furry feline creature. The painting of the pipe was not the pipe. A snapshot of Charlotte Cockburn on the beach, a private icon in my files, was not the haughty blonde whose blue eyes had tormented me, but a mere layer of fading emulsion on crumpled paper.

I put Barthes aside, still flinching at twinges of memory, both ancient and recent. For distraction I turned to my old esoteric tomes, which I liked to peruse as a contrast to the rigour of Wittgenstein or Russell. Instinctively, I pulled out A.E Waite's edition of *The Key of Solomon the King* and opened a page at random: 'The Mysteries of Goetic Theurgy'. Here indeed were intricate signs and symbols of the Goetia, demonic entities who could serve one's appetites, teach wisdom and defeat one's enemies - SYTRI with a leopard's head and the wings of a gryphon 'who causes women to show themselves naked', BUER, 'a great president who teaches philosophy' or VEPAR who 'occasions death in three days by means of putrefying sores...'

It was amusing, almost empowering, to reflect on how Charlotte might have yielded herself to me, how I might have risen to the presidency of some venerable academy, and how certain departmental managers might have been made to suffer for their arrogance, simply by evoking such grotesque spirits. Yet this was a sixteenth century fantasy. However frustrated I was in this very post-modern situation I could hardly inscribe these ancient symbols in my own blood on an emerald or on a sheet of virgin parchment, with the prescribed embellishments of a chalk circle, black candles or sulphurous incense. The notion was attractive but impractical.

Nevertheless the idea of creating a secret sign that embodied my desires was intriguing. Indeed, its absurdity was almost compelling, a rebellion against the materialistic consensus that pervaded our educational culture. Before taking up my ill-fated lecturing post I'd briefly joined a small society, meeting in the basement of a London bookshop, where members had delivered enlightening talks on arcane beliefs and curious practices. I unearthed some notes I'd made on Dr. Levi's enlightening talk about deploying 'the sigillum', the little sign or sigil, an operation much favoured by the artist Austin Osman Spare, who would create magical symbols, his 'monograms of thought' by fusing together the alphabetic forms of a written message of intent. He would - and I could, I realised with growing excitement - 'charge' a sigil by focussing on it in a self-induced trance state, so that it entered the unconscious and could continue to do its work of influencing events at the astral level. Maybe it was time for me to progress from a scholarly interest in the byways of historic esoterica to actual practical experiment.

To loosen the girders of the soul I drank several large whiskies and tried to formulate my message of intent. After a few rough drafts I condensed it as follows:

T-H-I-S-M-Y-W-I-L-L-T-O-H-A-V-E-M-Y-S-I-G-N-I-F-I-C-A-N-C-E-R-E-C-O-G-N-I-S-E-D-B-Y-T-H-E-U-N-I-V-E-R-S-I-T-Y

As recommended, I sigillised the alphabetic characters by removing repeated characters:

THISMYWLOAVEGNFCRSDBU

And then reversed their order:

UBDS RCNF GEVA OLWY MSIHT

The resulting mantra was almost unpronounceable and reminded me too much of the cumbersome passwords I was forced to used all the time when navigating the campus networks. So, with careful penmanship, using black ink on high quality paper, I drew a visual sigil, combining all the various letter forms, their curves, verticals, horizontals and diagonals into a single complex shape.

In the light of all that has subsequently happened, I have chosen not to reproduce it here. Suffice to say that its serpentine curves and contorted geometry symbolised all too well the thwarted energies of my overwrought psyche. And like a good signifier it bore no overt resemblance to what it signified.

I'd noted that 'self-pleasuring' was one of the techniques recommended by Spare for attaining a trance state when charging the sigil. At the time, the notion had seemed ludicrous but now, in a Bacchic state of ancient lust and new rage, I lost all my bourgeois inhibitions. Soon I was standing semi-erect and nude, like a crumbling statue of Dionysus in some overgrown Edwardian garden. With the sigil held before me, I focused on its intricate signage as I slowly aroused myself with the phantasm of a pale blonde woman, naked and chained, arranged for my total satisfaction across an oak desk in a dim-lit library of leather-bound antiquities. In the flickering illumination of fantasy her face morphed between Victoria Bormann and Charlotte Cockburn, blue eyes half closed in ecstasy as I finally possessed her, driving the burning outline of the sigil into the depths of my mind...

A while later I awoke, sprawled on the sofa. I felt cold, slightly nauseous and my head ached. The sigil lay on the carpet, stained and crumpled. As I lumbered towards the bedroom, I was already trying to forget this dubious episode.

In the weeks that followed I was overwhelmed with work, preparing slide presentations, seeking out digestible gobbets of critical theory, duplicating hand-outs, marking the students' confused and fragmented assignments with commentaries that were twice the length of their submissions. I worked, in fact, in a kind of asexual trance, the self-indulgences of the sigil rite thrust from my mind. Nevertheless I was surviving; Victoria Bormann kept her distance. As the module I was teaching was compulsory, attendance was adequate and the students seemed to appreciate that although the contents might be tedious for all of us, I was doing my best to make it comprehensible. I even allowed myself a few brief digressions into the symbology of the Rosicrucians and the supposed Illuminati - they had heard of the latter via various computer games.

As I sat in a stuffy overheated seminar room one Friday afternoon, I was struck by one striking difference between this generation of students and my own cohort. Scanning the brawny biceps of the lads in t-shirts and the necks and cleavages of the girls, I realised that every learner was marked with some kind of tattoo. I could see flowers, snakes, Celtic knots and swirls, butterflies and daggers. This gave me an opportunity to revisit semiotics and the concept of polysemy, especially as Ben and Holly were still struggling with it.

'Look at this way, Holly. What's the signification of Ben's tattoo?'

'It's a snake...' She squinted at me suspiciously, suspecting a trap.

'It's an ink pattern imprinted on the flesh of Ben's upper arm, signifying a reptile' interpolated Joe, one of the brighter sparks. Holly shrugged and turned to her laptop, probably to shop surreptitiously.

I turned to Ben. 'What are the connotations of your snake?'

'It's cool,' he said after a moment's reflection. 'Wicked...'

'Yes, to a devout reader of Genesis, the snake who tempted Eve would certainly be a figure of evil. But to someone who collected snakes, it might be a creature of outstanding natural beauty.'

I sensed this discussion was going to peter out, so I reverted to the Power Point and my approved script. A few students resumed making notes.

At the end of the session Ben shyly approached me. 'That was helpful about signifying. But could we have more on the website, some pictures or something?'

I thanked him for reminding me. In my haste to prepare the classroom content, I still hadn't met Victoria Bormann's target of adorning my virtual presence. Then Ben rushed off to catch up with his peers. As I passed them in the corridor, Holly was giggling as she traced the outline of the serpent motif on Ben's upper arm with her long manicured fingers.

I spent much of the weekend redesigning the website, struggling with broken links and templates that didn't fit. However with perseverance I managed to post pictures of various cultural studies gurus and sourced some graphics and video links on semiotics. I also added a section on Foucault whom I quite admired for his bleakness. Yet the work gave me little satisfaction. I was merely a conduit for other people's work. I wished I could add a more personal stamp.

Then, shifting a pile of books across my worn carpet, I was struck by an epiphany. My charged sigil still lay at the feet of the sofa. I could try to scan it and embed it in every page, or even in every email. It would be more distinctive than the po-faced mugshots my colleagues used to adorn their sites. And I loved the bizarre subversion of it, that the symbol of my secret intent would be publicly flaunted to the staff and student body, while Victoria Bormann would never know the auto-erotic ritual that had charged the mystery signifier.

Within minutes I'd marked every page of MM101 CULTURAL THEORY with my unique seal and also added it to my default email stationery.

The week that followed saw a noticeable increase in the number of hits on my digital fiefdom. Several students emailed to thank me for 'the awesome new learning materials'. When Victoria Bormann swept through the cafeteria en route to a senior management meeting she paused by my chair to pat my elbow, exhorting me to 'keep up the good work'.

But I should have known that something was amiss when Ben and Holly failed to attend my Friday session. 'They've been suspended,' Joe informed the class. 'For damaging uni property. Graffiti or something.' Some of the others exchanged significant looks, as if they were about to say something more, but I closed the register and made it clear we needed to plod on with representational issues in soap opera.

It was only later when I was walking over to the Library that I witnessed the first signs of the disruption to come. The glass and concrete ramparts of the new Business Studies Centre had been sprayed at least a dozen times, in thick black aerosol, with my sigil.

I escaped to London for the weekend, staying at a small hotel, so I could visit an exhibition of Austin Osman Spare's art work at the Gamaliel Gallery in Bloomsbury and then spend the Sunday trawling my favourite bookshops in the area, eschewing all contacts with the internet and the university. Gazing at Spare's exquisite draughtsmanship in works like Sentient Symbols and Resurgent Atavisms I was transported into a cosmos of archeo-psychic forces, inked into manifestation by his fluent line.

However, on the long train journey home, anticipating an unusual week ahead, I kept reassuring myself that Ben's adoption of my private sigil as a 'tag' had simply been a random choice, probably fuelled by a student drinking bout. The Dean could not possibly believe that I had perpetrated the offence or even encouraged it.

Nevertheless, I received a few curious glances when I walked into the staff room on Monday. 'Becoming a cult figure, are you, Arthur?' exclaimed Bob Perry, an extrovert Northerner who taught TV production. 'The kids are putting that squiggle of yours all over the place as if it was an election campaign. Just go over to the Physics Lab or the Library extension. It's everywhere!' I shrugged, mumbled and retreated towards the toilets, only to encounter Victoria Bormann en route.

'This stupid logo thing of yours, Arthur. It's got completely out of hand. I hope you haven't put them up to it.' I assured her I hadn't. 'Well, it may have begun as some weird joke on their part, but it's your professional duty to discourage them.' As she swung away, I noticed that instead of her usual spiky silver necklace, she was wearing a purple silk scarf, not her usual style.

In the toilet cubicle someone had used a penknife to scratch a clumsy copy of the sigil on the door.

After trying unsuccessfully to focus on an inbox full of marking, I went for a quick snack in the cafeteria. I joined the queue behind Tanya, a blue-haired siren in leather trousers, who usually sat at the back of my class reading Gothic fiction while I pretended not to notice. The whitish skin of her neck was freshly tattooed - with a purple iteration of the sigil. I watched her take her espresso to a nearby table, where she continued her perusal of H.P. Lovecraft's *At the Mountains of Madness*. I felt I'd already arrived at the foothills.

As I started to eat a sandwich, I glanced surreptitiously around the room. The chattering students didn't appear to register my presence. But I counted at least six versions of the sigil - on forearms, ankles, shoulders. There were perhaps others, in more private places. This synchronicity was beyond coincidence now; its enigma alarmed me, to the extent that my hand was trembling as I tried to pick up my coffee cup. I pushed the food to one side and got up unsteadily.

There had to be a rational explanation, an Occam's Razor that would cut to a simple reason for the flesh-and-blood replication of the sigil. Perhaps my 'brand' as Ms Bormann might have called it, coincided with the logo for some popular music group or modish fashion accessory that was quite outside my sphere of experience. Perhaps, more worryingly, a 'sigil craze' was an ironic gesture from the students directed at my alleged academic pretensions. Yet why take it to the extent of having it obsessively tattooed on one's youthful body? What did this mean? I decided I would take sick leave for a few days.

So I lurked at home for a week. I switched off my router and disconnected the phone. I shrouded my TV in a blanket and removed the batteries from the radio. The image of Charlotte Cockburn was finally sliced and burned, a painful yet somehow essential exorcism. Laboriously I boxed up my library of occult books and locked them in a cupboard. Instead I read the logical positivists and the analytic philosophers, in the hope that their brutal clarity might disperse the miasma of paranoid fantasy that was engulfing me. During the day my regime almost worked. But at night I alternated between sleeplessness and disturbing dreams, each one more nightmarish as the week wore on.

In one of them, I was hustled into a filthy tin-roofed hospital for 'one of our more interesting operations,' as the obese male nurse informed me, holding me down in bloodstained pajamas. Large horned beetle-like creatures, neither organic nor mechanical, swarmed all over my torso, leaving a pattern of dark purple scars before crawling towards my face... No need for analysis, as I woke up shouting.

Eventually I decided that human contact, however hostile, might afford me a better anchorage in reality. I could no longer evade my Monday-morning responsibilities at the campus.

I tried to keep my eyes down as I paced along the crudely sigilised concrete walkways that led from the car park to the Human Resources Department. I needed to hand in my sick note. Fortunately my GP had confined himself to hurriedly scribbling 'depression' and prescribing Prozac. Nevertheless, the female HR officer gave me a suspicious look. 'I'd say that you're quite lucky having depression. Other people around here have nastier things to worry about.'

I slunk out past the Medical Centre. A queue of students stood in line outside, huddled in their hoodies, despite the bright morning sun. Further down the line, I recognised Bob Perry, baseball cap pulled down over his forehead.

'What's the matter, Bob? Is this some new vaccination programme?'

He scowled. 'Fuck off, Arthur. You've got a nerve to turn up here. You knew what was coming, didn't you?' As he jerked his head away, his cap slipped sideways and I saw the angry red scar, my accursed sigil scrawled across his forehead.

I could only retreat, sick with fear. I tried to stumble on, eyes half-shut so that I might only partially witness the symbols daubed on broken windows at the Psychology building and an overturned litter bin outside the Library. The signpost where the pathway forked off to the student residences was almost completely obliterated by my psycho-tag. I brushed past a sobbing Asian girl clutching her hijab around her face, and a youth who'd dismounted from his skateboard to stare in bewilderment at a mark spreading across his calf muscles. By the time I'd reached the cafeteria,

I'd seen more than enough.

The space was almost deserted, the counter unmanned, the coffee machine silent. Only azure-haired Tanya sat at a table with her back towards me. She was writing intently in a notebook with one hand, and picking frantically at the back of her neck with the other. As my footsteps echoed across the tiled floor, she turned - and sprang to her feet, overturning her chair and dropping her notebook. She screamed, a loud theatrical cry as if I were one of her fantasy entities, and rushed to the exit before I could intervene.

But I picked up her notebook, to read her final entry:

...holly's so bleeding again -up all night tattoo's viral now like a replicant flowing all down her back - like black death particle chain reaction - and not just ppl who did 1st round tags & tats - it's gone airborne -joe ninety mister monty's star bursting out all over- same pattern coming through - and now something horrible on my back-i'm not turning found to look at it i'm not not

The jagged scribble broke off. Whatever the outcome, I could evade my responsibility no longer. The exit sign was no escape. I slipped and tumbled on the stone pavement outside, shivering, close to vomiting, overwhelmed by the implications of what was happening, for the causal connection between my signifier and its significance was manifest. The astral universe had played a diabolical joke in permitting me to make my mark on the university, imposing my stigmata of rage and vengeance. All I could do now was to get home to my grimoires and try to set up a magical counter-current, whatever the cost and however absurd the process. Credo quia absurdum.

As I staggered to my feet, face and hands bleeding, I tried to focus the chaos of my being into a form of words that could be compressed into a sigil, while the glyphs of Sytry, Buer, Vepar and their howling legions swam like oily streaks across my retina. But strong hands grabbed my elbows, the gloved hands of Campus Security. 'Dr. Bormann wants a word, Mr. Montague...'

I can't go on. The sign summons the signified. Too dangerous to recall those moments but I can't stop living in them. But spelling it all out might banish it? I need to get it down somehow.

They left me alone with her. But no blame to them, the odour was overpowering. Over-ripe meat mingled with heavy perfume. Sprawled across her executive chair, clutching the blood-stained silk scarf to her throat.

'You're doing it,' she rasped. Her every word was clearly hurting. 'Somehow you're doing this shit. The Dean's called the police of course. And specialist medics from the hospital. They'll probably have to quarantine the whole campus.' Her voice was raw with anger. 'Look me in the face, you old bastard.' I tried to evade looking at those bloodshot eyes, the drool on her lower lip. Automatically I lapsed into my lecturing mode as I tried to explain what a sigil was, that the outcome wasn't my true will. And so forth.

'Don't bullshit me with your supernatural nonsense. So clever to confuse people at first with the graffiti stunt. You've cooked up a virus haven't you? Or got it off the dark net. You must have done, to poison their tattoos. Some barbaric alchemy of yours. And then spread it over the cafe and the Library.' No way of challenging the confused speculations that she was so obviously desperate to believe for her voice filled my brain with her rancour and misery.

She tossed back her tousled mane of blonde hair and rose from the chair, ripping open her long black dress to expose the swell of her breasts and her pale belly. 'Just look what you've done. Go on, take a good look...' Impossible to read her body's language, as she stared into my eyes, her pupils dilated like black micro-planets.

She dropped the scarf and touched the sigil embossed at the base of her neck. The outline was raised like a wiry black scab and beads of blood were forming at points where the lines crossed and entangled. A small area around the wound was trembling like skin on a liquid simmering over a flame.

Despite the desecration of her flesh, I was for a few seconds horribly aroused by her defiant flaunting.

'Listen, all I need to do - ' I broke off as she pulled my head downwards, forcing me to confront the sigil, only inches away now. I could actually see it shimmering and blurring against her flesh, as if afloat in a tank of milky solution. It was centred on her clavicle area, but expanding upwards now towards the protrusion of her larynx. The aroma of blood and musky incense was overwhelming . I was sure that tiny nodules of light were flickering between the intersections of the sign. Something had written its way through me into her body. I was retching with terror.

So much I need to suppress, in case it manifests here in this musty bedroom among my tangled bedsheets. Although I burned the sigil and broke the pen I used to inscribe it, erasing the drives on my computer, even laboriously punching out this, my final text, on a clumsy mechanical typewriter, I shall always remain open to attack.

I know we fell to the floor together, unbalanced by forces surging around us, and I managed to roll away.

I can see her now, lying on her back, convulsing as if under electro-shock as a sub-creature - an aborted entity, that lumpen alien thing - I can't decode it - rotated slowly above her. I have given up trying to translate it into any normal frame of reference.

Her wound was spawning. An object emerged, to merge. Hot beasting breath between us. A buzzing noise, glimmer of failing electrics and/or vibration of veined wings. Filthy fur or flaking scales were part of it, extruding from her heart meat. Plasma of a time-worm for my tonguing in homage, a familiar suckling to fight off, in nerves and sinews of the sigil, I was resigned to it, it wants to melt me into its gory slippage.

It contained deformed elements of both vertebrates and invertebrates, a compacted pseudo-mass of our entire pre-human phylogeny congealing in blood, red clay and dribbles of amniotic mucus. It embodied my old random devils Sytry and Buer and Vepar and all the denizens of the dark texts, a myriad sub-demons and servitors compressed in a globule, pulsing like a newly transplanted heart. But trace the lineage of these old demons back, beyond all their gryphons and lions and horned goatishness and you tumble into the swill of our brains where our archeo-psychic avatars squeal and writhe in saurian fury, then flicker into chitinous articulated mandibles and webbings around a mass of hybrid viscera, bubbling molecules in a state of constant mutation. Imagery slowly floated in and out and around it like tiny holograms - a tiny human-headed dog-pig, horned hermaphrodites, the outline of my sigil like soft tubes of neon unravelling - before bursting in clots of jellied blood or urine. I dare not breath. When I tried move away I was mesmerised by this final manifestation of my Will.

For a few seconds it hung there, pulsing with reddish light - then imploded into a speck of darkness with a shrill cackling noise. Victoria Bormann stopped moving.

The emergency services tried resuscitation and men bustled round with cameras as I was led out through the blue-and white tape, blubbering or ranting. I understand the office has now been sealed, perhaps permanently.

I have been through all the procedures now. Victoria Bormann's post-mortem established that she died of a massive heart attack. Although the curious scar on her neck was beginning to go septic, it had no apparent connection with her death. I was of course arrested and questioned exhaustively about my professional relationship with her and any grievances that might have provoked me into assaulting her. However, DNA tests established without a doubt that I had no abnormal contact with her, sexual or otherwise. My story that I'd found her hysterical and half-naked was, at one level, quite accurate and I let it rest there, for the forensic psychiatrist had already found my account of the demonology most entertaining, a useful contribution to the professional literature regarding fantasy constructs. And the overworked detective inspector didn't want to know about sigils. What crazy students got up to was their own affair, or a matter for university deans. So I've been informed unofficially that the Crown Prosecution Service is unlikely to press charges.

The consultants at the local hospital took a similar line, especially when the sigils, self-inflicted or otherwise, began to fade quite rapidly. And the university PR department made sure that the 'student graffiti' were quickly removed and stories of unusual college pranks or the tragic death of a colleague never made it into the national media.

Nothing can proved of course, if one follows the current consensus reality model and possibly I could fight for my reinstatement. But it's been made very clear to me that I am persona non grata. I am, in any event, unable to teach. Neither Plato nor Aristotle can erase the Goetia from my mind.

It only remains for me to write my last sentence, suitably compressed.

IT'S ONLY THE GRANDA (A TRUE STORY)

by Sally Cochran

My late husband always said his grandfather haunted him. Most of our married life, no matter where we moved, we heard footsteps creaking on the stairs or passing us by. We used to laugh and say, "It's only the granda".

The haunting stopped when my husband died, or so I thought. I remarried and moved to California, but due to homesickness after twenty years I moved back to Belfast, Northern Ireland.

I moved into a house close to where we had lived previously, and where my late husband had been born and died. My two grown up daughters both said they felt their father's presence in this house and when either of them stayed with me, we heard footsteps on the stairs. Shadows caught our eye, a slight movement over our shoulder and a sudden unexplained coldness in the room, or the smell of Old Spice shaving lotion in an all female house. Now, they said, it wasn't their great grandfather but their dad that followed them about. So now the words had changed and they laughed and joked, "It's only my da".

Well, I'd had enough of their da when he was alive and I most certainly didn't want anything to do with him when he was dead, so after two years, I moved into a brand new house. "No one would be doing any haunting in this house," I thought.

My youngest daughter's twins were born that summer, 20th

June 1998, and strange occurrences began to happen whenever they came to visit or stayed with me. When the boys were about one year-old they started to put words together and one day Dylan, for no reason, picked up my daughter's handbag and gave it to her saying, "Phone mummy". A few seconds later her mobile phone started to ring. Or Leon would say, even though he couldn't see or hear anyone approach the house, "Bell ring", or "Bob bark", before the dog started to bark, or "Baby sick", meaning his brother would fall ill. Numerous little things that made us look and wonder, but never voicing aloud our thoughts.

One night, Dylan and Leon curled up beside me in my bed. Dylan as usual had awakened in the middle of the night and of course his twin bellowed in sympathy. Their mum and dad both worked for a major airline and unfortunately both schedules coincided from time to time, and this was one of those times, so 'good ole gran' babysat the eighteen month-old twins. Not an easy job. Leon quickly went back to sleep, but Dylan fidgeted, squirmed, wriggled, punched and kicked and then all of a sudden, he sat straight up in bed and stared at the dark shadows in the corner of the room.

"Dylan love, lie back down again, there's a good boy." I touched his small back and gently rubbed. Dylan ignored me. Again, I called his name softly. "Dylan," I coaxed, "Come on love, be a good boy for nanny and lie down and have a cuddle".

Dylan continued to stare at the dark shadows in the corner. His head twisted around slowly and then back again. He repeated this movement several times. I was starting to worry. He sat perfectly still, his hands for once lying limp on top of the duvet. In the quietness of the room, I could hear his identical twin breathing softly, hear the hum of the clock on the beside dresser, and smell the baby lotion and apple juice which scented the bedroom. I thought Dylan had fallen asleep where he sat, he was so still.

Cautiously I sat slowly up and pressed the palm of my hand

into the child's back and with my other hand tried to ease Dylan back down onto the bed. Dylan remained ridged. Afraid to move him, in case I frightened him, he sat like this for what seemed ages. All of a sudden, his head whipped around as though he was following something or someone and spread his tiny arms wide and said, "Man all...gone nanny". He lay down and promptly went to sleep.

I was worried. Dylan had been having little episodes like this from he was a few months old. He could be standing or sitting and all of a sudden he would stop what he was doing and stare into space. No matter how hard we tried to distract him, he ignored us. We clapped our hands behind his back, we called his name, whistled and played music, but still he ignored us and although we were worried, we were not too concerned, however no episode had lasted as long as the one in the bedroom that night.

My daughter brought him to a doctor and explained what was happening with the child. His ears were tested and he was given a series of card tests in which he had to identify objects and animals. He passed them all with flying colours. The doctor reassured us that Dylan was an intelligent and normal little boy. The episodes, however, got longer and more frequent.

A year later, after many visits, the doctor sent Dylan to the hospital for a brain scan. The scan showed some abnormality of the brain. He had a form of epilepsy, an unconscious closing down of the brain. My daughter was told that he might possibly grow out of it or it could get worse. The medical staff wanted to put Dylan on drugs, but my daughter said firmly, "NO, no drugs. Not until I can explore other options, or he gets worse and I can do nothing else to help him." The doctors respected her wishes.

We had to note the time, the day and how long the episodes lasted. Dylan attended the children's hospital on a regular basis for the next two years.

His photograph, name, contact numbers, and the nature of his condition were pinned on the notice board in his nursery school.

A few moths before the twins' fourth birthday, I was once again minding the boys while their mum and dad went to work. Over a week this time, eight very long days. I love my grandsons, I spoil them as most grandparents do and talk about them and show their picture to anyone who will listen and look, but I am so glad to hand them back after I have had them more than four days. It was the day before their mother was due home and I was exhausted, even though it was only six o'clock in the evening.

I filled the bath and watched the bubbles foaming and then dumped some toys into the water, quickly followed by the twins. They chattered and splashed and played with boats and action men. I sat on a small white stool beside the bath, listening and nodding, gazing out through the open bathroom door and into the landing beyond. I intervened when they fought and argued about toys. Suddenly Dylan jumped up screaming, and leaning over he grabbed me by the hair and pulled himself out of the bath. The water soaked the front of my tee shirt right through to my bra and ran down my legs to my feet.

"The man, the man nanny!" he screamed, his eyes wide, staring terrified towards the open bathroom door. His hands gripped tighter and tangled into my hair, pulling and tugging painfully at the roots. Leon had stood up simultaneously to Dylan leaping out of the water; he stretched his neck and raised his arms into the air, making a kissing noise.

The bathroom had chilled. Leon turned towards me and smiled saying, "I kissed the man nanny."

All the time Dylan was screaming, "The man, the man". I felt a presence I couldn't explain. I could feel the hairs on the back of my neck pull tighter as a shiver ran down my spine.

I felt apprehensive and uncomfortable as I tried to calm my little grandson's fears. "There is no one there love, shh...it's alright." I patted and stroked the child's back, all the while gazing at the open bathroom door and the bedroom and stairs beyond.

Leon waved, "Bye, bye man". The floor in front of where I kneeled creaked, the sound continuing outside onto the landing and halfway down the stairs. It's only the pipes, I thought, I'm only after giving the kids a bath. But I kept glancing around, fearfully listening for footsteps and watching for something I could not see.

Dylan went for another scan before he started school in September. His scan was clear, no abnormality of the brain was detected. He has never has another episode of staring into space and ignoring everyone and everything around him. Was it his granda looking after him, was that who 'the man' was? Or was it his great, great grandfather, or was it simply just the water or air in the pipes? The noises have stopped, the rooms heat up quickly, so has the granda finally gone to rest?

And which grandfather was it?

SHE'LL FIND YOU

by Ro Mierling

It was a small town, so small that it looked like a village. As a matter of fact, few people in the region knew that place. Maybe because it was an underdeveloped and underpopulated town. Maybe because it was located in a tiny valley, remote and inaccessible.

But because the town was small, all its dwellers were interconnected. Everybody knew each other. Everybody spoke with each other. And any uncommon event, like a wedding or a childbirth, made the headlines for weeks.

It was 2007. Jorge, one of the village dwellers, woke up earlier than usual on that morning. The sun hadn't risen yet. He had to start his car. It was an old vehicle, that operated on ethanol. And as the winter was coming and the weather was getting cold, the engine had to be left to idle for some time before he could drive away.

On that morning, however, Jorge's car didn't start. He had only two hours to make it work, because he had to go downtown to buy seeds for his vegetable garden. As he noticed it wouldn't work, he checked upon it to find out what was going on with his car.

As he opened the trunk to get his tools, Jorge felt his heart on his throat. He gasped and stepped back, not sure if he should scream or run away.

Inside the trunk there was a partially burned body. Jorge was assaulted by dread. He ran into his house and called the police.

The small town tranquility had ended. The corpse Jorge had found was identified as Silvia, the young niece of the town's baker.

The town's lone cop investigated it and found out that Silvia had left her house on the previous night, for a romantic date and didn't come back. How did her body end up in Jorge's car trunk, an old man that owned a ranch on the town's outskirts?

No one had a clue. Jorge kept his old car outdoors and unlocked, so the suspicion didn't immediately fall on him. Anybody could have dumped her body in that place. The cop thought that somebody could have kidnapped the young woman, raped her, as confirmed by the town's doctor, and burned her body afterward.

After that, the murderer had the unfortunate idea of hiding her remains inside the trunk of that old car, that he supposed was abandoned, near Jorge's barn.

Nobody could say with whom Silvia had met on the night she vanished. She had only told her mother that she had met a guy and would spend some time with him at the town's square. She had said she would soon introduce him to her family. But after that night, she would never be seen alive again.

Three days after they found Silvia's body, Marcos disappeared. He was a strong and big guy, who unloaded cargo trucks in the town for a living. He was the only son of Jandira, a woman who made her money selling candies. On that afternoon, Marcos had left his house after telling his mother he would go to the baker's shop to get some bread but had never returned.

Marcos's body was found inside a small shed that belonged to Sebastian. The old apple farmer made his living from his thirty apple trees. He sold his products to both town's grocery stores.

The body was discovered in an early Sunday morning, when Sebastian went into his shed that he kept unlocked because he trusted his neighbors. Marcos had been beheaded. His headless body and his head were found in separate plastic bags in the shed.

Sebastian had been investigated, but he was so old that he barely managed to take care of his ranch. He also had an alibi that acquited him of the murder.

Within four days, Silvia and Marcos were viciously killed and the town dwellers hadn't been able to realize that everything began when a strange guy called Bento arrived in town. A weird and recluse young man, that claimed that he heard voices. At dawn, Bento strolled through the streets, with a strange shadow by his side.

People who had seen it insisted that the shadow was misshapen, but few others believed them.

However, Bento didn't stay in town for long and days after Marcos's body was found, he was seen hitchhiking and boarding a truck.

After some time, bodies of truck drivers were found scattered in different small towns. Their bodies were burned, inside their trucks. And lots of witnesses claimed that a young man, weird and accompanied by an undefined shadow, had been seen alongside the truck drivers before they were killed.

INTO THE SPIRIT

by Rachel Sarah Glasgow

Flora and Rosie were the blondest little twins that Turf Lodge had ever seen. They had moved over with their family from the Vale of Leven in Scotland a few months previous and so far, they were loving Belfast.

It was 1991 and the two girls were due to start primary school later that year. Originally, they were to go to Christy Park like the rest of their siblings in the Vale but one evening the whole crew had upped sticks and moved country.

None of the children understood why, but Flora and Rosie seen it as a wonderful adventure.

When I climbed down into the underworld I was intending to get to heaven; I climbed down just over a wall at the top of the Whiterock thinking that I might finally see Flora again, my twin. I only vaguely remember her sweet smiling face. She was only like me in looks. She was a nice girl.

No one acknowledges our time spent in Turf Lodge, but I will not forget the day the brakes failed.

The underworld is a dark place but it is not particularly scary. Or at least the horrors of earth make it appear not so scary.

I have spent three days and three nights in the underworld during my stint in New Craigs. All I can say is that by comparison to New Craigs, the underworld was a welcome break: I was escorted to New Craig from Thurso to its geographical position on the map in Inverness by ambulance. I hated it. However, to be fair on the medical profession and the police force alike I was not in a good place at that time, but, to be locked up against my will under the mental health act 1998 did me no good whatsoever, in fact by the time I left hospital nearly five months later I would say my mental state was one hundred times worse. And I do not exaggerate.

On the morning of my detention under the act the police officers were horrible to me, taking me out of my flat to the ambulance in the clothes I stood up in, not allowing me shoes or a coat or even my pouch of tobacco. If it were not for the fact that the police officers who dealt with me through the night could not have done more to help me I may have developed a resentment towards the police. But that is not the case: For around a fortnight before this event I describe I had been drinking copious amounts of red wine on a nightly basis, spending my days waiting for the hangover to subside just enough so as I could walk to Lidl and buy yet more Chilean red. You see, a decent bottle of red from Lidl costs at most six quid whereas to spend that in, say, the Co-op for wine, you might as well buy mere flavoured vinegar at best. So, by the time I awoke that evening in September my brain was so addled with excessive alcohol that I had quite literally lost my memory. The last thing that I could remember was Belfast, so naturally I phoned the PSNI and reported myself missing, claiming that the only plausible explanation for my predicament was that I had been kidnapped from Belfast and dumped in Thurso. Yes, I really believed this and yes, the PSNI did respond promptly, sending two very helpful and nice police officers round to my flat.

On arrival, the two male officers found me with no electric and no food, also in complete dejected misery; they did their best to turn my electric back on. On failing that they bought me a chippy. So, by the time the evil sergeant turned up at my flat the next morning I had no ill feeling towards the police, just towards himself.

I have never gone into explicit detail with any doctor what exactly went on in that flat in Holbourn Avenue: I was seeing demons in the mirror and angels in the air.

Call me pure mental but I do see this as a spiritual escape from the degradation of society and my life in general. Possibly it was the drink making me hallucinate, that could well be said. But I do not buy into that line. I know the truth; however, I only have my word to give.

The vast machines of war scream forth across the Highlands of Scotland. Centuries of fire and force and violence have cemented the feelings of civil unrest and disappointment felt throughout the communities of the artic regions of this Celtic nation.

Mary had never once left Thurso throughout her thirty-five years upon this earth. The walls and gates around the towns prevented all, barring the police, from travelling across the terrain. But she did not resent them like most folk did. They had treated her well when she was a child, when that man had treated her badly.

Her childhood was fraught with fear; and not just from that man. The flashing lights at night and the evil pillar of light that stalked the darkness petrified her and everyone around her. The adults would never discuss the lights but as children they could not help but talk.

Mary imagined that the force that begun this war fired electrical forces at houses causing this phenomenon. Many believed without doubt that it was all caused by Satan himself. Whoever, or whatever, caused it all there was no doubt that the lights issued forced the oppressive atmosphere of war itself.

I felt my soul leave my body, just like it did when I was a child, the day that the nurses administered to me liquid cosh. Liquid cosh is a colloquialism for some sort of prescription medication reserved for apparently troublesome psychiatric patients and prisoners alike. It is nicknamed so for it comes in the form of a liquid injection and it also has the same effect as being hit over the head with a cosh; basically, it knocks you out for days.

The old familiar flashing lights filled my hospital room, the brick in my throat, the tears in my eyes and the pillar of light loomed all around me, everywhere and nowhere.

My soul soared and flew into the abyss. Down the ladder of doom, down the ladder of doom into the misty and dark underworld: It is not so bad there, not somewhere to spend an eternity but the people are nice and kind.

I met so many folks who were stuck within the mist, separated from the universe, unable to climb the ladder into the spirit: I helped as many as I could but there was an eternity of souls and before long my soul snapped like a cracker back into my body. Back to the misery of New Craigs and debilitating depression.

I remember clearly as a child sitting with my dad and my sister Ruth eating cream crackers and butter, drawing a picture of Ruth sitting cross legged before me. My dad was in his room in the home nearing the end of his life and myself and Ruth were thirteen and fifteen alike. I used to have such a close relationship with my older sister, but since my psychiatric treatment began as an adult she sees me differently as before, and I cannot stand her attitude any longer.

On the 3rd January, at eleven forty-five at night we were secretly watching *Interview with a Vampire* in her room. I knew within myself at that time that our dad had left this world for a higher consciousness. The truth was confirmed at one in the morning. We missed the end of the film and it was a long time before I could bring myself to watch it through: Confirmation that I would never in this life see his physical form again.

For around a week afterwards myself and Ruth slept in the same bed in her room, until my mum told me that she believed Ruth wanted her bed back so reluctantly I returned to my cold and lonely room. Mary, our older sister returned to Thurso just fifteen minutes after he passed on. Alexander, our oldest brother, did not attend his funeral. His funeral was the last time that I saw my other older brother, Robert. I am now thirty-one.

It confuses me as to why he does not keep in touch with me. I do not see what I have done wrong.

Mary had a vivid dream that the hell of atrocity rained down on Castletown, Thurso's neighbouring village. Somewhere that she had only seen on the telly. She awoke scared, as her dreams as such tended to be prophetic.

She had vague memories of early primary school and visits from nice American scientists. You see, for a long time there was a large NATO base up in Caithness County.

The nice American scientists talked a lot about ESP, Extra Sensory Perception, and its differing forms of gifts.

They tested Mary's reflexes and senses. They told her that she had the hearing range of a bat. They put her in a room and told her to draw what they were thinking. They told her that she was special and gifted. They told her that she was psychic.

I took an overdose and I cut my arm up once. I took too much zopiclone. Not all in one go, but over the course of one week. I cut tally marks on my left arm for each person I knew who had died.

I was everywhere and nowhere; I knew everything, the whole truths of the universe, I was into the spirit.

It was such a sublime experience, I was experiencing time as it really is, completely freed from the shackles of gravity. I was lifted beyond the wonder of the physical existence and while I was there, if I can call it there, for it was like no place imaginable in this life, a big part of me wanted to stay there forever. I hope that I am doing this level of existence justice in my explanation.

Before I joined with the universe I lay tossing and turning in bed in pain and torment. My arm bled and my head hurt. The lights flashed around me like colours I cannot imagine. At that point, all that I wanted was release through death. I could see faces in the curtains beckoning me to vacate the earthly realm, and in the flash of a still heart and the lack of breath I was away, travelling through blissful darkness and an eternity of knowledge.

I had the choice whether to stay or return, reluctantly I chose to return. I remember thinking to myself that to stay would be lovely but at the same time, I was only twenty-nine: I had better get back to my body. It was inexplicably painful, both physically and mentally, to return to my body.

Louise was twelve, she had no family or friends but she knew a lot of folk both in Castletown and elsewhere. A passing stranger once told her that if she were a cat she would most definitely be a feral one. That was a few years ago now, but she remembered the comment and the man well, not sure what to make of either.

When she had been a small, small child she had lived a normal life: She remembered a kind mother with red hair and a funny father with sandy brown hair. She had four older brothers and two older sisters, but one day something bad had happened and many of Castletown's residents had left this world for the next. A police officer had carried her from the wreckage to safety but somewhere along the line she had fallen through the cracks in the System and nowadays she lived as she willed.

Everyone knew about the doors that connected the world together but a very select few knew where to find them. Louise knew, she went everywhere. The police knew, they utilised them.

Down at the harbour there were many underground tunnels, and at the end of these tunnels were doors leading around and across the United Kingdom. Louise's favourite place to go was Belfast. Her earliest memory was of her daddy singing to her a song about Belfast, so when she found her way there she was happy. It was much in the same political state as Scotland, or at least that is what the telly told her, although she had to admit that she was not quite sure what the term political state meant. Although she had a faint idea that it had something to do with the reason why a lot of people tended to die.

She had an acquaintance in Belfast, a boy of nineteen, who would go to the off licence and buy wine for her, which she would drink at night with him in the Ormeau Park. Not just when she drank, but during the day also when she went for extended runs. You see, when she turned eighteen and three quarters she fully intended to join the police, so fitness was a big thing for her.

There was a lot of talk around Louise about peace, and again, she struggled to comprehend this concept but she imagined that after the process was complete folk would stop dying so much.

After I had returned from being into the spirit I realised how dangerously ill I had made myself. I was violently sick, I was shaking and I hurt to my core. I was terminally confused too and I could not get back to sleep.

To begin with I tried talking to the out of hours doctors but they all without fail treated me as if I was wasting their time, a Scottish pill popper after prescription meds. I considered phoning myself an ambulance but I did not want to burden the emergency services so I dialled 101 and asked for their advice.

Their response was instant, they told me I had every right to phone 999 and furthermore to hang up and do so; which I did.

They were nice in triage at the Royal Hospital. A nurse named Lyra took my bloods, and I took this to be a good sign as the blue star of the sky, Lyra the Liar, is my favourite star and the most beautiful by far. I drank coffee and took a gram of paracetamol in the waiting area.

When I saw the doctor, he tried to tell me that there was nothing wrong with me; maybe he was having a bad shift but I cried and argued so he sent me to 2F ward.

The following twelve hours were hell on earth. Unknown to myself my inherent psychiatric team were on my back holding up my physical treatment. For according to them I must be a hypochondriac.

When the psychiatrist did turn up to attempt to admit me to the Mater Hospital I articulately argued my case, I wanted to speak to a GP and a solicitor, which I was granted. I must say, the psychiatrist was livid that I could speak to the GP without his presence.

The male GP whose name escapes me, was nice and reasonable. He agreed that a psyche ward was not the answer. Although I cannot remember his name I would like to see him again and thank him for his support and his belief in me.

David was the sergeant in Thurso. His job tired him out every day. Passing through towns around Caithness. Using the doors to work between the various jurisdictions of the United Kingdom. He barely had time for himself so he did not blame his wife for taking the children back to Belfast where she was from. He missed them every day.

It pained him that the public mistrusted the police force. He had had the same upbringing as them. The same experiences as them of this bloody war-torn collection of countries but he was set aside. Separated by a cap and a gun.

He joined to help people, maybe naively so, but that was his intention. He wanted to at least attempt to formulate some sort of peace for society.

A young girl had decided to befriend David, he did not mind as she was the same age as his youngest. She would not say where she lived or who she was, just Louise.

Into the Spirit is a lovely place to be, right now I wish that I had stayed when given the choice. I say that I want to go up there again, but it was not up, or down, or anywhere at all. It was a different level of existence and I want to return, to be surrounded by peace and serenity and darkness.

The light hurts my eyes.

The truth burns my soul.

The days drag on into nothingness and I have no one to call my own.

The day that the social workers arrived I was in my dressing gown drinking coffee.

They rattled through my drawers looking for evidence to detain me under the mental health act of 1986 as I stood outside and chatted to the police officers who had accompanied them.

They were nice, we swapped stories and chatted for at least half an hour. The first thing that they told me was that they were there to help me, not to support the social workers. I do not think that the social workers were best pleased by this.

As I got into the ambulance, ready to be taken to the Mater Hospital, the police officers informed me of their names, that they were from Castlereagh and that if I ever needed help that

I could call up the station.

Nothing will ever change in Caithness.

Nothing will ever change in Scotland or in the UK.

We are merely experiencing a lull that will inevitably return full force; as sad as it may be, the fact remains as do the lights of truth.

Lights of truth fill up the sky.

Lights of truth return to the universe where all knowledge is held and give us the answer to peace eternal.

Where shall I go to find my friends?

Where shall I go to experience the solitude that I desire so and fear so?

In the cold light of morning when life remains, thoughts of the abyss seem so welcoming and pure.

THE STORM

by Andrea Bickerstaff

Wiping the condensation from the only window which hadn't been boarded up, a hazy view revealed the harrowing vision of the storm most of the non evacuees and I had tried to sit out. The postcard view of the small town street was now unrecognisable, littered with debris, fallen trees, family homes and businesses destroyed. Most people had evacuated to the city, but being a nurse I felt compelled to stay behind to help the emergency services.

The radio boomed the repeated message for a third time: *'All residents of Clonis town and the surrounding areas must immediately evacuate to Avenmore Caves, gather bedding and emergency rations and seek higher ground. The storm surge is expected to worsen in the next four to six hours and major flooding is expected'.*

"I suppose it's time to up sticks as they say, Olivia. I do hope my animals will be safe," said Mrs Napier with a worried look on her face. She was one of my favourite native elderly patients, with always a kind word for everyone and an animal sanctuary owner and one time activist, always a surprising story to tell.

"I think it is, Mrs Napier, you have done all you can at the minute and we need to get somewhere safer than this old battered town hall to stay, before we all get washed away."

I lifted a crepe bandage and started to wrap Mrs Napier's bloodied and swollen arm. She had been bitten and a deep gash ran the length of her forearm, I'm guessing in the frenzy to get all her animals into safe shelter. She really wasn't fit to be doing this kind of work at seventy years of age. I worried for her as she had no husband or children to look after her and had early onset Alzheimer's disease.

"Don't you worry, Mrs Napier, me and you will stick together. We will be up in those caves singing Kumbaya before tea time."

She laughed as I laid her crudely stitched and dressed arm back onto the chair. "Thanks, Claire, erm...no...Fiona."

"Olivia," I reminded her, gently .

The emergency coach arrived at Avenmore Caves laden with the elderly and sick, and the odd cat and dog thrown in for good measure. Smoke was already billowing from one of the three caves set in a sheer rock face towering over the town, a sure sign others in the community had been listening to the reports also. Gulls were screeching and flocking down against the winds, seeking the shelter from the torrential rain. The sound of the sea waves crashing against the ancient rock echoed in my ears. In true community spirit everyone helped each other up the steep climb to the top cave and across the rope bridge. Those who couldn't manage were hoisted up by the local abseiling club. By 7pm the last person entered the cave and past the Devil's Fork, which was a large two foot split in the cave mouth. One wrong step and it was into the abyss below.

Deeper inside the large cave silhouettes sat around one of the few fires. Sparks glowed and flicked from the orange blaze, ashen faces in puffy coats sat listening intently to the radio, drinking tea or bedding down on the dusty rock to get some kip. The smell of sausages and whiskey filled the damp room, candle flames danced in the draughty breeze. Safety in numbers. I couldn't help thinking about what kind of life I would have to go back to. I looked around for Mrs Napier and saw her laid down sleeping soundly on an airbed beside Mr Elliot, the town's butcher. Such an unlikely pair, he being an avid foxhunter and very much a carnivore, laying next to an animal activist vegan. Usually these two would have choice words for each other, but I suppose necessity changes opinion. I took sip of my British plaster - a hot steaming cup of tea - and wrapped a blanket around me and lay down. The voices, sound of the rain and radio faded into a lull as I drifted off to sleep, exhausted from the day's events.

A huge crack of thunder woke me from my sleep. The cave lit up electric white, the lightening's light reflected and danced through each person's eyes in front of me. The mood had changed, everyone seemed much more frightened, as the winds blew harder and the fire swayed, as if it could be extinguished like a birthday candle. The temperature had dropped dramatically and people hugged each other and wept. The rattles made it feel like the very rock was being stripped away in sheets to the wind. To make things worse, the minister, Mr Parsons, chanted prayers while people knelt at his feet praying, like he would be the one to wish the storm away. Looking around those once calm faces, now a despaired and veritable madhouse. My eyes moved to where Mrs Napier had been laying. Panic struck my heart as I saw she was missing from her bed, but no one I asked had seen her leave. Fearing the worst, because of her mental state, I gathered a torch and went searching.

The whine of the wind made my cries for Mrs Napier a waste of time, but a corridor turn and few feet away from the mouth of the cave I heard footsteps and strange singing - *"Who's afraid of the big bad wolf, the big bad wolf, the big bad wolf?..."*

I found her alone and in the dark, crouching dangerously close to the edge of the cave entrance, the apocalyptic storm raging in the scene behind her. How she navigated this far in the dark was beyond my comprehension. I shone the large headlight torch on her which startled her:

"Mrs Napier...Brenda...please come back inside. It's way too dangerous to be out here. Come back inside. You must be freezing."

She stood up and turned towards me, still singing although her voice had changed into a creepy demonic sound. I knew then that the darkest powers imaginable on this earth were at work, with the wind whipping up her dressing gown and silver-grey hair in a frenzy. Behind her the cloud parted and a navy night sky revealed a bright white and full harvest moon, Brenda's outline at its center.

"Brenda please," I pleaded, but her head sharply snapped up and she let out a guttural groaning growl, as her eyes grew larger in her head and turned a bright amber. Beneath her dressing gown her bones bubbled under her skin, popping and cracking while she screamed an ungodly scream. Patches of thick black fur broke through the skin and all over her body, her fragile pale face elongating and her mouth disjointed and stretching open to reveal a row of razor sharp fangs. Her thin hands each ruptured open to display a set of five huge sharp curved claws. In agony she slumped to the ground, her body heaving and expanding, taking on some sort of metamorphosis, neither woman nor beast.

I stood frozen in shock, gazing upon the events unfolding before me. I dropped my torch. A shout came from behind me and a flash from another torch beamed into the cave. It was Mr Parsons the minister. Startled, I stumbled back on my heels and tripped, falling into the Devil's Fork. My anorak snagged on a piece of rock and I dangled, held between the crack and the abyss, only by the hood of my coat. I pushed my feet towards the rock in front of me, my body in an 'L' shape and tried to take some of the weight from my hood. Mr Parsons knelt down beside me, not realising the events that had just unfolded and reached down to help me up.

"I'm so sorry, Olivia, grab my hand."

But before he had even finished his sentence, what was once Brenda stood up bathed in moonlight and howled a long drawn out howl, her muscular body doubled in size. She was no longer a woman, but a ferocious black beast. Mr Parsons screamed as he turned to see the beast leap onto his body, the razored teeth sinking into his torso and shaking him free from his grip of my hand. The beast ripped, clawed and shook his body until it was in two halves. Still alive he clawed his way back into the cave whilst the beast feasted upon his legs, chomping down and allowing me to hear the bones crack, as chunks of flesh dripped from its mouth.

Mr Parsons, bleeding heavily, prayed as he took his last breaths, his entrails and pooling blood splattered all over the dusty rock beside me.

The jaws of the beast couldn't reach me at the angle I had fallen into the Devil's Fork, but I could feel its rancid hot breath and saliva run down my neck and hear a sniffing sound, then a long black claw reached into the rock towards me, swiping at my head and leaving a deep cut on my neck and face. The beast wanted my blood too. I couldn't move. If I shifted I would fall, but if I didn't I would die anyway. I was stuck.

I screamed as loud and as long as I could, knowing that I would be next to die, as the beast stood completely unfazed, patiently waiting.

Muffled voices and footsteps in the distance came closer, but not close enough, yet I could make out the shadows of torch lights beaming against the corridor in the cave. Help was near and I needed it badly. I was weak and ready to give up and my voice wouldn't let me scream anymore. Pieces of the minister's legs and blood littered the cave mouth. The folkloric beast took a step back and clawed at the top half of Mr Parsons' body. I could see it bite down and drag him slowly past the crevice I was in and then sliding it off the edge of the cave rock face, its kill disappearing into the now dieing storm.

"Help," a whispered cry escaped my mouth.

I looked out towards the storm, the large moon blazing white, my eyes shut as my body slumped and hung upon the rock...

THE SHEEP

by David Brilliance

Returning from a late night party with friends was always a mixed bag of experiences for Larry David Crowther. On the one hand, he enjoyed going over everything that had happened - who he had managed to impress, who he thought fancied him, all the food and drink he'd consumed etc. On the other hand, he always had a nagging suspicion that he'd been a frightful bore who had crossed the line of being merely friendly with the women, and came within literal striking distance of getting chinned by the men.

Larry rolled his thoughts and memories of the night over and over in his head as he began the long walk home. He hadn't see Jeanette and Tom for a good few months, though in the latter's case, he wasn't bothered at all as the man was a complete prick and he was wasted on her. Larry had had a brief fling with Jeanette over four years ago, which had cost him his marriage and ended up with him being run out of town by the sanctimonious locals. That was when he and Jeanette had both lived in the same squalid little town - Heathsville - but both had moved on both physically and emotionally. Jeanette now worked as a detective in the Metropolitan Police, while Tom was in charge of the entertainment on a luxury liner. Denise had also been at the party and Larry was pleased to see there was life in the old girl yet, as she had spent the night flirting with all the men present and then getting uproariously drunk, ending with her urinating in the fish tank. However, everybody took it in good nature (apart from the fish, possibly), as Denise was a real salt-of-the-Earth type who would do anything for anybody, and if she was prone to getting drunk and urinating in fish tanks, well, that was just Denise, and nobody took offence.

Sarah was also at the party, getting drunk and a bit giddy but no urinating in fish tanks thankfully. She hadn't changed much in the few years since he'd last seen her - she was still tall and slim, like an elegant giraffe, and the funniest woman he'd ever met, with a laugh that reminded him of bubbling soup in a saucepan. She always teased Larry about his thin, lanky form and his knobbly, jutting bones but he always took it in good spirit. She'd done very well for herself, becoming a model who was currently involved with a mustard-making entrepreneur. Mark had also been at the party. He'd been an acquaintance of Larry's since they'd both worked together as security guards at an abattoir, and their career paths had crossed a few times over the years. They had a friendly rivalry going over who had the biggest house, and the most money, and Larry was confident that he was the winner, with a large mansion nestled away and a savings account with £356,000 in it.

It was while he was thinking about all this that Larry felt a fleck of rain on his cheek. Cursing, he started to walk a bit faster. It was a heck of a long walk home, a lengthy trudge down a long country road, then through a field, followed by a lengthy walk along another out-of-the-way country road, and finally, within sight of his home village. As he moved on, off the road and into the field, he was suddenly startled by movement ahead of him. He squinted through the gloom, and as his eyes focussed, he realised he was looking at a sheep, an ordinary, run of the mill, sheep. However, there was something a bit different about it. For one thing, it didn't turn and run away as he got nearer. Instead, it stood its ground and continued looking at him. It wasn't chewing anything either, as sheep normally do. It was stood, staring. There was something about its stare that unsettled him slightly - it seemed almost insolent...no, more than that...threatening.

Larry walked past it and on his way, but he could feel its eyes following him every step of the way. Larry wasn't a big fan of animals. He liked dogs (but only certain ones), was wary of cats and horses, and had no interest in fish, tortoises and the like. Sheep were in that same category as fish and so on for him; he considered them harmless and not really of any worth to him. But this particular sheep was making him a little edgy for some reason. He quickened his walk, but as he moved further on and came to be getting out of the field, he couldn't resist a look back to see if the sheep was following him. However, it wasn't there. Larry assumed it must have just wandered off to eat some grass, thought nothing more of it and continued his trudge home.

Larry crossed out of the field and into a long, winding road. He was about fifty yards along the road when he jumped slightly at the sign of movement ahead of him. It was another sheep! Or...wait, was it the same one he'd just seen in the field? It must have been the same one, as there were never any others about, and it was stood looking at him in the same threatening, in fact, downright hostile, manner. There was something...malevolent about the thing, as if it intended to do him some unspeakable harm. Larry silently cursed himself for his stupidity - imagine, being afraid of a bloody sheep?! What would all his friends say? He walked past it quickly, attempting to appear nonchalant but quietly wetting himself. If it had been daytime, it wouldn't have been so scary but at fifteen minutes past midnight on a dark and cloudy night in October, it was a very different proposition.

As Larry moved past the sheep, something happened that made him jump almost out of his skin - the thing seemed to speak! Actually, all it uttered was the usual 'Baaaa', but it produced the sound in such a way that it seemed to be deliberately trying to un-nerve him. And the bloody thing succeeded! All Larry wanted to do was get back home as quickly as possible - damn these bloody miles-long country roads! He continued walking and couldn't resist a few backwards glances from time to time, to make sure the sheep wasn't following him. Eventually, he got onto the last stretch of road that would lead home, and started to move even faster.

The path was next to a main road which adjoined several fields, and the road sloped downwards eventually leading to another main road which adjoined the pavement which led to his house.

As he walked, he was already more than half aware of what he would see. That wretched sheep again, and there it was, now silently chewing furiously and looking at him in that same, strangely frightening, malevolent and intelligent manner. Larry considered shouting at the thing, hoping to scare it off. As he came within a few short feet of the animal, it moved suddenly, causing him to almost choke as he suddenly inhaled with shock. The sheep made a sound that almost seemed like a laugh and ran at him...

The following morning at 8am, all was quiet, not a breath of wind to disturb the scene, just a slight noise from a solitary sheep which was stood in a field near to the winding road, and chewing furiously at a collection of knobbly, jutting bones which lay in a mound of discarded clothing, excrement and dirt.

SUICIDAL PARASITE

by Frank Bowes

If ever there was proof of evolution in action, it's the parasite. Imagine an organism so complex that it could take control of a host body, allowing it to hijack the host's self awareness and motor functions? Outside of a host, the parasite has no such cognitive capacity. It is consumed by an insatiable hunger, which can only be satisfied through the acquisition of a sentient host. However, therein lies the problem. Once the parasite acquires a suitable host, it must feed off the flesh to continue its survival. Over time, the host body is consumed. The parasite can replace the dying cells, but each host body has a shelf life. This particular host has almost served its purpose. In fact, by the current month's end, the parasite is confident that the host will bring about the circumstances which will end its own miserable existence forever.

The only other thing that the parasite can do is dream. Its dreams, however, were no release. It often had nightmares of being free from its everlasting search for a suitable host. This planet was not made for the parasite. The dinosaurs had served as useful hosts until they were wiped out by a world ending event. The parasite was forced to use unworthy hosts which it burned through in a matter of weeks. When humans came along, the parasite welcomed the opportunity to partner with a host that could sustain it for a moderately longer time period. They were nowhere near as resilient as large dinosaurs, but they would suffice until larger creatures once again roamed the Earth. Unfortunately, as centuries passed it became clear that evolution would never again take that direction. Humans, as the dominant species, ensured that the Earth would remain their playground until such time as they managed to destroy it through acts of greed and war.

For millennia, the parasite had been going through the same, tired, repetitious process. Hunger, host. Hunger, host. Hunger, host. Despite its age, it never occurred to the parasite that an end could be achieved. At the very core of what drove the parasite was an unmatched instinct for survival. It had coupled with the greatest leaders this species had to offer, always believing that only a natural world ending disaster would offer release from the bounds of an existence mired in pain and suffering. A long time ago, the parasite abandoned the notion of any sort of symbiotic relationship with the host. These creatures were stupid. They had a tendency towards destroying each other, if they didn't manage to destroy themselves first. This host, however, was different.

His host name was Donald J Drumpth, and the parasite had been riding his coattails since he was a young boy. Unlike other hosts in positions of class, 'The Donald' suffered from an unusually high level of cognitive dysfunction. This malady, which would have normally made society life untenable for young Donald, actually worked in the host's favor when coupled with the parasite. Due to the reduced neural activity, the parasite's metabolic rate slowed significantly. This allowed the host to sustain the parasite for much longer than previous vessels. Over the past two years, however, the host was beginning to show the telltale signs that it was reaching the end of its usefulness.

Once the parasite had access to the trappings of being the POTUS, it could end this pointless existence for good. The end would be bigly. The thought of that word made the severely compromised host chuckle. At the sound of their boss's voice, the two secret service agents assigned to the Oval Office detail looked at each other, unease clear in their eyes. The parasite knew that they knew something was amiss, but they couldn't quite figure out what it was. This president was like no other. There was a deep sense of apprehension among the West Wing staffers, which was only exacerbated by the POTUS dragging his emotionless carcass from room to room in the White House when most everyone else was in bed.

The parasite was finding it increasingly difficult to control the host's speech. So, instead, it came up with an ingenious way to communicate without speech. The host tweeted. A lot. Modern social media was the perfect tool for the parasite while occupying a dying host. It could conserve its strength for verbal interaction by using Twitter to communicate dangerous and provocative ideas in one hundred and forty characters or less. When a press conference was necessary, the parasite made the host speak in unintelligible sound bites. It didn't really matter. Opposing members of the American public were so polarized in their politic beliefs, the host could say anything and he was loved and loathed in equal measure.

As the parasite sat at in the oval office, musing about the destruction of this world, the host's mind drifted back to the campaign trail. It knew that time was running out for this host, and the parasite's own instinct would compel it to seek another healthy host. Running for president was its best hope of ensuring its destruction. The parasite could not commit suicide. Its primary functions would not allow it. However, if the host was successful in winning a seat at the most prestigious table in the country, it was all but guaranteed that a world ending war would follow. For all his blathering idiocy, Drumpth's silver spoon legacy provided him with status, which appealed to the low IQ voter in the United States. The parasite planned to use that legacy to paint a picture of a self made man, who had made it to the top through hard work and a take-no-shit attitude.

So far the plan was playing out exactly as the parasite had imagined. The host made calls to the various leaders of the free world, making outrageous threats that left both the leaders and media outlets baffled. By alienating long standing allies of the United States, the parasite was setting the stage for the next phase of the plan. Soon the United States would stand alone in the face of nuclear obliteration. The parasite was aware that congress and the various intelligence agencies were worried. Good. With all the Washington movers and shakers on edge, it wouldn't take too much of a push to start the war to end all wars. Americans are known for digging in when their actions have proven to create more problems than they solve. This would serve as the ultimate test. A test that the parasite was confident they would fail.

The host rose from his chair in the Oval Office and strode confidently across the room. Sometimes it was necessary to give the host a boost, just to keep the staffers guessing as to the extent of his physical decline. A number of ongoing FBI investigations were worrying the parasite. If the president were to be impeached, the plan would fall on its face and the parasite would need to find another host and start the cycle all over again. It could not allow that to happen. No, this was its best chance. If this president was removed from power, the Electoral College would not likely allow another brash businessman anywhere near the White House. The host's wealth was essential to the completion of the plan.

During the campaign trail the host had promised to release his tax returns. That was another mistake that had forced the parasite to exercise more control over the host. If the Donald had released his tax returns, they would have revealed the dodgy dealings that the parasite had orchestrated over the years. Many of those deals were part of the grander scheme, and they would have no doubt landed the host in a federal penitentiary for the rest of his short life. It was a rare error in judgment on the parasite's part. As it turned out, however, the people who voted for the host weren't at all concerned about his tax returns. His detractors continued to demand that he release the tax returns, but to no avail. There was no legal requirement for a president to release his tax returns, and that was that. Still, it was a level of scrutiny that the parasite could not afford.

The host had courted Russian players in his effort to win the presidency. The plan was orchestrated with great precision.

With the Russian propaganda machine on his side, the Donald shocked the world and snatched the presidency from the democratic candidate. Clintosh was a woman who had spent thirty years in politics, holding some of the highest positions in government. However, a large number of Americans did not trust her. She came from a political dynasty and the ordinary people of the United States were sick and tired of the same old, same old. All the host had to do was exploit their fears, keep talking about the propaganda leaked by Russian hackers, and sell himself as a champion of the people. The American people, for their part, couldn't get enough of it. From the very first chants of 'Lock her up! Lock her up!' the parasite knew that the plan would work. The Donald would take his place in the White House and the cards would begin to fall. There was no stopping this train, and no getting off.

North Korea had long been considered a running joke among the intelligence agencies of the free world. Their threats of launching nuclear weapons against the U.S. were thought of as no more than posturing. What the intelligence agencies didn't know was that the host had been funding North Korea's nuclear weapons program for the last decade. The country now had the means to launch missiles with a nuclear payload that could reach far beyond the shores of the Continental U.S. All they needed was a push. On the day of the attacks the parasite intended to ensure that the defensive systems of the United States of America would, unfortunately, go offline. Those Russian hackers had one more job to do, and this time it would mean more than just the end of a hopeful candidate's campaign for the presidency. The host would receive forewarning of the attack, allowing the parasite to ensure that they were both in the direct line of fire.

The host had been poking the North Korean leadership since he took office. His provocation was viewed as juvenile, even by the Chinese who were North Korea's closest ally. Still, it was the beginning of a grander plan. The North Korean leadership's every action was designed to hold onto control in a country that was under increasing scrutiny from the rest of the world. The parasite could have chosen one of the Middle Eastern countries; a hotbed of political unrest. But that would have been too obvious. When it comes to the Middle East, intelligence agencies have their eyes wide open. North Korea, on the other hand, is viewed as an unlikely threat despite all the bravado coming from the glorious leader. No, North Korea was definitely the right choice. Nobody would see it coming – least of all the soon to be compromised intelligence agencies of the U.S.

The host had actively encouraged campaign staffers to engage with known Russian agents. When it came time to pick his presidential dream team, it didn't take much to convince those same staffers that it was not in their best interest to divulge their connections to Russia. The dangling carrot of power and position was too tempting to ignore, so none of them had any qualms about lying when questioned under oath. Of course, the parasite knew that these indiscretions would eventually come to light, leading to numerous investigations, and leaving the president's cabinet in turmoil. The plan absolutely hinged on the distraction. While congress and the FBI were tied up with the investigations and the president's numerous, outrageous policies, the Russian hackers were quietly creating back doors into the National missile defense (NMD) and the other United States defense systems. Ironically, it was the hacking of the CIA's coding database that allowed them to create the exploit that would ultimately allow nuclear weapons to reach the U.S. Only the Americans would be stupid enough to store some of the most complex hacks, viruses, and exploits on a poorly secured server.

The End

As the bombs rained down on Washington, the host sat smiling at his desk in the Oval Office. The White House was a hive of panicked activity. A team of secret service agents burst through the doors and took up defensive positions around the room. This amused the parasite. What did they expect was going to happen when a nuclear warhead with a yield of fifty megatons landed on the president's lap? It was their training, of course. They had nothing left to grasp onto as their inevitable end came whistling ever closer to the White House. There was no stopping this party. The parasite would welcome death with open arms. It felt no sympathy for the countless lives that would be lost on that day, and nor did it care about the international fallout from the attack. Let the cards fall where they will. The sweet release of death was the only thing that the parasite cared about.

The security detail was surrounding the host, now. The parasite could hear them urging the host to leave for the shelter. The host, of course, could not move. His access to his motor functions had been revoked. He would sit there with a smile on his face until it was melted away by the powerful force of the largest nuclear explosion the world had ever witnessed. They were now trying to physically drag the host from his chair. However, the parasite was easily able to keep the host firmly seated at his desk. The U.S. secret service agents looked at the host in confusion, before deciding that their own lives were worth more than this bumbling idiot's. They hastily headed for the door, leaving the president to his fate.

There was a blinding flash outside the window, the deafening sound of an explosion, and then the windows exploded around the host impaling his body with sharp shards of glass. The shockwave of the nuclear explosion swept through the White House, laying waste to everything in its path. For a brief moment the parasite feared that the nuclear explosion would not be enough to destroy it, before it felt its physical form starting to melt away. The last thought it had as the nuclear firestorm ended its existence was of the host, standing at a podium and declaring that he would Set America on Fire Again. Those were, perhaps, the truest words to ever come out of this particular president's mouth.

TUBBY BYE BYE

by Joe Gardner

It was the third time I had that dream.

"One more time!" I said to my brother, somewhat with sadness, somewhat with excitement. He never did comprehend the first time.

"For what?" He asked, dismissively. "One more time for what?"

"One more sleep in our bedroom!" I said. "Tomorrow we move."

The location and layout of the house varied each time, but the content of the dream was always the same; it is my last day in the house in which I grew up; tomorrow my parents move, and I stroll the place melancholy, taking in each old, familiar and now functionless room a final time. My destination is never known. In one version, I had to buy a car from an old school friend I haven't seen in years, and I sat in his living room watching kids' TV while he looked for the keys.

My brother and I climbed the frail, splintered and uncarpeted steps to our childhood bedroom. Each step shuddered, cracked and fell away beneath us as it was used. I dared not look below and see where the useless wood was headed. We arrived at our destination and cracked open the door, for what felt like the first time in a hundred years for all it hazarded a refusal to properly give.

A wooden bunk-bed stood precariously in the centre of the

room. The far wall of the bedroom was almost entirely absent, exposing the strange world outside, but neither of us really cared. Beyond the charred, gnarly corner remnants of the wall lay a storm-bruised, twilit, screaming wasteland, flickering in thunder and burping with the aggressive creeks of myriad dead trees. Again, though, we did not care.

"We can play Sonic 2 if you want?" I suggested, shouting over the elemental commotion breathing into the bedroom. "Like old times. Or get out the Micro Machines. Remember when we made Pokémon characters out of papier mache?"

My brother let off a tut. "Christ, Frank, you're twenty-six years old."

"I know," I said with a sulk, climbing the ladder to the top bunk. "I know. Just an idea. Nighty-night."

The lights went out, and in the real world the sun came up.

I cracked my neck, did a fart and rolled onto my side. It was Sunday. Two weeks to the day in my new flat and I'd more or less finished unpacking everything. Twenty-six years old and already a fortnight out of flat-sharing in North East London. What a go-getter. The room was almost starting to look familiar to me by now, it's always strange when you move and for the initial few days the first waking thought you have in your supposed home is 'Where the fuck am I?'

Next up I did what I'd lately always been doing of a morning. I grabbed my phone from the bedside table and booted up Tinder. No new matches. I spent the next quarter of an hour absent-mindedly swiping left and right, forever binning women who didn't immediately catch my attention and putting those that did on hopeful reserve. A vacant grin behind a delicious looking meal didn't cut it as a first impression photo. There were a few too many of those. A woman on her knees, seemingly poking a chicken in the eye, cut the mustard. And on the swiping went, my left index finger and the agents of faceless social media gradually constructing the future of my romantic life from the comfort of my rented bed.

I got a match within fifteen minutes of swiping. A big, white smile, bordering on cheesy or even manic, peering up over a full glass of white wine, staring straight into the camera with piercing, unforgettable blue eyes. Tinder told me her name was Sammi, and as I swiped in approval, I was quickly informed that the feeling was mutual. I did, however, feel the need to blitz through my phonebook and Facebook contacts, as she looked so familiar, but I came away from that and into our first conversation convinced that we'd never met before.

We chatted, on and off, over the next couple of hours as I sat in my pants watching old Rugrats episodes on YouTube. I'd been hitting the nostalgia pretty hard since moving house, and the new, binge-worthy serious shows just don't hold my attention anyway. Not that Rugrats even currently was; my eyes were firmly on my phone as I anticipated responses from Sammi, who lived just down the road by Lea Bridge, shared my fondness for '90s Britpop and also shared my hatred of the words 'Bespoke' and 'Artisan.' Eventually we arranged to meet up for a drink at the Crooked Billet in Clapton. Equidistant from our homes, a short stroll for each of us.

When the time came, I recall no initial nervousness or forced small-talk. We hit it off instantly; at ease in each other's humours, never straying close to confounded silences, even drawing stares from some of the pub's other occupants for how loud we'd gotten in our banter. The only thing I didn't love about Sammi was her laugh, which I was nonetheless able to frequently draw from her, as she was from me, but it was of little concern. I'm sure there were things about me that she was less than taken with. But the look in her eyes, or perhaps the eyes themselves, made me feel as though we'd known each other all our lives.

I was more at ease in Sammi's company than I am with a

fair few of my closer relatives, and I knew it was mutual, because the night's climax never seemed in doubt to either of us. Drunk and laughing, we stumbled in the dark back to my flat down the road, where we made haste for the glorious crescendo for which we'd each initially booted up Tinder in the first place. Naked and lit only by my dim bedside lamp, we collapsed onto my mattress and got cracking. Incredible as it was on the whole, I did not enjoy it when she looked me in the eye while going down on me. I don't know why, her eyes just sort of made me feel guilty and I had to keep looking away in shame, with butterflies in my stomach, or, perhaps, moths. Besides, I didn't want to finish in her mouth anyway so I gently pulled out, rolled us over and went in for the main event.

That night I had the usual dream. But it had gotten worse. Things started out familiar enough, albeit with the expected changes, but as my brother and I reached our crescendo atop the stairs, it just wasn't right. That gaping hole in the wall unsettled me more this time; it was hard to pin down how my brother felt but the thick-black, howling maw that should have been my bedroom wall seemed to yell at me - to shriek at me - as I stared into it. Furthermore, things were stirring from within the black. Agitated imperfections in the shadows lurked closer, staggering upwards over the precipice of my bedroom floor from the raging outdoors. Drenched yet in all shadow, rising paws slithered into view and large, spongy fingers latched onto the floorboards. A strip of the surviving, left-hand wall peeled back to a thunderclap and fell into the night. There were at least eight limbs pulling up now, lifting four bulbous, misshapen bodies into view. Like overgrown babies they were; stubby arms, stubby legs, heads too big for their shoulders, ears too big for their heads. They came at me, laughing, giggling, speaking in a language both painfully familiar and utterly foreign. They remained shrouded in shadow, even when lightning struck. I flailed my arms behind me, trying to grab hold of my brother for comfort, but I think he was gone. The four things closed in on me and I sank to my knees.

I had no breath with which to scream, so I succumbed. Then the sun came up.

I hadn't gotten around to closing the curtains the night before, as we'd wasted no time in getting down to it. As such the sun shone in through the window and onto Sammi's face, lighting her up with something akin to divinity. I stroked her hair away from her eyes and joked that she was glowing, and this made her laugh. But when she laughed, I don't know if it was a grim recollection of the dream, the brightness of the morning, a subconscious dislike of her tone, or simply a coincidence of timing stemming from a sudden hangover, but it turned my gut. A thin layer of cold sweat overcame me, I felt my colour drain and I stumbled drastically out of bed, hoping to make the bathroom as quickly as possible. It was no good; before I'd even grasped the handle of my bedroom door the tide came, swelling and gurgling up from my stomach and spewing freely from my throat, a violent, scorching projectile that brought the taste of stale beer and garlic sauce and dashed milky-pink all up my bedroom door. With residual tears filling my eyes, I dared not look back at Sammi, who had called out all the same, and I retreated to the toilet bowl to finish the offence.

When I returned, Sammi was sat up in bed. "All okay?" she asked, with a hint of a giggle underneath the concern.

I rubbed my eyes and left my hand there out of sheer embarrassment. "I'm so sorry," I groaned, mustering courage enough to peer at the mess on the door. What a first impression, surely the time of our parting had now come. "I can't believe -"

"Don't worry," Sammi replied, the giggle more prominent this time. "We did drink quite a lot last night."

"Still," I said. "I never do that. I don't think - even once before - "

Gloriously, miraculously, Sammi didn't seem any the less taken with me after I'd hurled my guts about the place. I scrubbed the place clean as she showered, and as the time to laugh about it came sooner than expected, we made arrangements to meet again in two days' time.

It was on that evening that I first broached the topic of childhood.

"Where did you grow up?" I asked. "What was your childhood like?"

Sammi looked down and laughed, with an air of hesitation. "My childhood was alright," she finally replied.

I grinned at her trepid tone. "And?" I asked with a grin. "Why so embarrassed?"

"You might not believe me," she said. "But I had my first job when I was eighteen months old."

I paused for a beat. "What?"

"Seriously."

"Were you born in medieval times?"

Sammi laughed again. "Haha. No. It was TV. I was the Sun Baby on Teletubbies."

I paused again. "The... Sun baby?" I was less surprised than I let on. I'd feigned confusion, but I knew. I was a tad too old for Teletubbies but I still liked it when I was a kid. The Sun Baby opened and closed every episode; an infantile, smirking baby's face pasted on a rising and setting sun, giggling and gurgling into the blue sky as, over the hills and faraway, the Teletubbies came to play. Those four podgy, alien babies with big heads. Those - those fuckers! It was they who harangued me in my dream! From that second on, whenever I beheld

Sammi, the years were gone from her face. In spite of her luscious hair, her classy gown and full shape all over, she had the features of a baby. And her laughter, frequent as it was, was not that of a woman in her twenties. It was the giggle of an infant who was pleased to have milk to suck on, or a rattle to beat. I felt a shrinking sensation in the trousers; this night was onto a promise, what with the previous one's outcome. But what of it now? How could I look Sammi in her toddler eyes and let her do the things to me she'd done before?

But I did, all the same. Needs must. And for a little while it wasn't even a problem, as we stripped bare in the passion throes, and she lay back on her pillow ready to take me in, it was fine. Amazing even. I watched her beautiful body rock and glisten as we went at it and nary a laughing, anthropomorphic celestial body entered my thoughts. But then we turned over. Then it was my turn to rest back on the pillow. Sammi straddled me and, smiling down from on high, began to rise and fall with all the sensual grace of a.... of a... a rising... Oh Lord. There it was.

The flaccidity fell on me so quickly that I felt I'd disappeared. I gasped in frustration and squeezed my eyes closed, desperate to muster an image sexy enough to bring me back before Sammi became let down. She continued to rock upon me with urgency as I conjured the mental image of my member, in full, erect glory, with hopes to garner the real thing with such power, but the mental image of my hard-on quickly became the bright green, felt phallus that tops the head of Dipsy, the green Tellytubby. It rose and Dipsy's wide grin and tiny black eyes rose into view beneath it, and he waved at me violently.

"Eh-oh!" said the Dipsy of my nightmares, smiling and waving vigorously as my limp penis flailed uselessly inside Sammi's bouncing body. The other 'Tubbies stepped into view; purple Tinky-Winky with his red handbag, yellow Laa-Laa and little red Po, all grinning identical, black-eyed grins, all waving and giggling and shouting "Eh-oh!" like brain-dead toddlers as the whimsical, spritely fanfare of the Tellytubbies theme song bled into my brain with increasing volume.

With an almighty roar, I opened my eyes and the 'Tubbies, along with their hideous ditty, were gone. There was Sammi's toned, milky-white pelvis thrusting to a rhythm above my belly. She was unfazed all this time? My eyes rolled upwards, past her belly button, her bare chest and up to the unnatural, searing glow that now enveloped her face. Gone was her long hair, gone any semblance of womanhood about her aspect. All that remained was that infernal Sun Baby, dribbling and giggling and staring into my eyes as its inhumanly adult torso continued to fuck me. It opened its toothless gob and, in a man's booming voice, bellowed "Time for 'Tubby bye bye!" as it raised its body up and allowed me to flop out of her, before falling forward onto her palms and starting a slow descent.

The Sun Baby, unstopping, drew ever downwards towards me, echoing again and again its instructive cry of "Time for 'Tubby bye bye!" and, once it had reached the choice region, contorted its little, dribbling smile into an open-mouthed, gummy 'O', before putting me into its mouth. I expected the Sun Baby's lips to burn white-hot on my delicate skin, but they were just cold. Cold and moist. It hummed a final giggle as the Teletubbies fanfare trickled back into play, and as my body betrayed me and I turned erect against all better judgement, I began to weep.

"Please," I cried. "Stop, just stop." I wept and wailed, tears streaming down my itchy cheeks and into my pleading mouth. I protested again and again, crying like the baby she'd made me, but the thing just kept on sucking, and when I finally came there was no euphoria to be had, just a faint, desperate flicker of relief that surely this must all be coming to an end by now.

MICHELLE

by Stephen Clarke

Grandfather had nobody when he passed.

I was a stranger to him really, as an ignorance imbued by an all consuming thirteen year strong habit that got out of hand clasped at any straw of concern for anyone or anything else. He never acknowledged my existence either or that of my father's all our days so it didn't feel so bad rambling through the countryside primarily to rustle through his belongings for something of worth to keep the monkey satiated.

The funeral director with an ice cold grasp enlightened me that my grandfather was found by Mrs Orr, a neighbouring farmer's wife, face down, rigid and with a bizarre fixated ear-to-ear grin as he was flipped over. Perhaps he'd went out happy through pleasuring himself, which was an unwelcome thought that came with a chuckle and a grimace whilst walking the dirt road to the ramshackle dwelling he'd called home for forty-one years of his life. His cause of death was down on paper as pneumonia. I didn't expect anything from the horrid, emotionally hollow little four foot, seven inch, wiry-haired, bedraggled recluse with the obscure sneering in death from the open casket, but he left me his all.

I could see Grandfather's shack was in borderline ruins as I removed the padlock from rickety metal shards that may have been once considered a gate. Strewn all over the patch of land at the mouth of the foreboding nook was the weathered filth encrusted detritus of his compulsion to hoard the town's unwanted household discards amongst a lot of other obscurities. A child's travel cot cram-packed with dolls, plastic limbs and baby toys sent a shudder right through me as my expectations of what could be stockpiled behind the door was certain to toy with my heart rate.

A key was unnecessary as the door was a little ajar thus stepping my vigilance level up a few notches. My eyes beheld a pristine almost bare downstairs interior exempt from sunlight for the crudely handcrafted sackcloth layers hung and adopted as curtains.

I'd never met my grandmother and neither did my father, whom was removed from Grandfather's care as an infant. Dad was told of his mother's disappearance in his teens. He was told of her running away from the hospital and her marriage immediately after the birth. She made it into the local observer with appeal for her whereabouts, which then commenced to be a police investigation with no success.

Indoors was the complete opposite to the haberdashery of shit accumulated out the front as there was absolutely nothing on any surface or table and I was beginning to find this all a little eerie. I wanted to make my exit but not before checking upstairs.

The faint singing of a child could be heard from upstairs in the room just above. I froze with instantaneous palpitations as the solo became a choir of children's voices singing what seemed like an old Sunday school hymn in a low monotone drone. Leg muscles jellied swiftly.

Scaling the staircase, a musty odorous damp whiff, tinged with sweet sickly meat reminiscent of lamb soon became a stench of rotting animal carcass. My boots began to squelch with each hasty step on the saturated carpet leading to the turn of the banister, which in turn led to three closed doors. The singing receded with each foot's advance as I crept warily to the source and flung open the door.

Pitch blackness achieved by yet more sunlight swallowing

sackcloth layers forced me to erratically claw the wall for a switch, the room filled with whispers intermingled with sinister spates of giggling. The bulb exposed an unaccountable horde of pristinely kept porcelain dolls that packed every crevice the room could muster, every eye seemingly fixed on my racing retinas and leeching at my life force and inducing an excruciating heaviness beneath my skull, bringing me to my knees on the noxious gungy shag pile. Suddenly the light flickered with the noise of crackling glass as it failed to redeem me from an imminent swallowing darkness before a pallid plethora of acrimonious antiquities.

My brain throbbed with a searing level of agony forcing me to embrace the decrepit flooring. A crescendo of children's screams brought back to life the now wildly swinging lightbulb as it puppeteered shadow to twist, contort and animate each and every doll face that drowned my sight with a deathly macabre tide of facial modifications using human parts to fill the heads of these twisted collectible playthings that outnumbered one by hundreds.

As my eyes jolted from face-to-face the mouths of each and every doll appeared broken in, stuffed and bloodied with a raw liver looking substance coiling round jutted porcelain shards like teeth writhing as if alive.

A heavy set of footsteps began to tread the staircase as dwindling dregs of determination returned briefly to permit me to crawl weakly from the monstrosities to peer furtive from between banister spindles. A tall sluggish humanoid form was was almost at the turn into the upper hallway as an almost gurgled unintelligible chant was to be heard from those horrific little bastards in the bedroom growing louder with the figure's approach.

Now leering over me was the masked form of a naked elderly lady, wheezing heavy with overtones of a busted bellow, poised to strike with a crudely crafted harpoon-style bolt implemented with a gargantuan hypodermic affixed to the tip.

Her mask was a mosaic of porcelain shards intricately placed to display a spirit wrenching expression of darkest daunting anguish. Upon raising her contraption she lunged it repetitively into my fear-stunned gape, expelling acrid tasting glob into my gullet, intermingling with the hot flow from new gashes with every thrust. Perhaps God intervened in my last howl, I thought, as I felt consciousness ferrying me from the situation behind my tightly closed eyelids.

Coming round without pain, surprisingly I wasn't breathing just right and found myself staring blankly ahead through a window with the sight of fields vast and stitched by hedgerow stretching for miles. Just below that was the all too familiar junkyard of grandfather's accumulations. Escape was the primary intent before one acknowledged the full-bodied icy sensation of paralysis and with great effort to cast my eyes down I discovered my horrifying fate as my arms were no longer flesh and blood but fucking porcelain!

Labelled 'Michelle' and clad in a floral Edwardian frock I was imprisoned within this cold brittle exterior on the windowsill with nothing but my way home over the hills before me.

This hell is forever, it seems.

THE DEATH OF DAHLIA

by Lauryn Malcolmson

As the dust settled on the newly paved road; a deathly silence filled the cold and icy air. Spectators didn't dare move. Or even breathe. The only thought that was going through their minds was the question of who was lying there, motionless, coated in blood, beside the distorted clump of metal almost unrecognisable as the vehicle it had been before – tyre marks had tattooed themselves onto the ground, and the overwhelming effluvium of burning rubber was impossible to dismiss. The eerie silence lasted only seconds, although it seemed endless. Sirens began to sound on cue, disturbing the quietness in the atmosphere, and soon enough, policemen, doctors, and other seemingly important suits surrounded the scene. The distant, and sparse, irregular crowd stood still, not knowing how to act, or where to go; what was one to do in this situation?

However, that all changed after the site was cleared; all, it seemed, was back to normal. The sun dared to shine again. People sauntered the streets, unphased by the event that had occurred only moments before. Children skipped happily on the footpath, and countless others were struggling to carry all of their shopping bags, humouring passerbys who saw them. Just another summer's day.

My heart was pounding. Another text had just come through. Who was this? My hands shook unwillingly, and I felt an unpleasant chill run down my spine. Reluctantly, I dragged my eyes to the screen, to see what had been sent this time. 'What?' I asked myself, confusion taking over. All that had been sent was a picture of a car. A Mercedes. Blue. Followed by one word;

'Before'.

Like I had done with every other text, I simply replied with 'Who is this?'. No reply. Again. Maybe it was a wrong number; they hadn't even mentioned my actual name in a text yet. They had just kept sending me messages that didn't make any sense; and some that did. Anyway, it was just a wrong number. I collapsed onto my bed, tired, throwing the phone aside; forcing a laugh. I had to be worrying over nothing. Just then, my phone rang; my heartbeat sped up, but I answered anyway, and breathed in relief when I heard the familiar voice. It was my mother. 'Hi!' I chirped into the phone, but her reply didn't reciprocate, as it usually did. 'Mara, please come over to Dahlia's house. Your other friends are here too. Something has happened.' She hung up. Had she been crying? Her voice sounded hoarse, and overly formal. A feeling of dread began to swell in my stomach. Something was wrong.

The walk to Lia's house normally took 6 minutes and 14 seconds. Of course, today, due to a mix of anxiety, desperation, and other emotions, the journey was less than three minutes long. Unfortunately I didn't have any time to count, I was too busy with tripping over my own shoes and tearing flowers from passing shrubs and bushes. Cars had lined up outside of the Ester household, making it hard to find a path to the entrance. Luckily I was small enough to force my way through the 'barricade'. Most of the vehicles were unfamiliar, and so was the pale face of my mother when she answered the door.

I choked when my mother told me the news, through her own muffling tears; 'Dahlia...she's been..killed..in a car accident'. But I didn't cry, even though everyone else around me was. My heart ached for my closest friend, yet I couldn't even cry for her. No emotion would reveal itself. So I pretended too; bearing the heavy weight of my head and shoulders on my lap, flinching when others came close and clenching my fists when someone patted my back in condolence. Even with eyes closed, I knew exactly how the scene looked. I had visited Lia's house so often that it was as familiar to me as my own home. The main living area was filled with the same scent as it usually was; jasmine incense was burning. Lia used to say that this scent made her feel the most at ease. Right now it was just suffocating. I needed to get out of here. I stood up from the armchair where I had been seated and struggled to make my way to the nearest exit. Every time I saw another stranger's face, I turned the other direction - small talk concerning my dead friend was the last thing I needed right now - to instead see Lia's face smiling back at me, from one of the many wooden framed photographs in the room.

At last I was able to reach outside. It was hard to breathe in that room. Too many people. I was able to use the breathing exercises that Lia had taught me to use when I was feeling stressed – she had learned them from her mother, who was a yoga teacher - deep breath in...1, 2...

Buzz.

My phone. A new text flashed onto the screen, all in capital letters; 'AFTER!' followed by a picture of the blue Mercedes car I had received earlier. Except, now the car was crushed and misshapen. And then something unthinkable entered my mind. Despite being afraid, I ran back into the heavy atmosphere and caught my mother, who seemed to be speaking to a 'Dr Arden', a man whom I had never met. He winked at me, saying 'Don't worry. I'm going. Just wanted to pay my respects is all,' before limping away, which made me feel irritated. I pulled on her arm. 'Mum? Do you know what the car involved looked like?'

Seven weeks later.

Today was the last school day of the first week back since Lia's death. This morning, after receiving a good luck message from my anonymous contact; I believe the words were along the lines of 'be careful...death is around every corner..blahblahblah...'something like that. Nothing different. I made the journey on foot; Lia and I had always walked to school together, as it wasn't far from where we lived. I accidentally stopped outside her house, forgetting that I didn't have to wait for her anymore. Because she wasn't here anymore. In fact, none of her family were. Her mother, Mary, couldn't cope with her daughter's death; she couldn't bear to live in the same place where she had raised her now dead child (understandably). To the neighbourhood's surprise, the house was swept up as soon as it had been put up for sale; a lone man, aged in his fifties now owned it.

It had been strange, for the first time in years, having no one to walk beside in the corridor and no one to eat lunch with. I spent most of my day weaving through crowds of whispering voices. All conversing about the same boring things. Of course I had been invited over to sit with quite a few different groups of people, but that's only because I was now known as 'Dead Dahlia's' former best friend. I didn't want pity, or to be used to make other people feel better about themselves. At least as I sat by myself I could think things over – not that there was much to think about, I had isolated myself since her death; I haven't even spoken to anyone other than my parents and a crappy grief counsellor who I saw once, a week after Lia died. I'm not sure what my other 'friends' thought of this - I'm not sure if I would count them as 'friends' per say. To me they were only individuals who were also close with her. I realised that I'd never really gotten to know them as anything else. They had attempted to reach out; to talk to me. I'd ignored them up until this point, but now that we were in school together again; in class together, it would become troublesome to keep it up for much longer. So we had all arranged to meet today, after school. I'm not sure what I wanted to say. I'm not sure what there was to say.

It was me who ended up waiting for them. It made me look like I actually wanted to be there (which wasn't what I was going for). They had chosen the park as a meeting place; we all lived around the same area, and this is where we usually hung around with Lia when we had the chance. I sat on one of the swing sets; just to kill time. My phone buzzed a few times, which was normal for me now. I looked at what I had received this time; 'I know what you did.' 'I will find you soon.' Sigh. I wish that this person, whoever they were, would send threats that were at least a little more original. Honestly, they'd been sending the same messages for months now; which varied between either personal insults or vague remarks that I know could mean something, but without evidence, didn't cause me any fear anymore. Instead of waiting in suspense and dread, and letting my imagination run, I thought logically about the situation. If anyone really wanted to hurt me, they would do it. But I was still alive...

Eventually, familiar faces approached me from the distance. Almost everyone was there. One was missing I think. I couldn't help rolling my eyes as I was embraced almost immediately by Sarah, the annoying and cheerful one of the group. Coincidentally the one I liked the least. This was followed by Jade, who had her brown hair tucked behind her ear, and Poppy, who had hers covering her face from seeing eyes, who were the quietest and closest of everyone - they seemed pretty content in their own company, so I never really spoke to them much. Then there was Aiden. He was the only guy of the group, and despite my suspicions of him and his intention towards Lia in the beginning, I'm pretty sure he only wanted to be friends with her. Like everyone did. He waved politely, but he didn't look overly thrilled to be there – he'd probably been dragged along. While Sarah started some small talk about how her summer was, and how sad it was that we hadn't seen each other in school that much, I realised. I didn't like being here with them. 'Anyway, school has been strange without Dahl -'. 'Please stop. Talking.' My sudden interruption seemed to cause quite a stir within them all. I was always listening, and didn't speak much. 'I need to say something. I'm sure all of you will agree. We don't have to pretend anymore.' At this everyone made puzzled expressions. 'Dahlia was the only reason that any of us became friends in the first place. Now that she's gone, what's the point? I can't stand being here with you all. I know you feel the same.' Confessing my true feelings felt good. I couldn't help but twist my face into a smile. Even to me it felt distorted.

'I hope to God that you're joking Mara.' 'Why would we keep trying to get through to you if we didn't care?' 'I don't think anyone else feels that way...' For some reason these responses made me angry. Why did they have to be nice about it all? 'Honestly, even looking at any of you right now makes me feel sick. In a way, I'm glad Lia's gone. This way I won't have to deal wi - ' Ouch. It seems I made at least one person angry. I knew it was Poppy because I caught a glimpse of her blurred wild brown mane as her hand came into contact with my face. I couldn't help but stagger back; clutching my face from the impact. My right cheek stung and my eyes watered - I knew that it probably looked just as bad as it felt. Blood dripped from my eyelashes; Poppy's ring was smeared in blood, as well as my brow. 'You bitch. No wonder Sophie didn't want to come.' I laughed it off and before turning away she stared at me in disgust. The others followed her lead. Finally. I was rid of them. But I didn't feel as content as I thought I would. Instead I felt...guilt? Maybe I should go for a walk. Clear my head.

The sound of the cars zooming past soothed me. I was glad that the people in the vehicles only had a glance of my hunched over silhouette and then moved their gaze back to the looming road ahead. They weren't so unfortunate that they had to know me. One look was all they had to bear.

The whispers of the road seemed to be beckoning me. They wanted me to come closer, so I could hear clearly what they were harshly hissing and hushing about. I noticed my steps moved a few to the left; I was now walking in more of a higgledy line. But still, when I realised my footing I adjusted myself back to the inner depths of the path. I don't know why to be honest. Maybe because the trees were more comforting to me. For some reason they sang joyously about sweet nothings, and made me feel at ease. It was...just...comforting.

The birds, flowers that were growing and living among the trees were full of beauty and vigour; vibrant and colourful.

But somehow my head still turned to the dull greys and blurred migrainous whites of the road. What was it that I missed? I'm not sure. I think it was only curiosity. Of what would if I dared too, if anyone would care if I disappeared. But why would they? I stumbled over, catching myself before I hit the ground. They had left. Whenever anyone wants to do something nice for me it always turns out to be in vain. Why do I lie? Why do I want and wait for myself to fail? For people to hate me? I wish I knew that my self-titled 'selflessness' was more self-entitled than anything. Nothing more than a delusion. At this rate I'm never going to find anyone else that I could love. Trust.

I grabbed onto my long hair, tugging at the ends. I can't take it anymore. The more cars there were the louder the whispers. It was hurriedly turning to   screaming. Maybe they were trying to tell me what happened to her. To Lia. I wonder?

Before I knew what was happening I was standing between the cat eyes of the road. Everything blurred. His gun metal black hair. His determined face. His...? A harsh shove sent me diving back onto the pathway. Among the harmonious trees again. A silhouette loomed over me. His face blocked the sun, and I couldn't help but blankly stare when he outstretched his arm to me; almost shaking with anger, but obviously trying not to show it.

Aiden.

'I knew I was right in following you here. You idiot.' I grabbed onto his arm, pulling myself up from the ground.

'You're the idiot. You just had to save me, didn't you?'

'All of the others left. You really pissed them off, speaking to them like that. But I know you're just griev -'

'I wish everyone would stop saying that.'

'Sorry.'

'It's fine, thank you. I guess.'

'It's fine, I'm glad I got here in time. But you wouldn't have actually..done it, would you?'

'Hmmmm.' I wasn't sure myself right now.

'Promise me you won't do that again. Mara.'

'Well. If it means I won't have to owe you anything...I won't. Of course I won't. Do you really think I would want my mother to end up like Mrs Ester? After Lia...'

I immediately regretted saying that. Aiden probably thought that I was a disrespectful bitch. Like the others. 'Sorry. Forget it.'

I began to walk away, using the path I had strolled down just a few moments before. I felt someone grab my shoulder. 'Wait. Mara. I know that you and Dahlia were close. More than the rest of us. No one else talks about her. But, I want to.' He shuffled uncomfortably, scuffing his black combat boots on the gravel. From what I could see of his face he looked tearful.

I didn't realise that anyone cared this much. Maybe I wasn't the only one who hadn't moved on. I felt the corners of my mouth turn up into a smile. For the first time in months, it was genuine. A jolt of happiness washed over me, knowing that someone else was feeling something similar. Aiden and I were never really close. I had only ever spoken to him when he was with Lia. He jumped with surprise as I linked my arm through his. We walked back home in silence.

This was how my new friendship with Aiden began. For the next few weeks we constantly talked to one another. We called each other on the days when we couldn't see one another, and for the first time since meeting Dahlia I felt like I was having a proper relationship; it was nice to be myself. It wasn't strained. I hated inventing different characters and parts to play, depending on whose company I was in. It just became a nuisance and confusing to say the least. After a few weeks, I felt as though I'd be able to trust him. The threats still hasn't ceased, and I realised that I'd have to do something about it. (I often wondered if Lia would be okay with me being this close to someone other than her.)

He immediately embraced me when I told him. I forgot what it felt like to feel this warm inside. It was nice. 'I, I need help finding out who is doing this. If you can't, I completely understand. I mean, they might know that you're with me...'

'No. I definitely want to help you discover who this person is. I'm tired of seeing injustice. Another criminal already gotten away with Dahlia's death. Don't get me wrong,' Aiden threw his hands up in the air. 'Although I know it wasn't purposely, but running away like that...it's cowardly. Not right. They should've taken responsibility.' I explained to him the texts I received, the day of her death, and how I thought the two people may be linked. After a moment of thought, he hugged me again and told me that he'd 'do anything to help'. I felt such a rush of relief, that I collapsed into him, and released my emotions that I had been holding inside for months.

***

Aiden took a particularly long time to come back one particular day. He had given me a key to his apartment; I learned that he lived alone. I didn't know the exact details of his situation, but he told me that it was what was best for both him and his family, and that they still got along well. His home had been transformed into a base for me and him to use when we were investigating *them*. We hadn't come up with a name for the anonymous contact, but I felt as though we were getting closer. It was nice to have someone to help me. I didn't

218

think I would be able to be with someone again like this. Since Aiden began helping me, I seemed to be handling things a lot better. It was easier to sleep; my nightmares were less frequent, and I'd apologised to my other friends – Aiden said that this was a requirement if I wanted him to help me, although Sophie apparently still wanted nothing to do with me; I couldn't blame her though.

'Hey Aiden!' I smiled at him brightly, glad to see his face. 'What's the matter with you?' His face was discoloured and his black, spidery hair covered his face almost completely. I moved towards him to brush away the stray hairs to the side and as I did he grabbed my arm. 'Aiden.' I struggled to release myself from his grip, but it was no use. 'Let go of me! Now!' He didn't seem to be listening. With sudden, unnaturally jerky movements, he freed my arm and leapt into the corner of the room, facing the white wall. He seemed to be shaking. It was making me nervous.

'I spoke with Sophie today,' Aiden said.

'Oh. Do you think she's any closer to forgiving me? I mean, I suppose I don't deserve any of their forgiveness, after what I sai -'

'After what you've done, you mean.'

I froze. 'What are you talking about? Oh, I forgot to tell you, I think I've found a lead on who might be...' he began to laugh. It was a cold and grim laugh. Made me feel uncomfortable. 'I know who's behind it all.'

'You're kidding, right?' Surely he couldn't know.

Aiden dragged a chair, stopping in front of the door. Was this to make sure I didn't escape? So many thoughts were going through my mind right now. Was it him? If it was, what was he going to do to me? His green eyes seemed to pierce into me as I caught them. My palms were sweating and I felt a major sense of dread. 'I think I'm going to go now, once you have calmed down you can let me know what you've foun...' I sighed. 'Aiden, let me out.' He was sitting against the door, leaning back on the chair. He acted like I hadn't said a thing. 'You're freaking me out right now. I have the police on speed dial, so don't even think of trying anything.' I laughed but my voice shook. I walked slowly back to my seat, and sat down. We had a table between us; but I didn't feel any less at risk.

After what I'd done? That sounds like something *they* would've sent me.

'Mara, you've really helped me these past few weeks. I didn't think that anyone else loved Dahlia as much as I did. But you - you did.' Aiden dragged his hand through his sleek black hair, scratching his head in obvious frustration. For a moment I saw his eyes. They were darker than I'd ever seen them before. I could tell that whatever feeling he had right now was consuming him. Just like fear was overwhelming me at this moment. I fidgeted with my hands on my lap, which were sweating; I felt panicked. After a minute or two of agonizing silence, Aiden raised his head, to catch my eyes. He spoke slowly; 'I'm going to speak now, Mara. Please stay there, and just let me finish until the end.' He gave a small smile, before looking down. I fixed the crease in my skirt, needing to concentrate on something else while I listened.

'I – I spoke to Sophie today, as I said before. I needed to know why she refused to see you, speak to you even. Everyone else understood why you had to isolate yourself after...you know,' he nodded his head. 'And you really didn't mean what you said about them, I know that now.' I nodded frantically; although saying that I regret what I said would be a lie – I felt it wasn't the right time to disagree. 'I don't know whether you know this, since you weren't...available after Dahlia's death, but Sophie couldn't cope with it well, at all. She actually withdrew herself for a week or two, not wanting to see anybody. She finally came around, and she's doing a lot better now. But right now she's being homeschooled – she didn't want anyone to know, but it seems like she isn't ready to come back yet...' Aiden trailed off, staring into space. I suppose I'd been pretty selfish; I hadn't thought or even asked about how Lia had affected others lives. Just mine.

'Anyway, turns out it was more than that. Something else was bothering her. Which is why she chose to reach out to me. It seems that she has been worried for me.' He looked up at me. 'Because of you.' My heart sped up even more. I felt nauseous. What was he talking about? 'Truth be told, no one really liked me spending this much time with you. Before I got to know you, before I really became friends with you, I hated Dahlia being so close with you.' I quickly fixed my expression as I instinctively glared at him. 'Hahaha. That's what I mean. You could never control your emotions when it came to her. We all knew we were second to her.' He laughed again, coldly. 'You could have made it a little less obvious. I'm pretty sure even she knew about your obsession with her. Maybe it made her feel better about herself, having a follower that agreed and worshipped everything she did.' My blood began to boil, and I could feel my fists shaking; they felt hot. 'I think that's why she kept you around. It's quite sad, really. You were only a leash away from becoming her pet.' As he spoke, my fingernails dug into the skin of my palm, until blood was dripping down onto my wrists. It stung, but I didn't mind. Those words were the breaking point of my patience. I could feel the blood rushing to my head; blurring out my thoughts. My blood felt so hot that I was convinced that my veins were about to explode. Before I could think of my actions, I launched myself out of the chair I had been seated on, towards Aiden. Only fear was present on his face now; which I'll admit made me feel a little better. I shoved him from his chair, which flew into the wall beside us. With a thump he landed on his back.

On the old wooden floor, I fell next to him, and as soon as I could, I scrambled to my feet, and stood over my friend, my right boot leaning hard on his chest. He grimaced. 'She knew. She told me your secret. How you used to follow her around,' I told Aiden as he coughed. 'You thought no one would catch you?' My mind was going frantic. This wasn't happening right now. 'Sophie. It's her who has been threatening me! I'm going to make her -'

'Mara! Don't you realise what you've done?' My friend was looking up at me, puzzled and frightened. Why was I doing this? I was dragged from my thoughts by a sudden banging on the door. 'Help! Come in here now!' shouted Aiden. I heard hushed sounds from outside. Before I could even doubt myself, a voice in my head told me what I had to do. I grabbed one of the empty bottles that was lying on his table, and smashed it against the wall, fractals of coloured glass glittering as they fell. I could feel myself smiling as I walked back towards him; he appeared to be stunned, lying in terror. I raised up my arm, preparing for impact. As I did, a rush of memories came flooding back. That's when everything turned black.

I woke up, lying in an uncomfortable bed, in what seemed to be a damp, dull prison cell. The back of my head hurt like hell, and was smeared with blood that still felt damp. I mustn't have been in here for that long. For a few minutes I was confused as to why I was here. 'She's awake.' My eyesight was unfocused and unsteady; I could make out the outline of a person, whose figure blocked out the buzzing white light. Rattling keys scraped against metal, and with a creak the entrance to the cell opened. I stood up from my slumber, falling over. My hands were cuffed behind my back. I was lifted up by the same person who opened the cell.

I was roughly thrown into a small square room, which to me, looked as depressing as the cell I was confined to only moments ago. A table was present in the middle of the room, and a thin, black-haired woman sat on one side, with a file and a scowl. There was also one of those 'one way mirrors', that I'd only ever seen in TV shows and movies.

'Mara Rivers. My name is Detective Larsson, and I am here to question you. I assume you know why you're here. We have evidence that shows you were involved in conspiring to kill

Dahlia Ester, who died in a hit and run just over two months ago.'

'I have no idea...What are you talking about?' My emotions appeared to have gotten the better of me, and tears (on cue), streamed down my face. What was happening right now? I wanted to leave. Go home.

'We were contacted two days ago by a person who wishes to remain anonymous. They gave us this.' I was shown a black burner phone. I knew exactly what it was when I saw it. Who's it was. I nodded to myself. 'Yes, yes, now you understand don't you?!? Her – Sophie, it must be, she's been torturing me. For months. Even before Lia's death, sh -'.

'I am fully aware of the situation, Miss Rivers. I am also aware that before Dahlia's death, you and her were rather close, were you not?' I shuffled in my chair. Answering her questions seemed to be the only thing I could do right now.

'Yes. She was my best friend. This is why I don't understand; why do you think I would want to hurt my best friend? It makes no sense.'

'I'll tell you why, Miss Rivers. Jealousy is an unruly emotion, isn't it? You couldn't stand seeing Dahlia with others. We have witnesses that have admitted to seeing you following her on several occasions. And when we searched your room, we found this.' The detective reached for a journal; the outside was a plain black colour. 'Would you like to have a look inside, Mara?' My hands wouldn't stop shaking as the book was set in front of me. The handcuffs that grazed my wrists made it difficult for me to turn the pages. As I opened it, more memories returned to me. Photos of Lia lined almost every page. Of her in school, out with her family, in her home. I had written beside each picture of where I could buy her clothes, what I could do to look more like her, and how to act like her and even though I recognised the handwriting as my own, everything was unfamiliar to me. Yet I remembered doing it. I remember hiding this book underneath a loose floorboard in my room. I felt like I was recollecting thoughts that weren't my own; that belonged to another person.

'This - this is mine.' I admitted.

'When we were handed the burner phone, the carrier states that the reason they began to use it against you, Mara, was to collect evidence of your obsessive behaviour of your friend Dahlia. They were angry and frightened for their friend.'

I stared at the laminated floor and sighed.

'At first I thought that it was Dahlia who was behind the messages. I was completely convinced that she found out about how I felt towards her. When I tried telling her about it, she laughed it off. It made me angry that she insinuated that the threats were some sort of joke. I became afraid. My life was being threatened. I was being watched.'

'Ironic, isn't it?'

'I never once posed as a threat to Lia.'

'Of course not...until you did.'

The Detective reached into to her file once again, this time she brought out a photo; an old man, around fifty years old.

'You know him don't you? Dr Arden. He was the man who supplied you with the car. The car which you then asked him to use, to kill Miss Ester. Now, what I didn't understand, was why this man, this *stranger*, would assist you with such a thing. It just doesn't make any sense when you think about it logically. Dr Arden is a well respected man; he used to own his own practice, you know? Well. Until it was all shut down. Eight years ago, when Dr Arden was sued for malpractice, which resulted in a patient's death. The unfortunate man's name was Noel Esther; he paid for a private doctor, who was also a good friend to the family, as he was undergoing surgery. Nothing should've went wrong; it was only a simple tonsillectomy. Noel Esther was sent home after the surgery, only hours later to be found in his bed drenched in blood. Cause of death was confirmed to be post operative bleeding; he died choking on his own blood. Your best friend Dahlia lost a father, and her mother, a husband, all because of this man. I wonder would things have turned out differently if Dr Arden had bothered to properly clean his equipment before operating on his patients...'

Lia had always told me that her father died of cancer. What a liar she was. I turned up the corner of my mouth. Detective Larsson stared at me for a few seconds in thought before continuing; 'Dr Arden lost his patients, and eventually his practise; the Esthers are a respectable family in this area, and news travels fast. By looking at his records I can tell that he hasn't had a steady job since. He wanted revenge. On the family that ruined his career. And he got it. Both of you did, in your own cruel and evil way. I'm curious as to how you two met, by the wa -'

'How do you know all of this? Why?'

'Would you believe me if I told you that he is currently being held in the interrogation room across from us, after having admitted everything? You made a huge mistake, Miss Rivers. You trusted people. While you were preoccupied with blocking out memories of the horrible things you've done, you were being suspected by your friends, and betrayed by your accomplice, who choked up everything as soon as we offered him a fractionally less devastating sentence.'

Aiden. He didn't actually like me. It made sense. He must've just wanted to get close to me for for Sophie's sake. I couldn't even feel angry anymore. I was just tired. My mouth was dry, but I finally found the courage to speak. 'I remember. I did plan to...get rid of Lia. After I suspected that she was the one who was threatening me, I was scared. I started to feel hatred

225

towards her. But the night before Dr Arden...killed her...I contacted him. I texted him with the burner phone I had purchased. I told him to call it all off. That I didn't want to do it anymore. I swear. After that I met him again only once - when I heard that he had purchased the Esther household. My parents believed that I was going to a grief counsellor. He...he told me that he only did what we both wanted; we were both free now. That he was lucky to have only injured his leg. Apparently I sent him nothing but confirmation of what was to happen that day. But, detective, I swear. Go to my house, my spare phone should be hidden somewhere in my room. I can prove to yo -'. My voice was beginning to rise with desperation.

'We have already taken your phone in as evidence. I can tell you that all of the text messages that were exchanged between you and Dr Arden were only confirming your plans to kill Dahlia Esther. Nothing more. At 9.15am, 25thJune, you used this phone to lure Dahlia to her death.'

This couldn't be happening. Why wouldn't she believe me? Sure. I forgot some things, but I remembered now. I called it off. Maybe - maybe someone messed with my phone. That had to be it. But no one had been in my house except for me, my parents, and...and Aiden. 'They...'

Detective Larsson glanced at her watch. 'That's enough for now, we'll continue questioning at a later stage. For now, Mitch, show Miss Rivers back to her cell, please.'

The burly officer that I forgot had been standing there approached me slowly. 'No! Wait! I need to explain, please.' It was no use. It was over.

As I was dragged out of the interrogation room, I felt numb. Until I looked across the hall. I saw Aiden there, with his arm around someone...Sophie. She was crying. They looked close. I wished I could cry too. I could have always pretended. Like I did at Lia's house; at her funeral too. Sophie raised her head as I drew closer. She hadn't been crying. She smiled, along with

226

Aiden, and the glimmer in their eyes told me everything I needed to know. In her hand was a pink burner phone. It looked exactly like the one I had hidden in my room. That was the image that I couldn't quite escape from my mind, as I bowed my head, and was taken back into my holding cell.

'Please! You have to belive me!! It's them, they've done this to me!'

A phone sounded in the distance.

TUTU CABARET

by Druscilla Morgan

I've been sitting at the bus stop for at least an hour. Maybe it's only half an hour but I'm so wasted that it feels like forever. I could walk. It's not far really, maybe twenty minutes, but my legs have betrayed me - useless pillars of flesh, numb and shaky. There are people everywhere, gibbering, laughing. Some glance at me as they walk past. I lower my eyes, stare at the ground.

Cigarette butts. Spit. A discarded flyer. I read the flyer. Or try to. I can just make out the heading.

TUTU CABARET

The rest is blurred. My eyes have joined my legs in their rebellion. I try to imagine a tutu cabaret in a desperate attempt to take my mind off the wait. Ballerinas with top hats and fishnets, legs raised, smouldering glances into the smoky crowd. The concept amuses me, distracts me, and I almost don't hear the bus. In fact, I don't hear the bus. I hear the singing. Loud, raucous, drunken singing. Warily, I raise my eyes.

There's a bus but it can't be my bus. My bus is boring, standard State Transport fare. My bus isn't festooned with bright balloons and streamers. My bus doesn't have noisy party animals hanging out the windows. Their off-key warbling competes with the archaic rattle of the engine as the bus rumbles closer. I squeeze my eyes shut and open them again.

It's still there.

It's okay. It won't stop. It's not my bus.

It stops.

The singing stops.

Now it's just noise, a cacophony of laughter and bellowing, virile voices. I sit, glued, as the doors swoosh open.

Out they tumble. There are lots of them. Old ladies and men - big men, like footballers. They're dressed in blue singlets and tutus.

Yes, tutus.

They gather around the bus stop, laughing, arms linked, seemingly oblivious to my presence. I swallow, try to move. Nothing happens. I focus harder, willing my useless legs back to life. One of the men notices me. He pins me with small black eyes. His tongue flicks between his lips, lizard-like and hungry. I drag my eyes away from his and fix my gaze on the old lady beside him. She's skinny, her wrinkled skin falling in folds under her raised arms as she prances in an unsteady circle. As she spins, I see a flash of gleaming scales under the tulle. It looks like a tail. I'm sure it's a tail.

For fuck's sake, don't be stupid. It can't be a tail!

Panic sets in and gives me impetus. I spring to my feet and start walking, breaking through the bizarre circle like a bulldozer. Head down, determined, I take them by surprise. The sea of bodies parts and I break into a trot as I glance nervously over my shoulder.

They're right behind me, an army of chaotic pink tulle and party hats. They lap at my heels, fast for old ladies and oversized ballerinas. I quicken my pace. It doesn't seem to do any good. They're almost on top of me now. Their laughter echoes in my ears, in my head. I start to trot then break into a run, streaking through the late-night crowds. I'm a human bullet, fired by fear. Someone swears as I send them barrelling.

"Dickhead!"

I keep running, ignoring the insult. I want distance, not a fight. I zigzag my way past the closed shops and the open bars, my breath catching in my chest. I glance backwards. I can't see them but I keep running until I'm clear of the bars and crowds. I only slow down as I hit the south end. There are no bars here, no people. No ballerinas with scaly tails. Darkness cloaks me as the bright lights fall away. I slow my run to a power walk. I can't hear them now. I'm surrounded by a blessed silence, punctuated only by the occasional passing car. I look behind me again.

Nothing.

I've lost them.

Relieved, I exhale a stream of hot breath that frosts in the night air. I'm sweating, my heart is pounding, but I've made it. I relax and dial my pace back a bit more. I can see another bus stop ahead. I'm real close to home now but I'm run ragged, so I decide to chance it and wait for the bus.

My bus. Not some mobile carnival of freaks.

Maybe I imagined it. After all, I am wasted. I want to believe it was some kind of hallucination. I tell myself it was an hallucination. I'm almost starting to believe it when someone approaches and stands beside me.

"Excuse me, do you know what time the bus is due?"

Fuck! I don't want to talk. I don't want to answer questions. I just want everyone to leave me alone.

"Sorry," I mutter. "No idea." I don't look at the owner of the voice. He sounds young. Polite. Maybe he'll go away.

He doesn't. He stands too close and shuffles around nervously, like he's planning something. I move away, not far, but far enough to give him the hint.

"Have you been to the cabaret?"

His voice is weird, kinda raspy, but it's his words that make me raise my eyes to his. He has a round, soft face, like a child, but his eyes are dark and old. It's not the night air that makes me shiver.

"What cabaret?" Deep in my gut, I already know the answer but I ask anyway.

He grabs my hand, a predator pouncing on its prey. His fingers slither around my wrist. His skin feels rough and cold against my own sweating flesh.

"Come!" he hisses.

"No!" I try to snatch my hand away but his grip is deadly strong for a smooth-faced boy. His eyes bore into mine. They say the eyes are the window to the soul, but this boy has windows overlooking a graveyard.

Panic begins to rise. "Let me go!" I protest, still struggling to free myself.

He says nothing, just stands and holds me like a vice. Once more, I try to retrieve my hand, twisting in a desperate attempt to throw him off balance, but he's immovable. He looks past me, his eyes lighting up with recognition. I turn and follow his gaze. The bus is rumbling towards us. The balloons bobble brightly as it slows down and stops. The doors sweep open and the boy with dead eyes smiles as he pulls me towards them. His mouth is a gaping, hungry chasm and his razor-sharp teeth gleam under the solitary street light above us.

"Time to go, sweetheart. Let's dance."

DRIVE

by Lizzie Darragh

Cassie screamed at Lottie as she put pedal to the metal in her red Ford Focus tearing down a narrow dark country lane:

"Calm your ham and slow down before you get us both killed!"

Through her thick blonde fringe with piercing blue eyes, Lottie gazed at Cassie with a sinister smile, "You're not scared, are you?"

Grabbing Cassie's wrist and pulling on her freshly stitched wounds from the night before, tress whipped past her window and whistled as distant blared memories of a lonely pain-felt childhood she would rather forget came flooding to the forefront of her mind. Lottie slammed on the brakes, sending Cassie forward, and as she jolted up she was face-to-face with Lottie's ever darkening eyes, like a pond on a dark night reflecting the moon - no life of their own, just a reflection of something distant.

Lottie screamed into the bewildered face of Cassie, "You didn't think the pills would actually work, did you?!" before laughing coldly. "You're not that stupid, are you?!"

Cassie cried, "I can't turn any of this around! I can't do this on my own."

Lottie gripped the back of her head, slamming her into the dashboard as if tying to knock some sense into her, "Aww, big girl, aren't you, crying into your scarf?! Can't do it alone.

Boo-hoo, grow up! Get it into that thick skull of yours! I told you this when I first came to you - we're all alone in this pathetic game of a rat race we call life! You're pathetic! You're nothing!"

Cassie sobbed uncontrollably.

Lottie continued, "You've done all this to yourself. Why couldn't you be better, be nicer? Less of a nut job."

Lottie started the car up again and screamed at the top of her lungs, "WANNA PLAY A GAME, CASSIE?!"

Cassie screamed in fright, "Stop this! It isn't funny anymore!"

Lottie went even faster, barely managing to navigate the car down the winding narrow country lanes, "Was it ever funny? The self destruct, the ever growing darkness? The hours spent trying to bleed out? You're pathetic! You couldn't even do that right! But now you've come too far down into the darkness and this game ends tonight. This game ends now!"

Both girls struggled, fighting to control the wheel of the car. Tearing through the midnight air, tearing up grass and grit as they swerve. Cassie screamed, as she knew she has lost the battle:

"Why are you doing this?!"

Lottie stared at her with her dark empty eyes, "What do you mean, why am I doing this? This is your doing! You're the one in control!"

Cassie found herself clutching the wheel, struggling to remove Lottie's foot from the pedal. The Ford Focus accelerated over a verge and tumbled into a field, glass hurdling through the car as the windows and windshield smashed on impact. The seats covered in blood and the roof crushed in.

***

A new dawn was breaking as a farmer was beginning his early start to tend to his cattle. To his shock and horror he found a flipped car in his field. He managed to pull a female in her early twenties from the carnage. While calling for emergency services he searched for a pulse.

The quiet remote village woke to the news of a fatal accident. The tragic loss of a young woman, Cassandra Charlotte Hines, lone driver of a red Ford Focus.

ZOMBIE BLUES TRILOGY

by Owen Quinn

IRONY ZOMBIE

My mother always said that my headphones would be the death of me and sure enough, she was right. Worse still, it was a female pensioner that did it. I wouldn't mind but how embarrassing to be turned by a shuffling old timer that I never saw coming.

Sorry, meant to say I'm a zombie and before you all run screaming holding your brains, just hear me out. Nobody listens to our story. And let me tell you, there's a hell of a lot of prejudice towards the living dead. Although I do have a problem with that label but I'll come back to it. Let me tell you how it all began.

I'm Sandy (yeah Sandy the zombie, laugh it up fuzzball), twenty-four, single and as I said, it all began at a bus stop. It was a Thursday morning. I was going to work as a trainee manager for a big chain supermarket (do promo laws count now, dunno, not sure, brains). Dreary, boring and most of my time spent wishing I lived another life. Well as they say, be careful what you wish for. There I was standing headphones on in my virtual Facebook world with Miley Cyrus singing in my ears. I have to point out though before you make assumptions that I have no idea how she ended up in my music library. Just so you all know, I've never twerked before.

Anyway, the bus was late and you know that feeling that there's something out of the corner of your eye but you don't really pay attention? Well, that was me. I was half aware of a figure then there was pain.

A little old lady (I use that word loosely in retrospect) had bit into my arm just above the elbow. My first thought was my best suit was not ruined but the sight of blood seeping through quickly wiped that thought from my mind. I yelled in pain (haven't got a high pain threshold) and leaped away like a scalded cat, scowling at her. The scowl fell into disbelief as I realized she looked like she had just walked off the set of Dawn of the Dead. I thought for a moment it was one of those joke shows that set up the public but her lunging for a second bite made me do the unthinkable and punched her straight on the nose. She fell back, little old lady coat speckled with her blood and head scarf hanging off.

Several things happened at once. The other people waiting at the bus stop went, in a second, from about to lynch me for hitting a pensioner to terror as they saw zombie pensioner growling and gnashing at their lower legs now she had got me. There were screams and yells of fear as they scattered. Unfortunately, they didn't see the crowd of undead approaching. You could imagine what happened next.

Frankly I couldn't care less. Three things hit me all at once:

1: Headphones helped kill the human race.
2: What would my manager say for being late?
3: How much is a new suit going to cost me?

It's dumb what you think of at times of apocalypse. What I should have been thinking was:

1: I'm gonna turn into a zombie.
2: I'm never gonna shag again.
3: Fuck this for a game of soldiers.

I stumbled away towards the hospital but all the time trying to figure out what to do. How long before I turn? Would I even turn or was that a movie and TV myth? Maybe it'd be just like being bit by a dog. Put the dog down. Problem solved. Bite heals. But there was a voice at the back of my head telling me this was it. The clock was ticking and I had no idea how long I had. All around me there were terrified screams, cars crashing and the streets filling with the dead. I chuckled as I thought how apt starting the day with a breakfast set you up for the day. I sat there, feeling hotter and hotter, my legs weak and head fuzzing. I loosened my tie and opened my top button. I glanced at my bite mark and realized I'd be one of the best dressed zombies around. A couple of zombies shambled past and ignored me like dogs that could sniff cancer. That was when I knew for sure I was a goner. And that's my embarrassing birth as a zombie.

I was bitten by the only pensioner in the world that still has her own teeth.

It's been six months since zombie world was born. You know the drill, you've seen the movies; chaos, screaming, end of the internet but an unexpected bonus - no more X Factor or Strictly Come Dancing. Jesus, I hated those but my mum was glued week on week.

There are still lots of humans but scattered, scavenging like animals. They run when they see us or attack in sufficient numbers which isn't really cool. Yeah, we're corpses but we're still in here. No one tries to communicate with us. It's just slam bam, spike through the head. Has anyone ever tried to talk to a zombie? Probably not which is fair enough because they freak when they see us. But it's not our fault. I'm going to let you into a little secret.

When humans see us, they see dead people trying to eat them. When we see them, all we see is chicken. Humans taste like chicken. Sorry to break it to you but every time you munched into a chicken burger, it was a taste of yourselves. Who knew? And add to that diabetics taste like glazed honey chicken, old people taste like an over cooked chicken breast, body builders taste like drumsticks and heavy people taste like rubber chickens mixed with chicken skin. That came as a surprise to me to be honest and probably to those of you that haven't turned yet.

We don't stop at humans to be sure; anything goes but no zombie can run after a dog or climb up a tree for a cat. Those running zombies you saw in the remakes are false representation. But the good thing is life has become a stroll for the zombified human race.

There's no more rat race. We just shuffle along contentedly until we come across dinner and eat it. Weather doesn't bother us. Rain, hail or shine, it's all the same to us. Snow can be a bitch though. You fall down in a snowdrift and that's you until it thaws. Then we just get up and shuffle off again. I would never have believed there were so many benefits to being part of the undead community.

As I said no rat race, no wanker of a boss being the big man trying to belittle you, no bills, no scraping the money together for a fiver for the electric metre, no more being skint when you have a five week month. No bad relationships, no bad sex, no food poisoning, no more unrequited love, no religion, creed, no racism, no child poverty, no child crying at night because its mother or father are abusing them, no starvation, no war, no atrocities, no old person lying in the street mugged for a quid. There's no gay and no straight. There's no sunburn, no heartbreak, no more tears. I can see the world round me rather than having my nose stuck in my mobile phone. Pity I didn't see that when I was alive.

Zombies are one race united with no emotional baggage. With us comes peace.

Being a zombie does have its benefits but I know the drawbacks. We stink but then so do the humans that are left. Deodorant on the road not a big thing because they're fighting to survive so they can't really talk about us. Try using your

Boots clubcard now suckers.

We rot but at a slow rate. That surprised me but we do. My suit is pretty dirty now but still looking good. You should see some of these idiots. If they knew they were going to become zombies, I bet they would have dressed better. And don't mention the naked ones; even saggy tits and penis envy means nothing to us. But we have our attention seekers. Even alive, I would be embarrassed for them. And let's face it; I doubt any of them broke their ankles before they turned so why are they dragging one of their legs? Attention seekers, even now. Their legs suddenly heal when they see fresh meat but you just let them get on with it. No point in saying anything even if we could but we can glare. By the way, I love my new eye colour; yellow and blue. I know people that paid a lot just to have contacts like this.

I never really encountered prejudice in life but I get it all the time now.

If it isn't humans, it's bloody dogs. Even Lassie hates me and there are packs of them now, starving and certainly not candidates for Crufts. I always preferred cats. But cats rarely come near us except if somebody's leg falls off and they are crippled on the ground. But even that demonstrates the strong minded zombie way of thinking. Even if we fall, we keep going. No means nothing for us. Damn, my boss would love me as a zombie.

True we shall never again experience what we thought of as life but that's ok. We have lost nothing because we are not the undead.

We're seeing the countryside for the first time. We are seeing the Earth heal itself now pollution has stopped. We are hearing bird song even if they do try to peck at us like scarecrows, the bastards. Budgies are the worst believe it or not. Now I know why people kept them in cages, vicious little bastards. Tweet and peck, tweet and peck. It drives me mad because I can't swing my arms right to smack them away. The sky is bluer than before as nature takes back what man had almost destroyed. But that's the biggest secret of all that only zombies know. Maybe that's why we cannot speak to share it. If we could tell the humans would that make a difference? Probably not; I love chicken.

You see monsters when you see us but if you think about it, humans never could see what was right in front of them.

We're not zombies. We're the clean up squad. We're cleaning up the planet by chowing down on humanity. You see, the zombie virus was not man made. It wasn't a super secret government experiment gone wrong or germ warfare. Humans turned zombie all over the planet on the same day at the same time. Only the power of nature could do that and she determined the very thing that was destroying her would be the instrument through which she would take back the planet. Earth itself released the zombie virus into the air. Humanity had been hurting her for decades and she could take no more. The small minority that tried to save the planet were undermined by governments and their efforts were not enough.

Mother Nature turned humans into zombies to save the planet. The zombie plague would overwhelm humans, clearing them off the face of the planet so life could begin again. Cities would vanish under the spread of nature and all trace of humanity would eventually vanish. Oceans would be clean once more and skies would be brighter.

So what happens to us I hear you ask when every human is dead? Our job will be done and the dead will walk no more. Now we are the most unlikely environmental warriors you ever met and I can't even tell you about it if we meet. Well, we didn't listen when people were shouting about it so what's the difference now?

And you thought a pensioner with her own teeth was ironic.

I'm saving the planet. See you soon chicken.....

SAVE THE PLANET ZOMBIE

Hi, I'm Lily Taunton from Chicago and I'm a zombie. Not my first choice to be honest but it's hard enough to walk about when you're dead without the added weight of a backpack.

So what's in the backpack I hear you ask? I don't? Well, I'm going to tell you anyway because this is my story and if irony had a face, it'd be mine.

As you know, Mother Nature did something to bring about the rise of the undead to help clean up the planet from the scourge of humanity. The irony lies in what I did when I was a human. I was the ultimate save the planet girl. I sponsored animals in those adverts you see, I joined protests about the ozone layer both in person and online. I recycled, switched to energy saving bulbs, the works. I even got to go on a protest overseas to stop Japanese whaling ships. Any group that wanted to help stop and reverse the damage we as a species were doing to the planet, I was there. I even stopped using deodorant and got a bike.

Don't be smirking. A girl can keep fresh with an active life while saving the world. That's what my backpack has in it; leaflets and booklets to hand out to people on how the smallest change at home can make a difference.

I used to watch people bustle past me, blindly grabbing the leaflets from me with a grunt of an acknowledgment before dropping them in the nearest bin. That annoyed me and as I watched their retreating backs, I wondered if they had children at home and what sort of world those kids would see because their parents never took the time to listen just for a moment. Still, at least they didn't litter.

242

So it's ironic that even as an undead, I'm helping save the planet but stuck in this zombie body. We have no choice and I wonder if I wouldn't have been better dying in the accident. I came out of a side street on the bike and was hit by a car. I remember a thud, the world turning and then nothing. My last thought was that driver didn't watch the caution adverts on TV.

I know now the zombie outbreak had started so people were rushing home to their families. I was the ant under the boot so to speak. I must have died, my neck broke I think because I came to as a zombie. My helmet had come off with the impact of the crash and my penny glasses were gone. But the back pack had stayed.

Did I mention I was a vegan too? Now meat, well flesh, is my only appetite. I can't communicate but I hear the song of Mother Nature in my head. Her plan for the extermination of the human race and when the last one dies, the entire zombie nation will simply lie down on the nearest grassy patch and decompose. We will help fertilise the land again.

It's pretty clear my life and undeath, if you will, was always to follow the path of saving the environment but the zombie part never really figured into the equation to be honest. You'd think it would be the perfect dream for me, complete symmetry knowing that I achieved what my life had been about. The Earth will survive despite all we did to it and that's good.

You'd think I would be happy with that as a lifelong environmentalist. Mother Nature would thrive. Human cities would be reclaimed by the plants and trees. There'd be very few mammals though; we sort of eat them too.

Ever wondered about that guys? Why we eat anything that moves except fish and insects and birds? Well, the bird one is obvious. We can barely grab humans or dogs without sufficient quantities never mind something that can sit in a tree and give us one of those looks that only a bird can do.

It's very simple. You know humans taste like chicken to us but we see only an infrared thermal signature. Well, it's the same with any mammal whether it be a horse, cat or a rat. All we see is the hot spot and go for it. Animals taste more like barbecued chicken as opposed to breast of chicken but chicken's chicken.

I do remember actually coming across a hen coop on a farm in the countryside but don't ask me when because time means nothing to us. I could have been walking for months for all I know. The other zombies with me tore the wire apart and we got tore into the chickens. Yep, that was a real chicken day. Chicken is chicken is chicken no matter what the species now. So, I'm living my life's goal. I'm saving the planet thanks to good old MN. And you know what? Mother Nature is a twisted old bitch.

A real crone straight out of the fairy tales that brings chaos to the world. She doesn't swan about fields with flower chains hanging from her neck, barefoot, in a really beautiful, flowing green dress. No, she sits back and watches humans suffer, even the ones that fought her corner all these years. All she had to do was release some sort of virus and wipe us out or bring a meteor down ala the dinosaurs. A simple plan with a simple solution. But no. It's like being betrayed by your best friend or sister. You ask why and get no reply. I'm actually hurt and degraded because I feel she singled me out for this. What greater insult to a vegan than to make them eat meat?

Thing is we don't even really eat flesh. We just chomp on it but never swallow. We have no control over throat muscles so we can't actually swallow. What we are doing is breaking it down so it rots quicker on the ground for the big Momma herself. Even better, the scavengers and the carrions scoop it from any concrete/tarmac/tiled surfaces and take it to woods etc where it can begin decomposing. She has it worked out to a T. What a complete bitch.

I suppose the only upside is that we are not aware of time passing which is good because it would drive you insane. We are trapped in our own bodies until the last human falls. I don't want that to happen. I've seen survivors take down zombies all over and part of me is crying out for them to do that for me so this can be over. I hope there are enough humans remaining to wipe us out and screw her plan up. And you know what? I think there just might be.

All I wanted was to save the world on my terms, not someone else's. I recall the people who took our leaflets without acknowledging them and I'm envious now. They were doing the right thing, going home to their families, living their lives. I was fighting for the world for the day I could have a family but Big Momma bitch has taken even that away from me. I was a soldier fighting a war for her and all the while she had this zombie shit planned as her final solution. There's no gratitude. No thumbs up. More tits up now.

But if there is such a thing as reincarnation or some way to come back as a human, I will pollute and litter the bitch up like she has never seen. My advice to you out there?

Kill as many of us as you can. Run if you can't to fight another day. Reclaim the planet for humankind. Regardless of whatever mistakes we made, we can change and learn. Fight the war against her guys and make it count for something unlike mine.

CROSS DRESSER ZOMBIE

The day the zombies rose will be remembered for just that; the rise of the zombies.

But for me, it was the day I could shed my skin and be the person I had always wanted to be for the entire world to see.

Just like everything else in my life, the timing sucked. Now my undead ass is walking the city without even the dignity of the heels I had chosen. I think my ankle is twisted though or I have a cracked toe. Now when I walk all six foot of my bulky frame is up and down like an Amsterdam tart. Add to that my wig is twisted on my head so the right side of my face has a permanent auburn covering. I look like Frankenstein's frigging granny. Instead of becoming a butterfly, I became something that was slapped up the face with a frying pan.

But I digress. Let me start at the start which also became my end.

First up, my name is Frank Malone resident of Belfast all my life. I have never married but shagged my way round the town. I came close a couple of times but never bothered. I play darts, love a pint and the craic with the lads. I've a hard man rep, afraid of no one and would knock the bollix clean out of anyone. When people look at me they see the black leather jacket, baldy head and the gold chains. They see a hard man. But when I look in the mirror I see someone else entirely. No one knows, no one has ever even suspected not even my ma and she's sharp as a pin. At forty-six, it's not a big deal these days but it reduces me to jelly if anyone found out.

I like wearing women's clothes. Simple as that.

Maybe I've always been this way. I'm not gay nor have any intentions of getting the three piece out and a gas oven put in. I like shagging women but the feel of those clothes on my body just makes me so happy. When I look at myself in the mirror in full get up, it's my world. Problem is, that world has never left my bedroom or mouth. My ma stays out of my room because I bung her the money for bingo four times a week so I can become Majella. Those times when she isn't there are heaven and I can try different outfits without fear of her walking in. Privacy not a priority for mother as most of you will probably identify with.

I'm not sure when it became part of me but it was always there. I never looked at my ma's catalogue in the same way as she did. I flicked through the women's section and wondered what it would feel like to be dressed as they were. It looked so elegant and comfortable that I yearned for it. The first time I remember putting on a pair of knickers was when I was shagging Fiona Fisher. I was staying at her place and been dating for a few months. As I said, I'm not gay. I love sex with women and Fiona was a goer. She would lick my bald head when she got excited and all I could picture was her slipping a wig on my bonnet. Anyway, I got up for a piss and was standing there trying to hit the side so she couldn't her the crash of urine on water. (It sounds louder somehow at three n the morning.)

As I washed my hands, I saw a knickers and a bra drying on the radiator.

My heart raced. My breathing quickened. I slipped her knickers on first and stared at myself in the mirror barely containing my excitement. It felt right. It felt normal to me. I slipped on her bra next and couldn't believe the rush I felt. This was what I had been missing all my life. Quickly and reluctantly I put them back on the radiator as I found them and was so turned on went back into the bed and woke her up for another round.

It was easier after that. I could go into shops and pretend I was buying for the girlfriend but all six foot of bulky me couldn't wait to get home and try them on. I even started going to the gym to slim down and my secret stash grew quickly but lived in the back of the wardrobe. But I couldn't bring myself to go public for fear of shame and ridicule.

I almost told Fiona but finished with her instead. I couldn't afford anyone finding out. Like a teenager discovering masturbation, Majella stayed a bedroom secret behind a locked door.

But it was like a pressure cooker inside me, bursting to get out. I wanted nothing more than to walk down the street and show the world who I really was. So I decided to do exactly that.

The big day began in the changing rooms of a well known clothing store. I went into the men's changing rooms. My heart was racing as I opened my bag. This was it.

All I could think about were the throngs of people I waked through to get here. Would they notice or would I melt into the crowds? But in the end it didn't matter. All that mattered was that Majella was about to go public. I ran a hand over the outfit I'd chosen and I was elated. Red jacket with open neck blouse with knee length skirt to match. Black stockings with a shiny black pair of heels. Necklace with a thin gold chain rounded it off nicely as I applied my make up.

I remember staring in the mirror, heart pumping as I began to strip. Piece by piece, Majella formed right in front of me and when I bowed my head to put my wig on, I paused. I shut my eyes before raising my head. I nervously opened my eyes, slower than I should have and looked in the mirror. I couldn't have been happier as I looked myself up and down. I never looked better even if I did say so myself.

Suddenly there was a searing pain in my calf. Half in shock and half in horror, I let out a scream of pain and swore like a trooper in a most unladylike fashion. As I stumbled, I saw some bitch on her front had crawled under the curtain and took a chunk out of my leg. I fell back trying to shake her off. Unhuman eyes looked at me as she drooled and snapped trying to chew on me. I don't know whether it was fear or adrenalin or what but I somehow managed to kick her in the face which for my size and cramped space was a bloody miracle. I punched and kicked for all my worth, my stiletto sinking into the cow's skull. I saw her gasp and slump forward before I passed out.

I don't know how long had passed but when I came to, it was like waking from the hangover from hell. My tongue felt like a shrivelled sausage roll and I could only make guttural noises. I thought to myself that's weird as I struggled to my shoeless feet. I felt shaky at best and lurched from the changing cubicle almost tripping over the corpse with the stiletto hat I made for her. Bitch, I thought to myself. My mind was fuzzy, strange urges filling it, propelling me towards the exit. Part of me was saying to get my heels on to complete my outfit but I was moving out of hunger. I barely noticed the shop was wrecked and blood stained the floors and walls. All I knew was I could smell human flesh and how like chicken it seemed. I needed it, I craved it and there was nothing I wouldn't do to have it. A myriad of questions flashed through my mind. Where were the shoppers? Why wasn't I being noticed? A six foot man in women's clothes should have drawn curt sniggers and hidden laughs even in this day and age and yet...nothing. There was fire and screaming. There was whimpering and munching. The street was a canvas of fear and chaos and here I was, now in full Majella mode, lurching amid it like a virgin in a whore house. I felt like crying. This was supposed to be my big day, my coming out. This was the day when the world would meet Majella and my secret life would shred away like cobwebs in the wind. It was supposed to be red carpet and fireworks, a statement that I had a rightful place in the world where I didn't hide in shadow or run from phobic attacks. I was Majella, ready or not, here I come bitches!

But instead I was unnoticed, just another shoddy figure amid the other bloody shuffling shoddy figures, all driven by the need for chicken. In stead of shouting from the rooftops, all I could do was gurgle like those off the telly. My outfit is ruined by the way which I ain't happy about and my tights are laddered like nobody's business. The event that was to be Majella has been reduced to nothing special. All I can think about apart from chicken, is I should have had the balls to come out as Majella years before. All my fears of being ridiculed and shamed because I wanted to wear women's clothes were dust now. They seemed pointless, a curse that kept me from being who I truly was. How ironic that now as a zombie, I can finally walk the streets as I always wanted to.

And not one person can ever take notice. I'm just ordinary Joe/Majella Bloggs. I'm just a rotting hulk of regret now, trapped in this body until all the chicken in the world has been eaten. If by some miracle, humans survive, I really hope the new generation learn to grab life by the horns and just go with it. Do what you want today kids: don't let anyone stop you. Fear of other people's opinions kept me back and now here I am – cross dressing zombie. Don't be like me: live life. Savour every moment before all the chicken runs out.

So if you ever see a zombie, don't look at us just as the undead. We're not, well we are but we're people too inside inflicted by this condition, helpless at what we do because of a trick of nature.

And I suppose that if you read all our stories, you'll see there's a very real truth to life: never judge by appearances.

TOTEMS

by Rob Thomas

This is the story. It isn't my story. It was given to me in a dream to tell, so by obligation to the dream, I'm telling it.

Long ago, when the great forest covered all this place and the first people spent their days busy under the sun and sat at night by the fire under the stars, Raven gave voice to the eldest of all the animals to teach lessons to the first peoples.

Now, seeing this, the evil one grew jealous of the talking animals. In shadow he brooded as the first people listened to the lessons taught by the eldest of all the animals. Attention was not given to him.

Loathing the choice Raven made, the evil one decided to destroy all the animals given voice.

Now bright-eyed Raven knew the evil one's heart and would not have his purpose undermined, so Raven turned all the grandparent animals into totems and gave them to the children of the first people.

So when the evil one set out under cover of night to accomplish the deed that had consumed his heart, he could not find the eldest animals. Scour the forest as he might, their presence was lost to him. He could only find children playing with carved toys.

These he ignored and passed the children by. As a cold howling wind he scoured the great forest, but to no avail. Thwarted he returned to his dark place brooding, but Raven smiled. His purpose had not been undone.

In dreams the animals given voice still teach the lessons of Raven, saved by children, turned to totems. The lessons learned in dreams. As I said, this isn't my story. It was given to me in a dream to tell. And so by obligation to the dream I have told it.

GRIM

by Alex S. Johnson

Thomas Marcuse surveyed the books on the shrink's shelves. They had ponderous titles, and reflected the county doctor's interests. Dr. Gonzales, who was doing his residency at the clinic now, shared a few of Thomas's own tastes.

He enjoyed the revolving door aspect of the county clinic: service was consistent, every new doctor he saw added enough of their own personal touch without disturbing the thrust of the official narrative; and he got his meds.

Which would be enough for most clients, and indeed for Thomas, if he didn't have an additional reason for being there. One certain to fry brains to a crisp if he showed a glimpse of it, which is why he kept that reason tucked away—although for anybody with the verve and insight to catch it, Thomas was ready to admit all on the spot. Just that nobody would think to ask; or if they did, the question would automatically raise flags—on the wrong side of the doctor/client divide—that would be hard for any mental health professional to lower.

Psychiatry was a game Thomas enjoyed playing. It appealed to his sense of intellectual perversity. How far could you push it? Under what conditions could you admit the inadmissible—spike the drink in plain sight, so to speak; ravish the mistress of the house, in daylight, with witnesses?

Two hot-button issues determined the difference between outpatient status and an involuntary hold. Danger to self, danger to others.

Thomas was both. But it wasn't personal. In his own—larger, symbolic, holistic way, he too was a professional. He had his hand firmly on the lever, the throttle, what you will. Only his joystick was dipped in gore, slippery with blood.

Today along with his long, lanky blond hair—still pushing the slumming rock star dream in his forties—black denim jeans and scuffed tennis shoes, Thomas wore a T-shirt he had owned since he lived near an area of northeast L.A. called the Arroyo Seco. The cotton T had a black background emblazoned with cartoon stars and the figure of Death wearing a cowboy hat and playing an oversized guitar. Dr. Gonzales was interested in the T-shirt, asked questions. Answering truthfully, Thomas revealed he'd bought the T-shirt at a Latino bookstore that appealed to the vital, emerging youth culture in the region, more interested in punk rock than protest, fucking than fighting for their rights, unless it was Rage Against the Machine laying down the rhythm. Actually, that wasn't quite just. Thomas had come to terms with his wife's defection a long time ago. Now he was back in the Central Valley, struggling with the fallout.

"Yes," said Dr. Gonzales, excited that Thomas recognized the volume of Carl Jung laid out on the doctor's desk. "The archetypes. Very deep stuff."

"Indeed," said Thomas. He coughed.

Dr. Gonzales regarded his client through rimless glasses. His dark hair was cut short, but not anally so. Thomas liked him. He liked most of the practitioners that came through the clinic. And he especially liked that now, unlike when he was in his twenties and first recognized the need to address his issues, such as they were, the field of psychiatry had opened up. Now you could actually talk about things like archetypes and mythology without the shrink handing you a script for an antipsychotic, along with a slip of paper for another medication to deal with the side effects, such as tardive dyskinesia—or, in layman's terms, involuntary grimaces and nervous tics. When Thomas was an undergrad, the psychiatrist at the university student health center wouldn't write him a script for antidepressants precisely because he wanted to talk about the meta-language of psychiatry—the symbolism of the patient and the doctor, the priest and the petitioner. That was too far out for the 80s, and betokened crazy for Cocoa Puffs. Thomas thought it was ironic that psychiatry's insistence on strict physiological origins for subtle conditions of the soul created the monsters it saw—and very little had improved since the middle ages, when mad people were considered living embodiments of Hell on Earth.

Over the years, Thomas essayed ventures into those deep, dark, turbulent waters, and he'd seen a succession of clinicians show greater understanding, sympathy and appreciation for psychology. A vast relief to Thomas, who had always felt the patient's thought about his own illness had an important place in the discourse between him and the doctor.

"So, that's about it," said Gonzales, handing Thomas the prescription for Zoloft. Along the way, the conversation had glanced over the family portraits on the doctor's desk. They'd talked about Gonzales' son and his passion for paint ball, their cabin in the Sierras near a lake, his wife's career in nursing, even how they'd met. At the very end came those two questions, which in almost every instance with the shrinks at the county clinic were quickly disposed of—formalities. No, he wasn't interested in killing himself or any kind of self-harm, and of course, Thomas joked, he was too obviously a homicidal maniac to ever get away with it, even if he wanted to. He didn't always make this joke, depending as it did on split-second timing, smuggling the crack into the flow of conversation, but this time he chanced it, and Gonzales whimsical smile caused Thomas to glow inside.

When he reached the street, the scripts for antidepressants carefully filed in his wallet, Thomas decided to choose the day's victims randomly rather than using the more industrious, methodical approach he generally favored. When the vast cosmic forces chose you as the Reaper du jour, you could approach the job in several ways, but Thomas enjoyed a strictly classical protocol touched with just a stripe of aesthetics. Life had to be plucked and pruned to make way for new life; such was the way of the universe, and the official function he served.

The young woman behind the counter at the pharmacy couldn't be older than twenty-three. Thomas knew immediately from her nervous mannerisms and confusion with his order that she would welcome the solace he alone could provide, the sweet care of a lover combined with the efficient competence of a master mechanic.

Besides, which, they never felt a thing.

SACRED MONSTERS

by Alex S. Johnson

"Maybe you should wear the glasses," says the Supervisor.

"Sure," I say. I take the wraparound cardboard shades and slot them over my nose and ears. They look like old school 3D, cheap and disposable, with white cardboard frames, blue and red plastic lenses. "Well, there's also built-in enhancements," he adds.

Naturally.

We belong to a certain generation. You keep your cool, and if something sets up warning bells in your head, you pretend as long as you can that the threat lies elsewhere. It is essential never to betray your actual state of mind--unless you have the power of negotiation. I thought I might, but there were questions—always questions—and as long as these exist, I wait.

Walking along the crisscrossed catwalk above the vats, the walkways running like conveyor belts for people, like swatches of fabric, we are integers in a vast sea of numbers. We are uniforms plumped with protoplasm—no more or less important than the air vents, the bio-flesh switches, the grids. Squirts of steam issue from the dark, bubbling waters. I see a few of the creatures swimming.

"They are outstandingly beautiful," I say, which feels awkward and obvious. Surprisingly, the Supervisor agrees without betraying any sense of my utterance as trite or anything other than a frank—I'm being honest here—expression of my thoughts. Because they really are something. They remind me of John Keats.

"And dangerous," he adds. His silver-blue hair is cut grimly close to his skull. Berlin is his designer city of choice, obviously. Our suits are identical, like metal postcards from outer space. My hair is closer to blue-black, like my eyes. His might be purple. I try to avoid looking directly at them. They might tell me the truth.

Then I remember—it's my Imposter Syndrome acting up—that the Supervisor has a stake in my assessment as well. His people are watching how I respond, and my people are watching how his people crunch that data. Juvenal was right: nobody watches the watchers.

The Supervisor asks me if I'd like to interact with them.

"Sure."

As I haul myself down the sinuous synthmetal ladder after him, I wonder if it's a trick. A set-up. I can already smell the perfume, hints of tangerine and lilac. They summon a garden from my youth, a fountain, and a girl.

They are gorgeous beyond measure, up close. Now I feel better about my spontaneous outburst earlier. You can't really touch them with language. And spastic gyrations look silly.

The monsters are sexless, neither male nor female. Instead of sex, they have biological nodals. Ports that open from your eyes, your nerves, your humming senses.

They are more like music. Really, nothing exists with which to compare them.

The Supervisor says what's on both of our minds. We're very close in age—I think he's about two years older than I am, actually. When we were growing up, even, the thought of such rapturous unions between biology and machines, the synthesis and next logical stage of nanotechnology, myth and the digital rave-rupture, strained the imagination. Now it seems odd we weren't building the monsters—the Sirens, whatever—sooner.

"But we didn't know," I say, formulaic.

An oval face on a long stalk, its features half-sheathed with a shock of pink hair, swivels by me. I might touch them. There's no warning signs, no cautions, and I can't read the Supervisor's face.

Am I being tested for an upgrade?

Is this a mating thing?

Or, all other things being equal, did the Supervisor call up to my office to welcome me on board the new, experimental department, as stated, simple as that?

I feel the irresistible urge to touch the creature. A surge of emotion, something warm, soft and vaporous as the mists from the tanks, rises up in me.

Music *is* the secret, and the key. We'd been looking in the wrong place all this time.

I try to place my hand against the creature's neck. The Supervisor just watches. He looks down at the wafer-thin grey console that hangs from a leather strap from his neck. I consider removing my glasses, to see if the lenses were affecting me. Finally, I take them off and fold them up in my pocket.

Rather than enhancing, the glasses have been diffusing and muffling my vision.

I know now what she is: Lamia. The teeth.

The eyes—seductive, alien, vampire.

Sister. Lover. Friend.

I slip down into the water. My skin turns an instant pink. Hers is a translucent metal.

I'm not anything to her. I'm lunch.

Behind me, the Supervisor speaks in hushed tones into his radio. Pain shrieks through my nerves. And drowning—it's worse than they say.

Every cell in my body screams for oxygen. But something—her gaze, her hunger, her desire—holds me down. I sense that she will eat when my flavor peaks—a nanosecond before my demise.

If I can only hold on...but for what?

She rises before me in the tank as I sink down. Her body is somewhat like an eel, a snake, a worm, but only in the way of a supple quality otherwise impossible to speak of.

I see the Supervisor's face ripple and warp. He's abandoned the pretense this was anything but a feeding. The figure on his console resembles Beethoven.

Efficiency—he does my job better than I. The creature is hungry. Whatever assets I possess, she will squeeze from me and secrete as an oily solution. The Supervisor will get his promotion.

A very neat package indeed. It is not he, or she, or even the situation, that is monstrous.

Still, as her jaws close over me, I can't help but feeling like the whole thing might have been handled with more humanity.

And that's about it.

MOTHERS OF THE DISAPPEARED

by Dean M. Drinkel

For Romain

"Speak! Shall you not bring back those things sublime? Return the raptured hour?" - The Lake Alphonse de Lamartine

"Our love is good because it is impossible." - Frédéric Beigbeder

The voices.

They were being a right royal pain in the derriere tonight.

Nag. Nag. Nag.

They just wouldn't shut up.

But when the one true Voice sang and the subsequent carnage began, the others fell deathly silent.

Dissipating into the darkness whence they came.

***

Hunger.

Blood.

Power.

He felt exalted.

He was a god.

She would call him a monster but there was nothing he could do about that – everyone was entitled to their own opinion.

***

Admiring his handiwork he used his elongated talons to smear the viscera, the bloodied offal, over his hunched body, paying particular attention to his face. How he loved what was once the living (ironic obviously) spread far and wide under his nostrils – the aroma such an aphrodisiac.

When he was satiated, he flung the carcass across the room.

Howled with laughter when it splattered against the wall.

***

After all that pressure: more than one sigh of relief

At last. A weekend away.

Away from her.

The past weeks had been hellish but now she had the chance to head into the country. Spend some downtime with Mathilde.

Forget everything that had happened, everything that had been dragging her down.

Got to get away.

It wasn't her mother's fault, she knew that really – it wasn't her mother's fault she was old, decrepit, that she was her only family now, but boy did she never let up. On and on and on and on and on.

And the book – that novel...so damn good but there was something about it that lingered in her brain, made her a little nauseous if she was honest. She knew it was going to be a best-seller for sure but it did fuck with your head. Left a sour taste in the mouth. Made her feel dirty.

She needed fresh air.

She needed her best friend.

Odd though. She hadn't seen nor heard from Mathilde in a while. No letters or phone calls either. Not even an email. Her work as an illustrator could sometimes be more arduous than that of a publisher, perhaps then it was just due to work-load. That's what she hoped anyway.

Tough gig for sure, yet it had its rewards obviously: the riches, the grounds, the gardens, the chateau, the thatched roof, the open fire – the staircases...Jesus, those staircases.

Heaven. On earth.

Literally to die for.

Thinking of the pleasures which awaited her, Carole threw her bags in the back of the battered Beetle and ignoring the old woman staring down at her through the window with that constant look of disdain chiselled into her face, she got in the car, indicated right and pulled away.

***

Blessed.

Special.

The Holy One.

The Master.

The Voice.

Never knew exactly when his Deity would call him; could be any time. It wasn't a problem though, whenever it came, he would be ready. Actually, he was glad of the company. Life had been pretty lonely of late. Bouncing around the walls of this large country house...

...yes, there were other voices if he listened but they bored him with their constant noise. They would drain him if he wasn't careful...

...but he didn't have time for weakness. He had to be strong.

There was important work to be done.

He rubbed at the words scorched into his arm.

Milton.

I give not heaven for lost. From this descent celestial virtues rising, will appear more glorious and more dread than from no fall, and trust themselves to fear no second fate.

With his un-gloved claws he traced the words, felt their meaning. He could feel himself getting excited and whilst he tried to curb his urges, he slipped and one talon dug deep into his flesh. He left it there for several seconds before slowly retracting it. Exquisite pain. The blood dripped – he suckled upon the wound and wept. Not tears of sadness, no: jubilation. He closed his eyes and reflected, he had a moment of solitude, so where was the harm?

The Voice had been with him since his Awakening. His sixteenth birthday. His friend from school had stayed over the night several weeks previously (his dad hadn't even noticed) and showed him something that seemed so pleasurable, so exciting, so forbidden. Scared until his birthday to try it on himself - whilst his hand enjoyed that hanging lump of flesh between his legs and yes he would admit he felt some semblance of pleasure, it was only physical; his mind and spirit were dormant and the vacuum that swirled around his head invited the Voice to enter more or less as he ejaculated and he was overcome with feelings of such a black, black void of grief.

At first it was only a whisper.

Just his name.

Simplicity.

That's all it took. And he was smitten.

After that initial contact and as the days passed the Voice became stronger and stronger. Vincent played less with his friends and more with himself, desiring the ultimate orgasm where the physical and spiritual would merge – getting close on several occasions but never quite reaching the rapture. Only slightly disappointed however, because he knew one day it would come.

Eventually, the Voice told Vincent about his Purpose here on earth. The Grand Plan. The end of man in his present form.

Complete Transformation from one sentient being to another.

And with that whisper, his first instruction. Clichéd perhaps, but important if he was to succeed: he had to kill his father.

Which wasn't as difficult as he first anticipated.

Now, sitting in front of the roaring fire and looking back fondly on those days, he had seemed such a sissy. A coward. But then of course he only had conventional weapons at his disposal, he hadn't been graced with the tools he had now. He hadn't begun his own transformation. His father had fought back and at one point it seemed he might actually win the day but no, Vincent was triumphant!

His mother, she had died years before in childbirth. His father blamed him. Obviously. Every single minute of every single hour of every single day he reminded him of the fact with that curled lip, that snarl...those eyes...those fucking evil eyes...

...what an excuse for a man anyway...his father...who did nothing but sit at home, drink and watch porn films all day. One hand down his pants. Such a fucking layabout, whose main purpose it appeared was to yell at the boy he held responsible for the death of his wife.

It didn't matter to him that Vincent didn't have a mother now either; it was more the fact that there wasn't a woman to clean up after him, to cook his meals, to be a home for his cock.

Base terms.

Base facts.

Just when he thought all was lost though, the Voice offered Vincent a deal. It was simple. He took it. Why not? He didn't have anything to lose did he? Definitely not in his present situation.

He was going nowhere.

After (and on account of the noise the neighbours had heard) the police found Vincent in the kitchen, in the large cupboard chewing on one of his papa's thigh bones. The meat was succulent, salty and tasty. There was blood all over the apartment. Most of course on the bedroom walls, his father's head plumped up by the pillows. A surprised expression on his face. Genitals forced down his throat.

Vincent thought that it might have been a one off but interestingly though, it didn't stop there – the Voice demanded more and more of him...vagabonds, strangers, people he met on the internet, a teacher, a priest, a nurse...

...the thing was, and this was a little weird, as time went on, the Voice wasn't solitary.

It had been joined by another: the voice of his father, begging for his son's forgiveness; Vincent ignored the half-hearted pleas, it was only the drink talking – he could hear the words slurred: "Son, I love you. You are all I have left. I was a mons...no I was monstrous to you, forgive me."

Vincent didn't quite get it at first, thought it was just his mind playing tricks but this, it seemed, was actually part of the deal. When you snuffed out the physical part of the person that wasn't the end of them – oh no, their voice, their soul was consumed by the killer, stored inside his brain. He felt their pain, lived their pleasures. He knew so much now. And not all of it interesting (was everyone's lives really that boring?).

Of course, those were the early days when he didn't quite know how to control them or how to control himself - a lot of water had flowed under the bridge since then; here he was almost twenty years later, released from prison, released on his own cognisance. If only they knew what was going on in that (pretty) head of his.

The authorities kept him under surveillance at first because they didn't completely trust him and because he had no living family – he didn't actually have a home to go to. They stuck him in the remand centre on his release, and then came the half-way houses. The Voice helped him through those difficult times and the days when he was allowed out (though not too far from the centre or house of course) he was able to Transform into the real Vincent – it always surprised him how he was able to rack up such a large volume of victims without raising an eyebrow. Sure, once or twice he almost got caught – but that was it exactly: almost.

So obviously now, quite a conversation was building up inside his cranium – white noise; he tried to ignore them and sometimes he was successful, sometimes however, he wasn't.

He imagined his mind-palace as a large black velvet draped room. His Master, the one true Voice sitting on his golden throne, the others (and there were so many he'd lost count) supplicant, bowing...and him: Vincent? He was in the centre somewhere trying to control everything. Trying to keep the equilibrium. The status quo.

***

The sun in decline. Carole hoped that Mathilde was in because she wasn't in the mood for hanging around for long and she needed the bathroom desperately. She was dog-tired and the drive down had taken a lot longer than previously for some reason. She wanted to get inside, collapse in front of the fire and open the nearest bottle of Bordeaux (as well as emptying her bladder!). In their University days they had both quite a name for themselves around campus for their vast intakes of booze and getting into trouble. Nothing had really changed in the passing years, she supposed, except for the furrows and crow lines on their faces and she sighed, a little more responsibility - as much as they fought against it. With great power came great responsibility she had heard.

When Carole pulled into the grounds, several surprises jumped out at her from when she was last there: the gardens seemed wilder and the roof, Mathilde's pride and joy, was dilapidated. Bare patches here and there which needed immediate attention otherwise they would cause a lot of (expensive) damage to the fabric of the building. What was going on?

Once out of the Beetle, Carole tried the front door (knocked twice and rung the doorbell) but when she realised nobody was coming, she tried the handle but that was locked and having a quick look around, there was no obvious hiding place for a spare key.

She went around the back but that was locked too and the shutters firmly closed over the windows.

Carole knocked on the kitchen-door several times but again no answer. There was probably a way into the chateau somehow but she wasn't dressed for shimming up drainpipes.

On the drive down, she had passed one of those fancy country restaurants a couple of kilometres back, knowing Mathilde she was probably there right now, holding court with the local sycophants, getting smashed on the wine she loved so much. They'd been there a couple of times together in the past, so it was as good as place as any to start. Home from home.

Back at her car, Carole found a scrap of paper and pen in her glove compartment, jotted down a brief message, stuck it through the letterbox. Within seconds she was in the Beetle and heading towards the restaurant.

***

Vincent had a splitting headache. He was having a nightmare with the voices and the last one which had recently joined the cacophony...Christ, she never shut the fuck up did she? No matter how hard he tried to ignore...she just droned on and on and on – most of it nonsensical bullshit as well.

What made it worse for him was that the voices combined were like the waves of a violent ocean: one minute they screamed, then they whispered, screamed, whispered...on and on and on and on (yes, just like that bloody woman). Some might have found that pleasurable – but not him, not after all this time.

As the years had passed he wasn't sure which was worse, the screams or the whispers. With his Master's help he had been able to keep the balance but he knew their time was close when, if he let his guard down too much, they would be victorious and drive him ultimately around the bend. They'd turn on him if they had the chance, and snuff out him out. He'd become a zombie, pliable, totally under their control.

Death from the inside. An implosion of cells.

They were like that, those bastards – didn't they see that he had done them a favour by killing and releasing them? Obviously not. Some people never saw what was right under their noses.

After a couple of hours concentration and meditation he managed an element of calmness inside his skull and so, he prepared himself. He went to the bathroom, stripped off and stepped under the shower. As the hot water cascaded down his body, washing away the stains, he wished he could wash away the voices once and for all. He knew it wouldn't be that easy however, and for now he had to live with them or at least settle for some kind of co-existence.

His dick hardened, so he knew what that meant: his Master, the Voice, obviously had a new instruction to impart.

He ignored the ringing coming from somewhere in the house and got on with the job in hand.

***

"I'm sorry, do you have any coins for the phone, my cell doesn't have any coverage."

Carole was at the bar, there was no sign of Mathilde in the restaurant, so she'd ordered a wine, tried her phone and had thought all was lost until she'd spied an old pay-phone which miraculously still worked. She'd also rushed to the toilet (outside for goodness sake!) because there was only so long she could cross her legs.

"Sure, what do you want?" the cute boy behind the counter asked.

She took a five Euro note from her purse, handed it to him.

"Cool," he smiled as he went to his till – he returned a couple of moments later, placed a tower of coins next to her glass.

She grabbed a couple from the top, went to the phone, dialled Mathilde's number and let it ring for a while but there was no answer. She went back to her stool.

"No luck?" the boy asked.

"Sadly not...been one of those days."

"Yeah?"

"I've driven down from Paris to see my friend. She lives in the small chateau not far from here. Mathilde Collier? She's been in here a few times. I have too in the past but it was different then. At least I think it was."

"Refit. Sure I know Mathilde, the illustrator? I haven't seen her for a few months...she was quite a regular when I first joined, back in April...think last time I saw her was...June...maybe July at a push."

It was now September.

"July? That was probably the last time I spoke to her too!

I've been so busy with a big novel I'm publishing...a young writer from Cannes...called Past By One that I haven't had time for much else – not sure if it's your thing but you should check it out. I'll give you a card." She searched through her bag (ignoring the object her mother had told her to always carry and though she had refused, there it was, still in the bottom of her bag!), found a business card, handed it over. The boy pocketed it without giving it a second glance. Carole had the verbals (why was she telling this complete stranger about the novel?) and she hadn't even had a drink yet – she tried to be more serious for a second. "July...wow." The way she said it: she realised she had failed the seriousness test.

The barman nodded, walked away. As Carole sipped her wine she watched him. He spoke to some old timers at the far end of the bar, then she noticed out of the corner of her eye that he was searching through a pile of papers behind him. When he returned, he was pointing to a newspaper photograph.

"We had a big re-launch party here in June. Lots of local dignitaries. That's Mathilde isn't it?" He put the paper down on the bar next to her. Carole picked it up. Gave it a quick glance.

"Yeah, that's her." You couldn't miss the woman, front and centre of the photograph. Smiling. Beaming. Looked like she was having the time of her life.

Slightly odd perhaps, was that there was a man standing next to her who had his arm around her shoulders. He was smiling. Odd because Mathilde had never mentioned a significant other in her life.

"Do you know who that guy is?" Carole asked as she handed the paper back.

The boy studied it for a couple of moments before shaking his head. "No. Sorry. But ask around the bar, quite a few of the regulars in today are in that photo. I know this is going to sound stupid but you did try her home right? You know what these kind of people are like. Work unsociable hours. Sleep all day, come out at night." He laughed at his own joke because obviously he was also making reference to himself.

He was cute, Carole thought but then shook her head, as much as she was beginning to like him she was more than double his age and he probably hadn't even given her a second glance. She didn't want the embarrassment she just knew would come if she asked him out. She had a friend, an English writer, who was totally in love with a younger guy, she really loved him and he probably did love her back in some capacity but if she wasn't careful she was going to make such a fool of herself...

"I know how she feels," she whispered.

"Oh," the boy picked up a tray of freshly washed glasses, began to dry each in turn. "You paint as well?"

"She's an illustrator. I'm a publisher, that's why I mentioned the novel. Same sort of hours."

"Right, right...the guy from Cannes?"

"Yes," Carole smiled. "He's quite a talent. Probably make quite a name for himself if he sticks with it."

"I've never been there."

Which seemed the perfect answer. Carole continued to thinly smile, concluding that whilst the boy was cute, he didn't have much going on in that head of his and perhaps any talents he had lay...elsewhere.

The barman finished drying his glasses; put them away on their respective shelves. "I'd better get on, feel free to ask around though. If you need a place to stay let me know; we've got a couple of rooms we rent out. Reasonable rates too."

Carole looked down the bar, she felt a little self-conscious and although she had been here a couple of times before she didn't think she recognised anyone. "Thanks. I'll give it a little while before making that decision." Why was she speaking so strangely – yeah, she knew, she had a crush on the kid and that was scrambling her vocabulary.

"Fine, you want another drink?"

"What?" Carole looked down, her glass was empty. Damn. "Why not? Might as well try and enjoy myself."

"Great." He got her a fresh glass and filled it.

"Tell you what," she sighed when he handed it to her. "Make up that room will you, just in case."

"Sure. The name's Julien by the way. You can call me Jules." He held out his hand. She took it, gave it a gentle shake. "Nice to meet you. Carole."

***

Vincent admired himself in the mirror.

He was excited and had received some quite unexpected news.

The Voice told him that only one more soul was needed for complete Transformation. The future, his future, was about to be revealed. Tonight was the night. He had been waiting twenty odd years for this very moment. Even the other voices were quiet for once. Maybe after all their shouting, screaming and cajoling, they knew they had to let him concentrate. Tonight, everything was going to change.

At 21.00 Vincent took a walk.

Yes, he was a little nervous, and whilst that was to be expected, he was also so damn...energized.

Nothing would go wrong.

***

Carole was sitting at one of the smaller tables in the bar area. After those first few glasses, she'd felt famished so had followed Jules' advice and had taken several plates of Tapas which filled the gap. For now anyway. She'd also had three, four more wines and was starting to feel...jolly.

The alcohol had also given her enough courage to talk to one or two of the locals and though they had all professed their love and affection for the local celebrity, they admitted too that they hadn't seen Mathilde for a while. There were various explanations for this: she had moved away; she had run off with a guy; she had run off with a woman; she was a vampire; she was a witch but probably the most implausible: she had gone tee-total.

There was one other notion however, which once Carole had heard, she couldn't shift: maybe Mathilde had had an accident and living alone, had died in complete agony calling out for help?

At that idea, Carole felt hot and flustered. Maybe Mathilde was dead. No! No! Don't be stupid, she told herself, it was just the drink clouding her judgement and that she had spent a couple of hours (couple of hours? How long had she been there for god's sake? How many drinks had she actually had?) going through the galleys for that Past By One book on her phone – fucking creepy thing it was too. Intelligent yes, but fucking creepy all the same. It even had a monkey in it called Candide! Carole hated monkeys.

Seeing that one of the stools at the bar had come free, Carole dropped her phone into her handbag, rested it over her arm, picked up her glass and headed over. A guy bumped into her and mumbled something but she forgave him, he was probably as drunk as she was and anyway, she didn't want any trouble. She just wanted her friend.

Carole sat. There was a lot of noise coming from the restaurant. Disco music. Strobe lights flashing. Someone singing. People clapping. Fuck, karaoke – that was all she needed. She hated bad singing with a passion. She turned as she heard the door behind her bang close.

"Now there's a man with problems," she decided as she turned and stared right at him, probably for a little longer than she intended.

Whoever he was, he certainly did look troubled. Standing, rooted to the spot, frowning. Carole glanced away briefly, finished her wine but then moved slightly so she could make it less obvious that she was eyeing him up (she blushed – was that what she was trying to do...damn...a few drinks and she was getting horny? First the barman and now this guy?).

Despite whatever was causing those furrows on his forehead he did look kind of interesting. Hands in his pockets. Thirty-fiveish, she wagered. Very fancy clothes (i.e. expensive), which he wore well. Dark hair. Brown eyes. Tanned complexion. 175cm tall, 59kg in weight. Attractive. She took a guess at his job, A banker. An accountant. A spy?! She burst out at her own conclusions. Her imagination at times...

The more she stared...there was something familiar. Where did she know him from? She was sure she hadn't met him before...was he an author perhaps...damn, had she published him and now forgotten his name...this could be a nightmare if he recognised her...

Carole racked her addled brain...no, no, no...GOT IT...it was that man from the photo with Mathilde, wasn't it? She was positive. She had find out what he knew. She tried to sober up

– wasn't entirely sure she was capable of that.

As he headed towards the bar, she attempted to get his attention.

"Hey sir...sir...SIR! Yes, I'm talking to you!" Why was she being so LOUD?

A surprised look on his face as he realised she was shouting at him.

"Come here a moment will you?" Was she really that drunk? Well she was certainly acting as if she was – she needed to control herself. She must have seemed a right state.

"Hello," he replied somewhat strained as he joined her.

"You want a drink or something? You look as if you could do with one. What's the matter, girlfriend trouble?"

"No," he said rather too sharply, so added a brief smile. "Just a splitting headache. It's been with me over the years. Never really been able to shake it. We're old companions."

"Unforgivable." Her mouth slurred; her answer made no sense. She mentally counted to ten before speaking again. "Why the gloves?"

"Sorry..." More confusion.

She grabbed one of his hands. "The gloves. You're wearing gloves."

Did he redden? If he did it was fleeting. "Right. Force of habit really. Always wear them for this and that. You know the type of thing I mean."

Carole laughed nervously. "I'm sure I really don't." She coughed, her throat was dry. "You don't look the type."

"The type?"

"Yeah," she chuckled. "Labourer, engineer, painter, whatever." Carole signalled to Jules who put down his towel and came over. "What can I get you?"

"Two red wines. You'll be okay with wine right?"

The man nodded. "I suppose."

Carole repeated the order to Jules who was already pouring them.

***

The drinks flowed. The conversation stuttered. She asked him about Mathilde and mentioned the photo. He nodded as he knocked back his glass. She hadn't asked him his name and he hadn't told her. They were drinking their wine faster and faster, he ordered more. She talked about Mathilde again, he said that he remembered the photo but didn't know the woman, just put his arm around her when the photographer shouted: cheese. Carole changed the subject. Made it more casual. She was drunk but didn't believe him. Thought he was lying. Not sure why though. She'd get it out of him in the end, even if it meant she would have to sleep with him. Yeah, she was up for that. He smelt so nice. Hugo Boss she thought, her favourite. He was too good to be true. He had stayed quiet for a while and worried that she had offended him she started chatting about herself: she told him her name, her age, where she lived, what she did for a living. She told him about her mother (Christ, that proved she was smashed!) She told him about the guy down in Cannes. Yeah, she said so much about the guy down in Cannes, she hadn't realised she had such strong feelings for him. Fuck. Where had that come from? She tried to change the subject but spoke about the novel which was freaking her out so much. She spoke about the fucking monkey. He asked her if this guy she kept talking about and obviously had feelings for was her boyfriend. She thought about it for a while and said no, but she wished he was. They could have such a great life together, she knew it, even if he didn't see it. Yes, she was older, but fuck it, wasn't age just a number? FUCK! She wiped the tears from her eyes. She was thinking about the guy's cock now and getting her fingers, her lips around it. She shook her head. Stop. Stop. STOP! They had more drinks. The guy smiled at her. Put a hand on her shoulder and looked in her eyes. There seemed to be so much going on back there. He wanted the same as her. Forget that guy, he said, I'm here now aren't I. I can be your everything. Obviously, she forgot about Mathilde.

***

Vincent never removed his gloves. Even when he touched her shoulder. This was the one, he knew it, he had spent a long time searching for her. The Voice sung in his head. Synapses electric.

This was the one.

The final one.

He whispered into her ear.

***

"I'll be back in a second. I need to powder my nose." Carole laughed at what he had suggested in her ear. She wondered if the room was ready for her upstairs – she hoped the bed didn't creak. Did she have time for a shower? She needed to clean her teeth, wash out her mouth, too much wine...

***

The music thumps and pounds. Strobe light flash. Red. Blue. Yellow. Green. Outside toilet. Long walk. Made worse by how drunk she is. Weaving her way through the tables. Not always successful. People curse at her to be more careful. Someone is singing Bieber. Badly. English guy. Through the doors, into the night (when did that happen? Wasn't it daytime only a little while ago? Shit...) and the cold air hits her. She stumbles and falls. Someone picks her up. Not someone. Something. Something beside her. In front of her. In her clothes. In her body. Scratching at her soul. A creature. A man. A monster. Claws. Mouth. A snarl. A feeling. A dark brooding feeling. A creeping death. She is thrown against the wall, the wind is knocked out of her. She goes to scream but she is slapped once, twice, three times and she has no breath left to shout out. She wants to plead for mercy but knows it will be pointless.

"Master..." She hears and remembers she has her bag still on her arm.

The creature retreats and waits; she knows it will pounce again, bloodied, bruised, she searches in her bag and grabs hold of that object her mother always told her to carry because she would need it one day.

She never believed her mother.

Not until now.

***

"...Master," Vincent says. He holds onto his head, feels like he is going to explode. All the voices are screaming at him in unison to stop but of course he won't. They realise something is wrong. His trousers are around his ankles and he's hard but that's not the point of this. It's not rape. Not rape of the body anyway. He just needs the Voice to guide him through these next few moments and everything will be fine.

He has no choice in this after all. No point in fighting it.

Inevitable.

He grabs the girl with one hand. Screams. Howls. The music.

Piercing. Light.

With the other he grabs his dick.

The voices are warning him but when he realises why, it is far, far too late.

When they spoke about Transformation, but he wasn't expecting this.

***

She tears. She yanks. She cries. She bites. She slashes.

She has such power inside her.

She is a god.

He is a monster.

***

Confusion. The voices are falling silent one by one, they are leaving him. He falls to his knees as he holds onto his head trying to stem the flow.

What is happening?

What is happening?

Master...Master...

He is coming undone.

He is being unmade.

Something has gone wrong surely.

Is his Master angry? What has he done...

...his father is the last to leave him, shouts and screams and tells him he is a waste of space and that he couldn't even get this right!

Vincent's stomach is in knots. His shirt is wet, the top of his thighs. Is he still hard...did he ejaculate and the Voice...his Master...where is his Master? He can't see it but there is blood everywhere. Some hers yes, but most of it...most of it is his.

He screams and screams and screams and screams.

He stops and listens but the voices are silent. They have gone. He is alone.

He understands finally what the Transformation means – he made a mistake...it wasn't him it was her...

The music stops.

He falls to his knees – she kicks him backwards. She's powerful now. He doesn't get up. He lies there listening to the silence. He doesn't have to see her eyes, he knows what he would see.

He would see them.

He begs for his Master, he begs for to hear the Voice one final time.

He only hears misery and the sound of the void. He has been abandoned. He has been forsaken.

Until she whispers into his ear but it's not her voice she speaks with...

***

The lights come back on. She is illuminated. She's covered in blood, she's pissed herself. It doesn't matter. She looks over.

283

He's there on the ground. He's not going anywhere. She drops the knife. Her hand is drenched in blood. She leans down and whispers into his ear.

Slowly, purposefully, she walks back through the restaurant. She knows everybody's eyes are following her.

She goes to the bar, falls onto her stool. Jules is standing there – a confused look on his face. He has a phone to his ear but he is shouting, though she can't hear a word. For a moment, she exits her body, she feels that she is riding a wave – when she comes to there are police, paramedics all around her. A light shines brightly on her face but she's not sure where it comes from. She feels different now. She feels alive. She knows she is smiling.

"It's over, it's over," she repeats.

There is something different about her. She has been Transformed.

She's wrong though – it's not over, it's just beginning.

There are voices inside her head. They sing to her. They are children who longed for their mother. Ironic without a doubt. There is one voice in particular, one voice who pushes her way forward to the front of the queue.

"Carole, its Mathilde. Never fear the darkness because the darkness fears you."

She laughs.

Somehow this seems to be the answer to everything.

BLOWN

by Adrian Baldwin

Should you ever find yourself travelling along U.S. Route 82, roughly halfway between the small towns of Winona and Kilmichael in Montgomery County, Mississippi, you will surely spot Donny's Truck Stop.

Oh, the bar-and-grill looks kinda quaint in a good ol' boy kinda way with its sun-baked signage, peeling paintwork and wide dusty forecourt, but just like those tumbleweeds: keep on rolling, do *not* stop.

Just in case.

In case it's time for a beautiful monster to raise its head again.

Presently, the only customers in Donny's Truck Stop are two overweight truck drivers, both male, each as dog-ugly as the other. They sit a table or two apart but could just as easily have chowed down together, these brothers of the road. One belches, deep and resonant; the other rubs his bulging gut - and the two dip their heads to each other, no words necessary. Then, as if to prove the narrator unreliable, Trucker One speaks:

'Yep, that'll do it,' he concludes, sucking leftover beaver tail from a back tooth.

(No, really: Beaver Tail Gumbo, it's an actual thing!)

Trucker Two nods, pushes aside his plate, now devoid of pork belly and taters.

'Hey, honey!' he calls. 'Could use another kaw-fee over here, darlin.'

In less time than it takes Billy Bob, the tooth-sucker trucker, to run pudgy fingers through greasy hair and reset his Arizona Wildcats baseball cap, a waitress appears with a coffee pot ...

DAISY, announces her name badge; as good a name as any.

Daisy's appearance is mid-forties, fine featured and undeniably shapely; *extremely* pretty once, no doubt - but tired-looking now, with barely enough get-up-and-go left to drift from table to kitchen and back again.

Wordlessly, she refills Pork Belly's coffee cup.

Gumbo clicks his fingers; seems he'd like a fill up, too.

Daisy sidles over and pours.

'Aw, come on now, how about a little friendly smile fer ol' Billy Bob?' winks Gumbo. 'I done et all ma beans,' he quips. Daisy moves her mouth. Not so much a smile as a smirk - heck, a sneer if anything.

Billy Bob thinks about patting her butt. Would he get away with it? A hard slap to the face would be a small price to pay, but a pot of hot coffee in your lap? Not worth the risk. Not when there were, most likely, a whole horde of hookers just a short drive from here; on the big parking lot opposite The Lightning Bug Motel, up where Route 82 hits Interstate 55 - Exit 185.

'What's with the dark glasses, darlin? Late night? Or did yer boyfriend give ya a whuppin?'

Daisy snorts. 'Any man raises his hand to me and it'll be the last thing he ever does.'

She peers over her shades then produces a smile, but Billy Bob isn't buying it; the smile seems more threatening than friendly.

'Well, you ain't no huckleberry,' he mutters.

Daisy tilts her head, aims a stern face. She says: 'So, can I git ya anythin else, cowboy?'

A fat red hand scratches under the Wildcats cap.

'Yeah, I'll take me a cold one to go,' he decides. 'Hotter than blue blazes out there.'

Billy Bob is correct: it's a scorcher outside, furnace hot, even in the shade.

'That it?' sniffs Daisy.

'Yup.'

'You done too, FedEx?' - a reference to Pork Belly's cap and uniform. The colour and logo match the livery of his truck parked out front.

'You can call me Bubba, darlin. We're all friends here.'

Daisy moves her mouth. 'Uh-huh.'

Bubba wipes his beard with a forearm, thinks a moment ...

'Mudslide Sundae,' he drawls, decided.

Daisy scribbles on her notepad.

'One root beer, one Mudslide, comin up.'

On the kitchen side of the serving counter, Don Junior, current line cook and one-day future owner, watches Daisy haul ass back behind the counter, ponytail gently swinging. She bends to an under-the-counter fridge, extricates a beer and a pre-prepared dessert, straightens up, holds the cold bottle against her forehead for a few seconds then ambles back to the customers.

'Gonna take me a smoke break in a minute, Chief,' she calls out.

Don Junior hates Daisy. He hates the way she calls him Chief or Boss. To his ears it always sounds sarcastic and mocking and disrespectful. Mainly, though, he hates her because he'd like to get his hands on her killer body and fuck her brains out, but hasn't got the balls to make a move. She'd say No, anyway, he just knows it.

'Okay, steppin out, Boss,' calls Daisy, lighter held aloft, heading for the rear door. 'Back in a tick.'

The way she rolls and smokes her cigarettes by the dumpsters out back, grates him too; disgusting habit - stinky ashtray-breath all over the customers after she returns (which is usually quick, to be fair, but even so).

No smoke breaks when I'm in charge, thinks Don. And he'd surely be in charge any time now; just as soon as granddaddy and present manager, Donny Senior, an already far from well man, kicks the bucket.

(Don Junior's father, Donald J. Tyler, Donny Senior's only child, went missing over eight years ago. No note, no nothing, not a word; one day he was here, the next he wasn't; just *poof,* and he'd gone. With Donald J. officially declared 'Presumed Dead' in absentia a year ago, Don Junior alone stands to inherit the Truck Stop.)

Old-school Donny Senior might believe Daisy's lady-assets keep the truckers coming back, but Lord when *he's* boss - the *real* boss - things will change! And she's always swearing.

Thinks nobody hears her when she's lighting up her cigarettes but Don Junior hears. Tits and ass be damned, no woman should cuss like that; killer body or no. Not even when she's doing the nasty in her trailer with whoever. Probably a dirt-poor cousin! Bloody rednecks. That's if Daisy even has any family. Despite working here for weeks, the waitress is still a mystery to Don. All he knows for sure is: she's a sarcastic bitch; she likes a beer or three; often looks like shit in the mornings (presumably if she's had a long night after picking up some young gun in Dixie's Bar); and when his waitress is home alone, she watches crappy soaps all evening - all of them; is hooked on the damned things. Maybe she even watches them when she's got company - *while she's fucking!* It wouldn't surprise Don Junior. Not in the least.

Old, dark thoughts return: like how he'd love to break into her trailer late at night, wake her from her beer-fuelled snoring and knock her around - a lot! A *real* whuppin; until she broke - then he'd force himself on her. He'd porn fuck her like the haughty bitch he reckons she is; make her squeal like a stuck hog! Hell, she'd surely enjoy it if she wasn't so dang cold and standoffish; didn't have a downer on silly little things that don't really matter: lack of height, back hair, a rotten tooth, that kind of thing. And, when he'd blown his beans up her - at least twice, maybe three times, in Don's warped mind - he'd strangle her then set fire to the filthy fucking trailer, and no-one would be any the wiser. Not a soul would miss her. Heck, he'd even hang around, brush shoulders with the trailer park's other resident rednecks, and watch it burn.

Prick-teasing trash!

Don watches her now from under his receding hillbilly hairline. (For all Don's railing against what he sees as 'rubes', he's just as hick as any of them, maybe more so.) He sucks his rotten tooth as Daisy slips Gumbo's and Pork Belly's bills onto their tables; notes how the truckers crudely scan their waitress's tight body, neither of them making any attempt to hide the fact as they finger the crumpled dollars within their billfolds. And Daisy doesn't seem to care about the eyeballing. Just ignores their lecherous attentions. Does she even notice anymore? Don reckons she enjoys it really, the furtive, leering glances and sly scrutiny. He thinks all women secretly love that kind of stuff; which is why he doesn't feel so bad when *he* checks her out - which, though he'd deny it, is every chance he gets. Oh yes, Don Junior studies Daisy a lot; always has - every day since that afternoon she first walked in and asked if the place was still hiring. She'd seen the sign. Don saw how she was happy to flirt with the truckers in her first week or two - at least, she appeared to be - until she realised it didn't improve her tips. No matter how many times the truckers grunted smutty suggestions, openly pinched or patted her rear end or brazenly squeezed a thigh, they'd never leave more than a buck or two. Chump change usually. Truckers are the worst tippers - period. Everyone knows that. And, as if proof were necessary:

'Cheer up, darlin,' winks Billy Bob. 'Here's a tip fer ya.' And he drops an extra dollar onto the table.

'Really, a whole buck? Yer too kind.'

Sarcasm, for some, can be difficult to master - but not for Daisy. She'd mastered it as easy as she had the southern drawl, prevalent in these parts.

'Sorry, darlin, but there is a recession, ya know.'

'Tell me about it,' mutters Daisy. Her long painted fingernails scratch up the money then she walks to the FedEx guy's table. She raises her sunglasses an inch and stares at the money Bubba has laid down: payment in full bar a few cents.

(As a side note: Don Junior had told Daisy she wasn't to wear sunglasses to work but Donny Senior overruled him; said she could on account of her so-called 'sensitivity to bright light'. Junior thought that was bullshit. She just thinks she's better than everyone else, he believed. Pot kettle black.)

'Keep the change,' grins Bubba.

Wordlessly, her unseen eyes drilling into Bubba's skull, Daisy collects the cash.

Then, as Daisy turns to walk away, he grabs a pawful of her backside and squeezes hard. Billy Bob laughs and grunts a hearty 'Yeah!' of approval, perhaps now regretting he hadn't done the same.

But how will she react? Don Junior is still watching closely. She's supposed to grin and bear it. Them's the rules. Unwritten but binding nonetheless.

***

Donny Senior, a much older, skinnier, dustier version of Don Junior, hands Daisy her wages for the week. Paltry but welcome all the same.

Daisy folds the thin envelope and slips it into a back pocket of her cut-off shorts.

There follows an awkward silence in which Donny Senior exchanges a look with Don Junior, peering in from behind the counter, Don's high forehead sparkling under the kitchen lights.

'What's up?' asks Daisy, though she suspects she knows already.

'Fraid we're not gonna need ya back tomorrow, Daisy,' explains Donny Senior.

'Oh, yeah?' Daisy adjusts her sunglasses. 'So, Monday then?'

Donny forms an uncomfortable grin and says:

'How about we call you when things pick up?'

'Pick up?' glares Daisy.

Donny twists his lip. 'Dagnabbit, girl,' he fusses. 'We got to let ya go.'

'Ya do, huh?'

'Ya leave us no choice,' bleats Donny.

'Ya punched a customer in the face, Daisy,' smirks Junior.

'He grabbed my crotch, Donny!' snaps Daisy.

'I thought it was yer ass,' frowns Donny. He glances at Don.

'Ass first,' hisses Daisy. 'Then crotch. And it was full-on, Donny. I mean the fucker's fingers were—'

'I'm sure, I'm sure,' panders Donny. 'But even so.'

Daisy looks from one to the other and back again.

'Well, fuck me, don't this beat all?'

'And that's another thing,' grouses Donny. 'The cussin - it's just not—'

'Not what?'

'Ladylike,' suggests Junior.

'Oh yeah? Well, fuck you, Donny. And fuck you too, Don, fer takin that fat-ass trucker's side. Ya know I got me a bruise the size of a gator egg on my pussy *and* my behind from that motherfucker.'

Donny Senior flinches at 'motherfucker'. Junior shakes his shiny head. *Trash*, he's thinking. But neither says a word.

Daisy huffs in disbelief.

'We gotcha these here beers,' offers Donny Senior at last. He taps a six pack on the counter. 'As a kinda leavin present.'

'Pfft, *leavin present*,' mocks Daisy.

'Call it one of them there Golden Handshakes.'

Daisy makes a face. 'And you ain't even jokin,' she says.

'Ya don't wan'em?' grills Junior.

'Fuck yeah, I wan'em.'
Daisy takes possession of the beers and the three stand there, staring at each other, a charged silence hanging like a haze in the heat.

'Well, I guess that's that, then,' sighs Donny eventually.

'Un-fuckin-believable,' glowers Daisy.

Then she turns on a heel, heads for the exit, and after a few strides, holds up a middle finger.

'I know y'all watchin my ass,' she calls without looking back.

'Don't let the door hit it on the way out,' replies Don Junior.

'Fuck you, Don,' cusses Daisy. 'Guess yer gonna have to git yerselves a new waitress to lust over. Am I right, boys?'

Daisy's raucous laughter slips away into the shimmering afternoon.

***

A whiskery, ancient hobo jerkily pushes a loaded cart along a bumpy, dirt sidewalk.

'They live among us,' he advises Daisy when she passes. 'Ya know how?' he breathes. She stops. 'Cos they look just like us.' Daisy throws her hands wide. 'I've known it fer years,' she agrees.

The hobo waves her in. Daisy steps closer. He checks no-one else is listening - Daisy's green eyes, green flecked with gold, peer at him over her sunglasses - then he puts red-rimmed, red-veined eyes back on his audience of one.

'But see, they ain't like us,' he hisses quietly. 'They *ain't* the same. Not underneath.'

'Ya got that right, old timer.'

'They beam down,' he continues. 'That's how they git here.' Daisy makes a face. 'That ain't how we git here.'

'Them there space vee-hickles they got over in Nevada - Area 51?' He coughs, wheezy and hacking, before adding: 'That's just a CIA smokescreen.'

'If you say so.'

'But what do they want, these aliens?' (He pronounces it *ay-lee-yens*.) The hobo hawks on the ground. 'That's the real goddamn question.'

Daisy lowers her voice: 'Don't ya know?'

She leans close, as if about to share a secret, which maybe she is. Her long fingernails grip the cart.

'We feed offa *you guys*,' she informs the hobo.

He leans back, wide-eyed.

'All those missin people everywhere,' poses Daisy, 'where do ya reckon they go?'

The hobo shakes his head then raises wiry eyebrows and points skyward.

'Nope.'

Red eyeballs scan the area: pawn shop, liquor store, laundromat, strip-joint ... a cattle-truck packed with prime beef, standing shoulder to shoulder, crosses the intersection. Then the hobo's attention settles back on Daisy and he shrugs. Daisy points down.

'They do *not* bury'em!'

'Now who said anythin about buryin?'

'What then?' blinks the hobo. 'Throw'em in a sewer?'

'Somethin like that.'

'Well, shit,' spits the hobo. He nods, slow and thoughtful. 'My friend Larry, he disappeared a while back. I reckon they stored him in an underground bunker somewhere. Am I right?'

'Well, now, I *could* tell ya, old timer ... but then I'd be forced to kill ya.'

But the hobo is no longer listening: he's stepped back his weather-beaten shoes and is studying the earth between himself and Daisy. 'Holy crap, is that ... is that where they sleep when they ain't walkin among us?' He bends over for a closer view. 'Right beneath our feet?'

'Well, *I* don't,' shares Daisy. 'I live in a trailer.'

The hobo straightens up, suddenly proud. 'Nuttin wrong with that.'

'See, I like to hide in plain sight. We all do. And that's how it'll be - until, ya know, there's enough of us.'

The hobo narrows bloodshot eyes.

Daisy raises her sunglasses ... then winks.

'Oh now, yer just teasin,' rasps the hobo. 'But I ain't no crazy fool,' he tells her. 'And one o' these days—'

A blast from a Colonel Bogey horn and a pick-up truck pulls up sharply at the kerb, young gun at the wheel.

'Hey, Daisy!' hollers the kid.

Daisy rolls her eyes behind her sunglasses. 'Whatcha want, Cody?' she challenges.

'We was wonderin ...'

Cody's long-haired passenger, another college-aged fella, leans forward and presents himself. He makes a peace sign before elbowing Cody. 'Ask her.'

'I know, I know,' bleats Cody.

'Oh yeah, what was ya wonderin, Cody?' sighs Daisy; she isn't in the mood for teenage high-jinx. Not today.

'Me and Floyd here, well, we was wonderin ... bout a spit-roast?'

'Why, whatever do you mean, Cody? Ya mean, like a barbecue?'

'Aw come on now, ya know what we're askin. It could be a quick one.'

'Now, what did I tell ya last time you asked?' says Daisy. 'I don't do that kinda thing.' She elbows the hobo and tells him quietly: 'Not no more.'

'Ya sure?' asks Floyd. 'We got ten bucks witch yer name on it right here.'

'I said no, *Floyd.*'

Daisy starts walking.

The pick-up truck keeps pace alongside.

'What if we made it twenty?' hollers Floyd.

'Can't you boys find no college girls to play with?'

'Well, yeah,' laughs Cody, 'but they ain't got—ya know—yer experience like.'

Daisy keeps walking.

The pick-up keeps rolling.

'We got beers in the ice box.'

'I got my own beers, Cody.'

Daisy turns left, around a corner.

Cody's pick-up turns too.

An eighteen-wheeler big-rig passes noisily on the other side of the road dragging a cloud of dust behind it.

'Ya wearin any panties today, Daisy?' shouts Cody. 'Under those tight, skinny little shorts of yers; betcha ain't - hot day like today.'

Up ahead, off to the right, a freight train whistles past.

Daisy turns left again, into the trailer park.

***

Daisy's on the bed, feet up, boots kicked to the floor. She swigs from a beer bottle, eyes focused on an old, tiny, portable television set (bent coat-hanger for an aerial) perched on top of the unit which separates the sleeping area from the kitchen section. The fuzzy black-and-white picture, the only current light source, casts a twitching eerie glow that bounces unstable shadows within the space.

Presently, the channel is beaming a low-budget Mexican comedy/soap/drama. The actors' performances are as unconvincing as the sets, and yet Daisy appears captivated by the show; she laughs along raucously in tandem with the canned studio laughter. Her laugh is surprisingly guttural and deep, not like you'd expect from a slim white woman at all; it's almost unearthly - 'ay-lee-yen' as the hobo might say.

The combined hilarity, hers and the audience-machine's, echoes loudly within the trailer; a trailer devoid, it seems, of most of the usual, basic human comforts and conveniences. There is a sink, but no sign of cutlery or dishes; there are curtains (purple, currently drawn), but no cushions and not a single lamp - oh, and no carpet, only Linoleum.

A Mexican woman is shouting dramatically, hysterically, in Spanish, at a man she has just caught kissing some other woman. Her scolding rant bellows for an age. Then, after a final slap to the cheek, the harangued man is allowed to respond.

'Espera, ella es tu hermana?' he asks.

'Si!' shrieks the woman. 'Ella es mi hermana!'

'Estas casado?' shrieks the sister. She too slaps the poor schmuck's face. 'A mi hermana!'

The television emits chuckles and chortles. Daisy snorts and convulses. 'Mi hermana,' she parrots. But then the screen suddenly fizzes, fizzles, and dies.

'Motherfucker!' bleats Daisy.

Sitting in the quiet darkness, Daisy stares at the blank screen. She sniffs the smoke now permeating the trailer, sighs deeply, and then drains the last of her beer.

Eventually, Daisy turns her head and stares at the wardrobe. Though it's pitch dark, she can see the few clothes hanging inside through the gap in the slightly open door. And one in particular: a blue - *black* to our eyes - low cut top. She eyeballs it intensely, without looking away, as if she has a difficult decision to make.

***

In less than an hour, Daisy has bathed, dried, clipped her toenails, dressed in a micro-skirt, tied her hair in pigtails, stuck on false eyelashes, and applied just the right amount of smoky eye-shadow and orange lipstick.

Now, after slipping on the blue low-cut top, she checks her curves in the wardrobe door mirror. The reflection gazes back for a moment then it sighs and sits heavily on the bed. Daisy seems troubled; a moment of doubt. She snatches open a drawer in the bedside unit, grabs the little tobacco tin and shakes it; enough for one good-sized roll-up. She flips the tin onto the bed, reaches back inside the drawer, pulls out a packet of cigarette papers, and then a small cassette-player.

Turned on, the player jumps into 'Gimme Shelter' by The Rolling Stones.

Again Daisy stares at herself in the mirror.

She turns the music up higher, real high.

As Jagger, guitars and drums belt it out - '*It's just a shot away! It's just a shot away!*' - so too an angry determination appears to rise within Daisy.

She has nothing and yet was promised so much. She'd travelled so far but had got nowhere. Years of waiting and for what? Be patient they said. Her brothers and sisters are on the way.

Suddenly, Daisy growls, low and husky, then snatches up the tobacco tin. She rolls up a fat cigarette, flicks her tongue along the paper's edge and lights up. It never leaves her mouth. Her cheeks sink and she pulls so deeply, the end burns like a tiny sun in the dark of the trailer; but only briefly, oh so briefly, for the cigarette changes to a length of ash in one rapid movement as Daisy sucks it, instantly, down to the filter. '*It's just a kiss away!*' sings Mick. '*It's just a kiss away!*' And though Daisy's express smoke might have appeared accelerated, the song, playing in real-time, suggests otherwise. Daisy exhales a cigarette's worth of smoke at the ceiling, then, without looking, pitches the cigarette butt directly into the sink. Though you can't see it, the cigarette stub bounces a moment, as if in slow motion, and is snuffed out by a drop that drips from the leaky tap.

***

It's dark outside when Daisy pads out onto the trailer's porch. She locks the door then turns to leave, but as she does, her purse strap catches on the door handle and snaps.

'Motherfucker,' rasps Daisy. She picks up the fallen purse, studies the strap, then looks over to a neighbouring trailer ...
Daisy knocks on the front door. There are no lights burning inside but that doesn't mean Tenisha is out. After a few seconds, with no reply, Daisy knocks again, louder.

A moment later, the door opens.

Evidently, Tenisha is a large black woman. She has a friendly smile, dark brown eyes flecked with gold, cornrow hair, and hoop earrings. A loosely tied dressing gown reveals a long strip of dusky nakedness beneath.

'Wasn't sure if you were in,' smiles Daisy.

'My night off,' advises Tenisha. Tenisha works at the strip-joint, as a security guard. 'S'up, girl?' she beams.

Daisy's left hand hoists the purse for consideration; the broken strap dangles like a dead thing.

'Now, that's a damned shame,' sighs Tenisha. 'So, are you ...? Or are you ...?'

'No, just cash,' confirms Daisy.

'Which is why ya need the purse,' realises Tenisha.

'Yep, no room fer pockets in this.' Daisy turns and slaps her micro-skirt. Then a noise, from inside Tenisha's trailer, catches Daisy's attention. 'Oh, sorry, ya got company?'
'Yeah, but it's alright,' whispers Tenisha. 'He's already tied up.' She winks. 'Big fella, too.'

'Big fella, huh?' laughs Daisy quietly. 'Well, good fer you. Should keep ya goin a while, huh?'

'Ya got that right,' agrees Tenisha. 'Ya sure ya don't need to ...?'

'No, I et a couple of weeks back,' Daisy assures her. 'Just need some cash, is all.'

'Ya sure?' checks Tenisha. 'Cos like I say,' she peers inside her trailer, 'he's a big one.'

'Mumhfhh!' moans a muffled voice.

'No, really,' Daisy assures her neighbour. 'I'm good fer at least another week or so.'

'Well, okay, then. So, just a purse.'

'If ya don't mind, Tenisha, darlin.'

'Don't mind at all, sugar. Now you wait there just one second.'

'Mumhfhh!' groans the muffled voice.

'Quiet, you,' warns Tenisha. 'Be right back,' she tells Daisy. Waiting patiently, Daisy takes the opportunity to snatch a quick peek inside. Whatever she sees amuses her.

Seconds later, Tenisha returns.

'See what ya mean,' confides Daisy.

'Yeah, two-hundred pounds of prime call centre guy,' beams Tenisha. 'Sure ya don't want some?'

'No, I'm good. Like I say, just need a little cash. TV's busted.'

'What?! So, no soaps!'

'Nope.'

'Well, now, we can't have that.'

Just then a bearded biker on a Harley drives by. The pair shield their naked eyes from the headlight. Once the motorbike has passed, Tenisha holds up the purse she's fetched.

'Okay, will this do?'

'Yup, that'll do just fine. Thanks, sugar.'

'Welcome, darlin.'

'Mumhfhh!' grunts the call guy.

'By the way, where d'ya git him? Ya been up the lot?'

'Hell no, girl; I don't do that anymore. I got me a laptop. Use the Internet now. Craig's List. Meet'em in Dixie's Bar. Bring'em back here, then—ya know.'

The pair laugh at their mutual secret.

'That's what *you* should do, hun: git yerself a laptop. Save all that walkin.'

'Yeah, maybe yer right ... if I can make enough cash.'

'Girl, with that ass and those titties? You'd soon have enough - *more* than enough.'

'It's the damn crack whores,' bleats Daisy. 'They've driven prices down - driven'em right down.'

'Yeah, but nobody blows like we do. Am I right?'

The pair laugh again, then look around, checking the area remains clear.

'You still like to do yers slow?' asks Daisy. 'I don't mean like me, now, when it's fer cash - I mean when yer—'

'Making a meal of it?' laughs Tenisha. Daisy nods. 'Lord, yes. Savour it on the way in, sugar - cos, ya know ...'

'Yeah, not so nice on the way out,' sighs Daisy.

Tenisha asks: 'Do you still ...?'

'U-huh,' nods Daisy. 'Speedy Gonzalez. Once I start ...'

'Well, each to their own, as they say here.'

Daisy smiles. 'But ya know what's really funny?'

'How they always enjoy it at the beginning?'

'Yeah, at first,' grins Daisy. 'And even fer a brief moment *during.*'

'Right,' agrees Tenisha. 'Until—ya know.'

Again they laugh, again they look around; and then, with still not a soul in earshot - other than Tenisha's 'guest' - they say their goodbyes: a series of low hoots, shrill coos and resonating clicks.

'Lot lizard,' teases Tenisha, her voice deep and guttural and raspy, the earthly accent totally dropped.

'Online reptile,' retorts Daisy, without a trace of southern drawl; she too sounding harsh and husky.

Another shared laugh; this one low and gravelly - then back to 'normal':

'You take care, darlin,' smiles Tenisha, closing the trailer door.

'Always do!' calls Daisy, descending Tenisha's porch steps.

***

On the huge parking lot opposite The Lightning Bug Motel, up where Route 82 hits Interstate 55 - at the infamous Exit 185 - Daisy freshens up in the lot's restroom.

Not that she really needs to. Sure, it's a long walk from the trailer park, but Daisy had quickly and successfully thumbed a lift from a gentle Christian couple in a station wagon; they sang along to annoying Sweet Jesus songs on radio station GOD FM or whatever the hell it was, the whole way.

(On Daisy's home planet, no-one has any concept of God or gods or any form of religion. They believe only in patient expansion.)

No, 'Daisy' - she chose the name herself after her conscription - just likes to freshen up before walking the lot because, well, she thinks of it as mental preparation, a kind of 'clocking in' if you will; and she'd be 'clocking off' just as soon as she'd earned enough money to replace her TV.

(Daisy's kind needed to keep themselves occupied somehow, until the main contingent arrived: *armed* troops, amassed in sufficient numbers to launch a worldwide offensive.)

So, here she is, this 'advance scout', in front of a tarnished mirror, psyching herself up for whatever is required: handjobs, blowjobs, full sex ... when a familiar human voice barks from the doorway:

'Well, fuck me, look who's back.'

'Oh, hello, Lizzy, how's it hangin?'

Lizzy is a gap-toothed hooker with a skinny ass, saggy tits, and a drug habit almost as old as she is. She's one of the reasons prices have plummeted in the last few years. Her usual chat-up line is to whip out a tittie and wink: 'Ya want some?'

Surprisingly, the line works about as often as it doesn't.

***

The parking lot, a clearly popular truck stop, is extremely busy this evening; so many big-rigs - row upon row of eighteen-wheelers with their huge grills, high doors and sleeper cabins.

The girls - four or five on the prowl tonight - slink from door to door, across the potholed asphalt, offering their wares to men of all shapes and sizes: some guys are chatty, some not, many drivers simply want to be left alone to sleep; some are randy and responsive, others receptive but hesitant, and several are just plain uninterested.

'Ya want some?' asks Lizzy, left tit scooped out as an incentive.

'You got a nipple on that?' asks the trucker looking down from his open window.

'Yeah,' sniffs Lizzy, rolling the mammary back with bony fingers.

'Oh, there it is,' laughs the trucker. They can be a harsh bunch.

'So, ya want some?' repeats Lizzy.

'That is horrible,' frowns the trucker. 'Horrible.'

Lizzy beams up her gappy grin. 'Yeah, but do ya want some?'

Meanwhile, over by the semitrailer directly opposite, Daisy has had her first bite:

'Forty, sixty, eighty?' asks the driver. Shorthand for a fairly standard rate: $40 for oral, $60 for sex, $80 for both.

(Crack whores can be a lot cheaper, especially if they're rattling, but Daisy appears far too healthy to be a rock-head.)

'Forty, sixty, eighty,' echoes Daisy in agreement.

'Climb in,' instructs the driver.

Now, we could hang around for a few hours, watch the

so-called 'lot lizards' patrol the area, strolling from truck to truck, knocking on doors: the sleepy drivers complaining about being disturbed from their much needed slumbers; the horniest truckers partaking of the services on offer; dollar bills changing hands; girls climbing down and straightening their skirts and slinging used condoms under the trailers or into potholes; but we may as well jump ahead, to 4:45 AM, for that is when Daisy figured she'd made enough money to buy a replacement TV from the pawn shop - and that is the time she bumped into Don Junior next to the restroom.

'Well, well, well,' smirks a smug Don Junior. 'Fancy seein *you* here.'

'Oh hello, Don,' sighs Daisy.

'Yeah, weird, right? You just stopped to use the restroom, too? Oh no, wait, you don't drive, do ya?'

'I'm with a friend.' Daisy scans the lot. 'She's around here somewhere.'

'Oh really?' Don makes a show of looking for Daisy's missing made-up friend. 'Nope ... don't see'er.'

'Maybe she—'

'Unless she's that *hooker* over there; is that yer friend - *that hooker*?'

'No.'

'No?'

'No.'

'Okay, maybe just as well. Cos I doubt she'll get any joy at that truck. Ya know, cos heck, that's the one *you* just climbed down from.'

Daisy turns to confront Don.

'Yeah,' he nods, 'I been here a while. Seen you skulkin from truck to truck—'

'Fuck you, Don!'

'Aw, come on now, don't be like that. A girl's gotta do what a girl's gotta do. I know that. Am I right?'

'And is that why *yer* here? Lookin fer some action? Does yer wife know that you—?'

'Me? No. I'm just on my way back from bowlin. It went on a bit. Like I say, just stopped to use the restroom. But then I said to myself: *Is that Daisy, our old waitress?*

'Yeah, so? So, what?'

'Nothin. Like I said, a girl's gotta do what a girl's gotta do.'

Daisy studies Don Junior with suspicion.

'Come on, let me give ya a lift back,' he smiles. 'No strings. The trailer park's on my way.'

'Why are ya bein nice to me all of a sudden?'

'I'm not *completely* heartless. And how else ya gonna git back? Bit late fer hitchin a lift.'

He had a point.

***

An old Eldorado Convertible pulls off the main road and onto an unlit dirt track surrounded by trees. The car creeps forward, slow and quiet, trailing wispy clouds of dust, red in its tail-lights.

'What are ya doin, Don?' grills Daisy. 'Trailer park's half a mile yet and it sure ain't this way.'

Inside, Don is taking his sweet time, like he's in charge. He lights a cigarette, lowers his window, enjoys the nicotine hit then exhales slowly.

'Yer not *really* from here, are ya?' he challenges at last. 'Originally, I mean.'

'No,' sighs Daisy. 'I'm from Arkansas.'

'Now, that's not what I mean,' smirks Don, 'and you know it.'

'Are you high?'

'See, cos I know.'

'Know *what*, Don? You ain't talkin no sense.'

'*I ... know.*'

'You *are* high,' laughs Daisy. 'Now drive, dammit, or I'll just jump out here, ya see if I don't.'

'The aversion to lights.'

'What? *Aversion to lights?* Lots of people—'

'Never seen ya eat, neither, not once. And ya walk kinda weird, too. Like a bit ... stooped over.'

'I do not.'

'And yer cigarette breaks; they last, what, all of ten seconds?'

'Well, now, that's a good thing, ain't it? Fer you, I mean. Or it *was*, before ya fired my behind. See, all I need is couple of puffs and—'

'Then there's days, *some* days, when ya suddenly look like yer knocked up - like totally out the blue, ya know - belly all stickin out here.' Don extends a hand beyond his gut. 'Then next day, *poof,* gone ... and dagnabbit, if ya ain't all back to normal - back to yer skinny ass self.'

'That's just the-time-of-the-month, Don.'

'Uh-huh?' Don sucks on his cigarette. 'Heard ya singin to yerself in the bathroom, too. And more than once - a few times, in fact.' He exhales. 'When ya thought nobody was around to hear. All those coos and hoots and clicks and the like. Ain't no *human* noises, I know that.'

'Not human,' scoffs Daisy 'Now yer just talkin crazy.'

'What are ya, like inside, some kinda lizard-woman?'

'Have you heard yerself, Don? Ya sound plum loco, ya know that, right?'

'Never had me no lizard-woman.' Don sucks his bad tooth. 'They all look as good as you on yer planet?'

He ogles her body.

'Don, take me back, right this minute or—'

'So, is that yer *real* skin - or is it like a suit or somethin?'

Don strokes Daisy's breastbone with the tip of his middle finger.

'Son of a—' Daisy slaps the hand away.

But Don's hairy paw shoots back, grabs a fistful of tit and squeezes, causing Daisy to flinch.

'Well, that feels real enough,' grunts Don.

'Don!' Daisy pushes on Don's arm. 'Don!'

Don slaps Daisy's face, hard. 'Now you listen to me!' he barks, his hand jumping back to her breast. 'Yer gonna give me one of them there blowjobs you was handin out back at the lot.' He crushes the breast between his fingers. Daisy winces. 'See, I'm hopin a beejay from an alien will be-' Don winks, '-*out of this world*.'

'I'm not a fuckin alien, Don,' scowls Daisy.

'Well, if ya ain't an *actual* alien, I reckon yer an *illegal* alien - ya got that Mexican dark-skin kinda look about ya - but either way, my junk is goin ... as we say in these parts ... in yer perdy mouth.'

'I'm warnin ya, Don; ya really do not wanna do that.'

Don slaps Daisy twice more; top of the head this time. 'Now, shut the fuck up!' he warns, undoing his belt. He unzips his fly, lifts his spotty ass and drags his pants and undershorts down. Then he stares at her.

'Well, what are ya waitin fer?' he asks at last. 'It won't suck itself.'

Daisy makes a face; Don's smelly cock is even uglier than his face. 'Alright,' she sniffs. 'But yer payin me. Forty dollars.'

'I ain't payin you a goddamned thing, bitch.' And he slaps her again for good measure; back to the face, harder than before, jolting her pigtails.

'Okay, okay, jeez.' Daisy palms her hot cheek, anger rising in her eyes. 'So,' she growls, 'would I be right in thinkin it's a blowjob yer itchin fer?'

Sarcasm. Daisy learned all about human mockery and wisecracks in training; mastered it faster than a Voraxian swamp-hog unearths Qeagnusian mud-truffles.

'No, I'm sittin here with my undershorts round my knees fer the pure heck of it.'

'Fine,' she blinks. 'If I can find it, I'll suck it.'

'Now yer talkin,' breathes Don. 'Now, no more talkin.' He pulls on Daisy's head, pushes it into his lap. 'Show Daddy some love.'

Daisy's head bobs up and down. Wet, sucking noises fill the Eldorado.

'Good, good,' grunts Don. 'That's real nice, sugar. Mmmm.'

Don's head pushes back hard into his headrest.

Outside, below overhanging tree branches, the Eldorado rocks, squeaking on its suspension coils.

Quiet, muffled groans emanate from under the car's closed soft-top.

The rocking continues for several beats - *squeak* - *squeak* - *squeak* - and though the track remains dark, over in the east, beyond the woods and fields, the first blush of a lightening sky.

'Okay, Daisy, now suck it like ya mean it,' prompts Don harshly. He checks his wristwatch. 'If I'm not home before seven, my wife'll be awake. And if Darleen's up fer breakfast, it means I'll have to talk to the silly bitch.'

But Daisy's face has surfaced.

'Why d'ya stop?' barks Don. 'Did I say—?'

'If I do this, can I have my job back?' Pride is not an emotion suffered by Daisy's kind.

'Fuck no. But I tell ya what: ya make me cum in yer mouth - *and* swallow - and I *won't* report yer bein here to the authorities. How's *that* sound?'

'Swallow?'

'That's right,' grins Don, baring his rotten tooth. 'Can yer race do that?'

Daisy laughs. *Is he being sarcastic again? No,* she decides, *he can't be. He has no idea.*

'Oh, I can suck you dry, meester,' quips Daisy in a Spanish accent.

'Now, that's more like it.' Again Don pulls on Daisy's head; shoves it roughly, back into his lap - holds her there, by a pigtail ... until she picks up speed.

'Oh yeah, that's it, darlin,' urges Don. 'Good, good. Okay, now keep goin—Wow, you really—do know—how to suck.'

Daisy's head bounces up and down like a piston, sucking and slurping at Don's crotch.

Squeak—squeak—squeak—squeak—squeak—

'Jesus H. Christ, I swear ya could drain a swamp dry with those sweet lips.'

Don looks happy, *really* happy, blissful even: inhaling through flared nostrils, teeth biting his bottom lip; eyes rolling; mouth in an O shape, lips pouting, for each lusty exhale. But then his expression suddenly changes, from pleasure to: What the fuck is that!? Discomfort? Soreness? Pain? How can that be?

313

Daisy's head keeps pumping, regardless.

Squeak—squeak—squeak—squeak—squeak—

'Wait, are ya wearin a brace?' scowls Don. 'What *is* that? Is that yer teeth?'

Daisy gags. 'Just go with it,' she urges.

The Eldorado is bucking now, seats bouncing on their springs - *SQUEAKSQUEAKSQUEAKSQUEAKSQUEAK* -and the sound of sucking has become wilder, wetter, and intensely loud.

At once Don perceives his legs have turned weak, but not in a good way; he's intensely lightheaded, too - his mouth absurdly dry. He blinks rapidly, confused. But whatever's troubling him, whatever the unidentified problem is: he feels unable to act on it - helpless.

'Stay with me, almost there,' presses Daisy, all breathy. 'Keep yer eyes open. Don't want ya passin out on me. Not now.'

'Okay, but ...' Something *is* different; Don feels it ... his voice sounds weak, *really* weak ... and is—? Yes, everything around him seems larger!

'Down here, Don. Look at *me.*'

Don looks down, makes eye contact with Daisy's huge green eyes.

'Sexy, huh?' she chokes, her mouth full.

It *should* look sexy but ... Daisy's upturned head seems massive in his lap. And is that really his cock? It looks more like part of his gut extending outward, protruding like a strange tumour. No sign of any pubes now, only the line of hairs down from his bellybutton, and that line growing shorter by the second.

'Fuck!' peeps Don, the voice high-pitched and rodent-like.

His nipples are sliding, melting, chest hairs drifting south, his very flesh, sinking! And now his tiny eyes note something else: below his chin, the v-neck collar of his shirt grown roomy around his scrawny neck - and Don realises that he is, as one, shrinking, imploding! Head, body, limbs, all of him; definitely - if he's not mistaken, judging by the scale of the Eldorado and Daisy's head, his own head is already reduced to the size of a grapefruit.

'This *is* what ya wanted, ain't it, *Daddy?*' winks Daisy, breaking momentarily, eyes locked on Don's little peepers.

Then the noisy sucking continues.

Don's fear is written all over his drained, deflating face, but it's too late to do anything about it now: his horrified head just keeps on shrivelling, withering ...

'I'm gonna kill ya fer this, Daisy,' squeaks Don. 'Ya see if I don't! Gonna bury ya in a swamp where no-one will ever find ya—food fer the gators.'

It's already too late, though, and Don knows it. He falls silent, open-mouthed; he grasps at Daisy's hair but his shrunken hand is useless - the arm drops, his watch falls onto the floor by his vacated shoes, and Don's teeny hand disappears up a baggy sleeve.

'*No, please—what the fuck!* a final pipsqueak plea.

But Daisy doesn't stop, she keeps on sucking; sucking until Don's tiny desiccated, wizened head slips down inside his shirt collar and vanishes from view, until Don's trousers and shirt finally collapse in on themselves, empty and flat.

Then Daisy sits up, exhausted and full.

She wipes her chin and, pulling a hair from her forked tongue, studies the scene: Don has completely vanished. Only his watch, clothes and shoes remain. Everything else has gone: hair, skin, flesh, bones - the lot.

The passenger door swings opens and Daisy, pot-bellied now, steps out. Breathless, she leans back against the car, distended stomach sloshing and gurgling ... then she belches, long and loud.

After a while, composed and breathing normally again, Daisy starts walking, towards the rising sun.

***

Daytime in Daisy's trailer, a few days later:

The broken black-and-white portable television set has gone; in its place, a good-sized flat-screen TV. Colour. The sound is off but the News Channel ticker is reporting a local man missing. A picture-in-picture of Don Junior's face appears. He looks even more grotesque in the photo than he did in real life. And here comes some roving camera footage of an abandoned Eldorado.

Daisy, looking several months pregnant, turns off the set. Then she gags, as if about to throw up. And now she's running through the mauve-coloured interior, hurrying to the kitchen area. Here Daisy vomits violently and painfully into the sink: a large initial pink/grey splash of chunky goo and gunk, bits of which splash onto the closed curtains; then, in one all-out extra-loud spew, she regurgitates a gut-full of cruddy sludge - enough mess to fill at least two buckets.

A final retch and hawk leaves Daisy leaning on the sink, coughing, dribbling, and trying to catch her breath.

'Not so nice on the way out,' wheezes Daisy, not for the first time.

Slow to drain the noxious remains of Daisy's stomach, the sink is left brimming to the point of almost overflowing, with disgorged, gelatinous slime. Some less-digested pieces stick up at angles through the lumpy surface; an unpleasant image that resembles a scaled-down septic tank - one laced with what appears to be pulverised bone fragments and clumps of matted hair.

'Bye, Don,' spits Daisy, at last, her respiration finally under control.

After reaching behind the purple curtain and cracking open the kitchen window, she sprays air-freshener over the still full sink; the scummy mess might take an hour or more to drain but that vile smell - a foul mixture of sewer gas and used diaper, of spoiled meat and rotten eggs - will surely take a lot longer than that to disperse. In the meantime, Daisy intends to clean her teeth, gargle with mouthwash, and then take a long cold soak.

***

Early evening and Daisy is relaxing in a deep bubble bath surrounded by candles. On a chair, near the taps, the cassette-player once again rocks out The Rolling Stones.

Eyes closed, Daisy looks, for the first time in a long time, content and relaxed. She begins to sing along with Jagger ... and her singing voice is truly awful: pitch; tone; all those important parts - extremely unpleasant to the human ear. Not to worry, though; none of those around at the moment.

But, after crooning through several lines of 'Brown Sugar', the song seriously slows down; the music drags - Mick's droning vocals now the singing equivalent of wading knee-deep through a thick, muddy quagmire.

Daisy taps the cassette-player with a wet foot and the song returns to normal.

(Did you notice the four toes - three webbed; one heel toe - and scaly skin up to the ankle? Surgeons back home had been able to perfect body-modification procedures on everything but the colonist's feet: the earliest pioneers had quickly proved, as the surgeons had feared, that altering the foot's normal birdlike bone structure, so weakened it, as to leave Daisy's kind - what we might class a 'reptile' and a lizard of sorts - unable to bear their own body weight in Earth's stronger gravity.)

Jagger's still wondering, *How come Brown Sugar dances so good,* and all is well - until the slow-mo problem returns and persists.

Daisy's sud-covered foot jabs the cassette-player; kicks it twice - three times.

And now the drawn-out song abruptly switches to warp speed: '*Yeahyeahyeahwooo!*' rattles off Mick, sounding like a mouse on helium as spools of brown tape rapidly snake around inside the tape compartment.

Then the music stops dead and the player spits out the chewed cassette, its ribboned entrails caught within the mechanics.

Daisy sighs and lies back - the machine has clearly had its day. After a moment, though, she turns her head, and gazes through the bathroom's open doorway ... to the bed, where the purse Tenisha gave her lies waiting.

Time passes slowly, then Daisy's chin slips down to the sudsy waterline; a subconscious clicking noise rises in her throat, and her eyes glaze over, deep in thought:

How much were those CD players? The ones she'd admired

in the pawn shop. *Plus a few Rolling Stones discs ...*

What would that cost in total?

Forty? Sixty? Eighty?

WANDA THE BLOODTOSE INTOLERANT VAMPIRE

by Russell Holbrook

One

For years Wanda resented his mother for the name she had given him. He always wished he had been given a classier name like Cindy, Tiffany, or Gertrude.

His resentment toward his mother led Wanda into a turbulent and rebellious youth. For months on end Wanda refused to walk on the right side of the street. He became obsessed with Death Jazz music and head slouching. Then, thirteen days into his thirteenth year, in a fit of complete and youthful defiance, Wanda raised his voice to his mother and told her that as soon as he turned seventeen he was going to try out for Blood Waltz, the local vampire dance troupe, whom Wanda had idolized ever since he saw them perform live at the Mable Town Celebration of Awesomeness Day when he was eleven and a half years old. It was Wanda's greatest dream, and he really hoped the news of his ambition would show his mom the full scope and sincerity of his new direction in rebellious behavior. Wanda's mom could see how hard he was trying to learn to be his own man and it filled her heart with love. Still, she felt skeptical. A sliver of concern wiggled up her spine.

"I don't want you messin' around with those dancin' vamps," Wanda's mom said in her calm demeanor. "You can't trust anyone who wears shoes like that, all pointy at the tips and what-not."

Like any good-hearted, level-headed teenager would do, Wanda mumbled his dissent, walked away, and secretly plotted against his mother. Wanda decided that on the day of the try outs he would tell his mom that he was going to Captivity Playhouse with friends from school to watch the lashing of the Naa-Na-Nihnn.

"That sounds like a wholesome activity," Wanda imagined his mom saying. "Just be sure to wear dark colors in case blood spurts out of the cages."

Wanda's mom was both caring and sensible. That's something Wanda loved about her.

Two

The years passed by and Tuesday came without delay. Wanda was seventeen; it was time for try outs. He found himself in a back alley, waiting in line with dozens of other hopefuls who also aspired to dance with Blood Waltz. Wanda was nervous, of course, but he believed in himself and in his dreams. Leaning his head against the alley's brick wall and waiting for his name to be called, he thought back on the events that had led to this fateful day.

Wanda had wanted to join Blood Waltz ever since the seventh grade. After declaring his intentions to his mother, he'd secretly horded away lunch money and bought his own pair of pointy tipped dancing shoes and kept them hidden in the back of his closet behind his step-uncle's stash of mutant porn magazines. Pamela, his step-uncle, used to say that no one would ever look for his magazines there and he also really liked masturbating in seventh grader's closets. And Wanda's wasn't the first closet that Uncle Pamela had been in either.

Uncle Pamela had been spending so much time in various closets over the years that his wife hardly ever saw him. Her memories of him and of the times they had spent together grew more and more dim. Meanwhile, Uncle Pamela's mutant porn collecting habit completely took over his life and he forgot that he was married. He just wandered from closet to closet, stashing his porn and masturbating. One day when he was looking for a new closet to stash his most recently acquired magazines and videos in, Uncle Pamela accidentally wandered into his own house. He stumbled upon his wife, who was in the kitchen, on the table, naked and pleasuring herself with a spatula covered in cake batter. Overwhelmed with horror at the sight of a living human being, naked and in the throes of self-passion, Uncle Pamela ran from the house screaming and crying, mentally broken, never to return.

Two days later, Uncle Pamela left himself on Wanda's doorstep, wrapped in swaddling clothes, in a grown-up size cradle he had fashioned from twigs, used bubble gum, and discarded holiday ornaments. Judging by his appearance, Wanda's mother concluded that the odd man must be a step-uncle. She checked the local step-uncle registry, which included pictures and vague yet genteel descriptions of registered individuals, and found the man who rested in the cradle before her.

"Uncle Pamela...?" She said to him, looking up from the directory.

The man raised his head and nodded. Feeling compassion in her heart for the weirdo on her front stoop, Wanda's mother invited Uncle Pamela in for tea. That same day he moved into Wanda's closet, where he finally found a permanent and stable place of his own.

Uncle Pamela didn't mind Wanda hiding the pointy-tipped dancing shoes behind his mutant porno collection and he promised that he would never tell.

"They're very handsome shoes," Uncle Pamela would say. This made Wanda smile.

And Uncle Pamela kept Wanda's shoes safe, and he never

wacked off when he stared into their shiny orphan skin surface and thought of awful, far away things.

Three

Wanda practiced his moves every day during the in between hours, after school and before his mom got home from work, putting in extra time on the days his mom had to stay late. Because she was an officer at the local consumer correctional facility, she often led the shopper's recovery group which was held on Wednesdays and Fridays. She didn't get paid for the time but she didn't mind because she knew she was helping others learn to become better shoppers.

Wanda danced and danced and danced until his toes bled and his spirit ached. He bought all the official Blood Waltz instructional video cassettes and reviewed them until the family video cassette player broke.

"What the heck happened to the video cassette viewing machine?" Wanda's mother asked. Wanda shrugged his shoulders, but deep down inside he felt ashamed. He knew it was his fault that the machine was broken.

His mother sighed and unplugged the machine. In her private thoughts, Wanda's mother blamed Uncle Pamela, imagining him spending countless hours rewinding and replaying his videos while she was at work and Wanda was at school. But she didn't say anything out loud to anyone. That afternoon Wanda, his mother, and Uncle Pamela buried the video cassette player in the yard and had a small ceremony. Uncle Pamela sang the traditional step-uncle's lament and Wanda, reminiscing over all the good times he had with the deceased machine as well as feeling guilty for asking so much of it during its life, felt tears swell in his eyes. After the service, Wanda's mom walked to the New Machines Store and purchased another video cassette player because she believed that replacement was the best way to take the pain of loss away.

Four

Every year when his feet grew, Wanda bought new pointy tipped dancing shoes just like the ones his heroes wore. And he never ate lunch and he got skinnier and skinnier. Yet still he danced.

One day while Wanda was rehearsing a particularly formidable set of new moves that he was sure would help him win a spot on the dance troupe when he was old enough, he collapsed from exhaustion. It was a Friday. Wanda was 16 years old.

Wanda had been so enraptured in his new moves that he hadn't even noticed his mom come home from work early. When she saw her son lying still on the driveway, Wanda's mother had a totally super mega-tronic freak-out. Even though she recognized the tell-tale signs that accompany ferocious, diligent practicing of vampire dance techniques and she was wicked upset that her only son had lied to her, she ran to Wanda, swept his emaciated body up into her arms and rushed him to the clinic.

Wanda's mom always wanted Wanda to be well. She would do anything for him. That's how much she loved her boy.

They had never owned a car and Wanda's mom had never learned to drive. She never accepted rides from people either.

"There are two things I don't trust: Dancin' vamps, cars, and the people who drive cars. Well, I guess that makes three things..." she always said.

Wanda's mom had a good pair of shoes of reliable construction so she ran everywhere she went. This could be funny, especially when she was carrying home groceries.

And so she ran to the clinic with her dear and only son in her arms. It was an extra hot summer day and the sun was feeling especially ruthless and wanting to hurt as many humans as possible. But Wanda's mom didn't care about the mean, vindictive sun. She ran as fast as she could, faster than she had ever run before. She had to save her boy.

Three and three-eighths miles later they arrived at the clinic. Wanda's mom gasped and fell to her knees. Wanda tumbled out of her arms and sprawled out on the clinic steps. The aged oak of the towering clinic doors swung open and jabbed Wanda in the ribs. He mumbled and stirred. Two nurses leapt out of the clinic entrance. One tap danced to Wanda while the other twirled, did a back flip off the steps and bent down to check on Wanda's mom, who had fallen down on her side and was staring up at Wanda. The nurse grabbed her wrist to check her pulse.

Wanda's mom stretched out her hand toward Wanda. She looked at him with the love that only true moms have for their only sons. Her heart was beating out of her chest from running so fast. It tore through her skin and shirt and jumped and bounced on the concrete, squirting little sprays of blood out on the sidewalk and leaving a bloody hole in the loving mother's chest. Wanda's mom looked up at the dancing nurse.

"Take care of my dear boy," she said.

She turned her eyes back to her son. "I love you, Wanda, be a good boy. Make your mother proud. Stay in school. Make good grades. Brush your teeth. Go to an accredited institution of higher learnin'. Marry a nice girl, one that doesn't wear sweat pants to the mall..." spoke Wanda's mom, her eyes beaming with earnest concern.

The dancing nurse started tearing up because his mother had never spoken to him like Wanda's mom was speaking to Wanda in that moment; she'd only made fun of him for his dream of becoming a dancing nurse and joining the local nurses' dance troupe, Gestapo Ballet. He always thought that was the root cause of his bulimia.

While the nurse attendant to Wanda's mom was caught up in thoughts of the past and his resentment of his own mother, he didn't see the heart of Wanda's mom bouncing away. The other nurse saw the bouncing heart, though, and called out to his fellow dancer and healer.

"Hey, Gary, get that heart before it bounces away!" he hollered.

Gary's eyes darted around. He saw the heart of Wanda's loving mother bouncing toward the street.

"Oh geez!" Gary whispered in horror.

Gary the dancing nurse sprang up and spun on his big toe. He jumped and soared over Wanda's mom, who was still admonishing Wanda about being a good boy, and went into a series of twirls, each one bringing him closer to the bouncing heart. Just as Gary landed his final twirl and swooped down to scoop up the beautiful, caring heart of Wanda's mother, a rental moving truck sped down the street and squashed the bouncing heart. And in that moment one of the most true and loving hearts the world had ever known was squished underneath the tire of the Move Your Own Stupid Stuff You Lazy Puke rental moving truck company and splashed onto the face of Gary the dancing nurse.

Wanda's mother felt her heart get smashed under the weight of the unfeeling tire and all the love and the beauty went out of her heart and flew to Wanda.

Wanda's body shook as all of the love and care and good vibes from his mother's heart flooded into his own.

And Wanda's mom looked at her unconscious, exhausted son and smiled and spoke her final words: "...And please, Wanda, for the love of all that's nice and decent in this topsy turvy world, stay away from those frilly, pointy toed shoe wearin' dancin' vamps."

And Wanda's mom died right there on the sidewalk in front of the West Mable Town Clinic.

"Noooooooo!!!!" Gary screamed.

Gary was known in several circles for being a really emotional guy, but this would break anybody's heart because Wanda's mom was such an awesome lady.

Gary cursed the moving truck for its large tires and dependable transmission. He cursed himself for his slow twirling. "If only I'd twirled faster!" He screamed out loud to himself and anyone else who might hear him. He closed the eyes of Wanda's awesome mother and stopped traffic by doing the nurse's dance of sorrow in the middle of the street.

Five

When Wanda woke up he was inside the clinic, on a big fluffy bed, surrounded by a hundred deep red roses. Wanda saw the roses and started screaming. He was allergic to roses. Gary heard Wanda screaming and leaped and twirled to his bed side. Wanda put his hands behind his head, flipped up, spun sideways, and landed in Gary's arms. Gary carried him to the safety of a clean bed without any roses.

Gary sat Wanda down gracefully. He held Wanda's hand and looked into his eyes.

"That was some impressive flipping," Gary said.

"Thank you," said Wanda.

Gary's lips began to tremble. His eyes grew wet with tears. He was a really emotional guy. Wanda saw the pain in Gary's troubled expression. He squeezed Gary's hand.

"I'm Wanda," he said. "I love to dance."

Gary smiled a smile that was meek and small but that tried hard to be comforting and reassuring.

"I'm Gary," he said. "And I love to dance too."

Wanda searched Gary's eyes.

"How did I get here?" he asked. "The last thing I remember, I was out on the driveway practicing some new moves. They were particularly formidable."

Gary cleared his throat and told what he knew of the events that had brought Wanda to the clinic.

"I don't know the whole story," he began, "but it seems that you collapsed from exhaustion. You haven't eaten lunch since the seventh grade and you're underweight and dehydrated. Your mother brought you in."

"My mother...?" Wanda asked, looking around. "Where is she?"

"She's...she's..." Gary's voice cracked and broke. He turned his tear-filled eyes to the floor.

Wanda waited. Nervous dread filled his belly. His fingers tingled and his palms sweated.

Gary looked back up at Wanda. The dancing nurse's cheeks were flooded with sad tears.

"She didn't survive the run, Wanda. I'm sorry...I'm so, so sorry..."

Gary broke down in hysterical sobs and twirled away, leaving Wanda alone on a plain, fluffy bed that didn't have any roses on its plain white sheets. Wanda looked at his dancer feet and began to weep.

Six

Wanda was filled with anguish. The next day he left the clinic and went home and burned his collection of pointy toed dancing shoes. One pair for every year since the seventh grade went up in soaring flames. Bitter tears of lost love and lost dreams fell from his eyes. He felt all hope and reason slip away. And all the love and hope and care and good vibes that Wanda's mom had put into his heart was instantly buried under heaps of anger and resentment. A scowl etched across Wanda's face sang his hatred toward the universe.

"I'll never dance again," Wanda said to the whistling and crackling fire. "My dreams and ambition killed my mother. Now I will live a life of shame and the only shoes I will wear will be the soft, padded shoes of a home telecom sales representative without any sort of formal training."

Overhearing his lament, Wanda's melting shoes spoke to him from the fire.

"Wanda! Wanda!" the pointy toed dancing shoes cried out. "It wasn't your fault, Wanda, it was Gary!"

"What?" Wanda cried out, aghast. "I can't blame Gary; he did the best that he could."

"It was Gary! Gary killed your mother!" The melting shoes shouted. "He couldn't twirl fast enough to save her; it's his fault that she died! And he has a girl's name...a girl's name!"

Wanda felt a spark of anger ignite in his heart. He never really cared for twirlers or leapers. To him, that wasn't real dancing. Besides, he was easy to convince.

"You're right, melting pointy-toed dancing shoes that I starved myself to be able to secretly purchase, it is Gary's fault and he must pay for his slow twirling!" Wanda said. He flexed his toes with vengeful fury. "There's only one thing to do to make Gary pay. Try out for Blood Waltz, the rival dance troupe of the dancing nurses known locally as Gestapo Ballet. Then, gain super dancing skills and strength by becoming a dancing vampire and have my revenge by defeating Gary in a back-alley dance to the death competition."

Wanda smiled with insane glee and twiddled his finger-tips while the light from the fire played on his face and made him look creepy scary and wicked insane. Then, another voice came from the fire.

"Don't you do it, Wanda, revenge is no good and you know it!" The voice said.

"Mom...!" Wanda exclaimed. "But I have to avenge your death. Don't you want me to avenge your death?"

"It's a sweet sentiment, son, but you can't go and use dancin' for vengeance, it's not right."

"But mom...!"

"Don't you 'but mom' me! Now, listen, I've gotta make this quick because this fire is awful hot. I don't want you joinin' up with those dancin' blood suckers! They're up to no good. You can't use your dancin' powers for evil. Dance for good, Wanda. Be brave and let your feet sing and bring goodness into the world. Stay away from those frilly, pointy-toed shoe wearin' dancin' vamps! For the love of all the good and wholesome thingy-ma-bobs in this smurky-durky world! I love you, Wanda! Ouch, ouch...! Dang, this fire is hot--!"

"Mom...mom...come back!" Wanda shouted into the fire as his mother's voice faded away.

Wanda bowed his head and felt a rage stir within him. The fumes from the melting dancing shoes intoxicated him.

"Mothers don't always know best," the shoes whispered to

him. "Make Gary suffer. Make him pay."

Wanda's eyes lit up with a dark fire of their own.

"Yes," he said. "Make him suffer. Make him pay."

The shoes started to fill the air with maniacal laughter. And Wanda smiled and laughed along with them.

Seven

Wanda's thoughts leaped from the past to the present. It was Tuesday, the day of the try outs; the day he had waited for, the day he had worked so hard for, was finally here. He stood in the back alley behind Roy's Abortion Clinic Cupcake Café', leaning against the brick wall, waiting with a small group of other hopefuls for his name to be called, his new pair of pointy tipped dancing shoes slung over his shoulder. He thought of his mother and his heart ached. He remembered his plan of telling her he was going to Captivity Playhouse when he was really going to try outs. Wanda missed his mother. He pondered his revenge.

"Gary...," Wanda whispered under his breath.

His eyes burned with hate. His mouth burned from the twenty-seven whole jalapeño snacks he had eaten half an hour earlier.

Just as Wanda was getting into his vengeful musings and forgetting to be nervous about try outs, he heard his name echo down through the alley.

"Wanda Whorely," a shrill, high-pitched voice called out with authority.

Wanda stood up straight. He checked his shirt and ran a jittery hand through his hair. He held his chin up like his mom always told him to do and left his place at the back of the line.

The other hopefuls judged Wanda with their eyes as he passed them on his way up the alley.

Just up ahead, Wanda could see a short, pudgy man holding a clip board. The man wore blood red pointy toed dancing shoes. He was one of them. Wanda felt sweat prick on his brow. His heart began to race. He exhaled and tried to keep it cool. This is it! He thought. He smiled wide. His nervousness gave way to excitement. He was going to blow them away. He just knew it.

The pudgy dancing vampire stepped forward. "Wanda Whorely...?"

"Yes, that's me," Wanda said with a confident smile.

"I'm Nancy," the vampire said. "We're very happy to have you here with us today. We've heard of your plan to avenge your mother's death and we'd be delighted to help."

"How did you know of my plans to use the art of dance for vengeance?" Wanda asked.

"Your step-uncle, Pamela, told us about it when we all went out for milk and tarts last Thursday. He's really concerned. He knows how dangerous going up against Gestapo Ballet is going to be," Nancy explained.

"That Pamela, he's such a worrier. He must have overheard me talking about it in my sleep. I often talk about my plans for vengeance in my sleep, and, since he moved into my closet, I'm sure he's heard everything," Wanda said.

Nancy smiled and patted Wanda on the shoulder. "It's understandable," he said. "Well, come on, put on those shoes of yours, we've got some dancing to do!"

"All right...!" Wanda shouted, jumping up and throwing a fist into the air.

As Wanda laced up, all of the members of Blood Waltz stepped into the alley, their pointy toed dancing shoes clacking menacingly against the pavement. Wanda stood and joined them. Without a word, they faced down the group of wanna-be vampire dancers who stood at the other end of the alley.

Nancy stepped forward and addressed the left-overs. "Try outs are over," his shrill voice announced.

A chorus of muffled curses and sighs floated down from the huddled group.

Wanda felt bad for them because he knew that every person there had worked so hard just to be able to try out. He also knew what happened when you tried out and you didn't make it. That's when he heard the fingers start snapping. First one pair, then two, then three, then the alley filled with the rhythmic chatter. Wanda's legs started moving to the beat, then his shoulders. He noticed that he was in perfect sync with the other vampire dancers. He didn't even have to think, he just let his body move. They skulked and shimmied and snapped closer and closer to the group at the other end of the alley. The hopefuls stood hypnotized and helpless, caught in the dancing vampire's thrall, their eyes huge with adoration.

The Blood Waltz dancers broke out into a perfectly choreographed number, bouncing off the alley's brick walls, walking on their hands, spinning and flying. Wanda fell in and moved with a grace and presence that he didn't know he had. He heard grand themes in his mind, his body twisted and contorted and he threw down with the most formidable moves in an effortless fusion of rhythm and symmetry.

As he weaved between the dancing vampires, Wanda felt blood rain down on his mouth and cheeks. He licked his lips and tasted iron. Nearby screams crashed down on his ears; tender lyrics from the sweetest songs of death and dismemberment. A severed head rolled up to Wanda. He jumped over it and tapped his toes in mid-air. He triple-cart-whirled, went down on one knee and finished by throwing his hands up in an arc of triumph. A random pile of flying intestines flopped against Wanda's chest and fell to the ground in front of him. The members of Blood Waltz stared at him with huge, sincere smiles stretched across their blood and gut drenched faces. Hoots, hollers and hoorays erupted through the alley. Nancy ran to Wanda and pulled him to his feet and embraced him.

"You're brilliant!! You're amazing!!" Nancy shouted out with glee. "You're ready to become one of us!"

Nancy spun Wanda around to face the other Blood Waltz dancers. They licked blood from their lips and clapped and cheered. Nancy got behind Wanda while Wanda loosened his dancing pants and let them fall to the ground. Nancy dropped down to his knees, pulling Wanda's powder blue man thong underwear down with him.

Wanda winced at the pain when he felt Nancy's fangs sinking into his left butt cheek. The other dancers chanted as Nancy sucked on Wanda's butt.

"Wanda! Wanda! Wanda! Wanda!" They shouted in unison.

Tears of joy came to Wanda's eyes, mixed with tears of pain from the razor sharp fangs that were digging into his rear end. This is the greatest moment of my life, Wanda thought, and vampire fangs are wicked sharp!

Nancy came up, gasping for air and holding the severed head that Wanda had danced over earlier. He waited for Wanda to pull up his underwear and pants. When Wanda was fully clothed once again, Nancy handed Wanda the severed head. Wanda looked down at the bloody head and felt stricken with a sudden blood lust, like when you really want to drink your favorite soda and nothing else will do.

He licked his lips.

He tipped the severed head up and felt the blood flow into his open mouth.

Deafening cheers filled Wanda's ears as he gulped down the sacred crimson. He felt the change coursing through his body. He was becoming a dancing vampire. All of his dreams were finally coming true.

Wanda drank and drank and sucked on the neck stump of the severed head while the other members of Blood Waltz danced and cheered and threw down moves of jubilation.

The celebration was brought to an abrupt halt when the back door to Roy's Abortion Clinic Cupcake Café' swung open and slammed against the brick wall of the alley. A seven foot, seven inch tall woman with triple D breasts made of solid brass, known locally as Roy, came storming out, her pink apron covered in flour and liquefied placenta. The slamming of the door scared the be-Julies out of the dancing vampires. They jumped in the air and squealed in fright. When they saw that it was just Roy, sighs of relief and low but sincere laughter rumbled through the alley. Nancy swept a hand across his forehead.

Everyone loved Roy. For as long as Nancy could remember, Blood Waltz had been holding their auditions as well as their mostly legendary brawls, some of which are rumored to have reached mythic status, in the alley that runs along behind Roy's café'. From the very beginning, Roy always supported the vamp's violent activities and found their choice of location very amusing. She once asked Nancy about this. "I'm not exactly sure, Roy, it just feels right," Nancy had replied.

When Roy was a young girl she had dreamed of making cupcakes. Her father, although supportive of his daughter's ambitions, had encouraged her to seek a more financially stable career. "Why don't you try abortion? I've always heard its very satisfying work as well as being quite lucrative."

Never being one to want to let her father down, Roy carefully weighed her decision. When the time came for her to take her inheritance and leave home, she knew just what to do.

She took her several thousand dollars and invested in massive brass boobs. Everyone who saw Roy and her new boobs was so impressed they always yelled some kind of exuberant expression. Some fell down and worshipped her. Some cried. Some masturbated. Some went blind.

One day Roy bought a pink tutu and spray painted it gold. That's when she was hit by a flash of inspiration. She decided that she would combine the arts of abortion and cup-cakery and create a café' that would capture all the beauty, ambience, and magic of the world's greatest waiting rooms and combine it with the allure of Roy's favorite interstate rest stops. And it would be right in town. And everyone would come. And it would be called Roy's Abortion Clinic Cupcake Café'!

After taking some pink magic correspondence courses, Roy opened her café'. Her father was so proud.

"Roy, you are my dearest, most beloved first born daughter. You have followed your dreams yet retained a sense of realism and practicality which is rarely seen in people of your age. I am so very, very proud of you!" He said to Roy at the grand opening ceremony.

"Thanks, dad...!" Roy said with tears streaming from her eyes. Then they shared a big father daughter bear hug. It was so awesome!

A few minutes later a woman arrived in a panic. Her name was Tray. Yes, she spelled it with an "A". She was holding her tummy and hollering about the stupid kid inside her. He was beating the snot out of her from the inside. "Please help me!" She cried.

Roy knew she had to come to the rescue. For hours and

hours Roy tried every technique she knew to get rid of the menacing baby but the child thwarted her at every turn, outwitting her, fighting her off, always staying one step ahead. After eight grueling hours Roy called it quits.

"Father, I have failed," Roy said to her dad, who had been by her side throughout the tumultuous day.

"Only the truest warrior can accept defeat with honor," Roy's father said, comforting his daughter.

"Gee, you always know what to say," Roy said. "I love you, dad."

"And I love you too, my dear."

Just as Roy and her father were about to share in another great big bear hug, a tiny weeping voice came from inside Tray's belly.

"The love that you two share...It's just so beautiful!" The squeaky baby voice said.

"Our family is very close," Roy said to Tray's belly.

The baby cried out and kicked the be-Julies of out Tray's uterus.

"Ooowwww...!" Tray screamed. "Get this little maniac outta me! He's way too emotional!"

Tray grabbed a nearby knife and slammed the sharp blade into the bottom of her stomach.

"No...!" Roy screamed, lunging toward Tray.

Roy's father grabbed her and yanked her back.

"There's nothing you can do for her now!" He yelled.

Tray screamed as she carved across her stomach like a child carving a pumpkin, the knife's blade working up and down and in and out, sawing the flesh, blood spurting from the wound. When Tray had cut across the length of her belly, she threw the knife down and thrust a hand up into her body.

"C'mere you little runt...!" She shouted, working her hand around inside her.

"You'll never catch me, you big meanie!" The tiny child squeaked.

Tray reached back and shoved her hand deep inside her.

"Aha! I Got 'Chu, you stinkin' munchkin!" She yelled.

Tray jerked her hand out of her stomach and held the blood covered baby up in the kitchen's sharp fluorescent lights. The baby coughed and cried and rubbed his eyes.

"No, no, put me back in! I don't like it out here!" The emotional baby wailed.

"Too bad, you're out now!" Tray screamed at the baby.

She picked up the knife and cut her own umbilical cord. She held the baby out in the light for all to see. She looked the baby in the eyes and spit on the floor.

"And behold, the babe was a man-child and she named him Gary, which means "One who twirls too slowly"," Tray shouted.

Roy and her father gasped.

"You can't curse the child!" Roy's father protested.

"Hush up, you...!" Tray shouted.

"But it's not fair, to give him a girl's name like that," Roy protested.

"Life's not fair," Tray said, hobbling off the prep table. She handed the tiny baby to Roy. "Now, if you'll excuse me. I have an appointment somewhere to do something."

Roy and her father watched Tray walk out of the kitchen and tiny baby Gary wept in Roy's arms.

"She gave me a girl's name...!" Baby Gary screeched. "...A girl's name!"

Roy looked into his father's eyes. Her lips turned down in a frown. "My first abortion was a total disaster. How will I ever succeed and achieve my dreams of making abortion cupcakes?"

A smile lit across the lips of Roy's father. "My sweet, not giving up at the first failure is a success in, and of, itself."

Roy smiled. "Gee, thanks dad!"

Roy's father put his arm around his beloved daughter. They looked down at tiny baby Gary.

"What are we going to do with this little guy?" Roy wondered aloud. "He's quite a special dude."

"He really is," Tray said.

Roy and her father whirled around. Tray stood before them, holding her innards in her blood drenched hands.

"I overreacted. I shouldn't a got so mad."

She held out a bloody hand. "Give 'im here. I'll take care of 'im."

Roy eyed Tray suspiciously. "You know you can't change his name, though. You said it out loud and you can never take that back."

"I know, what's done is done. I'll do my best to raise 'im up right like a good man, even though I went an gave 'im a girl's name."

Tray continued to hold out her hand. "Please, give 'im here. Gimme my boy..."

Roy looked at her father for reassurance. He nodded and Roy handed baby Gary over to his mother.

"Now, if you'll excuse me, I got a son with a girl's name to raise," Tray said.

As Tray turned to walk away, she took one last look back at Roy. "Nice tits," She said.

"Thanks...!" Roy replied.

And then Tray and baby Gary left the café'.

Roy didn't give up that day. Every day she worked on her crafts of abortion and cup-cakery, growing stronger and stronger in her powers. When she met the earliest members of Blood Waltz eating some conjoined twins while tap dancing out in the alley behind the café' she felt her spirit move. She asked the vamps what was going on. The two founding members of Blood Waltz explained their dream of leading Mable Town's greatest, most vicious vampire dance troupe' to Roy, and asked if they could use the alley behind her shop for violence and special events. Roy admired the vampires' vision and told them it would be her pleasure. And ever since that day, Roy's Abortion Clinic Cupcake Café' has been like a second home to the generations of Blood Waltz dancers, of which this is only the second, because they really haven't been around that long.

Roy looked at Nancy and his friends with patience and love in her eyes.

"Could you dancing vamps knock it down a bit? I'm trying to make cupcakes in there," She said.

Utterances of apologies fluttered through the dance troupe.

"Okay then...thank you," the tall woman said. "And before you go, could you please put these bodies in the dumpster?" She swept her arm and pointed in a general direction at the butchered and dismembered corpses of wanna-be vampire dancers that lay strewn across the alleyway floor.

Wanda followed Roy's pointing finger. For the first time, he saw the bodies and body parts and entrails and puddles of blood that littered the alley through his new, blood-lusty vampire vision. Yum! He thought. That looks delicious!

"Sorry for the mess, Roy, we'll tidy up," Nancy said.

"Such a sweet, tiny man," Roy said to Nancy.

Roy waved goodbye and the door creaked shut behind her.

"What a nice lady," Wanda said to Nancy.

"And you should taste her cupcakes," Nancy said as he rubbed his belly. "Simply unbelievable, the woman is a culinary genius."

"Nice boobs too!" A voice from near the dumpster said.

Wanda spun around and looked for the voice. "Uncle Pamela!" He said. "What are you doing here?"

"Oh, me...? I was just masturbating behind that dumpster, like I do every Tuesday," Pamela said between giggles.

The vampire dancers all broke out in riotous laughter, swinging and punching and kicking each other.

"Dang Uncle Pamela, you're so crazy!" Wanda said, clutching his belly in laughter.

Wanda laughed so hard that he fell down to his knees. He wound his arms around his tummy. A sharp pain began in the center of his stomach and burned outward. Knots formed and twisted and tightened inside him.

"Ow...Oww...Owwww...!" Wanda cried.

In an instant Nancy was by his side.

"What is it, Wanda?" Nancy asked with eyes full of worry.

"I don't know," Wanda said. He squinted in agony. "My stomach is all up in burning knots. It feels like someone made me eat bricks made of broken glass and then after that, they made me drink fire."

Nancy gasped and put a hand over his mouth.

"Oh no, this can't be!" He said. "You're Bloodtose intolerant!"

Nancy punched the pavement and squealed. "Only two dancing vampires in history have ever been Bloodtose intolerant."

Wanda felt like he was going to cry. He was in serious pain.

Tears were forming in Nancy's eyes. He couldn't believe this was happening.

"We'll get through this," Nancy said. "You'll have to buy the special Bloodtose-free blood from the special vampire health food store, but you'll be okay. Children may stare at you and point and laugh and call you a freak, but you'll survive..."

Wanda grabbed Nancy by the frill of his frilly shirt sleeve.

"Nancy..." Wanda said. "None of that matters to me now...just tell me one thing...will I still be able to dance?"

Nancy laughed out loud. Tears covered his face. "Yes! Yes my dear Wanda, you will always be able to dance!"

Nancy grabbed Wanda's hand and squeezed it tight. Wanda looked deep into Nancy's eyes. "Then I will have my revenge," Wanda said.

Nancy's lips curled into a mischievous smile. "Yes, my dear Wanda...You will have your revenge."

And Nancy and Wanda held hands and cackled until the vampire ambulance arrived and took Wanda away.

Eight

Later on that day Wanda was all hopped up on goofballs and walking out of the hospital's front doors.

"Gary..." Wanda whispered under his vampire breath as Nancy helped him into the plush backseat of his luxurious, convertible eight passenger rickshaw.

Nancy was so proud of his rickshaw. His father had helped him build it when he was a teenager, just after he had been promoted to lead dancer. The frame was the brightest yellow. The seats were the deepest burgundy velvet. Bright pink plastic tassels cascaded out of the handle bar grips. The entire passenger cart was outlined with the human teeth of Nancy's victims. Mummified testicles dangled from the edges of the folding hood; which itself was made of human skin that had been perfectly aged and dyed a regal shade of the deepest purple. And, of course, the Blood Waltz logo was painted proudly across the back in huge, bright red, flowing cursive letters. Nancy's father had been a true rickshaw master craftsman and his legend lived on in Mable Town even to this very day.

"This is a hot rickshaw," Nancy's father had told him. "One day you will have sexual thoughts in this rickshaw."

Nancy loved his father. He thought of him whenever he saw a squirrel acting up because Nancy's father had died in the great Mable Town squirrel fiasco, when a hundred million squirrels had descended on the town and gone insane, drinking and cursing and fighting. Nancy's father had been on his way home from the vampire candy store, known locally as Sweet Fang, when he had been confronted and cursed at by a pack of the drunken squirrels. The foul language and lewd behavior of the tiny, furry miscreants was too much for Nancy's father, and he died of shock, right there in the crosswalk.

Wanda leaned back, holding his stomach, while Nancy got into the driver's seat. Nancy looked side to side, honked the horn and started pedaling. Nancy's pedaling was so loud Wanda thought his ears were going to explode. But everyone knew that Nancy was a loud peddler, so Wanda couldn't complain. He was also very thankful to have such a good friend who would give him a ride home from the hospital.

"First we're going to Trader Vlad's Whole Bloods Market to get you some Bloodtose-free blood. Then I'm taking you home, mister dancer," Nancy hollered over the loud pedaling in his high-pitched, manly voice. "What did the doctor say?"

"The doctor was very nice and helpful," Wanda shouted. "Her name was Hercules Valentino Menudo Gonzalez IV, Esquire, and she was as big as the Terminator. She used to goof off in the sand wars, and, after years of Approval Killing, her heightened self-esteem allowed her to pursue a study of the medicinal arts. She's very good at her profession! After carefully examining me for several hours and getting to know me on an intimate, first name basis, she prescribed me two days casket rest with no dancing."

"Dang, dang, dang...!" Nancy screamed. "That means we can't exact your revenge until Friday and Friday is when the powers of Gestapo Ballet are at their highest! And, as if that wasn't enough, this Friday is the full moon, and we all know what happens on the full moon. That's when Gestapo Ballet is able to channel even the most secret, most diabolical Nazi dance moves; moves that were believed to have been lost to the ravages of time and poor penmanship."

Nancy started fidgeting and wringing the grips on his handle bars. "What are we going to do...oh goodness oh my, what ever are we going to do...?"

The two dancing vampires came to a stop light. Wanda's heart filled with sympathy for his dear friend. He rested a reassuring hand on Nancy's shoulder. Nancy turned around. Their eyes met. Nancy saw the burning need for vengeance in Wanda's eyes and all of his anxieties vanished through his wiggling toes. He knew they were going to be okay.

"Gary..." Wanda whispered.

"Yes..." Nancy said. His eyebrows raised in an awesomely evil arch.

Wanda and Nancy both hunched their shoulders and the two friends began to cackle. The light turned green and the cycle started moving. And Nancy's super loud peddling drowned out the vampires' joy-filled laughter as they sped away down the street.

Nine

Gary was in the clinic bathroom puking. He was mad that his mother had given him a girl's name, but that wasn't the reason he was throwing up. Gary had tried to hide his bulimia but everyone knew even though, out of politeness, they pretended not to. All the other dancing nurses told themselves and their step-uncles that Gary just enjoyed vomiting. But, neither bulimia nor the sheer enjoyment of vomit was to blame for Gary's hurling that afternoon. He knew that Wanda and the Blood Waltz dance troupe would be coming for him to seek revenge for the death of Wanda's mother. Uncle Pamela had made a special visit to the clinic and told Gary all about it, taunting Gary and waving his fingers and masturbating and laughing in front of all the other nurses.

Gary knew there was no way to get out of the confrontation. He'd never been in a face-to-face, back alley, dance to the death dance off before, and he was wrecked. He was so nervous he could barely see. And it was only Tuesday.

Gary retched into the toilet one final time, and then he blew his nose and washed his face. He looked at himself in the mirror, staring deep and long into his own eyes. He felt a new strength and a steely resolve come over him. He heard the admonishment of generations of step-uncles in his mind. He remembered the dancing nurse's oath ("Ever my feet shall move and my hands shall heal, until death and beyond, I promise thee!") and a solemn grimace spread across his countenance.

"If I'm going down," he spat. "I'm going down twirling."

Ten

The sun rose and Friday arrived right on schedule. Gary shoved back the sheets and reluctantly crawled out of bed while, across town, Wanda raised the lid of his coffin and smiled to greet the day.

"Hello, Friday!" Wanda said to the sparkling air. His voice seemed to echo through the still morning and return his greeting. Wanda felt a sense of the sacred, a sense of awe. He knew that today was going to be a special day and that, centuries from now, dancing nurses would whisper of the horror and defeat that their brethren suffered at the hands of Blood Waltz on that day. Wanda smiled the biggest smile that had ever formed across his lips, jumped out of his coffin and headed for the kitchen to have a healthy breakfast of fruit, toast, grilled fingers, and Bloodtose-free blood.

Gary was halfway through a bowl of Sugar Mums when he gagged and puked, spewing partially digested cereal all over the kitchen table. He jumped up and ran to the bathroom. While heaving into the toilet, Gary cried and wondered if this was going to be his last day on earth. I like it here, he thought, I don't want to leave.

Eleven

Gary sat with the other Gestapo Ballet dancers. They were all gathered in the alley behind Roy's Abortion Clinic Cupcake Café'. The fragrant aroma of old blood, rotted flesh, and baked goods wafted through the air. The old iron door to the café' creaked and Roy stepped out carrying a tray of cupcakes. She saw the solemn looks on the nurses' faces. She knew the situation was grave. She hoped she could help brighten the mood.

"I brought cupcakes for everyone," Roy announced to the nurses in a cheery voice.

The dancing nurses grumbled and nabbed the little cakes. Orgasmic cooing and moaning echoed through the alley as Gestapo Ballet inhaled the delectable deserts, except for Gary, who sat alone, leaned against the dumpster, his head between his knees. Roy's brow crinkled. With one cupcake left, she went to Gary.

"There's one left, just for you," Roy said in a gentle voice, kneeling next to Gary and holding the little cake out to him.

"No thanks," Gary said. "I'm too sad to eat."

Roy's ears perked up and did a weird wavy thing. She thought she recognized Gary's voice.

"Why are you so sad?" Roy asked.

"Because I'm going to die today; I don't stand a chance against those vamps. Their skills are unsurpassed."

As Roy listened to Gary talk, her face lit up. Her eyes went wide. She remembered. Yes, it was him; Gary, the cursed one. She would know that voice anywhere. His mom was right, he is really emotional.

Roy looked deep into Gary's sad eyes. "Listen...You may not remember, but, you and I met years ago, and it was a meeting that changed my life forever. It taught me to never give up. I remember you, Gary, and I know that you're a fighter. Deep down, I know you know it too, you know."

Gary returned Roy's gaze. He felt a stir of recognition. "You do seem somewhat familiar. I can't quite place it, though."

"No need to worry about that now," Roy said. "Just eat your cupcake and do your best. I'm sure you'll be fine."

Gary smiled a tiny smile and took the cupcake off the tray.

"Thanks..." He said.

Roy nodded and stood up. Gary took a deep breath and bit into the cupcake. He felt a tingling sensation spread over his body. He looked at his fellow dancers and suddenly things weren't so bad. It seemed that abortion cupcakes did make a difference after all! But this was the secret that Roy had known all along: Abortion cupcakes make everything all better. Roy smiled at the dancing nurses and turned to walk back inside. Just before she stepped through the door, Roy stopped and twirled. Her massive brass boobs bounced. She looked at the nurses before her.

"Dance hard, boys..." Roy said. She twirled through the back entrance and the old iron door slammed shut behind her.

The dancing nurses of Gestapo Ballet swore an oath to honor the abortion cupcake lady. Then they gathered around the dumpster and chanted the summoning chant to summon the fullness of their powers. It was Friday and Gestapo Ballet was ready to dance!

Gary looked around at his fellow dancing nurses, at his friends, and felt overwhelmed with gratitude. His ears twitched. In the distance he heard the faint sound of obnoxiously loud pedaling. *They're coming*, he thought as his pulse began to rise.

Twelve

Shop keeps ran inside, bolted their doors and turned their 'open' signs to 'closed'. Mothers grabbed their children and whisked them off the sidewalks. Cats and dogs and wild townie moose fled into empty alleyways. And everyone watched from their hiding places as Blood Waltz tore through the empty streets of west Mable Town on Nancy's luxurious, convertible eight passenger rickshaw, top down, the vampires' hair blowing in the wind. Wanda sat in the front seat wearing his favorite frilly, bright blue button up shirt. He grimaced and thought of revenge.

Thirteen

The troupe of dancing nurses known locally as Gestapo Ballet stood in formation, listening as the pedaling got closer and closer and louder and louder. Gary wished for a way out. He couldn't believe what was happening. Sure, dancing vampires and dancing nurses had always been arch rivals, he could accept that, but he couldn't grasp Wanda's thirst for vengeance. Gary had done his best to save Wanda's mother and failed, but he had tried with all his heart. He just wanted Wanda to understand.

The pedaling grew even louder. Gary gritted his teeth. The stale taste of toothpaste and vomit lingered on his tongue. Beads of sweat formed on his eyebrows. His bright pink scrubs clung to his body in the humidity of the dank alley. The quickly approaching pedaling stung his ears. He heard giggles and glanced over his shoulder. It was just Uncle Pamela masturbating behind the dumpster.

Gary shrugged and returned his attention to the empty end of the alley. The sound of the pedaling was nearly deafening when Nancy's rickshaw roared into the alley and skidded to an abrupt stop. The eyes of the vampires were on the nurses as they leaped down gracefully from the bright yellow cycle.

With Wanda and Nancy out front, the dancing vamps strutted toward the nurses. Gary felt his skin crawl at the clacking sound of the vampire's pointy toed shoes against the pavement. When they were about ten feet away, Nancy held up his hand, signaling for the vamps to stop.

A breathless silence fell over the alley. The only sound was Uncle Pamela's furious masturbating, which was really pretty distracting. Nancy cleared his throat.

"Quit it, Uncle Pamela...please!" Nancy yelled.

"...heee...heee...sorry," Uncle Pamela mumbled.

Then it was silent for real. Wanda and Gary stared each other down. The nurses and vamps watched each other, waiting for someone to make the first move. Suddenly the big iron back door to Roy's Abortion Clinic Cupcake Café' flew open and crashed against the brick wall. Gary and Wanda flinched and jumped. The nurses leapt up and twirled in a panic. The dancing vampires, known locally as Blood Waltz, flew through the air in an anxious, perfectly choreographed group flip, landed, snapped their fingers and bobbed their shoulders up and down.

"Let the dancing begin!" Roy shouted in jubilation as she threw up her hands and sent cupcakes and amniotic fluid sailing through the air.

At the sound of Roy's words, Wanda felt his feet moving on the concrete beneath him. He glided across the alley toward a twirling nurse. Wanda spun down and flipped sideways. The twirling nurse stopped twirling and stared at Wanda's moves in complete amazement.

Gary saw his fellow dancing nurse stop dancing.

"Sheila...no...!" Gary shouted from across the alley. "Don't stop twirling! Don't look at him...he'll put you in a trance!"

But it was too late. Sheila's eyes were fixed on Wanda. He couldn't stop watching Wanda dance. Sheila's eyes filled with tears as he fell under Wanda's mesmerizing spell.

"I'm no good! I'll never dance like that!" he cried out.

Sheila punched himself in the throat. He grabbed a sharp, broken cotton swab that was stiff with the dried blood of a trillion disemboweled fetuses off the alley floor and began jabbing it into his eyes.

"I hate myself!" Sheila roared as he plunged the swab shank into his eyes again and again until his eyes turned to bloody goo and drained out of their sockets. Sheila stabbed the gore soaked Q-Tip into his throat and sank down against the alley's brick wall. With bitter tears flowing down his cheeks Sheila took his final breath.

Wanda giggled triumphantly and did a double back flip. The nurses were twirling and tapping, their eyes wide and desperate, clinging to the hope that they could defeat Blood Waltz with their Nazi dance moves.

Through his frantic twirling Gary caught blurred glimpses of his fellow dancing nurses falling victim to the powers of the vampires' vengeful dance.

Nurse Trisha was hypnotized by Nancy's pop-locking. Nancy popped and locked and pulled off Trisha's arms and threw them at the armless nurse. Trisha's severed arms went into a fit of confusion and started tickling Trisha. His arms didn't know that Trisha was deathly allergic to tickling. Trisha fell to the pavement, his body wracked with convulsions, foam pouring out of his nose and mouth. His eyes filled with terror and his heart stopped beating.

Nurse Susan was captivated by the flowing elegance of the movements of Rosalina; Blood Waltz's founding member and elder dancer.

Nurse Susan's feet stopped moving and his eyes and heart were fixed on Rosalina.

He's so beautiful, thought Susan, so graceful, so debonair. I'll never be like that...I stink! Nurse Susan's eyes closed. He fell down and died of disappointment next to the dumpster.

Wanda put his moves on Thelma-Lou, the nurse who attended to him on the clinic steps the day his mother died. Thelma-Lou's eyes bulged out, glazed over in hypnotic stares as Wanda's feet glided across the alleyway floor and his jazz hands threw shapes in the air. Thelma-Lou tapped a traditional Nazi tap dance as hard as he could but it was no use against the fury of Wanda's jazz hands. He tried to close his eyes. He tried to look away but Wanda's jazz hands had him in their thrall. It was all too much for the dancing nurse known locally as Thelma-Lou. He skidded sideways. He stopped dancing. He ripped the crotch out of his scrubs and tore off his good luck neon orange man thong to reveal a fertile garden of untouched, untrimmed, untamed pubic hair.

"Goodbye my lovely forest!" Thelma-Lou screeched. He ripped at his award-winning pubic thatch with furious, tearing fingers.

Blood and puss flew up as Thelma-Lou ripped the hairs out at their root. A huge bundle of pubes amassed at Thelma-Lou's feet. He picked the hair up. Using his knowledge from his pre-teen years of sailing and marauding on the high seas, he fashioned his pubes into a length of rope with a noose at one end.

"Goodbye beautiful dancers!" Thelma-Lou shouted. His voice cracked with pain. His words broke and spilled out hopeless sorrow.

Thelma-Lou tossed the pubic hair rope over the arm of the lamp post that held the light that illuminated Roy's backdoor after dark. He shimmied up the tall post and tightened the noose around his neck and the other end of the rope to the lamp post's arm.

Gary saw Thelma-Lou from across the alley. He started twirling toward him.

"Thelma-Lou...No...Wait...Get down from that lamp post! Get that handcrafted pubic hair noose out from around your neck!" Gary shouted.

"Dance on ye mighty nurses!" Thelma-Lou cried. "...Sieg heil!"

Thelma-Lou threw a fist into the air. He slipped and fell, crotch first, onto the lamp post's cold metal arm, wracking his naked balls and freezing his brain with pain and regret. He flipped sideways and spun off the post, the pubic hair noose snapping his neck and leaving his feet dangling inches above the dirty alleyway floor.

And Gary watched helpless as one by one, the members of Gestapo Ballet became spellbound by the charms of the vampires' dance and their lives came to a violent end.

This can't be happening! Gary thought.

"Oh, but it is! Muwahahaha...!" Nancy said from behind.

Gary whirled around. "What? How did you..."

"I heard your thoughts, doofus face! You shouldn't think so loud, you big doodie head! Muwahahaha! Muwahahaha...!"

Nancy laughed and danced away, leaving Gary alone with his loud thoughts. Gary stopped twirling and stood still. A bright light-bulb, as big as a birthday balloon, appeared above his head. Gary reached up, pulled the light-bulb down, and looked inside. There was an idea. It was bright and helpful and appealing. It showed him how he could fight the vampires. Gary smiled and took out the idea. He pushed the idea through his ear and into his brain. Then he twirled twice and threw the empty light-bulb into the dumpster.

Gary started tapping and twirling and thinking really loud and then even louder until he was thinking so loud that the sides of his skull felt like they might burst open, turn into birds and fly away. And he thought the saddest, most painful thoughts he could bring into his aching head.

Gary thought about the great Mable Town vampire massacre of '84, when hundreds of innocent vampires lost their lives to angry retail shoppers who were leading pointless and unfulfilling lives and needed a scapegoat for their misery and frustration. He remembered the faces of grieving vampire mothers that he had seen on TV as a child, calling out the names of their dead vampire children.

Gary recalled the news report he had seen on a school lunch food factory. He let himself see it all again. Hundreds of thousands of millions of trillions of innocent, squeaking kittens falling down shoots and into massive grinders, ground alive to be made into kitty cakes for the rich school children to eat with their government subsidized lunches.

Gary twirled, stopped, and glanced at the dancing vampires. They were slowing down. Nancy shook his head and rubbed his eyes. The sad and terrible thoughts were starting to drain the dancing vampires' strength. It was working!

Gary looked back at his fellow dancing nurses. He had been too late. They were all dead. Gestapo Ballet had fallen to the vamps and Gary was the only one left. His heart broke for his fallen brothers; Trisha, Susan, Thelma-Lou, Erika, Sheila, Tiffany, Kirsty, and, of course, Barb. Sweet Barb! He had been Gary's closest friend ever since their days at the dancing nurses' academy.

Gary watched as the lifeless corpses of the dancing nurses rose up off the hard concrete and ascended to heaven. He watched them until they floated into golden sky and disappeared from sight. He felt a punch to the gut. He never even got to say goodbye.

Gary's tear-filled eyes went back to the dancing vampires. Gary let them feel all of his sorrow. He thought about how much he would miss his friends and about all the good times they'd had together. Overwhelmed with grief, Gary started hyperventilating, his heart beating and pounding, stretching the skin on his chest. Before he could stop it, Gary's heart beat out of his chest and started bouncing down the alley toward the street. His heart was so sad that all it wanted to do was bounce into oncoming traffic and get squished so the pain would go away. Gary's will to live and to dance evaporated into the ether. He fell to his knees and watched his heart bounce away.

The dancing vampires, known locally as Blood Waltz, felt all of Gary's weepy sadness, and it was a lot of sadness, a whole,

whole lot, because Gary is a really emotional guy (and he has a girl's name). The vamps began to falter. They lost their rhythm. Their perfect choreography shattered and fell apart beneath the weight of Gary's anguish and loss.

Wanda lost his footing. He tripped, slid across the alley and slammed into the brick wall.

All the dancing vampires were tripping and slipping and bumbling around the alley, crying, wailing, pouring tears of sadness and regret, clutching their heads in agony at the pain of Gary's blaring, grief-filled thoughts.

Wanda brushed his frilly shirt off. He heard Gary scream. He felt the kind nurse's pain and his eyes filled with golden tears, the kind of tears that vampires cry only when they feel the deepest mourning.

"Come back...!" Gary called out, his eyes raised to the sky, searching for his departed friends.

Wanda looked in Gary's direction and saw the nurse's big, wounded heart bouncing toward the street. It was rush hour in west Mable Town and Gary's heart was about to jump out into traffic. Wanda looked at Gary.

Gary cried so hard that his tears turned to blood. His face was red with the crimson sorrow. He looked so lonely and scared and sad. Wanda's thirst for vengeance waned. He heard the voice of his mother, "Be a good boy, Wanda, and always help others."

Wanda's lips trembled and the golden tears poured down his cheeks. He tasted the bitter salt on his lips.

"*Gary...*" he whispered through tearful sobs.

Wanda's jazz hands formed into determined fists. He snorted and spat a huge loogie. Wanda spun, jumped and clapped his pointy toed shoes together in mid leap. He front flipped into an electric slide and headed for the street, straight toward Gary's bouncing heart.

The other vampires spun and bumped into each other in confusion.

Wanda felt the light in his heart. He spun. He leaped. He cartwheeled. He threw down moves so new that they hadn't even been dreamed of yet. He danced out of the alley and jumped over the sidewalk.

Gary's heart sprung off the curb and landed in the busy street. The sad heart bounced up again, high and determined, hurling itself against the oncoming traffic. Wanda landed in a perfect arabesque pose. His hand jutted out. Like a hero from an '80's movie, Wanda caught Gary's heart just before it sailed in front of the tire of a moving van from the Move Your Own Stupid Stuff You Lazy Puke moving truck rental company.

Wanda pulled Gary's heart in and clutched it safely against his chest. Holding the nurse's heart close, Wanda flipped off the sidewalk and backwards into the alley. He skipped and flittered. He spun and kicked and bounced off the alley's brick walls and went into a series of handless cartwheels, making his way straight to Gary. The other dancing vampires heard Gary's thoughts of sheer amazement at the graceful beauty of Wanda's dance. They stopped their broken movements and looked on. And the powers of love and of dance enraptured them all.

Wanda danced harder than he had ever, ever danced before. Sweat poured into his eyes and blurred his vision. His mouth was parched with thirst. His lungs burned with emptiness. And still he danced.

The air was electric. The alley was charged with anticipation. Every eye was on Wanda.

Wanda went into a jazz walk. Everyone gasped. Then he flapped and turned. Nancy squealed and threw up his hands, astounded by Wanda's combination of moves.

Wanda moonwalked into a backward, handless, sideways double flip. He landed on the pointy tip of his left pointy toed dancing shoe and spiraled down into a back spin. 'Round and 'round Wanda went, gathering speed until his legs whirled up and he made a flawless transition into a head spin.

Gary's mouth fell open.

Wanda twisted out of the head spin and flew into the air. Everything seemed to go into slow motion as Wanda did a triple backward somersault into a frontward flip transitioning to a sideways quadruple spin.

With grace and ease Wanda came out of the last spin and landed on one knee in front of Gary. He bowed his head and held the still beating heart out to Gary.

With happy tears of blood streaming down his already blood—soaked face, Gary took his heart from Wanda and placed it back in his chest. Wanda stood up and smiled at Gary.

With his heart back in its place, Gary felt love, hope, goodness, and new life and energy flowing through his veins. He stepped back and went into a twirl of pure joy. He twirled and he burst with happy laughs that echoed through the alley.

Wanda felt a wind pick up. He watched as Gary gained more speed. Gary was turning into a spinning blur of color and laughter. Wanda stood still, captivated, nay, hypnotized by Gary's whirlwind twirling, while the other vampires slinked back, hissing in fear. Gary went up on his toes. He started spinning so fast that he created his own gravity. The wind around Gary became a roaring funnel cloud. Wanda started to try to back away. The wind and the gravity yanked at his favorite frilly shirt.

"Not my shirt!" Wanda said as the fabric began to tear.

Buttons flew into the twirling vortex. Wanda struggled against the gravity of the human cyclone. His shirt ripped and flew off his body.

"No...!" Wanda shouted.

He grabbed on to the fleeing cuff and was instantly sucked into the twirling mass. The other members of Blood Waltz, and Uncle Pamela too, looked on as the tornado twirled faster and faster, pulling trash and pieces of uneaten cupcake and used syringes into its colorful mess.

"Wanda! Oh dear Wanda...!" Nancy yelled in fright.

The twirling nurse and his captive lifted off the ground and hovered and spun. The sky parted. A light from heaven shown down and a sweet, low feminine voice boomed out.

"Eat your cupcakes and be good to each other," the thunderous voice said.

All the vampires trembled and peed their pants.

And by slow degrees Gary stopped twirling and his dancing feet came to rest on the ground. There was a giant dust cloud surrounding Gary and Wanda and no one could see them.

Nancy peered into the falling dust, moving his head from side to side, squinting and trying to get a better view. His heart thudded hard, full of worry for Wanda. He moved his head to the left. Nancy's squinting eyes bulged out and his mouth fell open.

The dust cleared and everyone saw them. Wanda and Gary stood embraced, their open mouths pressed together in a passionate kiss.

"All right...!" Uncle Pamela said. He shoved his eager hand back into his pants.

Gary's hands moved over Wanda's bare, shirtless back. Wanda moaned and ran his fingers through Gary's hair and pressed his crotch hard up against Gary's. Wanda pulled back and looked into Gary's eyes.

"Oh Gary, even though you have a girl's name and you couldn't save my mom from her untimely death, I've loved you ever since that day I jumped out of that clinic bed and into your arms," Wanda said.

Gary's lips trembled at the mention of the death of Wanda's mother. "I tried so hard to save her," Gary said as new tears of blood gathered in his eyes.

"I know," Wanda said. "You did your best."

Wanda threw his arms around Gary and kissed him with all the love and passion that he had in his dancing vampire's heart.

"It's so beautiful!" Nancy cried out, wiping tears of happiness from his eyes.

All the vampires clapped and cheered and Uncle Pamela masturbated. Roy burst out through the back door. She ran up to Wanda and Gary carrying a single cupcake.

"This is a special, magic cupcake that I made to celebrate your love," she said, holding the small cake out to Wanda and Gary. "It's infused with the life-force of a thousand aborted babies and will give you long life and super strong erections."

Wanda and Gary leaned down to smell the cupcake. With their ears close to the desert, they heard the tiny cries of a thousand aborted babies. Wanda and Gary looked at Roy and smiled.

"Thank you Roy, this means so much that you would bless our love by giving us this special magic cupcake," Gary said.

Wanda nodded and smiled at Roy. Gary took the cupcake and held it up to Wanda's lips. Wanda bit in, then Gary bit in, and they chewed until their lips came together in a sugary kiss. Batter and saliva swirled back and forth through each other's mouths on their probing tongues. And everyone cheered and felt all tingly inside.

Roy turned to the other members of Blood Waltz. She crossed her arms across her huge brass breasts.

"I hope you boys have learned your lesson," she said.

"Yes, dear sweet Roy, we sure have!" Nancy said. "Abortion cupcakes make everything all better!"

Roy grinned and gave them the thumbs up. She knew, and they knew that she knew and she knew that they knew that she knew and everyone was glad that they knew because having a general understanding gave everyone involved a peace of mind which was necessary to move on to the next phase of their lives. Roy smiled at the vamps and walked back inside, the heavy iron door swinging shut behind her.

Wanda and Gary held each other, embraced in passion and wet, sloppy kisses.

And the fallen Gestapo Ballet dancers looked down from heaven with a smile. Wanda's mother stood by their side. She looked at Wanda and her heart swelled with pride.

"That's my boy," she said. "That's my boy."

THE BLOOD AND THE DARKNESS

by Dave McCaughey

The train rattled on through the cold winter's night, the steam hanging in the air like a long streak of cloud, fading into the distance. The moon was almost full and sat high and bold in the eastern sky, it's light giving the steam trail an eerie, silvery glow.

The engine was a large Norris model, trailing a train of seven carriages, tailed by a caboose at the rear.

Inside the caboose, five men sat in comfort in a small carriage which usually served as a tea room and lounge for the engineers. On this journey, however, the engineers were riding on the second carriage, having been paid to concede their usual comfortable habitation to the group of rough-looking men.

Three of the men sat around a small table, playing cards and drinking bourbon. The tallest sat beside the oil lantern, reading a tattered book in the flickering light. Their leader, a man in his mid-forties sat brooding in a chair in the corner of the carriage, his rifle propped up on the side of his chair. His name was Daniel Harrison, a lawman from the nearby town of Stilbury, Louisiana. Out of the entire group, he was the only one dressed tidily. He wore a long, brown overcoat with his sheriff's badge pinned to the lapel. His moustache was thick and well-groomed and sat neatly on his lip, speckled with the odd grey hair.

Daniel stared into the lamplight, watching its flicker dance against the glass of the window, his mind far away from the chatter and activity in the carriage. He thought about what he had witnessed over the past few days. Three days before, on the Monday afternoon, he had been in his office, filling in the papers for a prisoner transfer when his first deputy, Paul, entered through the front door.

Paul was a tall, very lean man with wiry hair and a scruffy face. He spoke with a voice which suited his appearance well. 'Sher'f,' he paused. 'Um, we got Lyle Rogers at the doc's. He's hurt pretty bad.'

Daniel stood and put on his coat. 'What happened?'

Paul shrugged nervously. 'I think it's better if you come see.'

Daniel strode out the door past Paul and headed across the street to the doctor's surgery. He noticed a saddled horse wandering free across the main street. He nodded towards it. 'That Lyle's?'

'Yessir, Sher'f' replied Paul.

'Well, go and tie it up,' ordered Daniel, shaking his head at his deputy's slow-wittedness.

Paul moved towards the horse, clicking his cheek to call the animal as Daniel approached the surgery. Already Daniel could hear a fuss of activity from inside.

The sheriff entered the surgery, at once noticing blood on the floor in patches, leading to the far side of the room where there was a surgical bed. The doctor had already gotten Lyle to the bed and was having trouble holding him down, as Lyle was squirming in both pain and anguish and speaking in gibberish.

Daniel quickly moved to the bed to help. Doc Kelly glanced up briefly. 'Hold him down. He needs a shot!'

Daniel placed his hands on Lyle's shoulders and could see

an open wound on his neck. Lyle was easily held down as he was weakened from his injuries. He was hysterical, his eyes streaming with tears. 'Annie,' he wailed. 'He killed my Annie! Oh God! My Annie!'

The doctor had prepared a syringe and knelt down by the bed, taking Lyle's arm in his hand, searching for a vein. Lyle's eyes were wild and staring and he locked his gaze into Daniel's. He gripped the sheriff's arm powerfully with his free hand.

Daniel was taken aback by the intensity of Lyle's stare and grip and he felt a shiver run down his spine. 'Annie!! OH GOD!!!'

Lyle's eyes suddenly rolled back and closed, his body going limp as the sedative began to work. Daniel released his hold on the older man and stood back, noticing the blood on his own hands.

Just then, Paul entered, looking curious and gently closing the door. 'How is he?' he asked.

The doctor spoke, but didn't look round, his attention was on his duties. 'I think he'll live, alright, but he's lost a lot of blood.'

Paul hovered by the doorway, keeping his eyes averted, obviously uncomfortable with the blood. 'Is he shot?'

Kelly paused for a second. 'Well, that's just it. These lacerations,' he gestured toward Lyle's arms, 'on his arms could have been done with a knife. Definitely something sharp.' He looked at the wound on Lyle's neck, and began shaking his head. 'This, though,' he said thoughtfully. 'This looks more like teeth marks.'

Daniel looked down at the doctor. 'Teeth marks?' he asked in disbelief.

Paul's jaw sat agape. 'What you sayin' Doc? Ain't nuthin' in these parts could do that to a man!' He started pacing nervously. 'Ain't no bears round here, odd coyote, sure, but even a pack of them wouldn't take on a grown man!'

The doctor shrugged, agitated by Paul's nervous demeanour. 'I'm just telling you what it looks like.' He pointed to Lyle's neck, then reached for a bandage. 'Look at these two marks here.'

Daniel leaned in to look, then his eyes narrowed as he remembered something. 'He said "he,"' he murmured, distantly.

Paul stopped and stared at his boss, quizzically. The doctor looked up at Daniel. 'What?' he asked.

Daniel shook his head faintly and met Kelly's eye. 'He said "He killed my Annie."'

Doc Kelly's face hardened. 'Who's "he?"'

Paul started again, his arms wide in a panic. 'Now, just wait a goddamn minute! Are you seriously suggesting that a person did this???'

Daniel crossed the room and began washing his hands in the sink. 'I'm not suggesting anything right now, because we don't know anything right now.'

'You're right, we don't,' hissed Paul intensely. 'We need to send to Baton Rouge and get some men out here so we can go up there with numbers an' kill this thing, whatever it is.'

Daniel dried his hands. 'It'll take days to get word out and even longer to get the help. You and I will go now and check out Lyle's property.'

Paul opened his mouth to protest, but Daniel wasn't finished.

He stared Paul down and continued, 'If what he says is true about Annie being dead, other people could need our help. Whether it's a bear or some kind of madman, maybe we can stop it, or him, before who, or whatever it is can hurt anyone else.'

Daniel turned to Doc Kelly. 'Doc, keep an eye on Lyle until we get back. When he wakes, tell him we're going to try and help anyone left at the ranch, and see if we can't get some answers.'

Daniel strode out into the afternoon sunlight, Paul following dutifully and slightly more resolved than he had been inside. The two men crossed the street and entered the sheriff's office, grabbing their rifles and ammunition. Paul lifted a heavy shotgun from the wall. It was an expensive model, double-barrelled and a relic from the civil war. Daniel kept it for nostalgia more than anything, preferring to use his rifle at longer ranges. Both men paused for a second and looked at one another. Paul knew how Daniel revered the weapon, but with the possibility of facing a potentially large and deadly animal foremost on his mind, he shrugged as if to say 'If ever we needed it..."

Daniel thought for a second, then overrode his first instinct, nodding reluctantly in approval. Paul felt a small pang of relief rush over him, the added firepower putting him at a little more ease.

Daniel and Paul carried the weapons out and loaded them onto their horses' saddles, mounting the creatures once they had finished packing, and spurring them off to a gallop, heading north in the direction of Lyle Rogers' homestead.

Several hours later, the men arrived at Lyle's ranch, the sun now setting in the November sky. They trotted slowly around the perimeter of the main house, looking for signs of struggle or damage. 'Outside seems fine,' spoke Paul softly.

They completed their circuit of the house and ended up back at the front entrance. The front door lay wide open, swinging gently in the breeze. Both men dismounted and stepped up onto the porch, cautiously approaching the door, their weapons drawn. Paul clutched the shotgun tightly, his nerves on high alert. Daniel was more focused, but still on edge. Neither knew what to expect.

Daniel called out; 'Annie?' He listened for a few seconds. The only sound was the breeze blowing softly through the main hallway of the house as he crossed the threshold, and the quiet stepping of boots and spurs from Paul, moving nervously behind him.

Daniel looked at Paul to see if he had heard anything. Paul shrugged and shook his head.

A staircase rose to the left and led to the upper floor. Daniel nodded towards it. 'I'll check down here,' he said.

Paul nodded, steeling himself, and began to ascend, creeping slowly upward, each step a milestone. Daniel turned and entered the lounge. It was well furnished with a large fireplace in the far wall. Lyle was quite wealthy because as well as farming cattle, he traded in furniture, working from a large, wooden workshop to the rear of the main house. All of his furniture was self-made and of a high quality.

Paul peered around the room, hoping that Lyle might have been wrong about Annie being killed, not wishing to find her body, but hoping that she was simply away visiting family or friends, and that Lyle was simply delirious from the attack.

There was nothing untoward to be found, however, and no signs of struggle. He breathed a sigh of relief, and left the lounge, moving on down the hallway.

Paul peered around the first door he encountered. It was the master bedroom. The sheets were unmade, but on the bed. He stepped into the room, pointing the shotgun ahead of himself. He checked inside the wardrobe, but there were only dresses and various clothes. He stepped back into the hallway and continued round the landing to the other door.

Daniel entered the kitchen, which had a large dining table in the centre and his heart sank. The table had been smashed into two pieces, showering the kitchen in splinters of wood. Daniel quickly stepped around the large half of the table that was between the doorway and the centre of the room and grabbed an oil lamp from the shelf.

Outside, the sun had all but disappeared, leaving long streaks of shadow, borne from its failing red light.

Daniel lit the lamp with some nearby matches, then turned to inspect the damage to the furniture. Of the six chairs that accompanied the table, only two remained intact, the others broken and splintered, their pieces strewn amidst the debris.

Daniel stepped closer to the wreck, wondering who or what could have caused so much destruction. He raised the lamp to get a better light. It was then that he noticed the blood amongst the wreckage.

Back in Doc Kelly's surgery, the doctor lit his lamp and moved to the surgical bed to check on Lyle. Over the past few hours, Lyle had been mostly quiet, stirring only twice. The second time was about an hour before, when he had awoken suddenly, in a high fever, delirious and flailing weakly. He had muttered and groaned mostly incoherently, the only words the doctor could make out were 'Annie,' 'No,' and 'Bit her'.

Kelly had given him another sedative and let him rest for a while, checking on him periodically, whilst continuing with other work in the meantime.

The doctor stood over his patient and eyed him curiously. Lyle wasn't moving at all and lay perfectly still. Kelly quickly put the lamp down on the bedside table and checked Lyle's pulse from his wrist. Finding nothing, he went to check his neck and noticed that his skin was cold and clammy. He realised that Lyle must have passed quietly in the last hour.

He shook his head in dismay, cursing himself for not checking on his patient more regularly, but also surprised, as given the amount of blood that he still had, he should have been weakened, yes, but surely not dead. He slowly removed the bandage from Lyle's neck, to inspect the wound.

When the wrappings came free, Kelly's mouth fell open in astonishment. The holes had now disappeared, replaced by two small nubs of scar tissue.

Suddenly, Lyle's eyes snapped open.

Paul lit the lamp in the guest bedroom and peered around. He squinted in the gloom, taking in as much as he could in the dim glow. He jumped as he noticed movement in the far corner, but breathed a sigh of relief as he realised that it was only the curtains blowing from the open window. He stepped closer to close it and noticed that the floor was littered with broken glass and the hinges were broken on the window itself. He saw that the glass had broken inward, indicating that something had come in from the outside. He saw that there was no blood on the glass from any injuries or laceration. He saw something glittering amongst the broken shards, and bent down to inspect it.

What he did not see was Annie's corpse, pallid, with clammy skin, her hair blowing in the gloom as the last of the sunlight faded, standing right behind him.

...TO BE CONTINUED IN A FUTURE WORK...

THEY TOOK HER

by Kasey Hill

It was 3:30 a.m. when I awoke into the stillness of the house. Beads of sweat rolled down my face and back as I sat up in bed and listened to the eerie quiet that settled throughout the night. I squinted my eyes and tried to remember the reason I woke up. I heard the wail of the dogs both outside and inside and groaned. Although I was grateful for being awakened from the nightmare, I was annoyed at the dogs. It had been three days in a row with them waking me from my sleep for no reason at all. They just stood outside or at the door and barked and howled.

I walked through the house and made my way to the front. Our main entrance doors were solid glass sliding ones, which made nights like these the easiest. As I peered out of the door and across the yard, I couldn't shake the heightened sense of paranoia that I awoke with. I knew it was the nightmare that caused the level of pandemonium and fear that rose in the pit of my stomach. However, no matter how much I tried to reassure myself that was the reason, I couldn't shake the feeling of being watched as I stood at my glass doors.

I squinted my eyes, peering deeper into the darkness that surrounded the outside, trying to see any of the objects without my glasses on. My husband and I lived on fifteen acres of land, which was pretty secluded from the world. You had to drive down a mile-long driveway to get to our house. I wanted to raise the kids away from the big city and away from violence, so I chose the hometown I had grown up in to raise them; Rocky Mount. Not only was this the same hometown I was raised in, but the farmhouse we lived in was the one I had lived in since I was a small child.

A few years before the kids were born, my parents were in a horrific car accident. A tractor trailer jack-knifed on the interstate, and they were caught in the middle with three other cars. They had to cut them out from the car with 'the jaws of life', but it was too late. It was my last year of school, and I was about to receive my bachelor's degree. I came home to take care of the estate and learned I had inherited the house as an only child. The only rational decision I could come to was to sell it off, and then I met my husband, Jack.

I had looked up on Craigslist a local handyman to do some minor repairs to the house to get it ready for auction. When he told me how much I would spend to get the house up to code, I realized that in the long run, I would lose money as opposed to making anything off the house and land. He convinced me to keep the house and instead, make home improvements to it. As he helped me with the repairs, we began to grow fond of each other. A year had passed when he got down on one knee and proposed to me. We took a minor break from repairs and slipped off to Hawaii to get married. Once we returned, we returned to what we were to call 'our home'. Before long, we had completely renovated it into a luxurious home, and I found out I was pregnant with our first child.

As my eyes scoped out the front yard, I came across a darkened figure moving in the shadows. I ran to the room, grabbed my glasses, and ran back to the door. The dark figure was no longer there. The dogs were running around the house outside barking and snarling. I walked window to window to try and catch another glimpse of what I had seen earlier. I gave up on trying to determine what the figure was and convinced myself it must have been a deer or something.

As I walked back to my room, I passed by my unruly mother-in-law as she made her way to the bathroom. I rolled my eyes and tried to brush past her. They had been staying with us while Jack's dad looked for work around here. They wanted to be closer to the kids, but living with them was a nightmare. They had no sense of respect for things that didn't belong to them, and it annoyed me as they pilfered through the objects I had set out of my parents and packed them in boxes to put their shit out as if they were here forever.

Jack and I had squabbled a few times over their presence, and after they had removed my mother's home interior from the wall to put up their crap, I told him he had to put his foot down. They had to go. Jack sat them down and talked to them to let them know that it was time for them to find a place of their own and a feud started with me being the center of it. I sat quietly letting them air their distaste of the way I raised my children.

"This is the exact problem I have with you two living here. What you don't get is this is my home; these are my children. You have no say over what happens to this house or what happens with my children. You don't pay bills here, you live here rent free, and have basically tried to take over my home as yours. Well, it ends today. It would be best if y'all left in the morning."

Jack ushered them to their room, irritated over the whole debacle. We had had many an argument over their temporary stay here, that to them, looked as if it would be long term. Separate families, whether blood-related or not, could not coexist under the same roof without some sort of spat arising. He went to bed early that night not wanting to talk anymore about the situation, so I stayed up a little longer to write.

That was one of the issues his parents had with me. I was a writer, an author, so to speak. They wanted me to put the kids in daycare to socialize them more with other kids as opposed to living out here without anyone to really play with. I said no. After all of the media coverage of fight rings in daycares instigated by adults, or the adults abusing the children with fly swatters or sticks, I was not putting my children in daycare. My children would not be abused in that way. Another of their complaints was that I spent too much time writing and not enough time with the children, while they were trying to make the daycare stake. I pointed out that in daycare they wouldn't spend any time with me, and while I wrote at home, I was able to take care of the house, spend time with them, and work from home. Excuse after excuse popped up for them to have a problem with me raising the children. I couldn't tolerate it any longer.

As I passed by Jack's mother heading back to my room, she let out a humph and brushed past me, bumping me into the wall. I breathed in deep and exhaled. They will be gone tomorrow. They will be gone tomorrow, I repeated to myself. I climbed back in bed and snuggled close to Jack. It was a humid night, but we kept our fan in the window to circulate the air in the room, which in turn kept it cool. Tonight, however, I was clammy and uncomfortable. My sixth sense was on high alert which hadn't happened in a while.

A few months ago, Jack and I had been outside star gazing after the children went to bed. As we watched the moon and Jupiter rise through the sky, we saw another light pop up out of nowhere. It literally materialized in the sky right before our eyes. We watched as it made its way across the sky. To our surprise, something shot out from the front of the mysterious lights. Purple trails appeared as the object shot from the front of it and abruptly stopped. It then shot to the right of the light leaving the purple trails behind the flashing-light object as it zoomed through the sky. A few minutes later, another object shot out in the similar fashion and we watched it go in the opposite direction of the floating light. As soon as the light had appeared, it dematerialized before our eyes.

Jack and I had goosebumps from the sight. He casually tried to explain it being new government equipment being tested. It was possible it could be the drones and stealth planes that were being upgraded by the government. I nodded my head listening to the explanation and reminded him of what he told me he saw the previous morning on his way to a job. Two objects were flying in the morning sky. It looked as if one was chasing the other. The one in front of the other flyer looked as if it had erupted into flames. After being reminded of that experience, he didn't know what to say could be the lights in the sky that night.

Being the writer I am, my mind was flooded with ideas. Alien invasion was number one. Since I was a child, alien research was always a thing of mine. Our little secluded area of land was always a hotspot for some type of anomaly. There had been nights when my dad and I would star watch with telescopes and see all types of strange activities in the sky. Solid red lights that would cut across the sky in a blink of an eye and disappear altogether. There was also the time my mother and I had seen some sort of 'unidentified flying object' slowly hover over a back road going the most of three miles an hour. I was a small kid then. When I explained to my classmates what we saw, I was laughed at and called crazy. I knew what I saw then.

Mysterious shapes had begun to show up in our fields. We would grow corn, barley, or even just hay, and at times, it looked like a round object fell from up high and dented the crops down. Other times it looked as if the crops had been burned and even the ground had crystallized into glass. These odd shapes upset my parents. There had been a few nights I would listen to them speaking in delicate tones in the parlor over the sightings. They were worried about 'them' coming for me. To do this day, I don't know who 'they' are.

I had the same antsy feeling fill me tonight as it had so many nights before. I closed my eyes to try and force my mind to quiet. They were forced back open when I heard a thump come from the area of the house my mother-in-law had been. I sighed in exasperation and sheer tiredness. She had more than likely fell and needed assistance to get up. I was about to throw the blanket off of me when I heard another noise that chilled me to the bone. It wasn't a sound I had ever heard. It was a procession of clicks and throaty sounds.

I slowly rose from the bed and walked to the door to peer through the crack of the door. In the dark hall, I could make out two silhouettes in the shadows. They were too short to have been anyone in the house. Their fingers moved as the sounds they made echoed as thy back and forth bantered with one another. It sounded as if they were arguing. I ran over to Jack to wake him.

"Jack," I whispered as I shook his shoulder. "There is someone in the house."

Jack wouldn't wake up. I shook his arm again more roughly, but he still kept sleeping soundly. I slapped him to wake him. My hands shook as he didn't awake from his sleep state. I returned my gaze to the door and stepped closer to the door jamb to look try and get a better look. The click sounds had stopped altogether, which made me extremely uneasy. I nearly fell on my ass as I saw the silhouettes right in front of my door. The door was unlocked, and I knew they would hear the click if I turned the lock to lock it. We kept the door unlocked so the kids could come in our room in case they had a bad dream or got scared in the middle of the night.

I clambered over Jack into my spot in the bed as quietly as I could and threw the blanket over my head. It was a childish move, especially if who was in my house were people there to murder us. I closed my eyes and pretended to be asleep. My breath caught in my throat as I heard my door knob turn and the door open. I didn't hear any footsteps, but before I knew it, the blanket was being peeled back from my head. I kept my eyes closed as my heart raced. I felt an unnatural finger caress my cheek and fought the urge to let out a scream. Instead, I casually swatted at the finger as if it were a bug and murmured something incoherent to make them think I was sleep talking.

A bright light flooded my eyelids and images flashed through my mind. I was being hauled away in a catatonic state, unable to move or scream out in fear. I was placed on a metal surface and strapped down, for formality was my guess. Four shadows stood around me. I squinted to make out their features. I felt my eyelids pried open and restricted from closing. Lights erupted all around me, and I was temporarily blinded. Once my eyes adjusted to my illuminated surroundings, I could see the figures more clearly.

They were tall, or I was down low to the floor on the table. Where there should have been eyes were gaping sockets. Small tendrils engulfed their heads and moved like snakes. They flicked around the room as if they were sensing. I realized that is how they saw. Like a snake uses its tongue, or how bats and sea creatures use sonar, these creatures use those tendrils as eyes. They were ghastly looking but each different. In a way, they seemed to favor humans that had failed in some sort of government experiment to make them fish people.

The wall to my left moved and opened into a huge atrium filled with cryotubes. There seemed to be millions of them, and each tube was filled with something different. It looked as if there was a pair of every species in the tubes. I saw male and female lions, I saw a bull and cow, a rooster and hen. There were different pairs of races for humans as well. If I didn't know any better, it would seem as if this was a Noah's Ark, like from the Bible tales of Genesis. Questions raced through my mind. Were Aliens really God? Were all the Bible stories illusions that were placed in human brains? Was there ever really a Garden of Eden? Was this like the Matrix. My brain overloaded.

"We have been around longer than your species, human."

Where did that voice come from?? I thought to myself. I looked around with my eyes and saw the owner of the voice that filled my head.

"What your race refers to as 'aliens' is in fact your species that exist outside of space and time. We have built and created earth millions of times trying to perfect our race, however, greed and envy always win. It seems to be a fault of ours. A fault that we have overcome, but you all cannot. We start from scratch each time. Building the prehistoric animals then creation of humans as cavemen. We start a special pair of humans each time out in the Garden of Eden and see if they can follow just the simplest of tasks. As of yet, no one has been able to forego curiosity and obey the command of not eating the Tree of Knowledge fruit."

"We then place them on earth to see how they do and add them to the already growing population of people. Every scenario has ended in total annihilation of the planet's inhabitants. So we rebuild every few billion years hoping to find the one pair of humans that will let go of envy, greed, and the urge to disobey. We take these pairs of races and use their DNA to create the world over and over again. All of them are direct descendants of Adam and Eve from different timelines. Each representing the many races of people upon Earth."

"Why are you telling me this?" I asked.

"Because we have studied you and your family for years. For generations. We believe that we do not have to start all over again, and instead, use your family as Noah's Ark. We will spare you, your husband, and children. The rest of the world will experience an apocalypse. I understand that your husband's parents are the only other family you have, but they are far too old to include in this. We will stay in touch with you and give you the future plans and final date of Earth as you know. The first thing we take care of is your mother in law for you. With her out of the way, things will run smoother."

"What are you going to do to her?" I asked.

"Everything you have ever heard people say happened when they were abducted." The creature felt like he smirked with his words. "Now, it is time for you to return home."

The alien touched my forehead and a bright light enveloped me. The images faded from my head, and I sensed complete silence. The room fell still, and I wanted so badly to peek out from under my eyelids to see if they were still in my room. The power had gone out a few minutes before I had heard the thump and the silence was deafening. A scream erupted through the air of the house, and I bolted upright from my bed. Jennie! I jumped out of my bed and ran to the room the kids shared. I opened the door to find them soundly asleep in bed. Another scream resounded from the first floor of the house, and I whipped my head in the direction it came from. I ran to the balcony of the steps and peered over the banister as I watched two disfigured things carry Jack's mother out the front door.

I ran back to Jack's room and started screaming at him to wake up. His dad popped out of his room after he heard my frantic calls for Jack to wake up.

"What's wrong? What's going on? Where is Shelby at?" he asked throwing his house coat on.

I whimpered with the tears free flowing down my face unable to answer him.

"Where is Shelby?!" he yelled at me, his voice echoing through the quiet house.

"They, they..." I stammered in between sobs.

We heard another scream, and he ran to the hall window as a bright light lit up the entire house and disappeared. Jack immediately woke up to the commotion. It was almost as if he were in a sleep paralysis state.

"What's going on?" he asked irritated.

"They, they," I repeated almost catatonic.

He grabbed ahold of my shoulders and shook me. "What do you mean they? Who are they? You're not making any sense!"

I looked at him as the room began to spin. It was a scene out of a horror movie, but it was really happening. It wasn't fiction; it was real life. She really was taken. What they said was going to happen most likely really was to happen. An apocalypse. An end to the world as we know it. Aliens have been God all along. Aliens are humans outside of time and space. We are our own gods, and we live such petty lives. We are gods that pray to a fake god, believe in fake religions. The world has been created and destroyed over and over into infinite outcomes. I needed a drink. The room began to fade in and out black. I watched Jack mouth words, but couldn't make any sense of what he was saying.

Before my eyesight went totally dark, I whispered, "They took her."

...TO BE CONTINUED IN A FUTURE WORK...

BIOGRAPHIES

Vitor Abdala is a Brazilian journalist and a Horror Writers Association (HWA) affiliate member. He's the author of two horror short story collections, both published in Brazil, in 2016: *Tânatos* (Giostri, 2016) and *Macabra Mente* (VCA, 2016). His stories appeared in the recently published *Horror Library - Volume 6* (Farolight Publishing) and *Night Shades #1* (Frith Books).

Soraya Abuchaim is a Brazilian author of terror and suspense, she is also known as Dark Queen. Author of two books and several short stories all available on Amazon.com, she regularly participates in literary projects in Brazil and, now, abroad. For more information visit:

www.sorayaabuchaimescritora.com.br

Leanne Azzabi is a full-time civil servant from Belfast, Northern Ireland, and single mother to two beautiful sons. She was inspired to write from a young age to impress her late grandfather, Matthew Cosby. Leanne aspires to be as good a writer as her grandfather someday and now uses writing as therapy in adulthood for dealing with obstacles life has thrown in her way. Her latest works have reignited her spark for the written word and she also had some of her work published in *Gruesome Grotesques Volume 1*. She can be contacted at leanneazzabi31@gmail.com.

Adrian Baldwin is an award-winning author from Manchester, now living and working in Wales. Back in the Nineties, he wrote for various TV shows/personalities: Smith

& Jones, Clive Anderson, Brian Conley, Paul McKenna, Hale & Pace, Rory Bremner, Terry Wogan, (and others). Wooo, get him.

Since then, he has written three screenplays, one of which received generous financial backing from the Film Agency for Wales. Then along came the global recession to kick the UK Film industry in the nuts. What a bummer!

Not to be outdone, he turned to novel writing - which had always been his *real* dream - and, in particular, a genre he feels is often overlooked; a genre he has always been a fan of: Dark Comedy (sometimes referred to as Horror's weird cousin).

His first novel, *Barnacle Brat (a dark comedy for grown-ups)*, won Indie Novel of the Year 2016 (Underground Book Reviews' Readers' Choice Award); his second *Stanley McCloud Must Die! (more dark comedy for grown-ups)* published last year, and he is currently writing his third book: *The Snowman and the Scarecrow (another dark comedy for grown-ups)*, due out summer 2018.

Blown is Adrian's third short to be published. He has also had his story *Pied!* (a dark comedy short inspired by Stephen King's *Misery* and *It* - but mostly *Misery)* published in the anthology: *Floppy Shoes Apocalypse 3 Cream Pie Freaks* with another dark short, *Egor's Emporium* coming soon in *Floppy Shoes Apocalypse 4 Greasepaint Inferno.*

Adrian cites his major influences as Kurt Vonnegut, Monty Python, Stephen King, and David Bowie.

For more information on the award-winning author, check out his Facebook page, Twitter feed, and, of course, his website (where the beginnings of *Barnacle Brat*, *Stanley McCloud Must Die!* and all of Adrian's short stories, are available for free).

adrianbaldwin.info
facebook.com/AdrianBaldwinAuthor
Twitter @AdrianBaldwin

Richard Barr lives and works in County Antrim, Northern Ireland. He's had several short works appearing in the last year published in *The Luminary* and *The Big Issue*, and also in comic-book anthologies *Courageous Mayhem* and *Hold The Phones, It's Alex Jones.* He received a 'Very Honourable Mention' in the 'Weekend Writing Challenge' offered by The Other Publishing Company. Previously, his screenplay, *A Place for Everything*, made the final round of Digital Shorts, a joint project between the BBC and Northern Ireland Screen.

Andrea Bickerstaff is a writer from the town of Banbridge in Northern Ireland. In the past she has contributed pieces to publications and plays, including for the John Hewitt Society, Heel and Ankle Community Theatre Company and *Gruesome Grotesques Volume 1*. She has also acted in several short films and other creative projects. Andrea has several more writing projects in the works.

Frank Bowes is a strange chap from Belfast, Northern Ireland. In his spare time he enjoys studying conspiracy theories, and conspiracy theorist behaviour. In his working life, Frank is the proverbial jack of all trades, master of none. He is known for his dark sense of humour and propensity for arguing with strangers on the internet.

David Brilliance was born in the North East of England, in a small town called Willington, which is about twenty miles from Durham City. He has always loved the genre of the Fantastique - horror, science fiction, fantasy, growing up with a circle of friends who loved the horror genre also, even if they weren't as mad about it as he was, and he was often followed around at school by kids wanting to see the various horror film reference books he would regularly bring in, and to ask him questions about the films. Anything he didn't know, he would just make up. Not having any particular career in mind, David has worked in a variety of jobs, and now, fast approaching fifty, he resides in picturesque Weardale in County Durham, where he works in a local care home. Writing has always been something David has enjoyed, and he has contributed to the horror film fan magazine *We Belong Dead* and spin-off books, *70s Monster Memories and Unsung Horrors*, as well as *Space Monsters* and the long-running UK horror mag *The Dark Side*. David's work also appeared in *Gruesome Grotesques Volume 1* and he describes himself as 'a hopeful guinea pig in the laboratory of fate'.

Stephen Clarke is a writer based in Belfast, Northern Ireland. He is a Carer and personal home tutor to his twelve year old child. He likes to express himself through writing, art and photography, mainly of a macabre nature.

Sally Cochran was born in Belfast, Northern Ireland in 1942. Reading from the age of three years old, she started primary school at the age of four, leaving at fourteen. She was married by nineteen and had three children. Sally moved to various places over the years - in London during her married life, then divorced and moved to Canada, later remarried and moving to California, USA for twenty years. In addition, she also went to college in California and studied creative writing. Sally later moved back to her home city of Belfast where she currently resides. She has kept a journal all of her life and has written various excerpts and had them read or published.

Raven Dane is a UK based author of dark fantasy and steampunk novels. Her first books were the critically acclaimed *Legacy of the Dark Kind* series. These novels were followed by a high fantasy spoof, *The Unwise Woman of*

Fuggis Mire. Her steampunk novels so far are the award-winning *Cyrus Darian and the Technomicron* and the sequel *Cyrus Darian and the Ghastly Horde*. She has had many short stories published, including one in a celebration of forty years of the British Fantasy Society, and in many international horror anthologies. In 2013, she was signed up by Telos Publishing to be the first author for their new Moonrise imprint, with her collection of macabre Victorian and Steampunk short stories, entitled *Absinthe and Arsenic*, and in 2015, an alternative history/supernatural novel, *Death's Dark Wings*.

Lizzie Darragh is an actress, presenter for Big Hits Radio UK and writer based in Belfast, Northern Ireland.

Dean M. Drinkel is an ambitious published author, editor, award winning script-writer and film director as well as being Associate Editor of FEAR Magazine – he has also contributed several non-fiction pieces to various publications. He has over thirty credits to his name in the field of genre writing (including short stories, collections, novellas, anthologies); has written and directed fifteen theatrical plays in London and the South East of England and during the years 2002 – 2008, he wrote and directed several short experimental films. In 2016 Dean moved to Cannes, France to write a script with Romain Collier which was to become entitled *The Tragedy Of The Duke of Reichstadt*. This went on to win two screenplay awards (Best Historical Drama / Best Independent Spirit) at the Monaco International Film Festival. In 2017 Dean directed the short film *15* for Midas Light Films and in October will direct (also for MLF) *Echoes of Mine* based on his own script. Dean and Romain currently own the film rights to Stephen King's short story '*Willa*' which they will be filming early 2018 in the South of France – Dean will be following this with *The Lake* – an historical short film about the Empress Eugenie and a young piano-tuner to be shot in Chislehurst, Kent at their former home – Camden Place. Dean has won five awards (thus far) for his script-writing and was runner-up for the 2001 Sir Peter Ustinov Screenwriting Award (International Emmys) – for his script *Ghosts*.

Joe Gardner is a thirty-one year old horror and comedy writer currently living in Greenwich, London. After attaining a degree in literature at the University of Reading, Joe has written film and TV reviews and blogs for several entertainment websites, such as *What Culture UK* and *The Time Warriors*, and has published several works of fiction. His most recent horror novel, *The Creeping Seawall*, is available now from Bloodhound Books.

John Gilbert has retired from editing to concentrate on his first love, writing. Based in Brighton, UK.

Rachel Sarah Glasgow has been writing for pleasure for the majority of her life. The first thing she ever wrote was when she was in primary two; an illustrated book called *Fiver's Adventures*, about her sister's pet rabbit. Her teacher gave her a gold star for it.

Paul Green is a writer whose work includes *The Gestaltbunker - Selected Poems* (Shearsman Books 2012), and the novels *The Qliphoth* (Libros Libertad 2007) and *Beneath the Pleasure Zones I and II* (Mandrake 2014, 2016), as well as *Space Virgins of the Third Reich* as Saul Wolfe. His plays for radio and stage are collected in *Babalon and Other Plays* (Scarlet Imprint 2015). Short fiction has appeared in *Canadian Fiction Magazine*, *New Worlds*, *Small Worlds*, *Brand*, *Unthology 2* (Unthank Books) and numerous on-line magazines. More information about Paul can be found at his website: paulgreenwriter.co.uk

Kasey Hill is an author and publisher originally from Virginia, USA. She runs her own publishing company - Azoth Khem Publishing.

Russell Holbrook is a reader, writer and rocker. Est. 1975. Mableton, Ga.

Alex S. Johnson is a writer, editor and publisher who finds one of the joys of being a horror fan lies in the awareness that, far from being wicked, monsters are only those dark forces of the subconscious that sustain the light. From the archetypes given such memorable form by Shelley, Stoker and LeFanu to today's icons of shred and slash, the creatures of the night have always been good company. Born on Halloween Day, he lives in Central California, and is the author of such works as *Shattergirl*, the creator and editor of the anthologies *Chunks, Floppy Shoes Apocalypse, Axes of Evil* and much more, who considers himself fortunate to have a place at the table among the ghoulish, the webfooted, the clawed and the hairy.

Rachel Johnston is a writer, for various publications over the years, a radio presenter, and model for Style Academy. She resides in the seaside town of Millisle, Northern Ireland with her three adorable children. Her work previously appeared in *Gruesome Grotesques Volume 1*.

Trevor Kennedy is a writer and editor based in Belfast, Northern Ireland, and creator of the Phantasmagoria horror series. In the past, he was a regular contributor for FEAR Magazine and has also contributed stories for several anthologies, including *The Thirteen Signs, Floppy Shoes Apocalypse 2, Chunks: A Barfzarro Anthology* and *Slashing Through the Snow: A Christmas Horror Anthology.* Upcoming works include *Phantasmagoria II: Danse Macabre, Phantasmagoria III: Theatre of the Absurd, Phantasmagoria*

Magazine and his first novel, *Time Travel for Junkies: A Beginner's Guide.* Trevor is also a presenter for Big Hits Radio UK and actor. He can be contacted at tkboss@hotmail.com.

Samantha Lee is a professional singer, actress, presenter, writer and general all-round creative originally from Northern Ireland. She used to pen scripts for the classic British kids' television series, *Rainbow.*

Lauryn Malcolmson is a seventeen year old upcoming writer from Belfast, Northern Ireland, with a very bright future ahead of her.

Dave McCaughey is a writer, actor and stand-up comic based in Newtownards, Northern Ireland. Dave and Trevor Kennedy used to work together in a Belfast-based call centre, many years ago. They spent most of their time there making animal noises instead of working.

Ro Mierling is a Brazilian writer, screenwriter and anthologist. Author of seven books published, including *Diary of a Slave*, which has enjoyed success on Amazon. Coordinator in more than forty collections of stories in the most diverse subjects, between the dramatic and the sinister, from the paranormal to sadistic crime. She believes that with a cruel, visceral and sinister story, it will show fear and raw reality to its readers. The author is writing her eighth book and currently lives in Buenos Aires, Argentina.

Ricky Mohl is a successful poet from Richland, Washington, USA, although is originally from Frankfurt, Germany.

Jonathan Mooney is a writer based in Belfast, Northern

Ireland, with quite a few upcoming literary projects in the pipeline.

Druscilla Morgan is an Australian writer and artist who loves cats, horses and vampires. She writes short stories and novels in the horror, fantasy and science fiction genres and designs book covers for many Indie publishers and authors. Her short stories have been published in several anthologies and magazines. Her debut novel, *Blood of Nyx*, co -authored with Roy C Booth, was published in 2016 by Indie Authors Press and is receiving positive reviews. Druscilla enjoys weaving a narrative that both entertains and challenges her readers. She is currently working on a stand-alone horror novel as well as the second book in the Nyx trilogy. Author's page URL:

https://www.facebook.com/pages/Druscilla-MorganAuthor/7 20568464695969

Jihane Mossalim, the cover artist, was born and raised in Montreal, Canada and is presently studying in the Art Education program at Concordia University and when she's not painting or working on new projects, she puts on her art instructor's hat and teaches art classes to college students. Her work has been shown in galleries throughout North America and Europe, including Montreal, Toronto, Vancouver, Chicago, Colorado, California and Ponte de Lima, Portugal. She is currently exhibited in Montreal as well as in private collections in Canada and Scotland.

Owen Quinn is a young at heart writer from Northern Ireland. He's a life long sci-fi and horror fan attending conventions up and down the country meeting celebrities from his favourite shows. This passion led him to create the *Time Warriors* series and the brand new *Zombie Blues* series. He is a keen photographer and is part of the 501st Ireland Garrison raising money for charities all year round, and which helps indulge his love of *Star Wars*. He can found on Facebook on *Owen Quinn The Time Warriors and Beyond* and *Ireland Loves The Walking Dead* as well as his website: www.thetimewarriors.co.uk

Carl Redding is a small town kid from the middle of nowhere, now living on the edge of the back of beyond UK. Occupations have included, amongst other things, aircraft technician, car mechanic, factory worker, artist, and shelf stacker. Thinks an imagination without a suitable outlet can be as much a curse as a blessing.

Rob Thomas was born 'n stuff, and is based in Canada.

Darren Webster is a decorated war veteran and has served in the police. This and other life events have given him an unquestionable sense of humour...though a smidge on the 'dark side'! He possesses a real 'joie de vivre' and helps support his local village school, the RNLI and other charities. But his children are his pride and joy. His motto to live by is - *You're better looking at it than for it.*

Allison Weir is a full time property consultant working in Belfast and STILL an avid Wolves fan, having being brought up in the Midlands. In what little free time she finds, she continues to write horror, fantasy and children's fiction and has recently taken up co-editing and writing for Belfast's very own bi-monthly horror publication, *Phantasmagoria Magazine.*

Her previous works include *The Christmas Collie* in *Ireland's Own*, *A Story from Valencia* in *Full House* magazine and in the first *Gruesome Grotesques* anthology, she was responsible for scribing *My Little Curcurbita (The Curse of Gretna).*

In her long list of hobbies, she has crashed back on to the ice rink (after a two year absence from injury) still teaches her beloved Spanish and German around her demanding job and helps friends out with radio broadcasting where possible, since presenting her former 80's radio show *Retro Randomness Sunday.*

This woman never stops!

Jennifer Wilcox (writing as J. K. Wilde) grew up in and around the historic town of Kingston, NY and found a passion for the macabre very early in life. With influences such as Mary Shelley, Bram Stoker, Stephen King, Anne Rice, H. P. Lovecraft, (and many, many more) it's not hard to see the influence of their creations and impact of their words on her work.

With a penchant wanderlust for the horror genre itself and an intuitively, creative mind, her work is rather new to the scene. But growing up near Woodstock, NY; she is no stranger to the 'strange and unusual'. Recently published works include short stories such as *The Hurt Locker* (featured in *Girls Rock Horror Harder* Issue #4), *Merry Go 'Round My Ass* (featured in *Floppy Shoes Apocalypse: A Clown Horror Anthology)*, *Changes* (featured in *47 – 16: A Tribute to David Bowie*) and dark (sometimes macabre) poetry, as well as her own anthology of work, *Musings: Writings of a Tortured Soul* (available on Amazon.com) and the novella length first installment of a story, *Blood Runs Thicker Under The Big Top*, as well as subsequent short story editions featured in the *Floppy Shoes Apocalypse* Anthology Series, with cameos from the beloved character 'Little Johnny Cotton' and 'Joey Diamantis' (Spawned from the evil minds of both herself and fellow colleague Alex S. Johnson), There are many treats in store for the months to come.

When she isn't writing she can often be found lurking about in the shadows looking for tidbits of the macabre and sinister in our daily lives. There is always some juicy tidbit of a story to be found in even the smallest of conversations. If you are patient and pay attention to your surroundings you might find some interesting stories yourself. Although, these days you might find her off near the lake in her North Carolina, country home; enjoying a good book, a frightful, chilling, horror movie, or just plain old relaxing with her toes in the cool, clear water.

Her author page is:

https://www.amazon.com/J.-K.-Wilde/e/B01ERY9RI0/ref=la_B01ERY9RI0_ntt_srch_lnk_1?qid=1461607891&sr=1-1

Made in the USA
Columbia, SC
10 November 2017